MY LADY OF
DECEPTION

MY LADY OF DECEPTION

Christi Caldwell

For more information about the author:
christicaldwellauthor@gmail.com
www.christicaldwellauthor.com

ISBN: 1514816679
ISBN-13: 9781514816677

ONE

1802

Bristol, England

Robert Emmet, a leader of the Irish nationals, has returned from the Continent with a contingent of Irish exiles. An organization of British spies is intent on stopping their revolution. It has plans to hunt these men down and execute them.

Signed,

A Loyal British Subject

I f children were guilty of the crimes of their fathers, Georgina Wilcox was going to burn in the eternal flames of hell.

Piteous moans from another of her father's victims echoed from the other side of the wood panel door. Georgina clenched her hands into fists to keep from opening the door. She could not go in. *Must* not go in. The angry purple bruise on the inside of her wrist throbbed as a subtle reminder of what happened when she questioned her father.

A groan more befitting a wild boar echoed from within the room. Georgina wanted to clamp her hands over her ears and drown out the man's pleas for help. *I cannot bear this.* She reached for the handle.

The floorboards creaked, echoing off the stillness of the corridor. On a gasp, Georgina spun around.

Jamie Marshall pinned her in place with his cold, hard stare. "What are you doing, Georgina?" The faintest hint of an Irish brogue lent his words a lyrical quality.

With his lean physique and black crop of curls, he had the look of a dark angel, only he possessed a soul black enough to rival the devil. To those in his traitorous circle, he was "The Hunter", enemy to the Crown.

To Georgina, he was also the orphan taken in by her father when English soldiers had murdered his parents those fifteen years ago.

"I-I…" She gestured to the door. "Who is in there?"

Jamie strode toward her and her heart climbed into her throat. "I asked you a question."

Not wanting him to see the effect his presence always managed to have on her, she met his gaze evenly, detesting the faint tremble of her fingers. Yet, she'd witnessed the cruelties he was capable of.

A moan punctured the silence and she thrust back her fear of him, renewed in her determination to help the stranger on the other side of the door. "I heard a man screaming."

An icy smile turned his perfect lips. "And you were compelled to help him?"

Long ago, she'd learned of his perversity; reveling in her fear, while delighting in her shows of defiance. She narrowed her gaze on him. "If the man in there is to be of any value to you then I must care for him."

In three long strides, he closed the remaining distance between them. "Do you presume to know what is best?" He grasped her chin between his thumb and forefinger, squeezing painfully.

"No." Georgina blinked back the tears that popped behind her lashes and glared. "Just what is right."

His fingers dug into her jawline. "Are you being insolent?"

Unwilling to give him the pleasure of seeing how painful his touch was, or the fear he sent coursing through her limbs, she gentled her tone. "Let me care for him."

Jamie lowered his head, his brandy-scented breath fanned her lips. Her pulse kicked up a beat. Life had taught her that liquor made him even more unpredictable. Then suddenly, he released her. His brows dipped as he appeared to contemplate her entreaty.

"Please, let me help him." She drummed up her best impression of a debutante's innocent smile. "I—"

Jamie pressed his finger to her lips. A shudder of revulsion snaked through her belly, and she pressed her lips into a tight line. Jamie had treated her first as a bothersome sister, then a useless servant, and now another shift had occurred. At some point, he'd begun looking at her in a way that made her flesh crawl with disgust. His obvious attraction, however, had also proven useful. A teasing smile and flutter of her lids had earned her the freedom to help prisoners in the past.

His pale blue gaze fell to her mouth.

She took a hasty step away from him. Her back thumped against the door. As if the unexpected movement had roused the beast within the chambers, a roar echoed through the house. "You bastard. Free me."

Georgina jumped.

The maniacal chuckle that spilled past Jamie's lips melded with the sheer terror of the stranger's shouts. "Still want to tend his wounds?"

Oh, how she wanted Jamie to suffer. His time would come and when it did, she would relish it. She tamped down the words she longed to hurl at his traitorous face.

"Hunter?" her father's voice boomed.

Jamie's broad shoulders stiffened beneath his blue, cutaway frock coat.

She said a silent thanks for the timely intervention, even if it was her father.

"Above stairs," Jamie called out. He paused, a black grin tilting the corners of his lips. "With Georgina."

Her heartbeat kicked up its rhythm as her father labored up the stairs. He stopped and studied her.

His astute gaze went from Georgina to his newest prisoner's closed door. He dabbed at his bald pate with a stained kerchief. "What are you doing up here, gel?" A wheezing cough escaped him and he spit into the cloth.

It was hard to fathom that this fat figure, known to the Irish Republicans as "The Fox", could be one of the organization's most powerful orchestrators in their plan to force an Irish revolt against British rule.

Georgina dropped her gaze to the frayed carpet and buried all hint of rebellion. "I—uh…I was—"

"Speak up."

Georgina looked up and held his stare. "I wanted to help." It wasn't altogether a lie. She had wanted to help—just not him.

"Help?" Father erupted into a fit of laughter until he began coughing. He swiped the back of his sleeve across his mouth. He dismissed her and turned to Jamie. "We have a meeting with Emmet. He's returned from France."

Jamie narrowed his eyes. "Does he know we have him?"

"He does."

Georgina held her breath and attempted to make herself invisible.

Father's talks of the Irish organization had been as common as a morning meal in their household. She had long heard the story of his mother, a delicate Irish lady who'd fallen in love with an Englishman. When her father had been a boy of five, he'd visited Ireland with his parents, a trip which had proven tragic. While riding one morning, the Irish beauty had been assaulted, and ultimately killed, by English soldiers. Her father had witnessed the whole horrific scene.

Georgina could imagine how such events would ever scar a person's soul. Still, England was the only home she'd ever known. She wouldn't blame an entire country for the sins of several, nor could she just sit idly by as witness to the wrongs done here.

Father continued. "Markham should break and give us the information we need." Her ears perked up. "He...we'll discuss the details later."

Without another word, Father and Jamie walked off.

It had been nearly a fortnight since she'd gotten information to the man known as "The Sovereign". Their absence had made it possible for her to pass along details about the Irish plot for independence.

She hurried after them. "When will you return?"

"We'll be gone the night," Jamie said, a dark frown curved his lips. "Lest you get the idea to do something foolish again, there is a guard stationed outside."

Her mouth went dry as she remembered the last guard they'd assigned to watch her. The blare of his pistol echoed in her memory. She shook her head to erase the face of the nameless prisoner and the blood that had blossomed on his chest like a crimson butterfly spreading its wings.

He'd been the last man she'd freed. They'd both paid dearly for it.

Georgina bit back the stinging retort on her lips. "Should I allow the guard entry?"

Father shot an annoyed glance over his shoulder. "You've got a lot of questions, gel."

"I just want to help," she lied.

Jamie's lips turned up in a sneer. "She is a dutiful girl," he said. He no more trusted her than she did him.

Georgina bowed her head and a wry smile played about her lips. "I strive to do my father's bidding."

Father and Jamie had come to expect small showings of disobedience from her, but neither suspected the truth—she stole information from them and dashed notes off to the Crown, providing details about their plans. All the while, she plotted to leave this hell. She was biding her time, waiting to find a way out of this lonely, dark life. The only thing that had kept her in this hellish place was a sense of obligation to the men brought here to suffer at Father's hands. That, and the fear they would hunt her and kill her themselves.

As if suspecting the deceptive path her thoughts had wandered down, Father glowered. "You aren't to let anyone inside."

She took a deep, slow breath when they finally left. Georgina locked the door and leaned against it. Her eyes slid closed at the blessed silence.

"I said let me out, you bastards!"

The thunderous shout above the stairs brought her back to reality.

Georgina hurried to the kitchens and prepared a tray of bread and cheese, a pitcher of water, and a glass of red wine to the sound of the captive's furious shouts. She sliced an apple into neat little pieces. Then she carried the tray to the captive's chambers and turned the door handle. For all intents and purposes, the room might as well have been an elegant bedroom for an esteemed guest. A four-poster bed sat in the center of the room and a small table with two chairs had been tucked in a corner.

She stepped inside.

One of those chairs was now occupied.

"You bloody bast—" His invective died a swift death. The stranger, his arms tied to the back of his seat, eyed her warily. The dimly lit room and the ten feet of space separating them did nothing to diminish the sparkle of wariness in his emerald green gaze.

With the tip of her slipper, Georgina closed the door and faced him. Her stomach turned over at his bloodied and battered face; his hard lips swollen and cracked, the green of his irises glimmered, like a wild animal's, full of the need for retribution. The slight tilt of his aquiline nose indicated it had been broken at some point. Her heart tugged. She, too, had known physical pain. "Hullo," she said quietly.

He studied her in mute silence. The black and blues marring his face did little to detract from his breathtaking beauty; the hard, chiseled lines of his angular face, a square jaw with the slightest indentation at its center. This wary man possessed the kind of power artists celebrated in stone. She cursed herself for thinking such thoughts at a time like this. Yet she could not take her eyes from him.

"Why are you here?" That hoarse question yanked her from her reverie.

Georgina rushed to his chair and set down the tray. Even strapped to the chair as he was, his long muscular frame filled the room. Her hand quaked as she dipped a rag into a bowl of water and gently wiped the blood from his face. It stained her fingers, and the potent smell that was sickly sweet and harsh metal combined, filled the air around them. Bile climbed to her throat.

A hiss slipped from between his teeth and she bit her lip, hating that she'd caused him further pain. Moments later, the blood was gone, but the bruises stood in dark purple contrast to the olive hue of his skin. Georgina knelt at his feet. When she picked up his bound wrists, a groan grumbled in his throat.

"Forgive me." Georgina lightened her grip and focused on his left hand, bound to the back of the mahogany shell chair. She'd done this many times before—loosened each prisoner's bindings one limb at a time in order to massage the bruised skin, knowing even as she did that it was dangerous. But compassion overrode logic. Within moments, she'd worked one binding over his wrist. Georgina probed the area for any breaks but found none. Wordlessly, she continued to rub his injured flesh.

The stranger held up his other wrist, clearly expecting her to release him.

Georgina shook her head. "I can't." With every breath in her body, she wished she could set him free of this hell. But it would mean death for him and other horrors for her. In time, she would plan a way to save him, but it couldn't be right now or her own life would be forfeit.

His hand fell back to the side of the chair.

In a sudden move, he trapped her chin with his large, strong hand. A startled squeak escaped her. She tried to shake loose his grip but he held tight. "What do you want then?"

"I only want to help."

"The men who brought me here, who are they?"

She shook her head. "I can't tell you."

He wrapped long fingers around her neck, his hold gentle, but firm. "Who are they?" Despite the furious demand, his thumb rubbed the spot where her pulse fluttered wildly.

She clawed at his hand, wanting to be free of his touch, to escape the vulnerable feeling of being helpless against him.

His grip tightened the slightest bit.

All Georgina's earlier resolve to set aside her own well-being and help this man at all costs, slipped. For as dark and lonely as her life was and always had been, Georgina didn't want to die. Not now. Not like this. She had given too much of her life to her father and the Crown to die here at the hands of this stranger. Enlivened, she raked sharp nails over the flesh of his forearm.

His lips curled in a sneering grin, as though he were amused by her ineffectual attempt at freedom.

"I could kill you right now." That whisper-soft threat chilled her. Still, he didn't harm her, proving with that hesitancy how vastly different he was than every other man she'd known. "Give me the answers I need."

Some of her courage restored, she forced words past dry lips. "Release me."

With a curse, he let her go. She stumbled backward and tripped over the empty chair. Instead of letting her tumble to the floor, he shot out his free hand to steady her.

Heart thudding hard in her chest, Georgina righted herself. She folded her arms close to her person. The greens of his eyes conveyed regret and some other indefinable emotion. She swallowed, uncomfortable. People did not worry about her and yet the remorse etched in the aquiline lines of his face indicated he cared. And no one cared of her or about her. Not her father, not Jamie, nor the men brought here as captors or captives. The stranger's concern pierced Georgina's soul. She cringed. What a silly, pathetic creature she was.

"Are you all right?" His quiet words slashed through her musings.

Well, my father is a traitor. I'm stealing his secrets and sending them off to the British government. Oh, and you nearly strangled me. How could I ever be better?

Georgina walked a wide path around him and paused at the small, chipped, wood table in the corner of the room. "I'm well enough," she said, with a touch of impatience. She planted her hands on the edge of the hard surface and used her hip to shove the piece of furniture over to the prisoner. All the while her skin burned under the intensity of his gaze. Studiously avoiding his gaze, Georgina picked up the tray and slid it toward him.

"You should eat." Georgina spun on her heel and hurried to the doorway. She'd come to help him, but this man had stirred a maelstrom of emotions beneath her breast that she didn't care to examine.

"Don't go!" His entreaty stopped her. "Please. I'm sorry..." He looked down, shame coloring his neck. "I would never have hurt you."

Georgina turned around and once more took in his battered features. The truth was etched in painful lines on his face. He wouldn't have hurt her, but that did not mean she had escaped danger. The longer she stayed here and talked to him, the more compelled she was to help him and risk her father's wrath.

Leave, Georgina. Leave.

Yet she moved to the empty chair next to him. "I am so sorry about what they've done to you." Even as the words left her lips, she flinched with the uselessness of them.

He arched a golden brow. "But not enough to free me?"

She poured a glass of water into the crystal tumbler and handed it to him.

The powerful man eyed it as though it contained witches' brew. A strangled laugh escaped his lips. "You're mad if you believe I would trust you."

He was right. This man didn't know about the previous prisoner she'd freed. Or the notes she dashed off to members of the Home Office. No one suspected the truth. This man only saw her as complicit in the ugliness that went on here. "You've no reason to trust me," she said at last. Georgina thrust the glass toward him.

Apparently, his thirst won out over his skepticism for he reached for the glass. His fingers brushed hers.

Georgina's skin heated at the brief meeting of flesh.

He drained the glass in one long, slow swallow. "What is your name?"

She stiffened and leaned forward in her chair, poised to flee. "Georgina Wilcox."

He gave no outward reaction to her admission. "I am Adam Markham."

Her shoulders relaxed as she realized he did not know who she was. Guilt niggled at her. She reminded herself she was not to blame for Father's crimes, but the thought rang hollow in her heart.

"I am sorry to meet you under such circumstances, Mr. Markham." Or really under any circumstances. There was no good in the world in which she dwelled.

He studied her intently and Georgina shifted in her seat. His gaze set a small flame alight in her bosom. The instinct for survival warred with her empathy. Except there was something more—some inexplicable feeling she didn't understand nor care to analyze. No good could come in any kind of connection with the men taken as prisoners here. She reached for his bindings then stopped. If she were ever to help this man, she'd have to plan carefully. After all she'd learned the perils in thwarting Father and Jamie's plans long ago.

The stranger's beautiful lips turned down. "So, tell me. What manner of woman would leave me tied here at the mercy of those bastards—" As if sickened by the mere sight of her, he jerked his gaze away.

She leaned forward. "If I free you, there is a guard outside who will shoot you dead. If that isn't enough, I will pay the price for your death. A price with my own flesh." Georgina let the weight of this dark truth sink in.

Silence reigned between them. They sat in uneasy silence until his stomach gave a rebellious rumble reminding her of why she'd come above stairs. Eager to give her fingers something to do, she reached for a sliver of apple and held it to his lips.

Something in his gaze softened. "Are you Eve?"

She angled her head. "*Georgina.*"

A sharp bark of laughter burst from his chest. The explosion of mirth seemed to rob him of breath. He coughed in obvious pain. "Christ, either you're an excellent actress or the most naïve woman I've ever met."

"Oh." Heat flooded her cheeks. "*That* Eve. Which, of course, makes you Adam."

"Adam and Eve," he murmured. He cast an almost empty gaze around the room. "And it would appear we've both been cast into hell."

Georgina's gut clenched at the all-too-familiar sentiment uttered by this man, Adam Markham. She cleared her throat. "Do you want the apple or not?" She waved it in his direction.

His lips parted, displaying an even row of pearl-white teeth. Georgina hesitated a moment, feeling a bit like a rabbit feeding a wolf, then slipped the fruit into his mouth.

He bit into the succulent fruit, all the while watching her as if he could divine her secret yearnings. When he opened his mouth again, she brought another piece of the apple to his lips.

"Why are you here?" he asked, after he finished his next bite.

Their gazes caught and held. "I have no choice."

Adam Markham's flinty stare threatened to bore through her. "They have you captive as well?"

In a way, she'd been trapped from the moment of her birth. "I am a victim of my circumstances, Mr. Markham."

Understanding dawned in his eyes. "You are a servant."

At his erroneous assumption, she stilled. She should tell him the truth. Confess who she was. *What does it matter?* a niggling voice whispered at the edge of her mind. *It is your father who is hell bent on an Irish revolution—not you.* "Why are you here?" She turned his question around on him, uncomfortable with his assumption.

"I, too, am a victim of my circumstances." A veil fell across his eyes, indicating he intended to say nothing further.

Georgina glanced over her shoulder at the closed door. "I should go." She stood.

He opened his mouth to speak. She had the distinct impression he wanted her to stay but she shoved the silly thought aside. Why should he desire her company?

Georgina reached for his bindings but the memory of his hand around her neck froze her mid-motion. She rubbed the sensitive skin where that possessive touch—firm but gentle—lingered. No one had ever handled her with even a modicum of tenderness. Reason had taught her to loathe such weakness. After all, compassion had brought her nothing but trouble.

His gaze went to her neck. "Forgive me," he said, his voice hoarse. "I've never mistreated a woman." Until now.

Considering her own experience with men and his earlier violent outburst, she didn't put much faith in his statement. Nonetheless, Adam Markham was desperate, an emotion she knew well. She waved off his apology. "You're not the first to...put me in my place." A niggling whisper of a dream flitted through her mind. In a different life she would have been the beloved daughter of a loving couple. She may even have a doting suitor. How different might her life have been if she'd been born a daughter to loyal British subjects? Georgina brushed back a loose strand of hair. "I wish there was something I could do to help you, but I can't." At least not now.

"You can free me." He was nothing if not persistent.

"I already said I can't."

His eyes ran a path over her face, but he said nothing.

Georgina bound his hands and hurried to leave before her father came home.

"Miss Wilcox?"

She paused.

"Thank you," he said in hushed undertones.

With a nod, she took her leave and made her way to the kitchen, where she gathered potatoes for the evening meal. Self-preservation dictated she forget Adam Markham. Yet her heart wouldn't allow her to do any such thing. All the while she prepared dinner, the visage of the handsome stranger danced through her mind.

He'd mistaken her for a servant.

Her skin tingled with the remembrance of his silken fingertips caressing her rapidly beating pulse.

If he'd wanted to strangle her before, what would he do if he learned she was really his captor's daughter?

TWO

In his meeting with Napoleon, Robert Emmet was informed the British have in their employ an agent who is assisting France. This person has pledged to also help the United Irishmen.

Signed,

A Loyal British Subject

Adam Markham had been betrayed. For seven years, he'd faithfully served the Home Office as a spy with The Brethren of the Lords. He'd uncovered the identities of Irish radicals trying to separate from England, had uncovered plots against the Crown, and seduced the secrets out of nefarious women all over the Continent.

None of his accomplishments mattered when coupled with his one great failure—the lapse in judgment that had earned him this month-long descent in the pit of hell.

Adam stared blankly at the cheerful floral curtains of his prison, at the sun's rays raining false brightness through the window.

The night Fox and Hunter had taken him prisoner, he'd been drugged. That much was clear. Adam had been in his townhouse, meeting with four other members of The Brethren, two of whom had been strangers. Someone must have slipped something into his glass of wine.

Who had handed him over to Fox? Fury licked at his insides, and he fed that anger because it staved off the mind-numbing fear. With a roar, he yanked his arms. The rope dug into his skin, rubbing the flesh raw until blood seeped down his wrists. Adam unleashed a string of black curses against his captors.

Adam comforted himself with the image of the day he would eventually be freed. He would use his far-reaching influence to see Fox and Hunter were made to pay. He would destroy his captors and all those who'd betrayed him. Their immediate death would be too easy. He would see that they suffered a traitor's public death so that any and all linked to them would learn the perils of interfering with The Brethren. Still, it wasn't only the thirst for revenge that kept him alive. Not anymore. Now there was also the young maid, Georgina.

As if his unspoken thoughts had summoned her, she appeared in the doorway. Georgina froze at the entrance and tipped her chin back a notch. A fiery light sparkled in her chocolate brown eyes. She put him in mind of a skittish cat.

He couldn't help but wonder what she'd be like if she lived in another house, in different circumstances. A cheery girl no doubt, with rose in her full cheeks, and a soft, sweet laugh that bubbled past her generous, bow-shaped lips. The thought made his heart twinge.

She carried a tray of food, on top of which rested a leather volume. "They've gone out," she murmured, the husky tone washing over him, as she closed the door behind her.

He remained silent, continuing to study her. The thick, dark waves of her hair always somehow managed to escape the knot at the base of her neck. Her slim figure was testament to the endless work she did in Fox's home. But for the bountiful breasts and generous curve of her hips, the maid's efforts had left her borderline gaunt. Still, there was something compelling about her.

Mayhap it was the determined sparkle in the brown of her eyes? Or the rigid set to her small shoulders that would have made a cavalry officer proud.

He'd tried to sort out her role in the household. With her regal carriage and cultured voice, she may as well have been any lady in a London drawing room. Her haggard figure and drab gown told a different tale. What had happened to bring her here?

As she did each time she visited, she released one of his bindings then took a quick step away from him. His gut churned with guilt as he thought back to the day he'd wrapped his fingers around her neck. Captivity did horrible things to a man. It turned gentlemen into monsters.

He eyed the bowl of chicken pottage. It was the third day in a row she'd prepared a meal of chicken. "Chicken, again."

She frowned. "You always eat the chicken."

"I eat all the food," he pointed out. "I am a prisoner."

"But you eat it faster, so I thought you preferred chicken and—" She clamped her lips shut. "I'll make something different next time."

As he shoveled another bite of broth into his mouth, he studied her. The quality linen dress she wore seemed more fitting of a lady than a household maid. He watched her fist and un-fist the silvery gray fabric of her skirts. Something seemed amiss, yet he could not put his finger on it.

"Is there anything I can bring you as a diversion?"

Her quiet question snapped him back to the moment.

Was that even possible?

"I draw."

She tipped her head. "Draw?"

He waved his free hand. "Yes, sketch. People. Buildings. I like to sketch."

"I've never known an artist," she mused aloud.

Adam chuckled, the sound rusty from ill-use. "I'd hardly consider myself an artist. My tutor once gave me a copy of Francois Boucher's work. I decided to try my hand at drawing." He didn't know why he'd disclosed such an intimate detail to her. Perhaps it simply stemmed from the bleak loneliness of his captivity.

When he said nothing else on the matter, Georgina gave a slow nod and rose. He called out to her, and she stopped at the threshold of the doorway.

"Thank you. You were correct. I prefer chicken."

She angled her head over her shoulder and a small smile turned the corners of her lips.

The next day she appeared with a dish of boiled chicken in a white spinach sauce and an empty sketchpad. She hovered uncertainly at his shoulder. His fingers flexed for the charcoal and parchment.

She reached for his right hand then froze. "Which hand do you use to sketch?"

"My left."

Without another word, she released his left hand and opened the sketchpad.

He eyed the page. A thrill of excitement coursed through him as it always did when presented with a blank sheet. He trailed the callused tip of a finger on the parchment. An image of Grace, Viscount Camden's elegant daughter—her wide, beaming smile, her violet eyes—flitted through his mind, and he froze. He didn't want to draw her face. He didn't want to bring her here into this bleak, violent world. He preferred her lakeside in the green pastures of Leeds where he'd last seen her.

In the end, the desire to see her one more time, even if it was just as a charcoal rendering in a sketchpad, consumed him. His fingers danced over the page, reacquainting him with the feel of the charcoal in his hand, the feeling of old lovers meeting. Grace took shape. The riotous crown of tight curls dark on the page but golden blonde in his mind gave him pause. A surge of pain climbed up his throat, and nearly strangled him.

"Are you all right?"

Adam blinked then forced himself to release a breath. "Fine." His fingers resumed their efforts.

Georgina sat beside him for the two hours he sketched. When at last he finished, he studied the face that filled the parchment. Beautiful Grace. He'd last seen her once upon a lifetime ago.

"She is beautiful," Georgina's reverent whisper cut into his musings.

His throat moved up and down. "She is."

"Who is she?" He ignored the slight catch in Georgina's voice, fixing his gaze on the page with Grace's image on it.

To speak of Grace in this den of traitors would be a sacrilege to Grace's purity and goodness. *Oh God*, what must she think? He'd promised to return for her and yet, between his last mission and his captivity, it had been nearly six months since he'd seen her last.

"She's just a lady," he lied. He snapped the folio closed, ending any further questions about Grace Blakely.

"Is she your wife?"

A spasm wrenched his heart. He tried to conceal the flash of pain, but the woman was perceptive.

"She is your wife," she concluded.

"She is not my wife." Mayhap in another life, at a different time.

Georgina leaned forward. "But you love her."

"Your questioning leads me to believe you are, in fact, working for the men here." The words came out as an animalistic growl.

An indignant gasp burst from her lips. She leaped to her feet. "How dare you?"

Adam hurled the book across the room.

Georgina recoiled, the color seeping from her cheeks.

He arched a brow. "Is my assumption so far-fetched?"

Seeing her frozen, with trembling fingers gripping the edge of the table, stabbed at him like needles of guilt. Still, he could not prevent the biting edge to his words.

"You come here and learn my interests. You bring me foods that are hardly the fare of prisoners. What is the benefit in learning anything about me?" He slammed a fist down on the table and it rattled, sending the remnants of his tankard of water sloshing over the sides. "Goddamn it! Who are you? What do you want from me?"

"I am merely a loyal British subject." She paused and gave him a lingering stare; as if that pronouncement was a monumental one that should mean something. Georgina sighed. "I only want to help you." Something else flickered in her eyes, but was quickly gone.

"Then, for the love of Christ, free me. I have a family waiting for me. Surely that must mean something to you?"

A sadness too profound to measure filled her eyes. "It does. But would you exchange your life for mine?"

Sensing she was wavering, his raspy promise burst forth like cannon fire. "I can help you! I will take you with me."

I will take you with me.

Despite the risks, despite Adam's beautiful lover, Georgina's pulse quickened at the promise he dangled before her.

Could she trust him? There had been others before him and they'd taught her that desperate men did and said desperate things. They'd bargained their families, their wealth, and all they had, to obtain their freedom. For all the help she'd given, they had left her behind.

Not one had thought her worth saving.

She studied Adam. In her breast, guilt warred with fear. He was in love. Her eyes wandered to the now-closed leather folio. Correction, he was in love with a stunning *lady*.

Georgina touched a curl and brushed it behind her ear.

He didn't deserve to be a prisoner in this vile place.

"Your expression is pained."

Georgina jumped at Mr. Markham's softly spoken words.

"And you always do that. Flinch as if you've been struck."

That was, of course, because she had been. On more occasions than she could count.

"Mr. Markham..."

"We've known each other for what? A month? You keep me company nearly every day. I think we can dispense with formalities." His lips turned up in a sardonic grin.

"Formalities?"

"My name is Adam," he reminded her.

"Georgina."

"Georgina," he teased in an almost seductive murmur.

Her skin warmed at the sound of her name on his lips. It was as though the one word utterance tumbled off his tongue like a lover's caress. She brushed her foolish longings aside. She'd not survived these many years by being foolish. "I mean, you should call me Georgina."

"Will you tell me about your family?"

She hesitated. His questions were dangerous. Nay, *all* questions were dangerous. If he discovered the truth...Her eyes wandered to a point beyond his shoulder as she imagined a very different world than the one she'd been born to.

"My mother was a maid. She was beautiful."

Well, the latter part was true. At least, that's what her father had told her of the woman who'd died giving birth to her. She often wondered if that was why he hated her. If he blamed her for her mother's death?

"She would sing to me. I would sit at her feet each night and she'd brush the tangles from my hair." Oh, how much more beautiful this image was than the horrid truth.

"What of your father?"

She closed her eyes and summoned an idea of the father she'd always dreamed of. "He loved to tell stories. Mother and I would sit beside him and he'd tell great tales." She paused. It was far harder to craft even false memories for the monster who'd sired her. A ruthless merchant who'd harbored a bitter animosity for everything English, including his own daughter.

"Your tones are very cultured for a maid's daughter."

Georgina stiffened.

"Forgive me. I didn't mean to offend you," he said.

His words danced too close to the truth. The Crown had known what they were doing when they trained this man to do its work.

"What happened to them?"

God, he was tenacious. Despite knowing exactly whom he meant, she asked, "To whom?"

"Your parents."

She looked out the window and shifted, her lies piling onto the already heavy guilt she carried. "They died." She directed her curt response to the gardens below.

"How did they—"

Georgina interrupted him before she had to add to her burden with further fabrications about her imaginary family. She spun around. "Why don't you tell me about your family?"

She expected him to go silent as he so often did when she asked him probing questions she didn't deserve an answer to.

"My father died when I was young. He suffered an apoplexy."

The anguish on his face squeezed her heart. It called her back to the seat beside him. "I'm so sorry." She sank into the chair.

Adam glanced down at his hands. "It was a long time ago."

"That doesn't make it less painful." Desperate to drive back the sad lines at the corners of his lips, Georgina asked, "Do you have any siblings?"

He nodded. "Two brothers."

A wave of wistfulness overtook her. "I would have traded my left hand for a brother or sister."

Adam chuckled. "Yes, sometimes I am lucky. It would depend on which given day you ask me."

"What are they like?"

His brow wrinkled. "Well, Nick is the eldest. He's four years older than I am and always assumed responsibility for us. My younger brother, Anthony, could drive a saint to drink. But they are a good, loving family." His throat bobbed up and down, and she had to look away again.

"And what of the woman?" Her cheeks blazed at the boldness of such a question.

He reached for his glass of water and took a long swallow. "I can't speak of her."

"Because she was your love?" She curled her fingers into the sides of the chair as she waited in hopeful anticipation of his answer.

"Because she is the only woman I'll ever love and it is a disservice to her memory to speak of her."

Pain knifed at her heart. What she wouldn't give to have a man speak with that kind of passion about her. The alternative; that his words resonated because they'd been spoken by this enigmatic man, were too terrifying for her to seriously consider. She shook her head, ridding herself of the foolish notion.

"Have you ever been in love?"

She started at his question. "Never." As much as she longed for an honorable suitor, Georgina didn't think she'd ever find a man who would love and care for her. She'd long ago ceased to believe that she'd find a way out of this hell. "If I marry, it will be for security and stability. Never love."

Adam's brow wrinkled. "Those are unusual words for a young woman. Women like you are supposed to be starry-eyed and dreaming of a handsome, young man to carry you away."

Bitterness made her laugh. "My dreams of fairy tale endings have long come and gone. There is no such thing as love." *At least not for me.*

He didn't counter her words. Instead, he eyed her with that warm concern that was chipping away at the defensive wall she'd constructed around her heart. He was dangerous to the self-protection she'd spent the better part of her life perfecting.

Georgina scrambled to her feet so quickly she upended her chair. She bit the inside of her cheek hard, drawing blood. She bound his hands and retrieved the sketchpad. "I have to go."

"Georgina!"

She raced from his room and down the stairs, sinking into a heap at the bottom step. She dropped her head into her hands. "What are you doing?" she mouthed into her palms.

The longer Adam Markham remained in her father's lair, the more she had to confront her own weaknesses in preventing his evil. This man, another stranger required her help in attaining his freedom. To not aid him would ultimately mean his death. Georgina captured her lower lip between her teeth. How could she manage to free him while taking care to avoid her father's retribution? Ah God help her. She could not fail. Not again. Not as she had before.

Her body trembled as the image of the stranger killed by her father's hand slipped into her mind's eye. He'd been the one to give her the contact information for key figures in the Home Office. In the end, Georgina had been unable to help him. She had sworn she'd never again be responsible for another man's death. Georgina folded her arms tight across her midsection as the stranger's face took shape—only this time it was Adam on the floor. Adam's chest painted red with blood. Adam's—

"What's the matter with you?"

She picked her head up and stared at her father's corpulent form. He stood over her, a dark frown etched on his face. She'd be damned if he saw just how much his presence unnerved her. He'd always taken a perverse delight in her fear.

Georgina schooled her features. "Forgive me, but watching a man suffer needlessly doesn't sit well with me." She rose to her feet and faced him.

Father chortled so deeply he broke into a fit of coughing. His rotund frame shook under the depth of his amusement.

Gooseflesh dotted her skin. How could she share the same blood as this loathsome creature?

His bushy, white brows dipped. "You got that look in your eyes, Georgie."

Georgina couldn't imagine her father knew her well enough to recognize any kind of look about her. "What look is that, Father?"

"The one that reminds me how you betrayed us in the past." Georgina did not answer fast enough for his liking and he launched into a stinging diatribe. "Did you forget about the soldiers who raped your grandmother and then slit her throat? Are those the people you are loyal to, daughter?"

Her heart ached for the faceless woman she'd never known, but Mr. Markham was alive now. "Mr. Markham is not guilty of those crimes, Father."

He slapped her hard. Blood filled her mouth where her teeth cut the inside of her cheek, and stars danced behind her eyes. She fought the urge to cradle her face, too proud to show him the hurt he'd caused. But she'd be damned if she allowed him to see even a smidgeon of the pain he'd caused.

Black rage danced in his eyes, giving him the look of a feral animal. He jabbed a finger in her direction. "You'll do what I tell you to do!" His rough hands closed painfully on her shoulders. "Now listen to me. You will make that bastard upstairs fall in love with you."

A haze of confusion descended. "You want me to what?"

"Stupid girl," he muttered. "We've tried beating the truth out of him. We've gotten nowhere. I want you to find out who his leader is. I want the names of all the men in his organization. They are the ones hunting down our members. We need to get to them before they get to us." A heinous smile tilted the corner of his lips and chilled her through.

Now it made sense—father's willingness to trust her with Adam even after she'd set his last prisoner free. She folded her arms and attempted to rub warmth into them. "And if I say no?"

Father's lips turned up in a black smile. "If you do, I'll let Jamie have at you."

Ice filled her veins. Having born witness to enough of his sins, she didn't doubt that vile pledge.

"Come, gel. You think I don't see the way he's panting after you? Why do you think he hasn't had you yet?"

Only, she'd believed her father at least valued her enough as a daughter to preserve her honor. Apparently, there were no redeeming aspects about him. He was a monster. *Didn't you already know that? Haven't you witnessed the lengths he will go to achieve his goals?* "Even with what happened to your mother, you would do that to me, your own daughter?"

He leaned close, fury dancing in his eyes. "I made a pledge to see Ireland liberated."

She gritted her teeth in thinly veiled hatred. Could she betray Mr. Markham to save herself from Jamie? "And how do you propose I make your captive fall in love with me?" The achingly beautiful woman in the sketchpad surfaced in her memory.

"I don't care what you do. Just do it."

Georgina slid her gaze away. Jamie would violate her. She knew that, knew it with a sick sense of inevitability. The part of her deep down, the part bent on self-preservation, embraced the promise of safety her father dangled before her. She closed her eyes and saw the hard angular planes of Adam's face, a face too beautiful for words. She saw his long limbs, imagined them twined with hers in thoughts no good, respectable woman should ever have. Her pulse fluttered in remembrance of his thumb stroking the soft skin of her neck. Georgina forced her eyes open. "I won't do it," she said in hushed tones. "I'll care for him, I'll feed him, but I won't play this game of treachery."

Her father growled and took a step toward her.

Georgina's chin ticked up a notch. She held his flinty stare.

He cursed and spit on the floor. "You'll do what I tell you to do."

She wasn't foolish enough to believe the matter concluded.

"Get up there and care for him. Jamie is untying him now." He jabbed another finger at her chest. "He is only unbound when one of us is present." A hard nudge between her shoulder blades propelled her feet forward. "I don't like keeping him around this long. As soon as I get the information we need, I can get rid of him."

Her tongue felt heavy in her mouth. She swallowed several times before managing to squeeze the words out. "Get rid of him?"

"Don't worry yourself with that."

Within moments, Georgina found herself staring at an unbound Adam Markham.

The door closed, the lock settling into place with an ominous click.

Adam's frame unfurled was more impressive than anything she could have imagined. He towered like the god Apollo, a golden warrior. Her heart missed a beat.

"You are taller than I'd imagined." She flinched.

Blast it! Shut your mouth, Georgina.

His lips twitched. "You are a tiny thing."

A startled laugh escaped her. That was the first time she had ever been referred to as tiny. Her laughter trailed off and she held up the leather folio in her hands. "I've brought you this," she said, belatedly realizing the foolishness in returning so soon with the same paltry offering. Heat slapped her cheeks.

He crossed the room in three long strides and Georgina panicked. She dropped the book and took a step backwards. Then another. Until her back met the wall. Her heart thumped wildly.

He froze. "You don't think I would hurt you?"

"No, I..." She let the words trail off. "Desperate men say and do desperate things."

Adam studied her. Silence stretched out before them and then he walked toward her. She studied the slow rise and fall of his chest, the indecipherable expression in his eyes as he came to a stop. He reached to caress her reddened cheek. "Who did this?" Barely suppressed violence underlay the whispered question.

Georgina relished the gentleness of his caress. Never had a man touched her with such tenderness. "Please," she rasped.

...don't stop touching me.

She was halfway to begging him to hold her in a way no one ever had.

He dropped his hand back to his side as though he'd been burned. "Forgive me," he murmured.

She wanted to weep at the loss of his touch.

"It was them, wasn't it?"

She nodded, grateful someone loathed the two men as much as she did.

A growl climbed up his throat and it was too much. This expression of someone caring about her welfare. About her. She clenched her eyes shut, willing back tears. He could not be allowed to see her weakness. A drop slipped down her cheek. Then another. Finally a torrent of long-suppressed grief poured out.

He groaned and pulled her into his arms. She recoiled, but Adam stroked the back of her head and held her to him with a gentle strength. "Shh," he whispered against her temple.

She sobbed against his chest, this man her father had asked her to betray. She selfishly took all the comfort and support he offered until her tears soaked the front of his rough cambric shirt.

Adam caressed the strands of her hair. "Shh," he whispered. "They are not worth your tears."

Except she didn't cry for them. She cried for the little girl who'd been beaten and forgotten. She cried at the unfairness of being dependent on a man to survive. She cried for Adam, who was as trapped as she was.

They stood that way until her tears drew to a shuddery halt.

Georgina wiped her eyes, suddenly feeling very foolish for her humiliating display of emotion. "Forgive me."

Adam brushed away a loose curl that hung over her eyes. "You are a brave woman. I meant what I said. If you free me, I will help you."

Suddenly it was very important that Adam understood.

"There was another man," she whispered. "I freed him and he…" She squeezed her eyes shut "He paid with his life. And I paid the price, too." Her father and Jamie had dragged her from the room and beat her until she'd passed out.

Adam cupped her face between his hands. His eyes met hers. "I would rather die than remain in this place."

His words transported her back to that dark day, when the last captive had lain dead on her kitchen floor. She would not lead him to his death. "No. You don't mean that," she rasped.

Adam steadied her. "What is it?"

She shook her head. Her breath came in deep, gasping pants.

He swept her into his arms and carried her to the bed. "What is it?" he whispered.

Adam held her and stroked smooth circles over her back. Georgina wanted it to go on forever. "Thank you. No one has ever…" Her pride prevented her from finishing her sentence.

He frowned. "No one has ever held you? What about your—"

Georgina tripped over the web of lies she'd already spun. To stop the question on his lips, she did the unthinkable. She leaned up to kiss him.

The shock of their lips meeting struck her like a flash of lightning. A foreign hunger for his touch snaked through her limbs and Georgina wound herself about him like a vine of ivy.

He groaned, the sound a primal, masculine grumble from deep within his chest.

She twined her hands about his neck and caressed the golden locks of spun silk in her fingers.

Adam put his hands on her waist, paused, and then, as if exploring, moved his search lower, down to the curve of her hips. She angled her head, opening herself to his kiss. Parting her lips, she allowed his tongue entry. He moaned as if in pain. Georgina's lids fluttered open and she studied this golden god as he kissed her. His eyes were clenched tight as if creased by agonized pleasure. All because of her.

With a small cry, she threw her head back, exposing her neck for his attention.

He set her away so fast she tumbled to the floor.

It took a long while for the cloud of passion to lift. When it did, she wished she could pull it firmly back in place. Horror wreathed the hard-angled planes of Adam's face.

Her heart sputtered to a slow halt. His revulsion had the same effect as a punch to her belly.

"Christ," Adam whispered.

As much as she hoped his horror came from having shoved her aside, she knew it was not. In a desperate attempt at preserving the little pride she had left, she rose and brushed out her skirts.

Adam's throat moved up and down as he seemed to force the words out. "I am in love with another woman. I will not betray her."

Not for a woman like you, her mind silently jeered.

A stinging jealousy for the woman who had laid claim to his heart filled her.

He'd merely been providing her with a comforting embrace and she had flung herself at him like a shameless wanton! A scarlet blush stained her cheeks.

Adam extended his hand.

Georgina looked at his long, gentleman's fingers. With every fiber of her being, she wanted to reject it, but pride dictated that she show him how unaffected she was by his rejection. She placed her hand in his and allowed him to help her up.

He took her chin between his forefinger and thumb. "This is not about you, Georgina. I told you before—"

She angled her chin away from him. "I know."

The last thing in the world she needed to hear was how in love he was with the nameless beauty in the sketchpad. It only reminded her that some women were born beautiful, with the love and adulation of good men, while women like her dwelled in the shadows.

In the grand scheme of lies she'd told this man, what was one more? "I am sorry I kissed you. I don't know what came over me." She had many regrets. Kissing him was not one of them.

"You are a lovely woman. I'm just in love with someone else."

And there it was, a second time. Punishment for coveting what belonged to the goddess on his parchment.

She wanted to find a dark corner of the house and nurse her wounds like an injured pup. Georgina managed a jerky nod and turned to leave.

Her father's yell carried through the door. "Georgina?"

The blood drained from her cheeks. "I'm coming!" she called.

She hurried over to the door just as it was flung open to crash into her hip. Georgina grunted at the throb of pain that shot down her leg.

Her father and Jamie stood in the doorway. Father held a pistol trained on Adam, while Jamie pinned Adam with a glare brimming with loathing.

"It's time to tie this animal up," her father growled.

Jamie escorted Adam to his bed, but the golden god sprang at Jamie and caught him square in the stomach, felling him. The men wrestled for power like lions vying for control. Adam managed to straddle Jamie. He wrapped his hands around the weaker man's neck.

Georgina watched in sick fascination as Jamie's eyes bulged from his sockets and drool spilled from his gaping mouth. She'd seen a dead man, but she'd never seen a man's last breath leave his body. She couldn't tear her gaze away.

Her father wrapped his arm around her forearm and tugged her to his side. He pinched the soft skin.

Georgina cried out.

Adam froze. His head snapped up.

"Stop. Or she'll pay for your disobedience." Father's promise seemed to penetrate Adam's single-minded purpose to destroy Jamie.

His eyes met Georgina's.

Father tightened his grip and she bit her lip to keep from crying out. She would not distract Adam again, not when he was handing out the beating Jamie so richly deserved. She gave a slight shake of her head and willed him to see that she was fine.

"I'll kill her," Father promised on a silken whisper.

It was a lie.

Then she felt the angry bite of a pistol against her temple. A chill swept over her. Father had descended into such madness she could no longer be sure.

Hot rage flared in Adam's eyes. "Stop," he barked. He scrambled up from his knees, hands held out. His eyes had the crazed look of a man who'd dueled with the devil...And lost.

Jamie turned over onto his side and gasped as he tried to suck in air, like a fish thrown ashore.

"Perhaps you don't care for your well-being, but should you choose to fight us, she is the one who will feel our wrath. Is that clear?" Father snapped.

Adam's chest heaved. He took several steps backward and sat on the bed.

Father released Georgina and nodded to Adam. "I see that we understand each other."

Except Georgina didn't see anything. A swell of emotion clogged her throat. Why would this man, a stranger, protect her—at the expense of his freedom?

Jamie managed to stand and dusted his hands along the front of his breeches. He took a step toward the bed.

Adam held his hand out as if in supplication. He could have killed Jamie but he hadn't. He'd saved her.

Jamie slammed his fist against Adam's temple.

Adam grunted and collapsed onto the soft coverlet. Blood trickled in a rivulet from the corner of his right nostril.

Georgina gasped and covered her mouth with her hands. Reminded of her presence, Father shoved her toward the door. She tripped over her skirts and caught the edge of the table to keep from toppling over.

Jamie set to work binding Adam's wrists and ankles to the corners of the four-poster bed. "Get out of here, gel," Father snapped.

She swallowed and turned back around to face Adam.

"I said, get out!" Father gave her another nudge toward the door.

Adam's roar of fury filled the small room and rattled off the windowpanes. "Don't touch her, you bloody coward."

His show of bravery was met with another fist to the head.

"No, Adam," she hurried to assure him. "I'm fine."

Father gripped her arm and steered her out of the room. "Go."

The door closed, the click like the crack of a pistol at night. Her breath hitched painfully in her chest as she waited. She leaned against the wood panel and knocked her head against the solid structure.

Adam cried out.

Her teeth sank into her lower lip.

He cried out a second time.

She bit the inside of her cheek.

Then silence. No more screaming. Nor shouting. Or vile curses. And, somehow, that was worst of all.

Georgina's fingers sought and found the edge of the doorjamb to keep herself from collapsing. Her heart climbed into her throat and threatened to strangle her.

Georgina didn't know how long she stood there but, as the seconds ticked by, her shame grew and grew. What manner of coward was she that she should leave Adam to face her father's cruelty? How could she have done that, when he'd sacrificed his own freedom for her safety?

She threw the door open so hard it slammed against the wall.

Two pairs of angry eyes swiveled in her direction. Jamie had a riding crop poised mid-strike over Adam's naked chest.

"Stop," she cried. She grabbed Jamie's arm. "Please, you must stop."

He shrugged her off.

Father spun around. "What's this about, gel?" he barked.

"Please, I—" She glanced at Adam. Their gazes caught and held. "I must speak with you," she said to her father. "Both of you."

Jamie straightened. The riding crop dangled forgotten by his side.

Her eyes slid closed for a moment as she sent her thanks up to a God she didn't believe in. For now, Adam had been spared this abuse. "This can wait until we're done here," Jamie growled, a feral gleam of bloodlust in his eyes.

"No. It cannot," Georgina protested. She gave her father a pointed look.

He shifted his mouth from side to side. "We'll finish this up later, Mr. Markham."

Georgina allowed herself to be dragged off, casting one last glance over her shoulder.

THREE

Emmet is amassing the power of the United Irishmen. His men have captured a British spy.
Signed,
A Loyal British Subject

When Adam was a small boy, he and his brother Nick had been as mischievous as any other young boy in England. They'd had a very stern tutor and, one time, he and Nick had carefully dug up earthworms from the lush soil and placed them in the man's gloves. As heir to their father's earldom, his older brother had escaped punishment. Adam hadn't been as fortunate.

For his troubles, the nasty tutor had locked Adam away in his armoire. Even as a man of now eight and twenty, he'd sometimes awake from his sleep, gasping for breath as he recalled the terror. The impenetrable abyss, the quiet hum of silence. He'd pounded away at the makeshift coffin, screaming until his voice had failed him.

His mother had been the one to find him. The tutor had been sacked on the spot but the horror of that moment would forever linger.

Tied up as he was now, unable to help Georgina, Adam found himself plagued by the same sense of helplessness that he'd suffered because of his tutor's abuse.

It had been clear she was lying. Fox's partner, known to Adam only as Hunter, had clearly realized that—Adam had seen the flash of understanding in his eyes. He couldn't stop flagellating himself with the image of what they would do to her. All because she'd protected him.

Why would she forego her own safety for his welfare? His torture was inevitable. All she'd done was bought him a momentary reprieve. She must have known that, yet she'd still shielded him with her body, as a kind of sacrifice.

Here he was; a faithful member of The Brethren of the Lords, a group sworn to protect and defend the Crown, needing the protection of a slip of a girl.

The memory of her anchored to Fox's side rocked through his mind and he wrenched at his bonds in vain. With a ragged cry, he lay back against the mattress. Sweat trickled from his brow into his eyes, stinging mercilessly. He ignored it, thinking of her. He'd go mad if he imagined them with their hands on her, so he allowed himself to unearth the other thought he'd buried.

She had kissed him.

He recoiled at the betrayal of Grace and yet…the taste of Georgina lingered. As much as he railed at himself for his fickle desires, he hungered for this capable maid.

She was nothing like the women he usually desired. Adam had always preferred fair women with long limbs and pale blonde hair, prideful.

Yet Georgina had drawn him in. With her well-flared hips and generous breasts, she was curved in all the places a woman should be. There was a sultry, seductive quality to her pouty lips. When he should've been thinking about Grace and his freedom, those goddamn lips would enter his imaginings. He'd envision her using her mouth for all kinds of forbidden pleasures.

Adam turned his head and stared at the small window in the corner.

He was a bastard and deserved every last bit of torture doled by Fox and Hunter.

Georgina's mind worked furiously as her father steered her downstairs with a firm grip around her wrist.

He'd always delighted in hurting her. She glared at him but he remained oblivious to her abhorrence.

When she'd turned eight and ten, he'd begun presenting her to his social circle and the beatings had stopped. He'd had grand hopes of her making a profitable arrangement with a wealthy merchant. Father had always been obscenely wealthy, but it had never been enough. He seemed to relish material things, status, and power a good deal more than he'd ever cared for any living creature—her included. She didn't care. It didn't matter.

Georgina hated that she still couldn't lie to herself after all this time.

In the two years Father had presented her to possible suitors, it had become obvious that even his wealth was not enough to entice the most eligible gentlemen. So the beatings had resumed and she'd faded into the background.

Jamie looked at her. The flecks of gold in his pale blue eyes sparkled with fury. "What could merit this insolence?"

She swallowed, refusing to answer him.

When they reached the kitchen, Father shoved her into a chair. He folded his arms. "Well come on then, I don't have all day."

"I agree to your request." In her lap, she crossed her fingers. "You are correct, Father. It is likely Mr. Markham will simply turn over the information you seek."

Father tapped his chin. "Why are you so suddenly willing to help?"

"It is conditional," Georgina lied. "I ask that when I find the names of those in his organization, you set him free. I'll not be responsible for another man's death."

Silence fell as her father appeared to consider her offer. "Hmm."

She waited, unfurling her fingers which she'd unknowingly clenched into tight fists at her side.

"I don't trust her," Jamie snarled. "She's protecting him." He turned to Georgina and stuck a finger in her direction. "You're falling in love with him!"

No! Georgina gripped the edge of her seat, her nails dug into the hard wood. She shoved aside the panicky fear that twisted in her gut.

She would never do anything so foolish as to fall in love with one of her father's captives. She was merely caring for him as she had many others before him.

Oh God, why did that feel like a lie?

Jamie slammed his fist down on the table. "You do not even deny it." His voice rumbled off the walls.

She stood firm even as her heart raced.

"Enough!" Father hollered. "She is doing her job, Jamie. Did you see Markham? I'd venture she could seduce the secrets out of him this day if we wanted."

Revulsion rippled through her at his crude words. What manner of father spoke of his daughter in such a way?

Jamie's eyes went wide. "No," he said between gritted teeth.

"No?" her father asked.

Father was across the room in an instant. He had Jamie by the shirtfront and pressed against the wall. "Have you forgotten our goal? We lost most of our leadership in '98 and cannot afford another set-back." He released Jamie and turned back to Georgina. "I'm proud of you, girl. Find out his secrets. Even if it means seduction. And to you, Jamie, each of us has a role. Georgina knows what hers is. I suggest you remember yours."

The hard glint in her father's eyes chilled her.

Jamie all but growled. "She's not a whore."

"Think of the information she can get out of him," her father needled. "We've been running from those bloody bastards since '93. Georgina destroyed our last chance...but she's agreed to redeem herself."

She kept her mouth closed. Better to let Father believe she'd agreed to his harebrained scheme. Father and Jamie could both order her to seduce Adam and she wouldn't do it. She'd not whore herself for their vile goals.

Father drummed his fingertips against his chin. "You haven't lost your courage, have you, gel?"

It took her moment to realize they were both studying her.

Georgina shook her head. She knew what she needed to do. "No."

"Very well then," her father murmured. "See to it. If you must seduce him, see to that as well." Her stomach turned. Father spoke of her ruin as casually as if speaking of the weather. He continued, directing his attention to Jamie. "I've a meeting with Emmet. I want you to remain here with Georgina."

Her mind screamed out in protest. She wanted Jamie gone. Only then could Adam be truly safe—even if for a short while.

Father turned back to her. "Prepare something for him to eat and return to his room."

Georgina watched him leave and stared blankly at the crusty bread atop the table.

So that was why Father had tolerated the lavish meals she'd prepared for Markham. It had all been a part of his deeper plot for Georgina to earn Adam's trust. Her stomach turned at her unknowing complicity in her father's plan.

She gave her head a shake and set to work making a plate of food for Adam. Even with her back to Jamie, she was aware of him at the kitchen door, watching her.

Gooseflesh dotted the skin on her arms. She picked up a knife and sliced the bread. How difficult would it be to turn around and bury the makeshift weapon in Jamie's black heart?

"I'm right, you know."

Her blade froze above the flaky, white bread. She brushed back the stubborn curl and resumed cutting. "I don't know what you're talking about."

He crossed the room in an instant and wrapped his hand around her wrist. The knife clattered to the countertop.

She gasped as he dragged her tightly against him, crushing her body to his chest. "You're falling in love with him."

"I am not," she said a touch too quickly.

It would be sheer madness to give her heart to a man who'd been taken captive by her father. Especially when *his* heart belonged to another. Why, it would be a level of foolishness that would merit committing her to Bedlam. She drew in a steadying breath. "I don't even know him."

Jamie lowered his forehead to hers. "I see the way you look at him and the way he looks at you."

The only way Adam ever studied her was with bitterness and sympathy. The thought lanced her heart. She detested the idea of being the object of anyone's pity, most especially Adam. "He does not feel anything for me."

Jamie's eyes went to her lips.

Her blood froze.

He snaked a hand around her arm.

She slapped at his hand. "What are you doing?"

He focused his hot, lascivious stare on her breasts. "Isn't it obvious, love?"

Bile burned in her throat at the idea of him touching her. She yanked her hand free and turned to flee. A cry tore from her throat as he dragged her into his arms and kissed her. His lips pushed against hers, hard and unyielding, punishing. She tried to plead with him to stop and he pressed his vantage, slipping his tongue into her mouth.

Georgina gagged at the cool, moist invasion. His breath, a sick blend of stale brandy and violence filled her senses. He worked a hand between their bodies and roughly squeezed her breast. A moan rumbled from deep within his chest.

Her body shuddered at his violation. She gave a hard nudge. Though stronger, Jamie was so engrossed in his efforts she managed to stun him into releasing her.

He stumbled backward.

Heart hammering wildly, she swiped the back of her hand across her mouth, trying to drive the taste of him away.

Jamie studied her from beneath hooded lids, a glimmer of satisfaction in his cruel eyes. "Finish preparing Markham's meal."

Her fingers shook as she followed Jamie's instructions. When she had the tray in hand, Jamie clasped her wrist. "Perhaps I should thank Markham for breaking you in."

Oh God, he was pure evil. She stared pointedly at his hand until he released her. With a flounce of her hair, she hurried above stairs. Jamie followed at her heels. He unlocked the door and pushed her inside.

From the bed he was strapped to, Adam studied her.

She flinched as Jamie brushed a curl away from her neck. He leaned down. His hot breath fanned her nape. "Remember me, love." With that, he took his leave and the door closed behind him.

The sound of the lock turning filled the small space.

Georgina set the tray down beside Adam's bed and immediately dropped to her knees. Filled with a restive energy, she set to work on his bindings. The memory of Jamie's advances so fresh and potent it burned like a poison, until she threatened to choke on the horror of his assault.

"Georgina?"

Adam's voice came as though down a long hall. The knots of his bindings came undone and she sank back on her haunches. "Hmm?" To keep from descending into madness, she fixed on the purpose of caring for Adam, taking his hand between hers.

"Georgina?"

She didn't pick her head up but continued to rub his bruised flesh.

He laid his free hand on hers, staying her movement. "Georgina, stop."

At last she picked her gaze up.

Adam ran his gaze over Georgina. A faint tremor wracked her stiffly held body. He thought of Hunter with his hands on her silken nape, his lips close to her creamy, white skin and had to fight to keep from tossing his head back and roaring like a wounded bear.

Hunter had touched Georgina. *What else did he do to her?* The silken whisper slithered around his brain, eating at his insides like a cancer. The idea of Hunter claiming Georgina—his lips on hers, his hands cupping her full breasts—ravaged him. "Did he hurt you?" Adam's voice emerged raw and gruff with emotion.

Georgina's chest heaved. "No," she said quickly—too quickly. She quickly stood and backed away

Her hasty retreat hinted at the lie.

Adam tried to quell the surging sense of panic. "Georgina?" This time his voice seemed to penetrate whatever horror held her in its grip.

She shook her head slowly then touched her lip, drawing Adam's attention to the bruised, swollen flesh.

And he knew. Before she even said it, he knew.

"He kissed me."

Rage warred with jealousy in his chest. It robbed him of speech. Hit him like a physical blow. He couldn't understand it. With his feelings for Grace, it shouldn't matter who Georgina kissed. Yet it did.

There was a wild, hunted look to Georgina, and she remained rooted to the floor.

His heart climbed up into his throat. "Did he do anything else?"

Her chest continued to rise and fall rapidly. "He touched me," she said quietly. She started to touch her chest and then her hand fluttered back to her side.

A loud humming filled his ears as imagined scenes flashed behind his eyes: Georgina with her skirts thrown above her waist; Georgina held down, defenseless while Hunter plowed between her legs. Adam's body jerked.

He forced words out past numb lips. "Did he...?" He couldn't finish the thought. God help Hunter; when Adam secured his freedom, he'd rip the bastard's entrails through his throat.

She seemed to follow his unfinished question. "No," she said quickly.

The empty hopelessness in her brown eyes ate at him. Hunter may not have violated her, but he'd still left an indelible mark. Adam could not bear seeing her like this; as if her inner light had been extinguished by his assault. A woman with her courage and strength deserved to live in a world of happiness and hope, untouched by the ugliness visited upon the world by greedy, manipulative men. When he spoke, he kept his tone calm and even. "Come here, Georgina."

For all that had happened between her and that monster, she didn't hesitate. She took a step toward him. Then another. And another. She froze when nothing but the span of a hand separated them.

"I want to kiss you," he said quietly.

Her eyes formed wide moons. "Why?" She wet her lips.

Because he didn't want her to believe a kiss was vile and ugly. Because she deserved to know gentleness in an ugly, cruel world. "Will you allow it?"

Georgina remained silent so long he thought she might not answer. The tick of the clock punctuated the quiet. She gave a tight nod.

"Lean close to me. I will not hurt you," he whispered as though speaking to a skittish mare.

Her breath, a blend of honeysuckle and tea, caressed his skin.

With infinite gentleness, he claimed her lips. The kiss lasted no longer than three heartbeats, perhaps.

Adam pulled away and placed a lingering kiss on her brow. "Run away from this place. You do not belong here."

Her lids fluttered open and she placed a hand against his chest.

His heart flipped over at her gentle touch. God, he wanted her lips again. He could no more stop the yearning than he could halt a runaway phaeton with his bare hands. "Will you sing to me?"

She paused and tilted her head ever so slightly. "Sing?"

"Yes, you know? You put music to words and—"

Georgina giggled, sounding for the first time since he'd known her, like a carefree young miss. She slipped the remainder of the ropes off his wrists. "What are you doing?" she squeaked as he stood up and settled his hand around her waist. Blood rushed through his legs and he gritted his teeth at the weakness months in captivity had wrought.

"Are you all right?"

"Fine," he lied. He twined his free hand with hers and found strength in her touch. "Go on then," he urged.

She started to sing and Adam nearly lost his footing. It was probably the inactivity that made him careless. He had to remind himself to count steps but Georgina Wilcox possessed a voice that would have made choirs of angels weep with envy. She closed her eyes, as if she'd drifted off on the soaring notes.

40

This is how he would remember her. If he died tomorrow, or the next day, or the day after that, or even if he was freed, he'd think back on this moment. Christ, he wanted her...

Her lashes fluttered open. A pale pink colored her cheeks and she dropped her gaze to his shirtfront as if embarrassed by the joyous interlude they'd both stolen.

All the while, he stumbled through the waltz, guiding her through the motions of the scandalous dance still not practiced in fashionable ballrooms in England, until Georgina laughed with breathless abandon. At one time he'd moved with grace, but his captors had stolen even that from him.

"What is this?" Her question pulled him back from the bitterness of his captivity and failings.

Adam managed a wry grin. "This is dancing."

She laughed again, the sound as pure and clear as bells ringing. "It is terribly improper."

Could there be anything more improper than a man being abducted and strapped to a chair like a filthy beast? He thrust aside those musings, not allowing them to intrude on this. "It is called the waltz. And most respectable hostesses would agree with you." For this wasn't about him, but rather Georgina and offering her a small sliver of happiness.

"Where did you learn such a thing?"

Adam stumbled once more, his legs stiff from ill use. "In the ballrooms of Paris." He squeezed her waist and she picked up his cue.

Georgina resumed her jaunty song and he twirled her in dizzying circles around the room until she was gasping for breath and singing was no longer possible.

God, in this moment, he was—content. With her in his arms, he could forget the horrors of his life—if even for a moment. When had he last known this happiness? His mind churned slowly. *Grace.* The muscles of his stomach contracted. Not since Grace had professed her love. The memory staggered him. The backs of his knees slammed into the nightstand, the abrupt movement making Georgina trip over his feet.

They crashed down atop the feather-down mattress in a twisted heap of legs and arms. Her frame bounced several times beneath his.

Adam braced his arms over her to keep from crushing her. He should move. He should roll to the other side of the mattress. Instead he brushed back a damp tendril from her brow. "If you could go any-where, where would you go?"

"Go?" Her voice was breathy from their exertions.

"If you could leave this place?"

A simmering heat pulsed in his veins. His body poised so close to hers. The sound of his ragged breathing filled his ears and almost drowned out her quiet response.

Almost.

He wished it had. Wished he hadn't heard the cynical edge that should never have been part of the lovely Georgina's words. "Why should I bother, Adam? Dreams aren't real."

Her words pressed on his heart. This is what she believed? "You must have dreams."

"Bah," she scoffed. "They are for small children."

No, they weren't. Dreams represented hope. Even in the direness of his circumstances he clung to something. For to lose hope would mean the end of him. "Wouldn't you want to see Paris?"

"We're on the cusp of war with France," she pointed out. "I hardly think Paris would be my most logical destination."

He chuckled. Ever practical Georgina. Too practical. He waved his hand. "Fine, Rome then, or Greece? Don't you want to see the world?"

She lifted her shoulders in a little shrug.

Adam trailed a finger along the satiny smooth skin of her cheek. An almost simultaneous awareness of the intimate nature of their posi-tion registered. Adam's whole body went on alert. His shaft, pressed against the vee of her thighs, hardened. *Roll away from her. Set her free.* Instead of doing the honorable, gentlemanly thing, he lowered his arms and pressed himself closer to her core.

Her throat bobbed up and down.

Get up. Think of Grace. Except, he'd been too long without a woman. This all-consuming desire was nothing more than a physical hunger. That was what he told himself.

"Adam?" she whispered.

It was a lie. He wanted her. "Georgina?" That word, her name, emerged as a hoarse groan.

The door flew open and slammed against the wall. In unison, he and Georgina looked toward the entrance of the room.

Adam awkwardly shoved himself to his feet, damning his unsteady legs. "Hunter," he growled.

Georgina scrambled up to a standing position.

Hunter trained his pistol on Adam, but his enraged eyes were fixed squarely on Georgina.

Adam stiffened as he switched his gaze between his captor and the young maid. It would appear he'd found the bastard's weakness.

"What are you looking at?" Hunter snapped.

And because it would infuriate the other man, he smiled. A deliberate, knowing smile.

Hunter's eyes lowered. He murmured, "Leave, Georgina."

She hesitated.

"Now," the young traitor roared.

Georgina flinched, but remained rooted to the spot beside Adam.

Adam leaned close to her ear. "Go. I will be fine."

She chewed her lip. Her soulful, brown eyes clouded with desperation.

Adam gave a small nod.

She turned and marched up to Hunter. "Remember what we agreed upon."

Hunter frowned, his gaze focused on Georgina as she sailed past him. And Adam was left alone with the beast.

"Did you make love to her?" Hunter's question gave him pause.

He blinked and stared at the man moving toward him. He stalked Adam, all but springing forward on the balls of his feet to get his hands on him. Never had the name "Hunter" been more apropos. Hunter moved the pistol to his other hand and dealt Adam a swift right hook that would have impressed Gentleman Jackson himself. "I asked you a question."

Adam flexed his jaw. Christ, that hurt. Still it was an interesting turn of events. As he'd suspected, his captor had feelings for Georgina.

Adam shouldn't have cared but, strangely, he did. Adam assumed a relaxed pose. He walked over to the window and folded his arms across his chest.

"I asked you—"

"Oh, I heard you," Adam murmured in casual tones. "It would hardly be gentlemanly of me to answer such a question."

Hunter rushed him. His reflexes dulled by captivity, Adam took a step back, but not before Hunter planted another fist in his cheek.

Adam crumpled to the floor with a groan. Blood spurted out his nose and made a sticky path down his cheek. Stars danced behind his lids. He forced them back.

Hunter towered over him. "You are not to touch her. Is that clear?"

From his work with The Brethren, Adam had learned the truth. Be it lords, ladies, or enemies to the Crown, everyone had a weakness. It would seem Georgina Wilcox was Hunter's. Could Adam exploit that valuable piece of information? Could he use Georgina to attain his release? *No*, he realized with sickening despair. In a short time, Georgina had come to mean too much to him. He'd never be able to use her...even if it meant his freedom. He gave Hunter a pointed look. "I'm not a coward who would force himself on a woman."

Hunter kicked him in the stomach.

All the air left Adam on a swift exhale. Through the agony lancing through him, he forced a grin. "Feeling guilty?" he rasped. "It appears you're not a total monster."

His captor brought his leg back, but Adam wrapped his hand around Hunter's ankle and yanked the other man down. Hunter hit the floor with a grunt. His gun skittered just out of reach.

Adam's heart kicked up a fast rhythm as he stared at the gun that represented freedom. Enlivened by this desire for freedom, he struggled through his weakness and managed to land a neat right jab. Hunter hissed then, with a triumphant yell, overpowered Adam. His captor raised his knee and buried it in Adam's gut.

Adam fought the flood of nausea as Hunter, gasping for breath, dragged Adam back to his chair and strapped him to the hard piece of furniture.

He retrieved his pistol and returned, glaring down at Adam. The gun dangled at his side, taunting Adam. So close. He was so close to it. If he could only reach out...

Hunter jabbed a finger in his direction. "I want you gone. I don't care if you're sent back on your merry nobleman's way or buried beneath the ground. Give me the information and I'll free you."

Hunter's words were a lie and they both knew it. Hunter would kill him because he knew too much. He knew what they looked like. Knew their code names.

Gasping for breath, Adam forced one of his "merry nobleman" smiles. "I don't have the information you seek. I'll say this. I will get out of here and..." He lowered his voice. "And when I do, Hunter, you'd better run. You had better run as fast and far as your pathetic legs will carry you, because I will gut you alive like the scum you are."

Perhaps it was the deadly calm in Adam's words, but all the color leeched from Hunter's face. "That may be, but you'll be dead as well."

Adam raised a single eyebrow. "We shall see about that."

A vein pulsed at the edge of Hunter's temple. Then a lascivious smile turned his lips at the corner. "You seem so very arrogant about Miss Wilcox's affections, but remember you are the one who is tied up and," he leaned down so he was nose to nose with Adam, "I'm free to fuck her whenever I choose."

Bile climbed up Adam's throat. Rage nearly blinded him.

In mocking fashion, Hunter winked. "In fact, I think I'll go see the lovely Miss Wilcox now."

The door closed on Hunter's taunting laugh.

FOUR

Emmet is using his own funds to purchase weapons that are being manufactured by an Irish sympathizer in Bristol.
Signed,
A Loyal British Subject

Adam had not gone mad.

Yet.

After three months of captivity, the thing that kept him from relinquishing control was not Grace but Georgina. He scrubbed his hands over his rough beard. Grace's features were becoming less clear in his mind. Adam reached for the charcoal and scribbled an image onto the paper. Grace's face began to take shape.

Except the heart-shaped lips he drew were too full. There was too much of a curl to her hair. And there was a faint birthmark at the corner of her mouth that most certainly didn't belong there.

His stomach clenched in a vise-like knot as Georgina's face materialized on the paper. He gasped and ripped out the page. Wrinkled it into a ball and tossed it aside. Somewhere along the way, Grace's face had dissipated in his memory and there was nothing Adam could do, aside from mourning the loss of a far simpler time.

The door to his prison opened. Hunter nudged Georgina inside then locked the door behind her.

She stood, poised by the doorway. Her words came out hesitant. "Adam?"

He reached for another page. His fingers trembled over the sheet. Closing his eyes, he tried to call up memories of the precious lines of

Grace's face. Adam made another attempt. When he'd finished, he sat back and assessed the result.

The woman in the sketch did not possess Grace's lean, lithe form but rather well-rounded hips and buttocks. He dragged the page out of the book, taking a perverse glee in the tear, and tossed it to the floor beside the other.

He didn't look at Georgina as she moved deeper into the room, but then he didn't need to. Her wide-eyed expression stared back at him from the bloody sketchpad.

His body went motionless as he realized there was just one more page in the book. With a roar, Adam tossed it against the wall. It hit with a loud thump and fell open on its spine.

Finally, he allowed himself to look at Georgina. All the color had left her cheeks. She moved with sure strides across the room and proceeded to undo his bindings.

When he caught her gaze, she focused her attention on the mess littering the floor.

"Georgina," he began hoarsely. This woman who bathed him, fed him, sat with him and kept him from descending into complete madness wasn't deserving of his fury.

Georgina shook her head. "It's fine." She continued to clean.

Adam blinked at her. Oh God, the sight of her on her knees at his feet did something to him. Her lips were mere inches away from his aching shaft. If she glanced up, she would see his erection reaching out to her, begging.

Georgina sank back on her heels in a flutter of skirts. She was an enchantress weaving a potent spell over him.

Don't do it. Do not look at her lips. If he looked, he would begin to imagine those tantalizing dreams that kept him from sleep at night: Georgina on her knees, her sweet mouth wrapped around him as he urged her on. He needed her. It had been too long since he'd made love to a woman. He glanced at her lips. The glance became a gaze. And he was lost.

Adam stood so fast, the chair went crashing to the floor. The room dipped with the suddenness of that movement and tingles shot down his ill used legs.

47

Georgina scrambled to her feet. "What's wrong?" Then she did the absolute worst thing she could have done in that moment. She trailed the tip of her tongue over those sinful lips.

With a groan, he pulled her into his arms. She tipped her head back to look at him.

Her eyes were wide, giving her a look of an unblinking owl.

Is it fear? He would've wagered his brother's entire holdings it was desire that flared to life in their brown depths.

"Adam?" His name emerged as nothing more than a whispery sigh and he lost the fight.

He kissed her as he'd dreamed about since she'd first entered his room, a Joan of Arc bent on saving him. He plundered her mouth as if it were the last time he would ever kiss a woman. She opened her lips and he slipped his tongue inside.

His efforts were rewarded with a purr. His erection thickened. Adam swung her into his arms. He stumbled and cursed the months of captivity that now left him weak.

"Adam—?"

"I am fine," he gritted out as sweat beaded his brow. He carried her over to the bed and then lowered her until her head rested on the pillow. Feverishly, he passed a hand over her body. Exploring. Teasing. Tormenting.

Adam released her breast from the confines of the drab, brown dress she wore. She sucked in a breath and his shaft throbbed with longing. A little moan escaped her.

"Adam," she whispered, and he didn't know if his name was a plea, a prayer, or a command but it urged him on, fueled his hunger and his desire to pleasure her. Then he cupped one breast, raising it to his mouth. God, her breasts were enormous, pale moons of silky flesh. The red tip of her nipple puckered in the cool of the air before he closed his lips over the bud.

She cried out, thrashing her head back and forth on the pillow.

A deep, primal groan of male satisfaction escaped him. He needed more of her. Now. He tore his lips away from her nipple.

"Please," she begged. She threaded her fingers in his hair and urged his head forward, a gentle woman turned tigress.

He lifted her skirts up. Higher. Until he'd worked them around her hips, exposing the soft flesh of her thighs. Her hips bucked in anticipation of his offering.

"Do you like this, love?" he whispered, taking a nip at her neck in the primal instinct of a man marking his mate. A man who'd had his urges denied for too long. "Do you want to feel my hands on you? My fingers inside you?"

Georgina cried out. "Oh God, yes. Touch me. Please."

That throaty entreaty drove him on. Adam moved a hand between them and found the thatch of dark brown curls shielding her center. He slipped a finger inside her hot, moist passageway. She clenched her thighs tight around his hand. He was a man possessed. Like an untried youth with his first woman. He stroked her. At that moment, his body craved her more than it did water or food. She was a molten flame beneath him. Never before had he wanted to play with fire as he did just then.

Adam returned his attention to her other breast, flicking his tongue over the engorged tip, trailing a circle over it until Georgina was bucking against him, keening his name.

He wedged his thigh between her legs and looked at her. She was close. Her eyes went wide in her face. Then she arched her hips into him, grinding into his upper thigh. Her rhythm became frenzied. He delved deeper, playing with her slick nub.

She came on a piercing scream. He continued to work her sex, bringing her to climax again.

Adam freed himself from the confines of his breeches and moved over her. Her quivering pale thighs fell open in invitation.

"Oh, Adam, yes!"

He positioned himself at her center, his shaft pressed against the entrance of her womanhood. And froze.

Do it. Take her. She is willing. You've been without a woman for more than a year. Take what she is offering you.

49

His chin fell to his chest and he rolled off her. Adam cursed. He flung an arm across his eyes, focusing on the rapid beat of his heart, the swift inhale and exhale of his lungs sucking in breath.

Except those sounds weren't enough to drown out her voice.

"Adam?"

"Quiet," he rasped. He gentled his tone. "Please."

What the hell had he done? Echoes of Georgina's cry as she climaxed bounced around the walls of his mind.

Adam flung his legs over the edge of the bed and dropped his head into his hands. He had betrayed Grace. Just thinking of Georgina was a betrayal. But this. This was the kind of sin that had gotten Adam banished from Eden. The kind of sin that could not be forgiven. His stomach churned.

He tried to blame his lack of self-control on his captivity. Tried to shift blame from himself.

His efforts proved futile.

The mattress dipped. The faint rustle of her skirts fluttered about them. Georgina touched his shoulder.

He recoiled and she drew her hand back.

Adam jumped off the bed and hurried across the room to retrieve the sketchpad on the table. "Do not say anything," he ordered. He needed her gone. He needed her to turn on her heel and leave him.

Georgina had worked her way into his innermost thoughts, had shoved out the face of the woman he'd left behind, and Adam had the sinking feeling this connection they shared was something more than mere lust—and it terrified the hell out of him.

A clamor from below stairs penetrated his thoughts.

The door flew open. Hunter filled the entranceway. His flinty stare honed in on Georgina's wrinkled skirts.

Adam placed himself in front of Georgina, eager for Hunter. He wanted to lash out at something, destroy somebody, and there wasn't a better target for his rage than his captor.

"You are needed downstairs," Hunter snapped at Georgina. She hesitated. "Now."

Georgina slipped out from behind Adam and raced toward the doorway.

Hunter grabbed her by the arm, whispering something into her ear. Georgina paled and cast a final glance in Adam's direction. With Georgina, gone, his loathsome captor grinned a slow, evil smile. "Come, Markham. It's time to tie you up like the animal you are." He kicked the door closed and started for Adam.

Georgina wound her way through the house. Jamie led her toward a series of grunts and loud thumps. "What is it?" Dread licked at her insides.

"Quiet," Jamie barked.

They reached the main foyer just as her father dragged a bound stranger past the parlor and into the kitchen. The man's hands were tied in front of him. As her father nudged him forward, the stranger kicked his legs and toppled the side tables in his wake.

The stranger looked over his shoulder and spied Georgina. Their eyes locked.

Then the door closed behind him.

She ceased breathing. "Another man?" Enough was enough. It would end, now. One way or another, she had to stop this.

Jamie's black glare cut into her thoughts. "I haven't brought you downstairs to turn fainthearted on us."

"Why did you then, Jamie?" She narrowed her eyes. "You didn't need me, did you?" she taunted. "You just didn't want me with Mr. Markham."

The mottled red that stained his cheeks confirmed her suspicions.

She gasped as his fingers bit into the soft flesh of her forearms. "What? No concern for our newest guest? Or are you too eager to climb back into Markham's bed?"

Her fingers twitched with the urge to slap his mocking face. "You're mad," she spat. Him and her father, both.

The sickening sound of flesh meeting flesh punctuated her statement. She wanted to flee to Adam's room and free him, rush past her savage family and into the free night air.

"I did bring you down here for a reason," Jamie drawled, wholly unaffected by the violent assault taking place on the other side of the door.

There was a loud crack, followed by a piercing scream.

Georgina clamped her hands over her ears to escape the agonized pleas for help.

Jamie had other intentions. He took her by the wrists, clenching them in his vise-like grip. "I wanted you to realize our need for Markham is not nearly as great, not with our most recent guest."

She shook her head. "No," she whispered.

Jamie smiled and released her. "Yes."

The world shifted beneath her feet as Georgina faced the ugly fact—she didn't want Adam Markham to go. He'd laid claim to her foolish heart, and because of that she'd not put real thought into how she might secret him away. Her unwillingness to free him had stemmed from a selfish desire to keep him here beside her. If he left, her heart, her very reason for living, would vanish with him.

Oh God, but now it was too late. The appearance of this new prisoner had rendered Adam useless to her father's machinations.

His life was forfeit.

Gooseflesh dotted the skin on her arms. Father and Jamie had no intention of releasing him. Her legs gave out beneath her. As Jamie slipped into the kitchen to torture their latest prisoner, Georgina caught herself against the wall and slid into a puddle of emptiness as she confronted the truth—if she didn't do something, Adam would be killed.

"Get in here, gel," her father shouted.

Georgina shoved the door open just as Jamie grabbed an older, graying stranger and led him down the cellar steps.

She closed her eyes. *Please God, make them stop.*

But there was no God. There was only her.

She continued to hover in the doorway.

Father gestured to the chair. "Sit," he barked.

Georgina rushed over to the seat. She froze. A stranger stood off to the corner. Her gaze swung back to her father and then back to the unfamiliar gentleman. She ignored her father and studied his guest. The man had the look of a demonic angel; an aquiline beauty with a sinister twist to his hard lips. His sky-blue gaze took inventory of Georgina. Her fingers trembled as she sat, her stare riveted on the cold, unflappable figure.

She jerked her gaze away from the angel-demon. "I'm sorry. What did you say?"

"Listen up, gel. You've failed with Markham. I'm trying something new. I have a meeting. This is Mr. Stone. He'll be the new guard."

Georgina sprang to her feet. "You can't leave me alone with him." She looked over at Mr. Stone.

He peered down his hawkish nose at her. A jagged scar ran along his left cheek and down a jawline that may as well have been chiseled in stone.

Panic gurgled up her throat and nearly strangled her. Danger fairly oozed from Stone's skin.

"Come, gel," her father said. "After you let Markham bed you, there really isn't much for you to protect."

Georgina gasped. Mortified heat climbed up her neck.

He didn't await a response. "Jamie and I have a meeting. You aren't to give Mr. Stone or the guards any difficulty. Is that clear?"

In other words, she'd be beaten as she'd never been beaten before. She squared her jaw. "Abundantly clear."

How had she stayed in this vile place all these years? Her efforts to help the Crown had all been for naught. She'd brought no real change. Father continued in his vile quest. The Irish radicals pressed on in their push for separation.

Her father's cruel gaze threatened to bore a hole through her. It was as though he sought signs of her deceit.

The steady thump of Jamie's boots grew louder. He stepped back into the kitchen and closed the cellar door behind him.

Desperate, Georgina turned her entreaty to Jamie.

His pale blue eyes slid away from her. And Georgina knew—there was no one who could protect her from Stone. No one other than herself.

While she listened with fast spiraling terror as her father and Jamie finalized their plans with Stone, her mind turned over possible ways to free Adam. The newest captive presented countless difficulties. How could she free them both? How, when they were imprisoned in two different parts of the house?

Then, as if she mattered no more than a chambermaid, Father and Jamie took their leave and Georgina was alone with the beast.

Squaring her shoulders, she walked a wide berth around the towering man who filled her small kitchen, careful to keep him in her sights. Georgina fetched a plate from the cabinet and proceeded to fill it with a large chunk of crusty, white bread and slices of cheese. Next, she reached for a glass and filled it from a pitcher of water.

All the while, Stone studied her through hooded eyes. "If you're preparing an afternoon meal, I'd welcome something to eat."

Georgina fetched a small bowl from the windowsill. She concentrated on grinding up the leaves, comfrey root, and mint leaves she'd blended together earlier that morning. "I'm not preparing a meal," she snapped.

Stone arched a brow. "Then what are you doing?"

Damn him for being an insolent, deliberately taunting bastard.

Georgina held his intent gaze, refusing to be cowed. "Seeing to my responsibilities." It was sheer madness to bait him, but Georgina would not give him the pleasure of toying with her the way a cat tormented a mouse. "I have to care for the man you and my father brutalized."

He bowed his head, gesturing to the door leading to the cellar. "Very well then, Miss Wilcox."

Georgina picked up the tray and hurried downstairs.

The murky darkness enshrouded her in its fold. As she descended, she gave thanks that Adam had been closed away on the main living quarters away from the nightmarish darkness of the cellars. On the heels of that was guilt for the poor soul her father had trapped down here.

"So you've returned, you bastard."

Georgina paused. A single candle had been lit. Instead of illuminating the constricted space, it cast ominous shadows around the room. This was the kind of place ghosts inhabited. She tamped down childlike fears.

"You're a bloody coward. Do you hear me? They'll find you and when they do—"

Georgina interrupted the stranger's tirade, sparing him his energy. "I've come to help you."

For the span of a heartbeat, the man said nothing. Then, "Are you here to free me?"

It was always the same. The vitriolic diatribe, followed by desperate hope.

She must. She couldn't wait any longer, but how would that be possible with Stone? Georgina said nothing.

The man sighed.

Georgina set the tray down and eyed him warily.

The stranger bowed his head. "I won't hurt you."

She moved closer. A gasp escaped her.

His face was swollen. He could barely open his eyes.

Through cracked and swollen lips, he managed a grin. "That bad?"

She swallowed. "That bad." She reached for the clean cloth in the washbasin as she swallowed the burning shame that her father had wrought such damage. Ringing out the scrap of linen, she held it out and froze. "May I?"

He inclined his head. "I'd be glad if you would."

Georgina set to work bathing the man's face. Her stomach rolled at the stench of blood.

"Blood bothers you." It wasn't a question.

"You are perceptive," she murmured.

"I'd imagine you see your fair share of it, here."

She managed a jerky nod. "I do."

"I'd imagine you must have a very good reason for staying."

Very perceptive, indeed.

Georgina gently grasped his chin. "Tilt this way a bit," she murmured.

He complied. "I take that as a yes."

She dabbed at his lip. He didn't even flinch. "I didn't think it was a question."

"Perceptive girl."

Apparently, the sentiments were mutual.

"What is your name?" he asked.

"Georgina."

He bowed his head. "Charles Blakely at your service."

His refined, regal tones indicated he was a man of importance. Surely, there were powerful people looking for Mr. Blakely? And Adam. Her father played a dangerous game and eventually he would be caught.

You too will be caught, Georgina. They will link you to Father and Jamie and find you guilty.

Georgina sat back and evaluated this new prisoner. He was closer in age to her father, but possessed the vitality of a man much younger. There was an intelligent glimmer in the obsidian depths of his eyes that unnerved her—a look that seemed to delve into her inner thoughts.

Mr. Blakely broke the silence. "I have a daughter. She is about your age. You remind me of her."

Her heart twisted at the stranger's admission. Another man. Another family. How many more good people would suffer to serve her father's twisted agenda?

She managed a forced response. "Do I?"

"Some people have an inherent goodness. A kind heart. I recognize that in you."

A bitter laugh climbed up her throat. It came out as more of a strangled sob. "Then you are a poor judge of character." If she were truly good, she would have released Adam months ago and to hell with the consequences.

The man reached for her and even with his bound hand managed to give her forearm a gentle squeeze. "You are here caring for me, aren't you? I know what it is like to do what you have to in order to survive."

Georgina fought back tears. "You don't know anything about me." Because if he did, he'd not be so magnanimous.

"Trust me, miss. In my life, I've had experience with all sorts of characters. You do yourself a disservice. I suspect it's because your life hasn't been an easy one."

His accuracy was too much. Here he was a stranger, whom she'd only just met, and he could so accurately gauge her life experience. She wanted to be free of her father. She'd had enough.

Georgina reached into the front of her apron and pulled out a knife.

The stranger stiffened. His reaction was much like Adam's and the two other nameless men before him. They were always waiting for the final deathblow.

"Forgive me," she whispered.

He flinched.

She slashed his shirt open then reached for a cloth inside the bowl of water. Georgina rang it out and pressed the cool water against his flesh.

He hissed and she glanced up at him. She'd borne the sting of the lash. Knew the searing agony of water as it seeped into the shredded flesh. "I am so sorry. I know they must hurt."

Blakely remained silent while she cleaned his wounds. Next, she applied the balm.

He sighed in response. "That is heaven."

"If this is heaven, I don't want to see hell." She dropped her cloth onto the tray.

"Miss Wilcox," Mr. Stone's voice thundered from above stairs.

She bit her lip, ignoring him. "Here." She loosened the length of the captive's constraints enough that he could reach the bread she placed on his lap. "Just a moment," she called over her shoulder at the still-closed door. Georgina reached for the glass of warm lemon water and held it up to his lips. "Drink," she said softly.

When he'd drained the glass dry, she picked up the empty tray and carried it over to the door.

"Can you help free me?"

Georgina swallowed hard. It was time to shove aside the selfish fear and cowardice that had driven her. "I will. I promise."

And Adam. She needed to free these men...somehow.

"I must go," she murmured.

She needed to see Adam.

Mr. Blakely nodded. His gaze seared her back as she climbed the stairs to confront Mr. Stone.

She nearly ran into him.

She would have tumbled down the stairs if Mr. Stone hadn't reached out and grabbed her, pulling her to safety.

She didn't want to be beholden to this man or anyone. "Thank you," she bit out.

He smiled but didn't relinquish her. "You sound like you'd rather have fallen down the stairs then talk to me."

Georgina looked pointedly at his hand. "I think perhaps I might prefer that than speaking with you." She arched a single brow. "You called me, Mr. Stone."

"I'm here at 'The Sovereign's' request. I've come to help. We must be quick if we are to get Mr. Markham and Mr. Blakely out of here."

Her heart stopped.

Other than that.

She did want to discuss that with him.

FIVE

Emmet is inordinately interested in pikes. He has made several trips to Bristol to meet with an arms manufacturer to discuss design innovations to the weapon.

Signed,

A Loyal British Subject

Surely she'd heard him wrong.

Or this was a neat, little trap orchestrated by her father to test her loyalty.

Either way…

"Miss Wilcox, I am here to help Mr. Markham and Mr. Blakely."

"Liar," she hissed and backed away from him. Her heart thumped hard against the wall of her chest. Oh, how she wanted to believe him, wanted to believe she wouldn't be alone in freeing Adam, because then maybe, just maybe, Adam could escape the guards stationed outside and live.

His onyx eyes snapped fire. "We don't have much time. Your father is off meeting his superior for directives on what to do with Blakely. When they return, they'll bring with them the order to kill Markham."

She gasped and, folding her arms under her breasts, imagined a world without Adam in it. Even if this was a scheme on Father's part, she had to act because the alternative would be watching Adam die in this place.

"There are men outside," she said.

"I killed the two guards out back while you were caring for Blakely," he said, his pronouncement devoid of emotion.

Georgina swayed.

Stone caught her about the waist. "You can't be weak."

Georgina nodded. If Adam were to live, she had to be strong. "What do I do?"

"See to Markham. I'll see to Blakely."

"He's in the cellar." Georgina gestured to the door.

"I know. We need to get them outside. There is a black carriage waiting out front. It has red drawn curtains."

A sob escaped Georgina's lips as she realized this was finally happening.

Stone misunderstood the reason for her emotion. He wouldn't know of the longing for justice that had burned in her since she'd failed the nameless man killed in her kitchen.

"You will be safe, too," he said. "We are not ignorant of how you've helped."

"How—"

He continued through her fog of confusion. "We appreciate that you've cared for our members, Miss Wilcox." He pressed a key into her palm. "Now go," he commanded, giving her a gentle push toward the door.

Georgina didn't hesitate. She flew up the stairs, taking them two at a time, stumbling over her skirts in her haste to get to Adam. She ran down the hall, gasping with the exertion of her efforts and the precariousness of their situation.

Still, an inevitable sense of doom hung over her.

"Adam," she cried against the door.

"Georgina!" His deep baritone, muffled through the door, shattered the rest of her composure. "What is it? What's happened?"

Her fingers shook so badly the key tumbled to the floor. She cursed. Georgina bent down, retrieved it, and jammed it into the lock. It made a satisfying click.

Georgina shoved the door open and tripped through the entrance. "We don't have much time," she rasped. "There is a man. He is here to help you. "

Us. He is here to help all of us.

Racing to his side, she set to work untying him.

The muscles in Adam's body went stiff.

He stared at Georgina in mute silence as she struggled to free him. He'd dreamed of this day for months. When Fox and Hunter had beaten him, nearly broken him like a battered animal, Adam had told himself that it had been the promise of seeing Grace again that had kept him alive. Only now could he be honest to admit to himself that it had been this woman, Georgina.

Close. They were so very close to freedom. A surge of desperate panic numbed his soul, froze his heart.

His stare alternated between the door to freedom and Georgina who knelt at his feet. He held his breath, expecting to see his captors storm in.

"Hurry," he rasped.

His words seemed to fuel her panic.

She lifted her eyes for a moment. "I'm sorry."

Adam forced himself to take a deep breath. Panic wouldn't help either of them. He managed a half-smile. "It's fine, love. Easy. Just focus."

Georgina returned to picking at his constraints.

And then the knots were loose. The cords slipped over his wrists.

She tugged on his hands. "Hurry," she cried.

He stood and nearly collapsed. Georgina wrapped her arm around his waist and led him to the door. She pulled it open and peeked outside.

She glanced back at him. "They are gone. I don't know when they'll return."

For the first time since he'd been captive in this hellish room, Adam stepped outside his prison cell. His heart thudded painfully against the wall of his chest. Fox and Hunter could return at any moment and crush all hope of his liberation. His jaw hardened. Not again. He'd not be their victim again. If he died trying, he'd not surrender to their foul clutches.

Georgina guided him down the hall toward the stairs.

Two men stepped into their path.

Adam froze. The air left him on a whoosh.

Charles Blakely, Grace's father, stared back at him. The graying gentleman's words emerged as a whisper. "Adam."

The dark stranger next to him nudged Blakely's arm. "We need to get you out front. There is a carriage—"

A door shut somewhere in the house. "Georgina? Where are you, gel?"

Georgina dug a talon-like grip around Adam's arm. Color heightened her cheeks. "They're here," she whispered.

Stone pulled out his pistol and pointed it at the closed door.

Blakely cursed. "Between me and Markham, we're no match for them. We have to go."

Three pairs of eyes turned to Georgina.

She gave her head a clearing shake. "The kitchen." She started forward.

Stone gripped Adam and Blakely by their arms and hurried them along.

Georgina opened a door, ushering them into the kitchen. "There's a door in the cellar that leads outside."

"Georgina," Fox thundered.

The color in her cheeks faded. She looked at Adam. "You have to go," she whispered.

"Come on," Stone murmured. He gave Adam's arm another squeeze and, physically supporting him, led him on to the cellar.

Adam dug his heels. They had to get Georgina out first.

His eyes caught hers. She gave him a sad little smile as though she'd followed the direction of his thoughts. "Go," she whispered.

"Georgina?" Fox's wheedling tone had grown impatient.

Georgina froze with her foot at the top step. "Now," she whispered frantically. She shot a glance over her shoulder. "I'll stay. Give you more time."

They looked at one another. Longing. Regret. Hope. All mingled.

"No…" he whispered, and turned around. He couldn't leave her. Not now. Not ever.

He was no match for Stone's strength. The other man kept him and Blakely moving downward.

"I'll meet you," she whispered and then disappeared.

His gut tightened but he focused instead on his slow downward climb deeper and deeper into the belly of the townhouse. For suddenly he was the small boy trapped in an armoire, banging and pleading for help. His own shallow panting filled his ears. He felt like he'd been tied down underwater and was clawing for the surface, longing to suck in a clean breath.

They reached the bottom of the stairs. Stone squeezed his arm. "Get control of yourself. We are nearly free."

The words called out to Adam from a distance.

He was sinking. Deeper. Down into an abyss.

He'd nearly struck bottom when Georgina's heart-shaped face penetrated his horror. In his mind, he saw her wearing a smile, holding a small, callused palm up in farewell. Some of the first words she'd ever spoken to him played again in his mind.

"You can free me."

"I already said I can't. If I do, my life is forfeit. Is your life more important than mine?"

Georgina, I was a fool—am a fool. Your life is more important.

She deserved freedom, deserved it more than he did.

Adam yanked his arm. He turned for the stairs. "I have to go back." Oh God, he'd promised to bring her with him, had pledged to help her. Instead, when his freedom had been dangled before him, he'd abandoned her.

Just as she'd always assumed you would, the voice jeered.

Stone snaked one arm around his waist, the other he draped over his shoulder, all but carrying Adam the rest of the way. "By God, I will carry you from this place if I have to," he bit out on a whisper. "It is time to leave. Now." Adam was no match for the man's strength.

Georgina. What have I done to you?

He had to try again. "I can't leave her. I must—"

Blakely interrupted him. "She will meet us. She is a smart woman."

That assurance wasn't enough. Until he had her in his arms, smelled the honeysuckle scent of her skin, he would not trust she was safe.

They came to a stop in the middle of the cellar. All three of them searched around for the door Georgina had promised.

Stone narrowed his eyes and scanned the space. His gaze settled on the corner of the room and he strode over. His fingers felt around then stilled. *Click.* A secret panel opened.

The sun's rays filled the inky darkness. Adam held his forearm up to block the blinding glare. Then he stepped outside. His eyes rose to the robin's egg blue sky dotted with fluffy, white clouds. He'd never thought of clouds as fluffy. Hell, he'd never given clouds much thought in general. They were just…there. Now, he saw them through the eyes of a free man. He drank everything in. The clean, ocean air climbed into his nostrils, filled him, until he was nearly intoxicated by the salty scent.

Blakely nudged him between the shoulder blades.

Adam crashed back to the precarious reality of their situation. They made their way down the side of the townhouse.

A hulking beast of a man stepped in their path. "Wot's goin'—"

Stone tugged a dagger from his boot then lunged forward, slashing the thug's throat. The man's eyes rounded before he fell silently to the ground.

They stepped over the prone body.

Stone gestured across the street. Adam followed Stone's gaze to the black conveyance. "Get to the carriage with red curtains. Don't look back."

The distance to the carriage was no more than a hundred feet. Stone grabbed Adam's arm, moving him along, and they both began to run.

Adam stumbled. His breath caught painfully in his chest as he braced for the bullet that would cut him down.

Stone cursed. He tightened his hold on Adam's arm and righted him. The loud thud of Adam's heartbeat filled his ears.

At last, they reached the carriage.

Stone pulled the door open and helped Blakely up. Next, he hoisted the weakened Adam inside and followed behind him. Adam pulled back the heavy, red velvet curtains in time to see the front door to the townhouse open. Hunter stepped outside, frantically scanning the area.

Blakely rapped his knuckles on the ceiling and the driver whipped up the team hurtling them toward freedom.

Adam's eyes darted around the passing streets. He shoved back the curtains. "Georgina."

Stone cursed and pulled the fabric into place.

A wave of dizziness gripped him. "She said she would meet us. We can't leave her."

Returning would be the height of foolishness, it would mean their sure death, but the alternative—her alone with Fox and Hunter, bearing the blame for freeing them—would mean untold horrors for her.

Adam collapsed against the squabs of the coach and clenched his eyes tight.

His stomach roiled as if he'd been thrown out to sea in the midst of a storm and the waves were crashing over him. His chest heaved. There was nowhere else in the entire world he wanted to be more than away from his prison.

Adam opened his eyes. "We have to go back."

Stone swiped a hand over his face. "We can't."

"She said she would meet us. I said..."

I would take her with me.

"We are in no condition to face Fox and Hunter," Blakely interjected with quiet insistence.

Adam ignored him, his attention reserved for Stone.

The younger member of The Brethren rested a hand upon his knee. "I made a pledge to Miss Wilcox as well."

Adam shoved his arm. "They will kill her."

Stone's gaze grew shuttered. "They won't."

"How can you be so certain?" Adam cried. He dug his fingers into his temples. He wanted to writhe and twist to escape this agony, but there was no escaping this hell of his own making.

"He's right," Blakely murmured.

A black haze clouded Adam's vision. He wanted Stone and Blakely to be correct, but the costs of them being wrong were too great. They didn't see Georgina the same way Adam did. They didn't know how her cheeks flushed red with every smile, or how her beautiful singing voice could move a man to tears. They only saw her as dispensable to the goals of The Brethren—just as Adam himself first had. It really wasn't anyone's fault but his own.

They hadn't failed Georgina.

He had.

Stone cleared his throat. "I understand you feel indebted to the young woman, but you have the organization to think about."

Indebted. This was about so much more than being indebted to Georgina Wilcox. It was about saving a woman who needed saving more than any person he'd ever known.

Adam looked down at his lap. The stitching of his well-worn breeches was frayed. He trailed a jagged nail along one of the threads. He suspected Georgina had taken a needle to them on more than one occasion. Had he ever thanked her? Had he ever said anything of it? No. His fingers curled into tight balls. "One way or another, I'm going back for her."

Blakely touched his shoulder. "Have we ever left a man behind?"

Adam felt like he'd just been kicked in the gut. He sucked in his breath. "She's a young woman." He remembered the day she'd come charging into his room, her lips bruised and swollen from Hunter's assault. A haze of blackness fell across his vision. It temporarily blinded him. Hunter would punish her. Even now, she might be paying the price with her innocence. Adam buried his face in his palms and sucked in slow, steady breaths. He would save her even if it meant he had to return and face Fox and Hunter—and when he found them, they would be praying for death because he would torture them within an inch of their lives.

Stone was saying something. "You will be perfectly comfortable. Eventually you will see them."

Comfortable where? See whom? Adam was spinning out of control again. "What did you say?"

Blakely explained. "For as long as 'The Sovereign' decides, you are to remain in hiding."

Adam clenched his teeth so hard a sharp, tingling sensation radiated up his jawline. "Are you saying I'm to be kept prisoner, still?"

Stone and Blakely exchanged looks. "You have to realize the suspicion you'll rouse if you appear in Society like this." Stone waved a hand in his general direction.

He'd had enough of all the bloody deception. His life had not been his own for a very long time. He'd accepted that—until now. Now it grated.

During his captivity, he'd tried to not think about his family. He couldn't think about his mother weeping at his absence or his brothers' desolation. Such images would have weakened him when he'd needed to be at his strongest. "What has my family been told?"

Stone reached into the front of his jacket and extracted a small stack of letters. They were tied with a black ribbon. He handed the pile over to Adam.

Adam took the packet, eying the bundle. He undid the knotting and pulled out the top sheet. Snapping it open, he scanned the parchment. It was his writing.

Except it wasn't his writing.

He picked his head up and glanced at Stone.

"You've been traveling," Stone explained.

"Traveling?" he said dumbly.

Stone motioned to the stack. "Italy. Greece. Spain."

Adam threw the stack down next to Stone. The packet landed with a decided thump.

"And you, Blakely?" Adam shot the question at the older member of The Brethren.

Blakely shrugged almost apologetically. "I've only been in the hands of Fox's men for less than a fortnight. I'm sure a trip to the country will explain my absence."

Of course, The Brethren had seen to everything with a needle-like precision, as they always did. With their far-reaching influence, it shouldn't have shocked him in the least that they'd managed to explain away his captivity.

They had taken care of everything.

His heart seized up. Except Georgina. They hadn't taken care of her.

During the long months of his captivity, he'd longed for the day he'd be free. He had expected his liberation would be sweet. There was nothing he'd wanted more in the world than his freedom—not even Grace. As the carriage sped along, putting Bristol far behind him, Adam realized again he'd been wrong. There *was* something he wanted more than his freedom—it was Georgina's.

But now she was beyond his reach.

He closed his eyes.

SIX

Irish radicals are planning to establish communication with United Irishmen in the Metropolitan area. Fox is being charged with the task of building an army of men to help the French in a fight against England.
Signed,
A Loyal British Subject

Adam, Blakely, and Stone had made their escape in a firestorm; now all that remained were the dying embers of inactivity. Georgina had learned early on that silence was never a good thing.

As expected, the explosion came fast.

Father shoved the kitchen door open and scanned the space. "I've been calling. Why didn't you answer me?"

Georgina wet her lips and took a step backward, placing the kitchen table between them. "I—"

"Why is the cellar door open?" he snapped. He rushed over and slammed it closed, turning the lock in place.

A giggle of hysteria bubbled up from her throat.

"What's so funny, gel?"

Mayhap she could leave before her deception was discovered. If she could get Father to go into the cellars to visit his recently released prisoner, she could make her escape to the waiting carriage.

A roar more fitting a savage beast reverberated from the floor above, followed by footsteps thundering down the stairs. She flinched.

Jamie ran into the kitchen.

And Georgina accepted that all hope of escape was gone.

"She set them free!" he shouted.

Georgina turned on her heel to flee. She made it past her father. Jamie wrapped his hand tightly around her forearm, cutting off the path to freedom.

He shoved her.

Father caught her and turned his glare on Jamie. "What are you talking about?"

Jamie spit. "Markham's gone!"

Father cursed. "When?" He shook Georgina until her teeth rattled. "When?" He looked to Jamie. "Go see if you can stop them. There are three men and two of them badly injured! They cannot be far."

Jamie rushed to do his bidding.

Please let Adam be free.

"It is too late. They are long gone," she lied, praying it would quash Father's efforts and provide Adam with much-needed time to escape.

Her father slapped her across the cheek with a speed and intensity of a man twenty years his junior. She went down hard, landing at the base of her tailbone. Pain radiated along her spine. His face blurred before her eyes.

Georgina tried to shove herself backward, away from him, but her back met the kitchen wall.

"Do you have any idea what you've done?"

Blood seeped from the corner of her right nostril. It traveled a moist path down to her lip. She opened her mouth and it trailed in. She gagged, which was why she didn't see her father rear back and kick her with the tip of his boot until it was too late.

Her hip absorbed the shock of his attack.

Georgina curled up on her side, wrapping herself in a ball.

She knew this latest transgression could not be forgiven. Father wrenched her by the hair and dragged her to her feet.

She cried out as the strands tugged at her scalp line. She looked around the room for help in vain. Adam was gone and Georgina was as she'd always been—alone.

Her father shook her until Georgina feared he'd knock her teeth loose. "I asked you a question!" he roared.

Georgina's head swam too much to make sense of any questions. "What?" she managed through numb lips.

"Did you free him?"

She met his question with stony silence.

He threw her away from him and she collided with the table. The hard oak bit into the flesh of her hip. She reached behind her and gripped the edges to keep from falling.

Her father brought his fist back. She hunched her shoulders, bracing for the blow.

Jamie appeared, granting her a reprieve.

Father turned his attention to him.

Jamie nodded. "It's as you feared. They're gone. All of them. Stone. Blakely. Markham. The guard Roberts is dead out back."

Adam is free!

Georgina's heart warred between joy and aching loss. Adam would no longer know hurt at Jamie and Father's hands. Now only she remained a prisoner to pain.

Adam will return for me.

Hope crested in her breast. There was no one more honorable and he'd pledged to help her. He would return.

The smiling, regal beauty in the sketchpad surfaced in her memory. Emotion clogged her throat. The woman Adam loved existed beyond the hell here, and now, now he had his freedom. There was no reason for him to return.

With a curse, Father slapped her across the face, but the pain of losing Adam was so much greater than any assault she could suffer at his hand.

Georgina inched around the table, placing the surface between them. Through cracked and bleeding lips, she smiled.

In his quest to get to her, he nearly leaped across the furniture. Georgina turned on her heel and staggered away.

Jamie caught her against him.

She jammed the heel of her slipper into his boot. Her ineffectual attempt at escape seemed to amuse him. He chuckled against her ear, the sound cold and merciless. He snaked a hand around her waist and jerked her against him. His hard shaft pressed against the small of her back. A shiver of revulsion coursed through her body as she realized he was aroused by her struggles.

Georgina stilled.

"We're not happy with you, little dove," he whispered into her ear. He dug his fingers hard into her hips.

"It was Stone!" she cried out, desperation guiding her lie. If she could convince them he'd acted alone, mayhap she could escape punishment.

Jamie shoved her at Father and Georgina was grateful to trade one beast for the other.

"Liar!" Father cried. "When did you free him?"

The lie sprang easily to her lips. "Yesterday."

Her father raked a hand over his bald pate. "Christ! What have you done?"

She held up a hand. "Surely you must see that you could not keep them here?"

"You traitor! Those men raped and killed my mother!"

"They did not!" she said, her tone desperate to her own ears as she tried to reason with him. "Not all Englishmen are guilty for the crimes of a few." Her bravery was rewarded with a fist to the side of her head.

A humming filled her ears. She drew in a deep breath.

"We have to go, Jamie."

Georgina noted the tightly drawn lines at the corners of her father's mouth, the telltale tick of the vein bulging from his temple. Goodness, he was nervous. As long as she'd known him, she'd seen him cruel, unbending, and vicious...but never nervous.

"Get Roberts into the cellar," Father instructed Jamie.

Jamie hurried from the room, sparing her a single, black look.

She looked to her father. "Where are you going?" She bit down hard on her lower lip, wincing when she further bruised the flesh.

Be quiet, Georgina. Just be quiet.

Father leaned down. His fetid breath, a blend of French brandy and garlic, wafted over her face. "You won't get a single piece of information from me, you whore."

The blood drained from her cheeks.

Her father's gaze narrowed on her, dark and threatening. "Do you think I don't know about you and Markham? Even the guards outside heard your cries."

A wave of humiliation slammed into her. It seemed sacrilege that anyone should have heard something so precious, so private. She tilted her chin back and glared at him. "I thought it was to help the mission." It was, of course, a lie. Nothing she'd ever done with Adam had been to help her father.

"But it never was, was it, Georgina? It was all about having that bastard scratch your itch," Father taunted. "Did you fancy yourself in love with him? Were you foolish enough to think he loved you?"

His jeering tone dug at her like a knife.

He twisted and turned the blade infinitely deeper. "Did you think he would take you with him?" He grabbed her by the shoulders and shook. Rage fairly seeped from his trembling frame. "How does it feel to know you're nothing but a damn fool? How does it feel to know that when presented with his freedom, he left without giving you a backward glance? How does it—"

She tossed her chin back and spit at him.

He felled her with a single blow.

She crashed to the floor. Her head thumped against the base of the table. Consciousness receded like the tide going out to sea. She fought to keep her eyes open.

At least Adam is free, she thought, before fading into blackness.

When Georgina came to, she became aware of several things all at once. One was the inky black sky, which indicated she'd been unconscious for quite some time. The other was the eerie hum of silence.

She pushed back the cobwebs wrapped around her sluggish mind and struggled to her feet.

The stabbing pain pressing on her ribs nearly brought her to her knees. She smothered a cry with her hand and winced. Her cheek ached like the devil. Georgina inched toward the kitchen door, which stood ajar. Closing her eyes, she struggled to put one foot in front of the other.

The floorboards creaked and her eyes flew open. She winced at the sudden movement, but then her heart stilled.

A tall, muscled stranger filled the entryway.

Through swollen eyes, she studied the imposing figure. His had been the face to haunt her dreams since he'd been shot dead in the kitchen. Apparently the sins of her past had come back to greet her.

"Hello, Miss Wilcox," he murmured. "My name is Nathaniel Archer."

Georgina fainted.

Outside of Bristol

Adam could scarce believe he was free. The wheels of the carriage that brought him to his next destination churned at a fast clip. It was the only sound in the harsh silence of the carriage. Blakely and Stone remained silent for which Adam was eternally gratefully. There was nothing he cared to discuss with them, just then.

When the sun had begun its descent, heralding the end of the day, the coach rocked to a sudden halt.

Stone shoved the door open and leaped down. He reached back and offered a hand to first Blakely, then Adam.

Adam paused. He stared at the lone farmhouse.

"This way," Stone directed.

They walked the remaining distance to the thatched cottage. Stone knocked once.

A stocky man, several inches shorter than Adam greeted them. He passed a cursory glance over Adam and his upper lip curled back in obvious disdain. "Is this him?"

Stone nodded. "Yes."

"Cedric Bennett at your service," he drawled.

With his aloof coolness and nasty condescension, Adam suspected Bennett was at nobody's service.

"Come in, come in," he said at last.

They filed inside the farmhouse. Bennett led them through the cozy space too small for a room full of gentlemen of their stature, to what appeared to be a makeshift office. A fire roared from within the hearth. Flickering shadows danced on the walls and played off the worn leather sofa and winged chairs.

Out the corner of his eye, Adam detected a figure stepping forward out of the shadows. His body stiffened as he mentally prepared for an attack.

"Hello, Adam."

The tension left his body.

"Fitzmorris," he gasped. His knees grew weak beneath him.

Fitzmorris had been the one to recruit and train Adam for The Brethren all those years ago. A sheen of tears filled the usually unflappable Fitzmorris's eyes. "We've got you back, Adam. It's going to be all right."

His friend was wrong. He'd never shake the horror of the past three months.

Fitzmorris took him by the elbow as if he were a small child and guided him over to one of the seats. Adam collapsed into its folds. The springs groaned in protest.

Someone handed him a drink. He downed it in one swallow, not even feeling the burn of the brandy. His glass was immediately refilled. This one he sipped. He savored the tingle in his mouth. The warmth spread down his throat, soothing, calming.

He stared into the dark brew and started. Georgina's face stared back at him. The tumbler fell to the floor and liquid sloshed onto his boots.

A hand came to rest on his shoulder. Adam cried out. He reached for his captor's fingers and squeezed.

Fitzmorris's hiss ricocheted through the barren farmhouse.

Sanity returned.

He released his friend. "I'm sorry," Adam managed between labored breaths. He raked a hand through his hair.

"Think nothing of it, my boy," Fitzmorris said in hushed tones.

I'm an animal. A savage beast.

His gaze flitted among the men. Stone looked on pityingly, Fitzmorris with concern. Blakely couldn't meet his eyes while Cedric Bennett eyed Adam like he was a despicable cur.

Fitzmorris followed Adam's stare. "Mr. Bennett is 'The Delegator'."

"The Delegator", one of the key figures for The Brethren, served as counsel to the elite organization. Members rarely saw or heard from "The Delegator".

Bennett cocked his head. "You wonder why I'm here."

Adam waited.

"You've served us well, Markham." The words rang hollow.

Shame rose in Adam's throat. In being captured, he'd failed. It didn't matter that he'd been drugged. It had been his error. He deserved Bennett's scorn.

"This is as good a time as any to free you from future missions," Bennett was saying.

Adam gave his head a shake. "What did you say?"

Bennett tugged his gloves free. He beat them against each other, looking bored.

Rage clouded Adam's vision. He surged to his feet. "This is how I'm to be repaid for my service?" He took a step toward Bennett. "After almost three months of captivity, this is all you have to say?"

Fitzmorris and Blakely caught Adam between them. "Calm down," Blakely said quietly.

Adam pulled free with a bitter laugh. "I was drugged by a member of the brotherhood and turned over to Fox. You do know that?"

Silence met his question.

He looked at each of them, stunned. "Fitzmorris?"

His friend glanced away.

Adam's gaze flew to Grace's father. "Blakely?"

Blakely gave an imperceptible shake of his head.

With a growl, Adam spun away and presented them with his back. They didn't believe him and he was too bloody exhausted from his efforts to fight them on the truth.

"Markham, I'm being patient with you because of your ordeal, but I expect a certain degree of respect," Bennett said in clipped tones.

A muscle ticked in Adam's cheek.

Bennett continued. "You'll need to spend some time here and then you can return to London."

"How long?" Adam squeezed out between clenched teeth.

"All in good time, Markham," Fitzmorris assured him.

He paced the floor and listened to their plans for him.

He would remain in this ramshackle farmhouse. He'd have Stone and Fitzmorris for company. He'd return to London, at which time he'd be reunited with his family. Adam stopped in front of Blakely. And Grace. He'd be reunited with Grace.

Adam looked away, unable to meet the man's eyes. Guilt snaked around his belly. During his captivity he'd thought of Grace. But it had been more a sense of guilt that had dragged her memory into his thoughts. At some point, Georgina had stolen a spot inside his heart and made him question everything he'd thought he'd known to be true.

Bennett tugged on the lapels of his black coat. "So it is decided." He made a move as if to leave.

"Bennett," Adam barked.

His superior froze.

Adam looked the cold bastard in the eyes. "There is a woman. A maid. Her name is Georgina—"

"Wilcox," Bennett finished for him. He slashed the air with his hand. "No need to worry. We're well aware of Miss Wilcox. She'll be taken care of."

Adam glanced over his shoulder out the grimy windowpane.

Bennett insisted The Brethren would see to Georgina.

When Adam wanted nothing more than to be the one to return for her and secret her away from the hell she'd been left to dwell in.

SEVEN

Emmet will accompany Fox to France to discuss the predicted resumption of the Anglo-French War. Orders have come down for Fox to kill the British spy in his possession prior to departure.
A Loyal British Subject

For nearly a fortnight, Georgina wavered in and out of consciousness. Her every moment was bathed in pain. Her every dream was an alternating universe of happy memories with Adam and the pain of her father's fists.

Then there was the faceless ghost who'd carried her off to his underworld to torture her for her sins.

Her body shuddered as cruel fingers poked and prodded at her, and she retreated deeper and deeper into oblivion—embracing it, welcoming it.

But just when the pain threatened to carry her off, a kind and sweetly caring voice would call her back. In her dreams, the woman cared for her as if she were a small girl—the mother Georgina had always yearned for, and just the dream of that was enough to keep her within the cocoon of unconsciousness.

At last, she forced her lids open.

"Georgina? My dear, can you hear me?"

Georgina burrowed into the stiff mattress. She didn't want to acknowledge the question, because the agony of merciless hands on her body would follow.

"Georgina?"

She tried to turn on her side.

Gentle hands held her down. "Your ribs were very badly sprained, my dear. It's best if you lie on your back," the voice murmured.

With sheer determination, Georgina opened her eyes. She squinted as a bright shaft of light penetrated a small windowpane, nearly blinding her. Rays of sun beamed off the satiny silver of the stranger's hair. She had to be an angel. There was no other accounting for how she knew Georgina's name.

Georgina forced words past her sore throat. "Am I dead?" She didn't imagine angels would weigh anything, but still the mattress dipped under the plump woman's weight. A wide, white smile creased her cheeks.

"You must feel pretty close to it, my dear, but no, you are not dead."

Georgina flung her arm over her eyes to blot out the sunshine and a moan escaped. Her face felt like it had been used for a pummeling target.

The flutter of skirts indicated another woman had moved next to the bed. Georgina peeked through her fingers at the young woman now pouring water into a white basin at her bedside. With a crown of pale golden hair and kind hazel eyes, she didn't look much older than Georgina.

She smiled at Georgina and rinsed a towel, handing it to the kindly stranger.

Georgina looked back at the older woman. "Who are you?" she managed past dry lips.

"You may call me Catherine. I'm a nurse at Bristol Hospital. Close your eyes."

Georgina obliged.

"They were badly swollen," Nurse Catherine explained. "But you look much better than when you first arrived."

A sea of questions filled her. "Who? How…?" She didn't know where to start. Georgina tried again. "How did I come to be here?"

There was a pause. "There will be time enough for questions later."

"Please," Georgina managed.

The woman hesitated. "A man brought you here."

Georgina's heart sped up. She shoved herself up on her elbows. The now-cooled compress fell into a damp heap at her side. She remembered a man sweeping her into his arms.

Adam! He'd come for her. "Adam," she breathed.

Nurse Catherine's brow creased. She waved off the young woman hovering at the bedside and gestured someone else over. "Do you remember Mr. Archer?"

White spots danced behind Georgina's eyes and she tried to get air into her lungs. She dug her nails into the sides of the mattress and screamed.

Nurse Catherine's voice could not penetrate the fog of horror.

She yelled until her throat burned and her lips were numb. But he didn't go away.

The face of her nightmares. The stranger who had died on her kitchen floor, whose ghost had visited her after Father had beaten her, now stared back at her with solemn, violet eyes. "Hello, Miss Wilcox."

Georgina clenched her eyes tight. A ghost back from the grave should possess a wrathful tone, not this gentle, quiet warmth.

"I didn't die," the ghost continued.

Her eyes opened. Not a ghost. A man. A very alive, very healthy-looking man. Her logical mind screeched in protest.

"You were dead," she gasped out. "I saw you. I saw—"

"You didn't see what you believed you saw."

No. She squeezed her eyes shut again. She'd been there. She'd scrubbed his blood from the floor until her fingers had been raw and her own blood mingled with the imprint his body had left behind. "I'm going mad," she said, the eerie acknowledgement chilling her to the center.

The man reached a hand out and she withered into the folds of her mattress.

He pulled back his fingers. "You're not going mad."

She bit down hard on her lip, drawing blood. The sweet, salty drops fell unchecked. "No," she said, this time more forcefully. "You were dead! You—"

"What happened after I was shot, Miss Wilcox?"

Her mind raced. Shouts of fury. Father had been enraged that she'd set him free. She pressed her palm into the side of her temple.

"They dragged you away, didn't they?" he asked quietly. "They took you upstairs and they beat you."

Tears blinded her. Fell in large rivulets down her cheeks. Jamie had dragged her across the kitchen by her hair. That had been the kindest thing done to her that day. The message Father had delivered in the form of raining fists of fury had been quite clear: no one's intervention in their plans would be tolerated—including Georgina's.

"I wasn't dead, Miss Wilcox. I was very badly hurt. I nearly died, but as you can see," he opened his arms. "I'm very much alive." His kind eyes grew somber. "When they were beating you, I escaped." He folded his hands together and looked down at them. "I'm so, so sorry that I did not help you. I had promised to help you if you freed me and I failed."

She swiped the tears away, but the blasted drops continued to fall. For the past four years, she had flagellated herself with the lash of guilt because she'd failed the stranger in her kitchen. All along, he'd been alive. Giddy joy filled her until laughter blended with her tears.

"I want to help you, Miss Wilcox," he said.

"Miss Wilcox needs her rest," Nurse Catherine murmured.

Mr. Archer nodded and, with a deep bow, he left.

The graying nurse spoke. "He brought you here nearly a fortnight ago. He's come by each day to ask after you. He's sat by your side for many hours."

Georgina collapsed against the pillows, turning her eyes away from the prying questions she saw in the other woman's gaze. "Why?" Nathaniel Archer had been nothing more than a poor soul captured by her radical father. She'd cared for him and set him free. He'd received a bullet to the chest for her efforts.

"It would appear that Mr. Archer has set himself up as a kind of guardian, Georgina." There was a question there. "And it would appear you are in need of guarding."

"Why did he bring me here?" Georgina didn't believe her delivery to Bristol Hospital was sheer coincidence.

Catherine rested her hand on top of Georgina's head. "Over the years, you've provided some valuable information to the Home Office." Her voice was a mere whisper that Georgina strained to hear. "There are many of us scattered around to help when needed."

Georgina swallowed back a lump. All these years she'd provided details about her father's plans—damning information that could have gotten him hanged. She'd believed there was no one out there concerned about her welfare, but that hadn't been altogether true. Mr. Archer had been sent to help.

"Where is your father, Georgina?"

A chill raced along her spine. Georgina's teeth chattered.

Catherine pulled a coverlet up to Georgina's chest.

It didn't help.

She took Georgina's hands in her own and rubbed them. "Shh, you are safe here."

For how long? It was only a matter of time before her father came looking for her. Georgina knew too many of his secrets.

What am I going to do? Where will I go?

Oh God, how she wished Adam was here. Georgina wept. Not the pretty droplets shed by young debutantes and flirty beauties. And not tears of self-pity. She cried over the loss of Adam Markham. After twenty years of being nothing more than an afterthought in life, he had treated her like someone to be cherished and cared for.

Hers were great, big, gasping tears that shook her whole body. Uncaring about the pain in her torso, she rolled onto her side and hugged herself.

She'd known it was the height of foolishness going and falling head over silly heels in love with Adam Markham. There were a thousand and one reasons she shouldn't have done it. The most obvious being that he loved another woman. The second most obvious being that she shared the same blood as his captor.

Defying the logic that had dictated her life, Georgina had tossed it aside—all for the love of a man who would never, could never, love her in return.

She cried until her eyes were dry. Until her lungs ached and her muscles hurt from the exertion of her efforts. Through it all Nurse Catherine sat at her side and rubbed soothing circles over the expanse of her back.

Adam hadn't returned.

Mr. Nathaniel Archer had come for her.

She squeezed her eyes tight. Adam hadn't had a choice but to leave. He'd had to escape. Even as she told herself that, in her bone-weary fatigue, she hated him for being as much of a liar as the rest of the men in her life. It had been just as she'd said from the beginning—when presented with the opportunity for freedom, he would invariably forget her. He'd put up a convincing denial each time but, in the end, Georgina had been right.

And she found she hated herself even more for having been such a fool.

She drew in a shuddery breath. She had to mourn Adam, but not at the expense of her well-being.

"What will I do?" she whispered into the quiet.

"You'll stay here as long as you need."

And Georgina did just that. For another week, she spent time resting. Nathaniel Archer came and went like a phantom.

"Miss Wilcox?"

She glanced up from the chintz-patterned chair. The hard angular planes of Mr. Archer's face were softened by the smile that curved his lips. She made to rise, but he held his hand up, motioning her to stay.

She stood anyway and dipped a curtsy. "Mr. Archer."

He held his arm out. "Will you walk with me?"

Georgina hesitated before placing the tips of her fingers on his sleeve. He led her into Nurse Catherine's office and closed the door behind them. "Mr. Archer—"

Catherine stood off to the side of the room, hands clasped in front of her.

Georgina's words for Mr. Archer were forgotten as she studied the woman's snow-white visage, the way she fisted the brown fabric of her skirts.

A cold sheen of sweat popped up on Georgina's brow. She unwittingly took a step closer to Mr. Archer.

The plump, older woman cleared her throat. "Georgina, would you please sit?"

Georgina looked from Nurse Catherine to Mr. Archer and shook her head. "I-I'd rather not." She didn't want to hear what either of them had to say.

Nurse Catherine sighed. She sat. Then proceeded to pinch the bridge of her nose. "My dear, you received a visitor today."

Georgina curled her hands into tight fists. She closed her eyes.

Don't ask. You do not want to know. If you don't ask it then it's not real.

"W-who?" she whispered.

Mr. Archer spoke. "Miss Wilcox, your father has come by several times looking for you. In spite of Nurse Catherine's adamancy that she's not seen you, he has not believed her. And he's growing impatient."

Georgina reached out for the nearest piece of furniture to keep herself upright and found support from the back of the leather sofa.

For too long she'd allowed herself a false sense of security, hoping beyond all hope that Father and Jamie had taken themselves off to wherever it was that traitors to the Crown went. That they'd left her alone.

She sank into the chair. Her momentary reprieve from the hell of her life was now at an end. Father and Jamie wouldn't rest until they found her.

Why? She raged within.

She couldn't go back to them. Not ever again.

Mr. Archer dropped to a knee beside her. He spoke in hushed undertones. "We need to get you away."

Georgina continued to study her lap. "Why would you help me? Why after..." She fell silent and buried her head in her hands.

A delicate hand came to rest on her shoulder. "You saved my life."

"I have to leave." Her mind spun. She had no one. No family, no friends, and it was only a matter of time until she was once more at the mercy of her father.

He looked at Nurse Catherine. "We need to get her away from here. Miss Wilcox will need to find suitable employment, in a place her father will not expect. She'll need letters of reference."

Georgina tried to muster some kind of care that they discussed her as though she were invisible.

She came up short.

Catherine nodded and hurried to her desk. She reached for a blank sheet of paper on her immaculate desktop, dipped her pen in a crystal inkwell, and proceeded to write.

Georgina embraced the frantic scribbling of the pen as it tapped away, because focusing on that staccato rhythm prevented her mind from trailing down the path of the unknown.

The older woman finished and stuffed the parchment into an envelope. "It's done," she murmured. Catherine stood up and came back around to Georgina. She handed the letter over.

Georgina accepted the offering. It may as well have contained the Holy Grail for what it represented: freedom, security, and something more, something she'd been without for such a very long time—hope.

Nurse Catherine spoke, bringing Georgina to the moment. "Here." She reached into the front of her apron and withdrew a small, red velvet sack. She pressed the sack into her palm. "I want you to take this."

Georgina pulled back the drawstring and peered inside. She made to return it. "I cannot take this."

Nurse Catherine gave her a stern look. "I'll be insulted if you don't."

Georgina wanted to protest but the reality of her situation, the uncertainty of her future, killed the polite rejection.

She bowed her head. "I can never repay you."

Nurse Catherine took her hands between her own. She gave them a gentle squeeze. "There's nothing to repay."

Mr. Archer held his arm out. "Miss Wilcox, we have to leave."

Georgina swallowed hard and, with a final thank you, left with Mr. Archer.

EIGHT

Forgive my silence these past months. Emmet has plans to travel to Fort George in Scotland and meet the United Irishmen interned there. He will then sail from Yarmouth to Hamburg.
Signed,
A Loyal British Subject
3 months later

Adam fumbled for his tumbler of French brandy, inadvertently tipping the bottle of whiskey on the drink cart.

He swiped a hand over his eyes. The Brethren had nurtured him back to health—and questioned him about Fox and Hunter. He'd given them everything he had on the bastard traitors. What had his work gotten him? For all his efforts, The Brethren had seemingly washed its hands of him.

He'd dedicated his life to the organization. All for the good of England.

His lip curled.

With his free hand, he located his glass of brandy. He tossed back the contents. After six tumblers of the stuff, his mouth had long gone numb. And his fingers. And toes.

It was his blasted heart that remained wholly unaffected by the alcohol dousing.

He'd returned to his family. It would appear he'd been one month too late.

He glanced down at the open sketchpad next to him. His lip curled. Grace Blakely's angelic face leaped off the page. Adam ripped the image from the book and shredded it with a gleeful precision. He sprinkled the scraps on the floor.

Because he was a glutton for pain, he fumbled for the four-month-old copy of the London Times beneath the sketchpad. He picked it up and crushed it in his fist. The paper cracked and crinkled like kindling for a fire. His gaze wandered over to the roaring fire across the too-warm room. He surged to his feet and stormed over to the hearth.

Setting his glass atop it, he tortured himself with the words on the page.

Miss Grace B, daughter of the 5th Viscount Camden, was wed to Lord Edward Benedict Helling, brother to the Duke of Aubrey.

After everything he'd lost and all he'd suffered, this was the final lash across his back, the kick to his gut. Grace had wed another. It didn't matter that at some point Georgina had needled herself inside his heart and thoughts. The loss of Grace served as a reminder of all he'd lost because of The Brethren.

He tossed the paper into the flames. Fire licked at the edges, singeing it black, then consumed it.

Adam reached for his glass and brought it to his lips. He downed the fiery brew in one long swallow.

For three months, he'd battled like Achilles not to succumb to his sexual desire. Oh, there had been plenty of times when he'd wanted nothing more than to lay Georgina down, spread her legs, and plunge his aching shaft between her pale thighs. But he hadn't. There had been the one instance when he'd very nearly betrayed Grace, but he'd stopped himself. How many times had he lashed himself with the proverbial whip for lusting after her?

A bitter laugh escaped him. It turned out Grace Blakely hadn't cared as much as he'd believed. The muscles in his belly tightened as he focused on Grace's betrayal. In doing so, he didn't have to think about Georgina Wilcox with her chocolate brown eyes and bow-shaped lips. He didn't have to think about how she'd cared for him. He didn't have to think about how he'd promised to help her. Or how miserably he'd failed.

His clenched his eyes tight to try to blot out all the ways in which he'd failed Georgina. For the remainder of his days he would punish himself with imaginings of the horrors she'd endured at Fox's hands. He'd gone back there, to the place of his imprisonment, with Bennett and Blakely, but the house had been silent. Silent and empty. And just like that she was gone…without a trace.

There was a knock at the door.

"Go away!" he roared.

The door opened. His brother stood framed in the entrance. His lips tipped in a perfect rendering of aristocratic disapproval. "May I come in?"

"I said go away."

"Lovely to see you as well, little brother," Nick said dryly. He waved off Adam's butler. The door closed behind them. When he turned back to face Adam, he didn't waste any time. "Mother is concerned about you, as well."

Adam fumbled for a new glass and the decanter of brandy. Finding it nearly empty, he grabbed the whiskey. "And Tony, don't forget Tony."

Nick's lips tightened in a flat line. "No, Tony isn't concerned. He told me to tell you he's annoyed with your childlike behavior."

Adam filled his tumbler to the rim. Amber droplets spilled onto the floor.

Nick placed himself directly in front of him. "I believe you've had enough to drink."

In a show of defiance, he tossed back the contents.

Nick placed a hand on his shoulder. "You've been like this since you returned from your travels. Where were you?"

Adam fed him the same rote answer his superior Fitzmorris had drilled into him. "I was traveling. I spent time on the canals of Italy…"

"Fine," Nick interjected. "Then what happened to you while you were there? You are a different man. I hardly recognize you."

That made two of them, because Adam hardly recognized the half-savage he'd become.

His brother spoke haltingly. "Is this about a woman?"

Georgina—her cheeks rosy with mirth as he waltzed her around his prison cell—flooded his mind. God, the memory of her hurt worse than the physical abuse he'd suffered at Fox and Hunter's hands. He needed to speak of her. "There was a woman."

Nick's eyes widened. "Ahh, I see."

Adam didn't want to sit here and listen to his older brother march out an array of inaccurate theories. "She married another man." It wasn't altogether untrue. Grace had married another.

"I'm so sorry, Adam."

Adam took a step. His brother mimicked him. He stepped the other way. Nick did the same.

"I need a drink," Adam said hoarsely. And he did. For the past months, his strength had been found at the bottom of a bottle. His need for the drink was a physical craving.

Nick placed a hand on his shoulder. "Enough. It is time you move on. We'll get through this. I promise you."

"Don't make promises you can't keep," he snapped. It would never be all right.

Not as long as Georgina is out there, alone and unprotected. Or worse…

His gut clenched at an image of her lifeless body.

Nick seemed unaware of the wicked fears ravaging Adam. He stroked his jaw with his thumb and forefinger. "I don't expect you to tell me the truth, but I do think there is more to your surly behavior. You've never indulged in spirits like this. You are a different man. I suspect if I press you, all you'll do is feed me more lies about canals and museums."

Adam froze.

Nick sighed. "You need a diversion. Why don't you take a mistress?"

Georgina's face flashed behind his eyes. He sucked in a breath. The thought of betraying her memory by taking some nameless woman into his bed sickened him. "I don't need a mistress."

A small smile tilted one corner of Nick's lips. "I wasn't referring to you taking a mistress. I was referring to you finding something else to do with your time." He glanced at the empty whiskey bottle on the table. "That is, something other than drinking and gaming." Disapproval underlined his words.

He swiped a hand over his eyes. "I don't need to be saved, Nick," he growled, hating the lie that pounded at his breast. He did need saving, but it was not the kind his brother could help with. Adam had failed Georgina and nothing could make it right.

"I can help you, Adam."

A denial sprung to his lips but he couldn't force the words out. Adam blamed his blurred vision on the alcohol he'd consumed. "I missed you, Nick."

And just like that long ago day of their childhood when Adam had been freed from the armoire, Nick folded him in his arms. "I'm not going to let anything happen to you. You're safe."

Adam trembled. It was like the faint rumblings of a distant thunderstorm that grew, and grew, until it opened up into a fantastic display that cracked the sky and shook the ground. He sobbed. Tears poured from him like a deluge.

"G-god, I-I missed you," he choked out between the great, gasping gulps.

Nick just held him and allowed him to cry.

Adam cried for the loss of the simple, uncomplicated love he'd known with Grace. He cried for the time he would never be able to recapture. He cried for the abuse he'd suffered at Fox and Hunter's hands.

And he cried for Georgina. He cried until his body ached. Until there was nothing left but a shell of the boy who'd been locked away in an armoire.

Nick ushered him over to the leather sofa and helped him down. Then, as if he were a valet, and not the powerful Earl of Whitehaven, he proceeded to tug Adam's boots free. "It will be all right, little brother. I promise."

Except, it could never be all right. Not again. He was broken and scarred in ways he would never recover.

Nick stood and appeared as though he wished to say more. Then, he turned to leave.

Adam couldn't be alone. "Please." He held a hand out. "Don't.

His brother returned to his side. "I'll stay with you."

Adam closed his eyes. "There was a woman." He yawned.

The leather wingback chair opposite Adam groaned in protest, indicating that Nick had taken a seat. "Oh?"

"Her name was Georgina."

NINE

Emmet is concerned by the apparent leak of information. The persons suspected of the leak are known as The Brethren of the Lords—a group of English nobles who are acting as spies for the Crown. A plan is in place to determine the identity of other members of The Brethren.
Signed,
A Loyal British Subject

A dull pounding filled Adam's ears. He squinted into the bright sunlight and glared up at the towering façade of the imposing white structure. When he'd awakened several hours ago, he'd convinced himself he'd imagined the emotional exchange with his brother, the haunting memories of Georgina, and the promise to join Nick at Middlesex Hospital where the earl served on the Board of Directors.

Adam couldn't think of a place he wanted to be less.

Fox and Hunter's cruel laughter echoed off the walls of Adam's brain and he flinched.

That wasn't altogether true. There were places far worse than this dreary institution.

"This is your idea of a diversion?" Adam mumbled.

He groaned at his brother's booming laugh. Nick thumped him on the back. "It is an improvement from the company you find in a bottle of spirits." There was a hint of reproach in those words.

Adam peered at Nick from the corner of his eye, heat making his cravat incredibly tight. He resisted the urge to tug at it, unwilling to let Nick know how his admonition had shamed him.

The truth that Adam kept from him—the tale of his captivity and the countless rounds of torture he'd endured—were not grounds for Adam's dependence on spirits. His stomach tightened. He hated that he had lost so much of his self-control. After months of indulging, he had to accept that the intoxicating pull of brandy was not strong enough to dull the pain that haunted him. It was the type of agony that couldn't be healed with a soothing balm or tonic.

He curled his hands into tight fists at his side. And all this because of the two bastards who'd taken him prisoner. If he found them, he would take great delight in—

"Adam?" Nick interrupted.

He started. "Fine," he answered the unspoken question. He gave his head a shake. "Let's get on with it," he snapped, and started up the steps.

Nearly twenty minutes later, Nick had gone off to his meeting and Adam remained rooted to the entrance hall of Middlesex Hospital. He shifted his weight from side to side, unable to stave off the surging sense of awkwardness. What had possessed him to allow Nick to drag him here? The last thing the men in this hospital needed was a visit from a former spy and current reprobate brother to the Earl of Whitehaven. Feeling foolish that he'd allowed Nick to drag him along, Adam spun on his heel and hurried to take his leave. He had nearly reached the front door when an older, graying nurse appeared before him, cutting off his path to freedom.

"Mr. Markham, might I show you around?"

Bloody wonderful.

"Yes," he growled.

If the nurse detected the spark of impatience in his laconic response, she gave no outward indication. He followed her down the long corridor, the echo of their footsteps sounding off the wall.

He noted how she continued to steal surreptitious glances from the corner of her eye at him. He may as well have been a two-headed demon for the way the woman eyed him.

Adam's jaw set stonily. At one time, he could have charmed the heart of the coldest dowager. Fox and Hunter had destroyed his ease around other people. Now whenever he moved around strangers, it felt more like visiting a menagerie of exotic animals.

"The men will be so very grateful for your visit."

He rather doubted it. He didn't offer much in the way of company. In fact, they'd probably prefer empty silence to anything he had to say.

They entered a large room with several rows of neat, white hospital beds. Adam started. He'd expected a quiet, sterile space, not this bright cheery room with pictures adorning the walls. At the tables beside each man's bed was a small vase of flowers. The winter sun glinted through the windows, wreathing the room in an ethereal glow.

His gaze followed one of the sun's rays and he froze, suspended in a world where dream met reality.

Her back was to him, but he'd recognize that untamable mane of brown curls in a crowded ballroom.

His heart pounded hard and fast within his chest.

Georgina.

She poured a glass of water and handed it to a graying man.

"Mr. Markham?" the nurse at his side prodded.

He shook his head. "Georgina!" he called.

Her body stiffened.

The nurse gasped. "I'm sorry, sir. This is most improper. Why don't we return to the front hall?"

Like hell.

Adam started toward Georgina. He'd found her at last—the proverbial needle in a haystack—and he did not intend to lose her now.

TEN

Diplomats for the United Irishmen will be received in Paris. The leader Emmet will go to France. He has appointed Fox as the English lead during his absence.
Signed,
A Loyal British Subject

O ver the years, Georgina had lost count of all the bad things that had happened to her. Yet, she could count on two hands the number of wonderful things that had happened to her, and all of them involved Adam Markham.

Since she'd found work at Middlesex Hospital, she'd lived in constant fear that Father and Jamie would find her and punish her for her role in freeing Adam. Whenever a stranger visited the facility, tendrils of fear would fan out and wrap around her lungs, making breathing difficult. At those times, she wished she could curl herself into a ball of invisibility. She'd done a remarkable job of going unnoticed—until now.

The tall man striding across the room like an avenging archangel was different than she remembered. Although lean, his body had the healthy weight of muscle to it. At the furious pace he'd set, his unfashionably long, golden hair whipped free of the queue at the base of his neck. Her fingers all but trembled from the urge to brush back those strands kissed with golden sunlight.

"Adam," she whispered.

Georgina's lids slid closed. It couldn't be. Moments like this didn't happen to people like her. Magical moments were reserved for good, deserving people who didn't share the blood of evil men.

When she opened them, Adam stood in front of her, very masculine and very, very real. She had to tilt her head back to look at him.

Hot emotion glinted in the moss-green of his irises. He studied her as if she were the sun, moon, and stars all rolled into one.

Adam took her hand and with infinite slowness, brought it to his lips with the sweet tenderness of which dreams were made.

Nurse Talbert gasped. "Miss Wilcox!" The woman's owl-like eyes were wide with disapproval.

Propriety could go hang. Just then, nothing else mattered. In the months since she'd lived in London and worked at the hospital, Adam had remained with her as a life-sustaining memory.

He continued to hold her hand. Some indecipherable look filled his eyes.

"Miss Wilcox, I must insist—"

Adam shot the nurse a withering look that silenced her.

Regardless of the fact that Adam was here, Georgina had to have a care for her reputation. By the grace of God, she'd secured a position at Middlesex Hospital. She could not risk being thrown out in the dead of winter without work.

She tried to tug her hand free to no avail.

Adam leaned close. His breath tickled her skin. "I am not letting you go. Is that clear, Georgina?"

When he looked at her this way, as if she were the most important person in all the world, it made her yearn for foolish, unattainable dreams.

The silence of the room seemed to reach Adam. His hard, powerful stare surveyed the wide-eyed patients, and when his eyes returned to hers, they gentled. "I need to speak to you, Georgina."

God, how she wanted that. She wanted to be with him and only him, now and forever. But there was Father and—her heart seized—the woman he loved. "I can't, Adam." If she spent any more time with him, it would destroy her with the promise of the things that could never be.

He growled and began tugging Georgina from the room as if he were a conquering lord and she the lady of the castle.

She tripped over her skirts and Adam caught her against him. He slowed his step but did not halt the determined course he'd set.

With the same force of a mountain crashing down atop her, Georgina became aware of the impropriety. She dug her heels in.

"Adam, you must stop!" she implored. In the span of a heartbeat, he'd destroyed the security she'd come to covet.

She cast her eyes back at Nurse Talbert. The woman clutched at her side as she tried to keep up with the rigorous pace set by Adam. Her pale blue eyes flashed sparks of disapproval.

A knot formed in Georgina's stomach. Her employer would never countenance such scandal. The woman was prouder than King George himself and would rather welcome the mice scurrying around the facility than Georgina, who would become a constant reminder of this humiliation. Georgina would be cast out, and this time there would be no reference, only a ruined reputation. Who knew that panic could be deafening and blinding at the same time? It filled her senses and consumed her until she didn't know which way was up and which was down. For all the damage Adam had wrought this day, he may as well have been dragging her into the pits of hell.

Adam, however, appeared unaffected by the tremor wracking her frame. He moved like a man possessed. His gaze snapped left and right down the long hall then narrowed on a closed door. Without a knock, he shoved it open.

The two women folding bed linens and towels glanced up. Their eyes widened.

"Get out," he snapped through clenched teeth.

The women shrieked and, in their haste for freedom, knocked over a small table with folded linens. Their efforts came crashing down like a crumbling, snowy white mountain.

Nurse Talbert caught the edge of the doorway. Her chest heaved as she struggled to catch her breath. "What is the meaning of this, sir? You cannot simply accost one of our maids!"

Adam closed the door in her face.

She pounded away at the door. "Open the door this instant, sir. Do you hear me?"

Adam's response was to turn the lock.

Georgina slapped a hand against her mouth. *Oh, blast.* With his powerful, commanding presence, Adam would make it through Nurse Talbert's rage unscathed. Georgina, herself, wouldn't be as fortunate. Her knees knocked together, and this time she was glad for Adam's sure grip on her elbow because it was all that prevented her from dissolving into a puddle at his feet.

The pounding stopped.

Adam released her. He stood staring at her through thick, golden lashes. Georgina inched away from him until her back met the door.

He reached for her, but she held up a single finger.

He stopped. "Georgina," he murmured.

She thrashed her head back and forth. "Stop. Please," she said, when he tried to reach for her hand.

As much as she loved him, he could never be hers. A spasm seized her heart. It had taken Georgina months to accept that Adam would not come charging in on his white steed and rescue her from the hell that was her life.

Adam had another. There would always be that beauty upon the sketchpad who held his heart.

Georgina sucked in a breath, nearly doubling over from the pain of it. Why, even now he might be wedded to the beauty. Georgina would've preferred to spend the rest of her days with nothing more than memories of Adam, rather than knowing he'd married his glorious goddess.

She rushed toward the window, covering her mouth to smother a sob. Oh God, it was too much.

"Georgina, please." His hoarse entreaty threatened to shatter her.

She couldn't look at him or the damned tears blurring her vision would fall and she couldn't bear for him to see what a silly-heart she was. "Y-you are well?" she managed, not turning around.

He placed his hands upon her shoulders. Georgina's body tensed at the unexpectedness of his touch. "Look at me, Georgina."

She shook her head. If Georgina looked at him, the thin control she had of her emotions would snap, and she'd be left exposed.

"Georgina, look at me," he commanded. With the care he might have showed an ancient relic, he turned her around.

Despair streaked her cheeks, and in that moment she hated him for not allowing her to hold onto the only thing she had left—her dignity.

He tipped her chin up. His thumb brushed back a single tear. There was another to take its place. He shouldn't be touching her. It was making her yearn for things that would never be hers.

"Why the tears, love?" His gentle whisper only made the tears flow all that much faster.

"H-how is y-your wife?"

Adam's finger froze. His arm fell to his side. "My wife?"

"Mrs. Markham. Is she well?" Georgina bit the inside of her cheek.

Adam's body stiffened.

Georgina used it as her opportunity to escape. This was too much. She'd rather endure the lash than this pain. Her hand was on the door handle before he stopped her. This time with words.

"Grace is married."

Grace. Her name somehow made her all the more real. Bitterness, as sharp as acid, burned the back of her throat. What remained of her heart cracked into a million shards, jabbing at her insides until she wanted to twist and writhe to escape the pain of losing him—but then, he'd never been hers to lose.

"Congratulations." She didn't know how she managed those words. Not when she wanted to hiss and snarl like a wounded cat. There was no way Grace could possibly love him like Georgina did.

"If I ever see her, I'll be sure to pass along your felicitations." His response was dry as leaves in winter.

She spun around.

"She is married," he held his palms up, "just not to me."

All the air left Georgina on a whoosh. His Grace had married another? The woman must be as mad as a hatter.

With the sketches he'd made of his love, it had been clear that Grace had been the light that sustained him through his captivity. The foolish, foolish woman. "Oh, Adam," she murmured. "I am so very sorry." Georgina should find happiness in knowing the woman had wed another. How odd to find she was not so very selfish. She would embrace the agony of unrequited love if it meant Adams's happiness. After what he'd endured—at her father's hands—he deserved nothing less.

He clasped his hands together and stared down at them. "Apparently I was gone too long."

Needles of guilt pricked at her. Adam's captivity had cost him the woman he loved. She hated her father, and herself, all over again.

"I should have freed you sooner. If I had…"

He closed the distance between them in three long strides and pressed a finger to her lips, silencing her. "I didn't lose Grace because of you."

She moved his hand. "That doesn't make it all right, Adam. It is because of…of them that you lost her. I could have helped you. I could have made sure you got back before…" Beautiful Grace married some other man. Georgina didn't finish. She imagined those words would be too painful for him.

He rested his palms on the door, framing her between his arms. "Lovely, lovely Georgina," he murmured.

Then he did what she'd longed for him to do since she'd spied him across the ward. He kissed her. The crown of her head. The tip of her nose. On her closed eyes. She waited, breath held, until he claimed her lips with his in a moment so fleeting, Georgina wondered if she'd imagined it.

"You worry about everyone else. Do you ever think of yourself?"

If he knew the depth of her betrayal, he'd know that all she'd worried about her entire life was her own safety, her own comfort. "I'm not good, Adam." She was as tainted as a witch's black mark. Her continued deception only proved as much.

The green of his eyes sparkled. He cupped her cheek in his palm. "Dearest Georgina, I have lain awake so many nights thinking about you. Worrying about you." His hand clenched reflexively on her flesh. "The day I was freed, I nearly went mad knowing I'd left you there." A tick in the corner of his mouth made his skin twitch. He leaned down, his breath caressing her skin. "Did they hurt you?"

Georgina hesitated. A feral gleam glowed within his eyes and she knew. If she told him about what she'd endured that day, he'd hunt her father down and kill him. She could not let Adam risk his life. Not for her.

So she lied. "No. They didn't hurt me."

His eyes slid closed and a prayer escaped him on a whispering sigh. "I thought…"

She touched her fingers to his chest. His heart thumped fast and true against her palm. "They didn't hurt me," she assured him. There were so many lies, sometimes she felt she was slogging through a quagmire of deception.

If this brings him peace, what is one more falsity to the hundred others?

There was a faint scratching at the door. "Mr. Markham?"

Oh God, Nurse Talbert.

"Your brother, that is, the Earl of Whitehaven has arrived."

Georgina scooted out from under the bridge of his arms. Nurse Talbert's voice grated like fingernails being scraped across a windowpane. She clamped her hand over her ears, trying to blot out the sound.

Nurse Talbert would sack her. She tried sucking breath into her constricted lungs. It felt like someone had dragged her below water and was holding on to her feet, as she was seized by the same desperation she'd felt in Bristol after her father had beat her and left her for dead. Then the woman's words registered.

"The earl?" She swung confused eyes to Adam and her stomach dipped. "Your brother is an earl." And she was a traitor's daughter.

Adam called out to her. "Georgina, it will be all right."

Even his tender concern couldn't drag her from the dark abyss. She was sinking. Deeper. Deeper. Soon she'd disappear, forever gone. A panicky laugh bubbled up from her throat. Disappearing was the preferable option to being discovered with Adam here.

Her gaze scoured the room for escape. It landed on a solitary window. She squinted.

Is there a tree out there?

Someone jiggled the door handle. "Open this door." It was a man. The clipped tones indicated it was a man of some power. An earl. Adam's brother. *Oh, God.*

Georgina could only assume the voice belonged to the Earl of Whitehaven, a mythical beast she'd rather not face. Austere, regal, and polished, he was everything Georgina was not.

She looked to Adam for help. His lips were turned up, revealing even, pearl-white teeth. "How can you be smiling?" she choked out.

"My brother is going to be furious."

Georgina dropped her head into her palms. Bloody perfect. She was going to have to contend with an austere, regal, polished nobleman who also happened to be furious. Being thrown out in the streets without a reference seemed the more palatable option. Almost.

The earl murmured something to Nurse Talbert, the words indecipherable through the door.

He tried the handle again.

Adam went to open it.

Georgina gasped and flew across the room, her pale white skirts fluttering about her. She reached him before he turned the lock. "What are you doing?"

Adam's lips twitched. "I assure you, Georgina, we will have to face him eventually."

How could he possibly find anything humorous about their situation? The wheels of her mind spun. Surely there was something—

"Adam, the door."

She jumped as Adam allowed the Earl of Whitehaven entrance.

Adam's lips formed a rusty smile as he greeted the earl. "Hullo, brother."

If looks could shoot fire, Adam would've been nothing more than a pile of ash at the earl's feet. "What is the meaning of this? When I said you needed a diversion, this is most certainly not what I had intended." His blue eyes, sparkling with fury, did a quick survey of Georgina. He returned his attention to Adam. "I was called from my board meeting by the head nurse, who informed me that you had abducted one of her..."

"I'd hardly call it abducting," Adam drawled.

The tight, drawn lines around the earl's mouth indicted that he didn't care to debate the merits of word choice. He arched a perfectly "earlish" brow.

Her stomach curled in knots. The Earl of Whitehaven chose that moment to glance her way. His upper lip curled back as he looked down his aristocratic nose at her.

Georgina inched away from Adam, who shifted his attention to the earl.

Georgina saw her chance and took it. She pulled the door open and flew down the hall as though the hounds of hell were nipping at her heels. She might actually prefer those sharp-toothed dogs to the condemnation she'd seen in the earl's eyes.

By the time the thick fog of confusion had lifted, Georgina was gone. His heart threatened to pound a hole out of his chest. He'd not lose her now!

"Georgina!"

Nick planted himself in front of him. "Where do you think you're going?" he snapped.

Adam took a step around him.

Nick again placed himself between Adam and the freedom he craved.

Adam gripped him by the shoulders and snarled like the caged captive he'd been. "By God, if you stop me from going to her, I will thrash you within an inch of your life. Is that clear, Nick?"

Nick's mouth fell open, but he remained frozen in place. "There will be a scandal," he snapped. He waved his hand around the sterile office. "The staff here will talk. The other board members have already caught a whiff of scandal when I was summoned from the meeting. I will be damned if you throw away your reputation for a common maid…"

Red dots of fury nearly blinded Adam. A roar rumbled deep within his chest. He slammed his fist into Nick's unsuspecting face.

Nick crumpled to the floor, landing hard on his knees. He pressed his fingers to a slightly-hooked nose and winced. He tugged a kerchief from his pocket and blotted the crimson blood. "By God, you broke my nose!"

Adam stood over him. "You're my brother and I love you. But if you disparage her, I will lay you flat again. Is that understood?" He held his hand out.

Nick knocked it aside and shoved to his feet without assistance. "I will not continue this dialogue in this very public forum. If you don't have a care for your reputation, have one for mine and mother's." He glared around the edges of the embroidered fabric.

A twinge of remorse hit him. Nick was the type of brother who'd battle a thousand foes for his family. But being reunited with Georgina had set a blaze burning within him and his thoughts raged like a conflagration, threatening to burn reason and logic to cinders. His brother would never understand, because he would never know the hell that had bound Adam and Georgina in an unbreakable bond. Still, he had to try. "I need to help her."

From behind the kerchief, Nick's eyes grew shuttered. "Tell me this is not the woman."

Adam didn't say anything.

Nick sighed. "Very well. I'll have her summoned." He walked over to the door...just as it was opened. The wood slammed into his nose with a sickening crack. He cried out.

The plump nurse with her silly, white cap stood there wearing a nasty scowl. She had her fingers wrapped tightly around Georgina's forearm. Nurse Talbert spared a glance at Nick's bloodied kerchief and wrinkled her nose in a manner hardly befitting a nurse. "My apologies for injuring your nose, my lord," she said with all the sincerity of a sinner taking sup with a man of the cloth. She didn't make a move to help.

Adam's gaze fell on Georgina. He tried to imagine her, a beautiful glowing nightingale, silenced by this harridan. The red curtain of rage fell back into place. "Release her now."

Nurse Talbert released Georgina's arm with alacrity.

Georgina's downcast eyes and pale skin indicated it was her spirit that had been wounded. Having suffered at the hands of Fox and Hunter, he knew some things were far worse than physical pain.

It made him want to throw her over his shoulder and run off like a conquering lord, saving his damsel.

He slipped his hand into Georgina's.

Nurse Talbert's eyes nearly bulged from her head. She pointed a quivering finger at Georgina. "Your services are no longer required here, Miss Wilcox."

It was perhaps a testament to how helpless Georgina had become. She showed no outward reaction to what was surely a devastating turn of events. Somehow, the lack of emotion from Georgina was even more bothersome.

Nick flicked an imaginary piece of dust from his shoulder, looking for all the world as though he'd never been more bored. "I'm sure that is a bit extreme, Nurse Talbert."

The woman's lips flattened into a hard line. "I have a reputation to maintain, my lord. I cannot allow women of ill repute within my halls. And I most certainly will not allow this wanton to destroy my hard efforts."

Adam had never hit a woman, but if ever a woman deserved it, this was the one. "If you disparage Georgina Wilcox one more time, by God, I'll see to it that you'll never work in this hospital or any other hospital, again. Is that clear?"

Nick dabbed at his nose. The blood flow had trickled to a near stop. He folded the cloth and tucked it in his front pocket like it wasn't completely bloodstained. "I'm sure, Nurse Talbert, there is something we can work out so the woman—"

"Miss Wilcox." Adam had tired of Nick's lofty use of the term "the woman". He spoke of her as if she were a teacup or settee.

Nick gave him a pointed glare. "So Miss Wilcox might retain her position."

"She doesn't want her position," Adam snapped.

"Yes she does!" Georgina said, hastily. She looked at Adam with such entreaty in the brown of her eyes, that he was struck speechless.

She turned to his brother. "I do, my lord. I want my position here. I need my position here."

Nurse Talbert was already shaking her head. "The moment you created that scandalous scene on the main floor, you sealed your fate."

A muscle in Nick's jaw ticked, a telltale indication of how very close he was to losing his temper. As the earl, he'd become unaccustomed to having people gainsay his wishes.

"Nurse Talbert, I'm going to say this just one more time. I would greatly appreciate it if Miss Wilcox was permitted to keep her position. Is that clear?" He raised a single brow.

Nurse Talbert raised her own brow. "Oh, it was quite clear, my lord." She looked to Georgina. "Pack your things, my dear. This is your last day."

Georgina pressed a hand to her mouth, as if she were trying to stifle a scream. Panicked eyes flitted around the office. They met his.

"I will help you, Georgina," he said quietly. Surely, she had to know that?

The guilt that had robbed him of sleep pricked at him. Then again, what would make her believe he would help her? He'd abandoned her with those foul beasts.

Ever proud, Georgina dropped her trembling hand to her side. She tossed her head back. "Very well, Nurse Talbert."

Like hell. He planted himself in front of Georgina and effectively blocked her path. Over the crown of her head, he shot his brother a look.

Nick held his stare then sighed. "I'll find work for Miss Wilcox in my household."

Nurse Talbert snorted, indicating just what kind of work she expected Georgina Wilcox would find in the earl's home.

Adam clenched his teeth. He had not survived the hell with Fox and Hunter to fear society's snide recrimination. "She will not be working in my brother's household."

Georgina picked her head up. Her full, red lips quivered.

He reached down and stroked her cheek. It was like silk against his fingers. "She'll be my wife. I'm marrying her." He turned to Georgina. "Will you marry me?"

And indomitable Georgina Wilcox fainted dead-away in his arms.

ELEVEN

Fox has made an innovation to the folding pike. The weapon can be concealed beneath one's cloak and possesses a hinge. Fox and Hunter have now devoted their efforts to locating members of The Brethren.
Signed,
A Loyal British Subject

When Georgina came to, she realized several things at once. First, she was in a carriage.

Two she was entirely too cozy, warm, and comfortable. In her twenty years, she'd been all those things...but never at the same time.

Thirdly, were the clipped tones of two men in a heated argument. Her brow wrinkled.

Two men?

Arguing?

She came crashing down to earth and her eyes flew open.

"Don't fight me on this," Adam fairly snarled. His hard body against hers thrummed with the same charge as a lightning strike. She expected most men would've cowered under Adam's lethal glare.

Apparently, the Earl of Whitehaven was not most men. He appeared bored, stifling a yawn with his hand. "You'll do no such thing."

What such thing?

"I'm marrying her."

And she remembered. Adam was speaking of her. Not Grace Blakely. Her. Short, plain Georgina Wilcox. Her heart soared.

Until the earl spoke.

"You cannot wed her." He looked down at her and realized she was awake. "She is a commoner. A mere maid. You will not marry a woman of her station."

Georgina returned his bold stare. The earl was as broad and muscular as an old oak tree. From the harsh angles of his cheeks to the square jawline, this was a man who would rouse fear in man and child alike. Noblemen weren't supposed to be hulking figures. They were supposed to be painted and clad in all the nauseating colors of an artist's pallet. And he should've been wearing padding. Didn't all nobles wear padding?

Her eyes narrowed on his waistline. It looked like it could be stuffing.

He shifted and the expensive line of his sapphire coat tightened across the rippling muscles of his abdomen.

No, there was no stuffing involved.

Perhaps it was her bold perusal, or mayhap just his utter disdain, but his upper lip curled in a sneer and Georgina thought of the tale her father had told of her grandmother's murder. Was this how her grandmother had felt when the English guards spat on her?

She scrambled off Adam's lap, landing on the floor with a loud thump.

"Georgina!" he cried. He picked her up and returned her to his lap.

Her face colored furiously. "You must release me, Ad... Mr. Markham. This is highly improper."

Adam held firm. "I am going to marry you."

As if that would make any of this right? Surely he realized that what he proposed was not possible?

"You cannot marry me, Adam." She shoved herself off his lap and sat down on the seat next to him.

"I can. I will."

He fell silent and, tugging back the curtain, peered out at the passing scene.

Georgina studied him. When she had been a young girl, before she'd made her come out, she'd dreamed of her someday husband.

He would be wickedly handsome, excessively kind, abundantly caring. To be precise, the man she'd dreamed of was Adam.

It had taken her no time at all to learn that marriage was reserved for beauties...like Adam's Grace. Georgina's silly hopes had died a swift death when Father had paraded her around all the wealthiest merchants driven by their goals of securing an advantageous connection. Georgina had been a failure. A miserable failure, to be precise. After that, she'd not given much thought to marriage.

Until now.

She wanted to marry him with a physical hunger that ate at her. But there were too many differences, and lies, between them. "You can't, Adam."

The fabric fell back into place, and he jerked his neck around so fast, she imagined he'd given himself a wicked pain.

She glanced at the earl.

He stared back at her with a first, faint sign of appreciation. "She's correct. You cannot marry her."

Adam cursed. "I've already decided I'm going to wed her. I ruined her reputation."

It felt like her heart was being kicked around her chest. The only reason Adam wanted to marry her was because she'd been turned out of her position. His offer, which had never really been much of an offer, was driven by his sense of honor. Of course. Had she really been foolish enough to hope that he cared for her?

She curled her fingers into tight balls. Her nails dug into the flesh of her palms, but she welcomed the pain.

The earl folded his arms across his broad chest. "Have you asked Miss Wilcox what she wants?"

Adam's gaze snapped to her. The green of his eyes was a stark contrast to the dreary gray of the cold, winter months.

There was the answer she wanted to give his irrational request for marriage. Then there was the answer the Earl of Whitehaven expected of her.

"I don't want to marry you," she said, her voice hollow.

Adam flinched like he'd been kicked in the stomach. He pinned a glare on his brother. "It's because of you."

The earl shrugged. "The lady has her own mind." The carriage rocked to a halt, ending the discussion.

Adam had different ideas. He leaned close to Georgina. "This is not finished."

Nearly an hour later, she was perched on the edge of a small, pale blue settee in a pale blue parlor, and it was still not done.

Georgina glanced at the ormolu clock on the fireplace mantel, watching the minutes tick by. After Adam had helped her out of the carriage, he'd led her up the front steps of the Earl of Whitehaven's home. The earl had marched ahead in stoic silence, and there was little Georgina hated more than silence. Quiet was a good indicator of many things—none of them usually good.

A bellow resonated from a distant room, and she clambered to her feet and all but climbed over the settee in her haste to use it as a protective barrier against the threat—that didn't come. She drew in a shuddery breath, closing her eyes. Shouts of fury were usually accompanied by a heavy fist or the sting of a lash.

"Well, I say, did you leap over that settee?"

Georgina shrieked and slapped a hand to her breast.

The young man in the doorway lounged with his hip against the frame, his arms folded across his chest. Not as tall as Adam, he still towered over Georgina by a good seven inches. He had a familiar squared jaw with the tiniest hint of a cleft and pale blue-green eyes the color of sea foam. At her obvious inspection, full lips tipped up in an amused smile.

Heat rushed to her cheeks.

This had to be Tony, Adam's younger brother.

She bowed her head and sank into a deep curtsy.

He shoved off the wall. "Tsk, tsk. Any lady who can jump as high as you shouldn't be wasting her energy on things like curtsying and head-bobbing."

She blinked.

He laughed, bowing low at the waist. "Anthony Devon Markham, at your service," he said, confirming her suspicions. "But please, call me Tony."

She'd do no such thing. She wasn't nobility, but she'd suffered through enough governesses and instructors to know it was highly improper to be alone with a young man, exchanging introductions.

Another bellow shuddered through the house.

"Georgina Wilcox," she said hastily.

Tony all but threw himself down onto the small, blue sofa she'd occupied. He swung his legs over the arm of the chair and folded his arms behind his head. "I'm assuming you are the source of that."

Georgina bit her lip. Perhaps it would be better to feign ignorance; it would invite less questions. "The source of what, Mr. Markham?"

"Tony," he corrected. A thundering roar, like that of a wounded bear, rocked the room. "That is the *that* to which I referred." His lips twitched with amusement again.

She felt like she'd been spun around in a dozen dizzying circles.

He clarified. "The shouting."

She worried her lower lip. "Uh…yes, I did think that may have been the *that* to which you were referring."

"You're going to chew right through it, you know."

Another shout and Georgina jumped, looking back at the door. Finding no immediate threat, she turned back to Adam's younger brother. "What did you say?" The last thing in the world she wanted to do in that moment was exchange banter with Adam's vexing, if abundantly charming, brother.

He motioned to his lip. "You keep biting at your lip like that and you're going to go through it."

"I've bit my lip enough times to assure you that will not happen." As soon as the words left her mouth, she realized by the glittering specks of gold in his eyes that he was jesting. "Oh," she said, another blush heating her skin. "You were making light of me."

Tony shoved himself upright and frowned. "I wasn't making light."

She raised a brow.

He sighed. "Very well, perhaps I was. I apologize."

Then he smiled. It fairly oozed roguish appeal. He was going to be deadly to the young debutantes—and, she'd venture, the older dowagers, as well.

"So, tell me, what's that all about?" Tony nodded toward the doorway.

Georgina had her lower lip between her slightly crooked teeth before she realized he was looking at her pointedly. She stopped immediately. "I-I…have no idea," she lied.

He snorted. Fortunately, he was wicked but not deliberately cruel, for he didn't press her for details.

Not that Georgian would have given them. What was she to say?

Oh you see, my father abducted your brother, took him captive, but I helped free him. Now the honorable lummox has decided to marry me…whether I like it or not.

"Mother is going to be quite disappointed that she's missing all this," Tony mumbled beneath his breath.

She fanned her cheeks. His mother! Goodness, Adam had brought her into his family's home, through the front entrance no less. Why, the scandal would surely rock his family. Suddenly, taking her chances alone on the streets seemed infinitely preferable. She glanced at the window.

"Oh no. It's far too high a jump."

Georgina jerked her gaze back to Tony.

He nodded toward the window. "You look like you were thinking of jumping to freedom." With a beleaguered sigh, he added, "I've considered it on many occasions myself."

Being reunited with Adam, losing her position and security, being dragged into the middle of a battle between the Earl of Whitehaven and Adam…all of it was suddenly too much. Georgina began laughing. She covered her mouth to stifle the giggle but it was little use. Laughter poured out of her like a torrential London rainstorm. Of course, it was infinitely better than crying, but there'd be time enough for that later, when Adam and the earl decided to include her in a discussion that pertained to the rest of her life.

Suddenly she was tired of waiting. To be rescued. To be taken care of. To have a decision made about her fate. She looked at Tony. "Will you show me the way to his lordship's office?"

Tony smiled, revealing a very Adam-esque row of perfectly straight, pearl-white teeth. "It will be my pleasure, Miss Wilcox." He held out his elbow.

Nicholas sat with his hip perched on the edge of his mahogany desk. The façade of nonchalance was belied by his broken nose and crumpled clothing.

It had been a good six minutes since they'd last shouted at one another. It would appear they were making progress.

Nick swiped a hand across his brow, dashing back an errant trace of sweat. "Surely you see the wisdom in my words. You cannot marry this woman. Why, it would be ruinous."

Apparently they were making far less progress than he'd hoped.

Adam closed his eyes and counted to ten. When he still felt like hitting his brother, he counted another five. He tried appealing to Nick's sense of honor. "As a gentleman, you have to see that I've ruined Georgina. She is alone in the world. Without work…"

In a wholly un-earl-like show of emotion, Nick slammed his fist down on the desktop. "Christ, you are not thinking with your head!" He drew in a deep breath, and when he spoke again, his tone was even. "I don't know anything about this woman other than that, in addition to being a maid, she was the reason for your overindulgence in whiskey."

Adam looked away. His role with The Brethren precluded him from sharing key pieces of himself with his brother. He couldn't mention how he'd come to know Georgina, nor did he care to get into details about Grace Blakely.

Nick placed his hand upon Adam's shoulder, and Adam met his gaze square on.

"There is something about her I simply do not trust, Adam. You offer me very little about her background, and if I might speak plainly—"

Adam shrugged off his touch. "You haven't been up to this point?"

Nick ignored his sardonic question and continued. "If this is about work, I'll find her work. I am not suggesting you leave the woman to her own devices."

Adam gritted his teeth. "Her name is Georgina."

"Very well, then. I'm not suggesting you leave *Miss Wilcox* to her own devices. I can have my housekeeper set her up with a position in the household. Hell, set her up as your mistress but, by the good Lord, you cannot wed her!"

"He's right, Adam. You cannot marry me."

The color leeched from his skin as he swiveled on his heel, his heart lurching in his chest.

Georgina stood there, a perfect, pale, porcelain doll—small, fragile, and helpless amidst a room of life-size beasts. Based on the faint quiver to her lips and the white-knuckled grip on her skirts, she'd heard Nick's scandalous proposal. A wave of hot fury licked at his insides and he wanted to hit his brother all over again.

Tony popped up behind Georgina. He wagged a finger at Nick. "Ain't the thing, discussing a mistress, in front of a young lady."

And now he wanted to hit his younger brother for showing Georgina to Nick's office and exposing her to his brother's priggish, bombastic views on status.

"Get out," Adam ordered quietly.

When Tony didn't move, Nick pointed to the door. "Out."

Adam locked eyes with Georgina. Her gaze bled with hurt and humiliation. This was a wrong he'd committed. He'd be the one to soothe those wounds. "You, too, Nick. Out."

Georgina braced for the earl's protest, but to her surprise, he turned on his heel and left his office. The door closed behind him with an ominous click, leaving her and Adam alone. She rather suspected the earl's willingness to leave had more to do with his confidence that Georgina would not capitulate to Adam's harebrained offer. She studied the tips of her serviceable black boots atop the Aubusson carpet, the stark contrast a glaring reminder of who she was and who they were.

"Aren't you going to look at me?" Adam asked quietly.

No. It was too hard to have all she'd ever longed for stretched out before her, hers for the taking. Except, as the minutes ticked by, she remembered Adam was the only other person who could weather silence with the same aplomb.

She glanced up and gasped, forgetting her dismissal, cruel Nurse Talbert, and the lofty Earl of Whitehaven. Adam looked horrific. "Adam, your face!" She rushed over and gingerly touched his swollen lip. He flinched. His blackened eye was a blend of purple and blues. Transported back to those hellish days of his captivity, she closed her eyes.

Adam rested his hands on her shoulders. "Georgina, this isn't your fault."

She swallowed, not opening her eyes because she didn't believe him. It was. All of it. More than he knew. To compound all the ways in which she'd wronged him, she was now responsible for this friction between Adam and the earl.

"Adam, you mustn't argue with him."

Not for me. Not about me. I'm not worth it.

He lowered his brow to hers and inhaled deeply, as if she were a fragrant bud, and he wanted to forever remember her scent. "I'll not allow anyone to disparage you, Georgina."

If only he knew what kind of blood flowed through her veins, he wouldn't so much as sully his hands by throwing her out onto the street. She couldn't continue the lie, not to a man who was willing to battle his powerful brother—a brother he loved—for her honor.

"I-I n-need to tell you something, Adam." Her insides fairly shriveled in fear of the condemnation she would see once she made her revelation. How long did it take a glimmer of admiration to die? A heartbeat? A second? The blink of an eye? "I don't deserve your kindness."

He held a finger to her lips. "Shh. You are a good woman—"

"Stop saying that," she cried, spinning away from him. She hugged her arms to her chest. "I am not a good woman. I'm the opposite of a good woman." Evil. Vile. Cunning. And a coward, because she couldn't even say those words aloud. "I can't marry you."

He stood there for a long time, watching her through hooded eyes. Finally, he said, "You can."

"Fine, I won't marry you. There are a thousand reasons," or more, "why I can't marry you. And only one reason I should."

She shouldn't have said that last part, because he dug his teeth into that statement and clung on. "What is the one reason, Georgina?"

Her throat swelled with emotion. She shook her head.

He closed the distance between them in four long strides and framed her face with his strong fingers. "What is the reason, Georgina?" he pressed.

It was the gentle prodding that weakened her resolve, shattered her, and humbled her enough to admit the truth. "I love you." The words came out strangled.

A fat teardrop squeezed out the corner of her eye. He brushed it back with the pad of his thumb.

"Oh, Georgina," he pressed a kiss to the top of her head, "that is reason enough."

Not, "I love you, too". Her heart wilted in her chest.

What did you expect, Georgina?

"You took care of me," Adam continued in a husky whisper. "You protected me, and what did I do, Georgina? I left you. Let me marry you."

Good, honorable Adam. He would marry her all out of a misplaced sense of obligation. She'd never imagined that a marriage proposal from this man could cut like a knife.

"I didn't protect you—"

He made a sound of protest. "You did. You—"

She held a finger up. "Please!" she cried.

He fell silent.

"I could have helped you. I could have done more. And…" She sucked in a fortifying breath. "I'm just as evil as they are."

117

Adam growled low in his throat. "Don't say that!" He closed his eyes. When he opened them, calm had been restored. "You are nothing like them—"

"I—"

"Enough!" The one word resonated off the plaster of the Earl of Whitehaven's palatial office. "This is not the time to discuss what happened in the past. Marry me. If for no other reason than because you have no employment prospects and nowhere to go."

She wanted him. Oh, how she wanted him. Yearned for him with the same intensity that had gotten Eve cast out of paradise.

The Earl of Whitehaven's vile suggestion twisted around her brain like a slithering snake, shaping an idea. "I..." Her cheeks burned hot. "I can be your mistress."

TWELVE

Another man has been taken captive. His name is Adam Markham.
Signed,
A Loyal British Subject
I can be your mistress.

Adam had to remind himself to breathe. His body stiffened and an uncomfortable ache settled in his groin. Throughout his captivity, he'd longed for her, but then there had been Grace and because of that—his love for her, his honor—he'd not succumbed to his base desires. Instead, he'd tortured himself with thoughts of her pale, white thighs quivering as he stroked her center. He'd imagined himself plunging into her heat.

Now she was offering herself to him. He needn't wed her. So why did he persist? Because she didn't feel worthy of him. That much was clear. Considering Nurse Talbert's condescension and Nick's priggish treatment of her thus far, why would she feel any differently?

Jagged fury slashed through him. Georgina had braved more than lauded war heroes. She was a better person than all members of the *haute ton* combined. It was he who didn't deserve her. And, suddenly, it was very important that she say yes to his suit. For reasons he didn't fully understand or care to examine.

"I don't want you to be my mistress. I want you to be my wife."

She troubled her lower lip, the ruby-red flesh he had dreamed about. "Why?"

Her question brought him up short. He suspected his answer would determine hers. "When I…left Bristol, I tortured myself imagining the

119

worst. I..." He looked beyond her shoulder, seeing the chambers that had served as his prison. "I feared they'd killed you and the thought of that almost killed me. I looked for you. I need you to know that. I didn't forget you."

A brown tendril escaped the harsh bun at the base of her neck. She brushed it away. "I—I know." The strand bounced right back, refusing to be tamed.

It didn't take an expert spy to detect the lie in her words. He caught the dark curl, rubbing the silky tendril between the pad of his thumb and forefinger. He brought it to his nose and inhaled the pure, clean, honeysuckle scent that was Georgina.

She'd thought he'd abandoned her. He tried to imagine the terror she must have felt as a young woman without references, family, or money. Most women would have dissolved into a puddle of nothingness. Not Georgina. Sweet, determined, resourceful Georgina. At one time, he'd thought her weak. How wrong he'd been. There was a resolute determination in her to survive. She'd stared down some of the most unimaginable horrors and still managed to retain the aura of innocence and beauty that all but radiated from her.

Finally, he found the words to her question. "Georgina, I care very deeply about what happens to you. After I'd been freed, I recalled your smile, your laughter, your pain. And I yearned to see you again. So marry me. I promise I'll never hurt you and I'll tear any man who tried limb from limb."

Georgina's lids fluttered like the delicate wings of a butterfly. His eyes roved a path across her heart-shaped face, settling on her full lips.

He leaned down and claimed them as his, searching, tasting. He explored the flesh, sucking at her slightly fuller bottom lip and, when a breathy moan escaped her, swept his tongue into the moist cavern of her mouth. Adam settled his hands on her hips, dragging her close to him, his swollen shaft pressing against the soft flesh of her belly. She cried out and her tongue met his in a violent parry and thrust.

He tugged her skirts up, caressing the silky skin of her thighs, cupping her buttocks. Her whimper melded with his groan in a symphony of erotic delight. For too long, he'd imagined plunging his shaft deep inside her. Now, there was nothing stopping him. There was no Grace. No sense of honor. No—

A knock sounded in the room like a gunshot. "Adam?" Nick called out. The interruption killed Adam's desire faster than being dumped head first into the Thames.

Adam yanked his lips away from Georgina's with a violent curse. Her chest heaved and her lashes fluttered against the pale skin of her cheeks. God, he wanted to kiss her again. Craved it like a starving man did food. He lowered his head—

Nick's peevish tone penetrated the hard oak door again. "Adam?"

It seemed to shock Georgina back to the moment. Her body stiffened against his and she made to pull away.

He held firm.

A lone brown curl fell across her eye. Brushing back the silken strand, he dropped a final kiss on her brow. Her eyes widened and the remaining color faded from her cheeks. She looked like a woman about to battle a beast, armed with little more than her pride.

And he knew. He sucked in a breath. This is why he wanted to marry her. Not out of any silly sense of obligation. Not because she was alone in the world, though that would have been reason enough. He wanted to marry her because of her strength. Her goodness. Her courage. Adam trailed a finger over her jawline, tipping her chin upward, forcing her to meet his eyes. "Marry me, Georgina. I'll take care of you."

She wet her lips. "I—"

"Adam, if you don't open this door, by God, I'm coming in—"

Adam growled. "Go to hell." He tossed the insult over his shoulder.

A shocked gasp met his curse. Then silence.

Adam rested his forehead against Georgina's, sending a silent entreaty to the gods.

It would appear the gods were otherwise engaged.

The door opened, admitting his mother. Nick stood over her shoulder, arms folded, his mouth set in a hard, flat line of earlish disapproval. He slammed the door behind them, the reverberations echoing off the walls.

His mother's shrewd gaze narrowed in on Georgina. She pursed her lips. "What is the meaning of this, Adam?"

⁂

Georgina wanted the floor to open up beneath her feet. She wanted it to swallow her whole and then have the carpet pulled above her mortified body for good measure.

Meeting green eyes so like Adam's, and so filled with stinging rebuke, robbed Georgina of breath. Attired in Wedgewood blue satin skirts trimmed with fine lace, the tall and gracefully elegant woman could only be Adam's mother.

She jerked her gaze away. Only to have it land on the Earl of Whitehaven's lowered brows, the pinched tension around his narrow lips.

The years and years of her father's sneering looks and hurtful barbs threatened to sweep her away into a sea of old hurts—hurts that still stuck like pinpricks.

Standing beside Adam, with the hard muscles in his chest straining the fabric of his jacket, she should have found solace. Instead, it only served to remind her of her own inadequacies and failings.

Then Adam slipped his hand into hers. His warmth pumped strength and support into her trembling fingers.

"Good afternoon, Mother," Adam drawled.

The countess frowned. She cast another glance at Georgina. "Adam," she murmured.

Apparently, the earl had tired of false pleasantries. "For the love of God, release that woman's hand now."

Georgina's toes curled in her boots.

You are worthless, Georgina.

She swallowed, almost choking on the memories.

Father is not here. He is gone. You are free of him and the pain he caused you.

When she shoved back the pall of her father's memory, she became aware of the quiet enfolding the room.

She stole a peek from the corner of her eye. Adam studied her through hooded lids. Fury melded with something else; something that looked remarkably like...love.

"Mother, would you tell Nicholas that if he disrespects Miss Wilcox one more time, I will lay him flat on this office floor?"

The countess tapped a finger on the edge of her skirts. "Perhaps this might be a good time to introduce me to...what did you say it is? Miss Wilcox?"

"He'll do no such thing!" the earl barked. He took a step forward. "This woman is a maid." He cast a glance toward the door, as if fearing that some passing servant should hear the horror of all horrors.

The countess showed no outward reaction, with the exception of her elegantly arched golden eyebrow. "Is this true, Adam?"

Adam's fingers tightened around Georgina's. She winced from the pain of his grip. He immediately loosened his hold but did not release her. "She is a nurse. And," he looked down at Georgina, holding her eyes with his, "I'm going to marry her."

Silence met his pronouncement.

His mother inclined her head. "Is that so?"

Georgina pulled her hand free. "No!" She couldn't marry him. Not with all the lies between them. When he finally heard her confession, he would withdraw his offer faster than her racing heart.

Adam glowered at her. "I'm marrying her. With or without approval." That statement was directed at the earl.

Georgina expected a vitriolic outburst from the staid nobleman.

It did not come.

"Is..." His mother paused and, for a moment, her mouth opened and closed like a trout out of water. "Is there a reason for...for haste?" she finished, ever so hesitantly.

The meaning was quite clear. Heat flooded Georgina's cheeks.

Adam shook his head. "There is no child."

"Thank God," the earl muttered beneath his breath.

She failed to hear the heated conversation that ensued.

A child. Suddenly, the cold within her melted beneath a single frisson of warmth. It flickered like a small flame in her womb, spiraling and spinning, and catching her afire. It grew and grew—the longing for a child sucked her into its fold, and she embraced it, wrapped herself around it, letting it consume her.

She wanted this marriage. Needed it for reasons that were entirely selfish. Not all of which had to do with her and Adam, but also for the hope and dreams of a child. Yearning filled her—for the unborn child she would cradle to her breast, love, and protect with all her heart. In her mind, the babe had the look of a cherub; he had Adam's pale golden curls and moss-green eyes. He was so real. So close, she wanted to reach out and caress his satiny skin. Her child. A person who would love her unconditionally. A person she would never fail. Not as her own mother and father had failed her.

"Georgina?"

She jumped, her heart racing.

Three pairs of eyes were leveled on her.

Adam claimed her hand. "If you don't wish to wed me, I will not force you. But I—"

Selfish, greedy creature that she was, Georgina's answer sprang to her lips. "Yes!"

The earl cursed.

She ignored him. "I want to marry you. I…that is, if you still want to wed me. I—"

Adam held a finger to her lips, silencing her. "I'm marrying you, love."

Georgina smiled. It would appear that sometimes people like her managed to find their own slivers of heaven, after all. Reality jabbed at the corners of her heart, but she forced doubt away. She shared her father's blood, but they were not the same person. And she would be a good wife to Adam.

Wife.

Still the guilt twisted within her.

"We'll need to prepare her for London," the countess was saying, her mouth pinched at the corners. "We'll need to have a story for Miss Wilcox." She looked at Georgina. "I imagine since you are to be my daughter-in-law, it would be appropriate for me to address you by your first name."

"Georgina."

"This is madness!" the earl shouted. He took two steps toward Georgina, jabbing a finger in her direction. "This woman isn't fit to grace the front stoop of this townhouse, let alone marry Adam. This—"

Adam had his brother by the collar of his shirt. The countess cried out, but fury thrummed through him. He dragged his brother up until they were eye to eye. "Do not say one more word. If you value me as a friend and brother, you will quit your insults. I'm marrying her." He released the earl so suddenly the other man stumbled back, gasping for breath.

"You'd choose this...this interloper over me?" he asked, a solemnity to that question.

"I would."

Georgina's heart lodged in her throat.

Oh God, I do not deserve him. He is good and loyal and I am destroying the bond he shares with his brother.

She opened her mouth, but no words came out. She tried to force them up through her constricted throat. To no avail.

The earl took a step toward Adam, eyes ablaze with fury.

But the countess placed a staying hand on his arm. "Stop," she murmured. "It is done."

The other man wrenched free. "Surely you cannot agree to this! We know nothing about *her*." He used the word as if discussing the lowest whore from the streets of London. He looked at Georgina, his eyes shooting sparks of fury and distrust. "She will hurt you, Adam. Mark my words. This woman is not to be trusted."

Georgina curled her fingers into tight balls. Jagged nails bit painfully into the palms of her hand, leaving indentations of guilt.

The earl was right. Adam deserved better than a deceitful creature like her. Moments ago, she'd managed to silently convince herself that her birthright didn't matter, had tried to separate herself from Father and Jamie's treachery. Though she'd trade her right hand for this marriage, she couldn't trap Adam this way. A confession sprang to her lips.

Adam placed his hands upon her shoulders. "You don't know anything about her. She is good, loyal, and loving. And you aren't fit to touch the heels of her boots."

Screeching silence followed that definitive proclamation.

The earl's head whipped back as if he'd been punched on the chin. "Very well. I see how it is to be then." He pinned Georgina with a final glare full of icy loathing. Then he spun on his heel and stormed from the room.

The countess bowed her head. "Welcome to the family, my dear," she said.

THIRTEEN

The United Irishmen have been stalled by talks of peace between France and Britain. Now Fox and Hunter alternate their time between interrogating Mr. Markham and searching for centers of Irish support.
Signed,
A Loyal British Subject

They were married two days later.

For all his brother's protestations, he'd still agreed to procure a special license from the Archbishop of Canterbury allowing the banns to be waived, even if it was, as Adam suspected, to avoid public notice.

Georgina stood across from him, attired in a pale yellow gown. In spite of the dark glower Nick directed her way, an ethereal smile graced her bow-shaped lips. With the flecks of gold dancing in her eyes, she had the look of a fey fairy creature. In all the time he'd known Georgina, he'd seen her smile, laugh, but never had he seen this unabashed joy.

The vicar turned a page in his book, though he did not even glance down at it. "I require and charge you both, as ye will answer at the dreadful day of judgment when the secrets of all hearts shall be disclosed, that if either of you know any impediment, why ye may not be lawfully joined together in Matrimony, ye do now confess it. For be ye well assured, that so many as are coupled together otherwise than God's Word doth allow are not joined together by God; neither is their Matrimony lawful."

Adam held his breath, half-expecting a barrage of protestations from Nick. They didn't come. With a smile, he glanced down at Georgina. His gut clenched.

Her cheeks had gone a sickly ashen gray, her eyes bore a tragic glimmer. Then she blinked and it was gone.

Her smile was firmly back in place, but the skin at the corners of her lips was stretched tight. He gave his head a clearing shake. Anyone's happiness would be marred with Nick glaring holes of disapproval at their back.

The vicar cleared his throat and Adam yanked his gaze away from his bride. "Wilt thou have this Woman to be thy wedded Wife, to live together after God's ordinance in the holy estate of Matrimony? Wilt thou love her, comfort her, honor, and keep her in sickness and in health; and, forsaking all others, keep thee only unto her, so long as ye both shall live?"

Love her. Comfort her. Keep her in sickness and in health.

Georgina worried her lower lip between her teeth, and it struck him like a bolt of lightning…she thought herself unworthy. She didn't believe herself deserving of his vows.

Oh, Georgina, my heart.

"I will," he said, willing her to hear the promise in those two words.

The vicar turned to Georgina. She balanced on the tiptoes of her yellow satin slippers, like a bird poised to take flight. For the span of a single moment, he thought she might turn and flee. He sucked in a ragged breath as he faced the realization—he wasn't marrying her out of any sense of obligation. He needed her just as much as she needed him. Mayhap more. She'd sustained him at his darkest time and even now, when the nightmares came, it was Georgina's face that called him back to the living and kept him breathing.

Breaking with custom, he reached for her gloved hand. The vicar's shocked gasp blended with Mother's. He ignored them. His touch seemed to infuse courage into Georgina. Her spine stiffened. The tension in her mouth eased and her lips parted. A gentle sigh escaped her.

And the ceremony continued. When it came time for Georgina to recite her vows, she looked up at him. Everyone and everything else fell away—Nick's heated anger, Tony's grin of amusement, Mother's quiet concern. The vicar's words faded to a droning murmur.

She would be his wife. Prior to this moment, he'd not really wrapped his brain around the reality of it. He'd only ever entertained the prospect of marriage to Grace Blakely. Yet when he'd learned of her betrayal, he'd crushed thoughts of the future.

But Georgina, he wanted her with a need that threatened to shatter him.

The ceremony ended as it had begun. With silence. Even Tony had become a reserved bundle of formality. There was no breakfast. No well wishes. And, God help him, just then he hated his family for not welcoming Georgina into their fold.

He took Georgina by the arm and steered her from the room, past the unsmiling faces. She let out a startled squeak, but he didn't stop. He'd not allow them to mar this day. Georgina didn't deserve a wedding that felt more like a funeral. They could all go hang.

"Adam," Georgina murmured. She dug her heels in.

He didn't stop.

"Adam!"

Adam finally stopped in the foyer. Winningham, the family butler, stood with his fingers poised on the front door.

Georgina took his face between her hands, forcing him to look at her. "You cannot leave like this. They love you. Please, speak to them."

He spoke through clenched teeth. "I've nothing to say to any of them." He'd not tell her that for the past three days he'd done his damnedest to make Nick see reason. He'd sung her praises and virtues to Mother, Tony, and Nick. In the end, it hadn't mattered.

"Please," she whispered forlornly.

His eyes slid closed. Christ. When she looked at him with those soulful, brown eyes, he could not deny her the Queen's jewels, if she desired them. He tried one more time. "I do not want to leave you. I—"

She pressed her gloved fingers to his lips. Even with the thin, white layer of fabric between them, her skin nearly singed him.

Passion roared to life. The last thing he wanted to do was speak to his brother. "Go," she urged. "I'll be fine." Her lips turned in a crooked smile. "I've encountered far worse treatment than your family's disapproval."

Her reminder didn't make it better. In fact, it made him want to hunt down his elusive captors and kill them with his bare hands. The thought of Georgina suffering clawed at his insides.

"Go." She gave him a gentle shove.

Adam claimed her lips in a swift kiss. "Okay, I shall, but only for you. Otherwise they could all go rot with their opinions."

She made a small sound of disapproval. "Don't say that. They love you and care for you. Now, go to them."

Adam captured her hands in his. He raised first one then the other set of knuckles to his lips. Without another word, he turned on his heel and headed for Nick's office. It was as he'd said to Georgina—his brother's approval didn't matter. But he would do this. For her.

Georgina stared after him, feeling as lonely as an angel who'd been cast out of the gates of heaven.

"Hullo there, sister."

She spun on her heel. Adam's younger brother lounged against a marble pillar, arms folded across his chest. His lips turned up in a roguish grin.

"H-h-ello." Her insides shriveled with shame at the humiliating stutter. Adam and his entire family were the epitome of all that was graceful, elegant, and urbane. She, on the other hand, was…just Georgina.

He shoved away from the pillar and closed the distance between them. "You got him to speak with Nick. That was no easy feat."

"How did you know?"

Another rakish grin. "I'm a younger brother. I make it a point to know these things."

Georgina smiled weakly at him.

"He's really not a bad chap, you know."

The earl might've been a loyal, loving brother, but he was just as arrogant and snobbish as the rest of the *ton* so she chose to neither agree nor disagree.

"He's not, you know," Tony defended, correctly gauging her silence. "He's not as stodgy as he might seem to you. You know, one of those priggish, stuffy noblemen."

Georgina hadn't seen anything to indicate otherwise.

He carried on. "He loves us. Oh, he's overbearing and quite annoying most times. But when Adam was gone..." Tony's blue-green eyes grew shuttered. A solemnity replaced his veneer of brevity.

She needed to hear the rest. "When Adam was gone...?"

He gave his golden head a shake. "I thought Nick would go mad. He would lock himself away in his office, reading each of Adam's letters. He was convinced there was something amiss." He slashed the air with his hand. "Said there was something not quite right with the notes, though he never said what exactly. He never wanted Mother or me to worry." He leaned down, so close Georgina could count the odd smattering of freckles along the bridge of his nose. "So how did you meet my brother?"

At his blunt questioning, Georgina shifted. She didn't know how Adam had explained his absence and had no intention of violating his confidence. Of a sudden, she became aware of the vulnerability of her situation. With Adam closeted away in his meeting, she was alone with Anthony Markham. She would venture neither the countess nor servants would notice if something were to happen to her.

She took a tentative step backward. Tony followed. She continued retreating until her back knocked against the front door, barring further movement.

"Hmm?" he asked.

Georgina had to remind herself that this was Adam's brother. He wouldn't try to beat the answers out of her. Still, after years of being kicked around, she'd learned that most men weren't to be trusted. Tony might appear debonair and charming, but for all Georgina knew, he could've been one of the many men who brutalized helpless women.

She cleared her throat. "I believe that is a question for your brother."

His lips turned down, with what Georgina suspected was annoyed disapproval. "What can you tell me?"

Georgina flattened her palms against the door. "Mr. Markham, I will not speak about Adam's personal life to you, even though you are his brother. I'd imagine you wouldn't want either of your brothers running around and pressing young woman for details about your relationship with them?"

He dropped his gaze and his eyes narrowed on her trembling fingers. Then he reached for her hand.

Georgina bit her lip hard.

His gaze flew to her face and he took a hasty step backward, nearly stumbling over himself in his haste to get away. His eyes had gone round in his face. "You think I would hurt you?"

Georgina tossed her head back and forth with such alacrity that her simple chignon came loose, displacing a mass of curls. She shoved them behind her ears. "No," she lied.

"Then why are you shaking?"

Nervous laughter spilled from her like bubbling champagne. "Are you not violating some rules of propriety with your questioning, sir?"

He folded his arms across his chest. "I'm no simpleton. It hasn't escaped my notice that you've not answered my earlier question. Do you believe I would hurt you?"

Apparently, she still hadn't mastered the art of lying.

"I didn't mean to frighten you," he said quietly.

"You didn't frighten me," she said, though the assurance tumbled from her lips a little too quickly.

Tony's brow scrunched up in what appeared to be deep contemplation. Several minutes passed before he again spoke. "I'd imagine Adam handled those responsible for your fears."

In spite of his youth, Tony had quite aptly determined that there were certain individuals to blame for her skittishness. But no, Adam had not punished Father or Jamie for the pain and hurt they'd inflicted. Nor did she want him to. Georgina was content with her father and Jamie being consigned to whatever hell they'd scurried off to.

Tony held his elbow out. "Would you join me in the parlor while you wait for Adam?"

Georgina hesitated, but then placed her fingers on his coat sleeve. She needed all the friends she could get.

Adam stood at the doorway, staring at Nick. Seated behind Father's great mahogany desk, scribbling away in some ledger, he looked more like an earl than the brother who'd wrought havoc on the same household throughout their boyhood.

Nick dipped his pen into the crystal inkwell.

"Are you going to ignore me for the rest of our lives?" Adam quipped.

Nick paused, pen frozen above the paper. The vein pulsing at his temple and the black ink making a splotch on the desktop were the only real indications that his brother was a hairbreadth from losing control of his temper.

He threw the pen down. "Oh? I thought you'd said all there was to be said."

Adam winced. For all his anger with Nick's treatment of Georgina, he'd never wanted to hurt him. He loved him and, as much as he was loath to admit it, Nick's approval meant a great deal to him. He could not be happy if his wife and any member of his family were at odds. "I'm sorry if I hurt you," he said quietly.

Nick shoved back his seat. It scraped a grating path along the hardwood floor. "To which hurt do you refer? My broken nose? The embarrassing scene at the hospital? Your total disregard for our family?"

Adam dragged a hand through his hair. "Yes. I'm sorry for all of it—"

"Then you shouldn't have married her!" Nick exploded. He cursed. "Christ, what possessed you to—"

Adam cut his brother off, not allowing him to say something he would regret and something Adam couldn't forgive. "I am not sorry for marrying Georgina. And any time you disparage her, you widen the wedge between us."

Nick's lips tightened. "Then it would appear we are at an impasse."

A sharp bite of regret lanced through him. He'd spent months as Fox and Hunter's captive, longing for his family's embrace. This frigid, unyielding tension between them hit Adam like a punch to the stomach. He forced himself to nod. "Very well." He turned on his heel.

Nick cursed. "Would you rather I didn't care about you? That I didn't worry after your well-being? If that is the case, then many felicitations on your nuptials."

Adam stared blankly at the ivory plastered walls. He'd endured hell at Fox and Hunter's hands. Considering all they'd suffered, he and Georgina were deserving of whatever joy they could grab.

"I wish..." The words died on Adam's tongue. What did he wish? That he'd never signed on as a member of The Brethren? Then he would've been living a carefree life, cavorting around town with his family's approval. He would never have known the cruel torture exacted on his mind and body...nor the bitter hurt of losing Grace.

But then there would be no Georgina and he couldn't fathom a life without her in it.

His brother rested a hand on his shoulder.

Adam stiffened.

"What do you wish?" Nick encouraged, his tone devoid of all the acrimony of these past days.

Adam swallowed past a ball of regret. "I wish you would be kind to her. She is a good woman."

I wish I could tell you how she saved me.

Nick squeezed his shoulder awkwardly, in a manner more befitting two strangers. His hand fell back to his side. "I will be kind to her and I'll encourage mother to be more...welcoming." The swift surge of relief died at Nick's next words. "But I need to say this. I don't trust her, Adam, and I fear that in marrying her, you've done something you will only look back on with regret."

A chill stole along Adam's spine at Nick's prophetic words. He shook his head. No, he had a lifetime of regrets, but marrying Georgina would never fall into those ranks.

"Adam?"

"Thank you," he said. "Thank you for being willing to try. I know you'll find her to be good and kind."

Nick inclined his head. "I certainly hope so, for your sake."

Hardly congratulatory words, Adam thought wryly.

He started to turn when Nick held out his hand.

Adam stared down at his brother's peace offering then placed his hand in Nick's.

"Congratulations, little brother." Nick's voice broke ever so slightly. He cleared his throat in an obvious attempt to cover his show of emotion.

"Thank you," Adam said, his words gruff to his own ears.

Nick thumped him on the back one more time. "Now go. I'd imagine you have better things to do on your wedding day than stand around talking to me."

Adam chuckled, appreciating Nick's willingness to try to restore levity. After the events of these past days, and the hurtful barbs hurled by the both of them, their relationship would require more delicate mending. But Nick's efforts were certainly a start.

He exited his brother's office and started toward the foyer.

The doddering butler—who was a good many years older than his late father—blocked his way. "If I may wish you much joy, sir?"

Adam inclined his head. By nature of his tenure with the family, and having known Adam since he'd been born, Winningham was more of a close family member. "Thank you, Winningham. Your words mean a great deal." And they did. Adam and Georgina had been remarkably lacking where well-wishes were concerned.

The normally staid butler then did something remarkably out of character with his cool reserve. He winked. "They'll come around, sir. I've known each of them long enough to know that." His face settled back into an implacable mask and stiff formality was restored. "Mr. Anthony is coming around in the Blue Parlor at this very moment."

Those words rejuvenated Adam's spirit. He could always count on young, irascible Tony to throw his support behind him. With a jaunty step, Adam hurried toward the Blue Parlor. Even as he approached the doorway, Tony's booming laugh blended with Georgina's breathy giggle.

Adam's steps faltered and his smile slipped as he caught sight of Georgina. His wife sat beside Tony on a too-small sofa, a leather folio open across her lap. She sat so close to Tony that the pale yellow fabric of her skirts had become crushed against his rakish brother's tan breeches.

Vicious spears of envy stabbed at his insides and Adam was possessed by an animalistic urge to throw Georgina over his shoulder and carry her away from Tony. It was Adam's first real taste of jealousy—and it had a bitter flavor.

He folded his arms across his chest, tapping his foot as he waited for them to note his appearance.

Adam might as well have been invisible.

Georgina brushed back a stray brown tendril and turned the page. Tony leaned down and whispered something close to her ear. She laughed, the sound as clear as crystal glasses clinking together.

His scoundrel brother joined in...and then glanced down at Georgina; his gaze focused on the enormous spill of her lush bosom.

Adam narrowed his eyes, as he was besieged by the kind of madness that robbed a man of self-control and reason. Of course, Tony would never betray him. Except...the young rake continued to leer at the swell of her breasts...and the green-eyed monster within Adam roared to life. He'd seen enough. With a snarl, he stalked into the room.

Georgina and Tony's heads jerked up. Guiltily?

Georgina jumped to her feet. The leather folio containing some of his earliest artwork fell to the floor, lying open on its spine. He paid it no heed.

"Hello, Ad—" A startled squeak escaped her when he took her by the hand and tugged her from the room.

Tony's knowing laughter trailed in their wake.

She shot a glance over her shoulder then looked back at Adam with wide, blinking eyes. "Is everything all right?"

His attention snapped forward. "Fine, just fine," he muttered.

"How—"

The fragile thread of control snapped. "Stop asking questions, Georgina."

She fell silent.

He felt like a bastard who'd kicked a puppy but, goddamn it, he was too blinded by the gut-wrenching, twisting bite of jealousy to apologize. He could not rid his mind of the lecherous stare his brother had affixed to her breasts. By God, she belonged to him. He'd not tolerate her being ogled by any other man—including his own brother. When Adam had discovered through the scandal sheets that Grace had married, he'd felt hurt. Betrayed.

This—the mind-numbing loss of sanity he'd felt on seeing Georgina beside Tony—was something altogether different.

The butler held the door open and Adam swept Georgina through it, down the steps, and into his black carriage. He didn't wait for his driver to close the door, but saw to it himself. The carriage lurched into motion.

Georgina sat on the seat opposite him, chest moving up and down as she panted. He stared at the low line of her décolletage. There was surely no more magnificent bosom than Georgina's. And those luscious pale moons of flesh were his. All his.

With a groan, he pulled her across his lap and explored her mouth with a hungering intensity. He slipped his tongue inside and stroked the tip of her tongue. She responded with a feverish wantonness that threatened to drive him wild.

Georgina pressed her breasts against his chest and wrapped her arms around him as if trying to climb into his skin.

He groaned in approval and hoisted her skirts above her thighs, guiding her so that she straddled him. He told himself she was an innocent, that he should show a modicum of constraint, but he'd denied himself this woman for too long. He could no sooner stop the flood of desire than he could stop the moon from rising in the sky.

Her thighs fell open. The heat of her moist center penetrated the thick fabric of his breeches. He wrenched his mouth away from hers. Shoving aside the mass of brown curls that had escaped her chignon, he paid homage to the soft skin of her neck.

Georgina arched her back on a breathless moan, opening herself to his exploration. He trailed his tongue, lower, lower, until he reached the edge of her bodice. With a single tug, the mounds spilled free, the glorious vision his, and only his, to see. The red tip of her nipple pebbled in the cool afternoon air. He took the tip between his thumb and forefinger, rolling it back and forth.

Georgina cried out and tangled her fingers in his hair. She shoved his head downward toward the eager flesh. He trailed a kiss around the peak in a ritual designed to torture.

"Oh Adam, please!" she begged.

He paused, mouth poised over the straining peak of her generous breast. "You're mine," he rasped against the satiny flesh.

She nodded. "Yes!"

"Say it," he ordered with a scratchy hoarseness. "Say you belong to me."

"I belong to you. I'm yours. Only yours."

Then he gave her what she craved. His mouth closed around the red bud. He drew it into his mouth, sucking deep.

Georgina dug her fingers into his scalp, her jagged nails biting hard enough to draw blood. "Don't stop," she pleaded on a breathy moan. "Please don't stop."

Adam didn't. He continued his torturous exploration of first one breast then the other. Georgina cried out when he worked a hand up her skirts to find her center. She was dripping—hot, wet, and hungry for his touch.

He slipped his fingers into her undergarments and found the delicate nub hidden beneath her thatch. She clamped her legs tight around his fingers in a desperate attempt to keep him there and ground herself against him. "That's it, love," he whispered, encouraging her frenetic little movements.

There was an unrestrained fervor to her movements that served as a heady aphrodisiac. He continued to work her nub. Faster. Faster. All the while, he lavished his attention on her breast.

And then she was coming. In a violent explosion of mewling cries and panting moans. He toyed with her until he'd wrung every last drip of pleasure from her hot center.

She collapsed atop him. Her chest jerked up and down as she desperately tried to draw breath.

Adam stroked the sweaty brown curls that had fallen across her eye.

"How was that, love?" he asked.

A tiny little snort rustled the skin at his neck. He leaned back to study his wife.

He smiled. It would appear he'd pleasured his wife thoroughly enough to put her to sleep. Masculine pride made him grin. He dropped a kiss at the corner of her temple.

Georgina was working her way into his heart.

And he found he rather liked her there.

FOURTEEN

Emmet is attempting to secure the help of Michael Dwyer's Wicklow
rebels. Hunter has been dispatched to meet with Dwyer.
Signed,
A Loyal British Subject

G eorgina jerked awake, her heart racing. Her eyes struggled to
adjust to her surroundings.

She blinked back the fog of confusion.

"Hullo, love." With the teasing tone underlying Adam's words, a
reminder of all that had transpired, a reminder that this hadn't been
a dream.

Georgina yawned sleepily, relishing the warmth and security
provided by Adam's strong, sure arms. "How long have I been
sleeping?"

"Oh, fifteen minutes."

Fifteen minutes? It felt like she'd been sleeping the whole winter
season.

A knock sounded on the carriage door. She let out a gasp and
tugged the fabric of her gown back into place.

Adam watched on in amusement before taking pity. With
quick movements, he had her skirts down around her legs, her
cloak properly latched, and her hair...well, he did the best he
could with the helpless mane of curls. She colored furiously at
the thought of what his staff would think of their scandalous new
mistress.

Another knock.

Adam didn't give her an opportunity to protest. He allowed the tiger to open the door. Without waiting for the steps to be put into place, Adam leaped down and held his arms up for Georgina.

He lifted her effortlessly from the carriage and cradled her close as though she were more valuable than the Queen's crown. Adam managed to do something no other person had ever done before—he made her feel cherished. It was quite the heady sensation.

Adam leaned down until his lips nearly brushed her cheek. "Come along, love." The warmth of his breath dissolved into a puff of air in the cool winter air.

Georgina allowed him to lead her up the stairs of his townhouse.

All her hopes for a quiet, unobtrusive entrance were spoiled by a long row of servants lining the marble foyer. A man attired all in black rushed forward, an older graying woman at his side.

This had to be Adam's butler.

Adam took her hand, giving it a small squeeze as if attempting to pump support from his veins to hers. "May I introduce you to your staff? This is your butler, Watson, and your housekeeper, Miss Gayle." He turned to the staff. "May I introduce you all to your new lady of the house, Mrs. Markham?"

Silence met his pronouncement.

Watson hesitated a fraction of a moment and then grinned. "Mr. Markham, on behalf of the entire staff, it is my pleasure to wish you congratulations on your nuptials!"

Adam inclined his head and, either unaware or uncaring of the gaping stares being shot their way from the row of servants, proceeded to speak to Watson.

The plump housekeeper at his side looked at Georgina with suspicion in her narrow-eyed stare.

Georgina's gut clenched. The staff here was really no different than any other person she'd known in her life—cool, unfeeling, judgmental.

Still on this, Georgina's wedding day, she'd longed to revel in the joy of her and Adam's union. Instead, she'd encountered everything from hostility to unspoken disapproval.

She had to dig her feet into the soles of her slipper to keep from turning on her heel and fleeing out the front door.

"Miss Gayle, would you please show Mrs. Markham to her chambers?"

Georgina jumped when Adam's words registered, and a wave of heat climbed up her neckline. His staff surely knew just why she was being shown to her chambers. She suspected she should've felt more embarrassment and not felt this breathless sense of anticipation.

Miss Gayle's lips turned down at the corners. She clapped her hands once and the servants all dispersed like caged birds set free. With a curt nod, she spoke to Georgina. "If you would follow me, Mrs. Markham."

Without waiting to see if Georgina did as bid, she turned on her heel and started up the winding staircase.

Adam leaned down and grazed her cheek with his lips. Georgina's heart tripped at the tiny, telltale gesture of support, and suddenly Miss Gayle's disapproval mattered naught.

"I'll be up shortly." His husky whisper bespoke wickedness and desire.

Georgina felt her womb stir with anticipation. Adam had to nudge her toward Miss Gayle, who'd frozen on the stairwell. She matched the taller woman's stride up the remaining stairs and down a long hall. The housekeeper stopped beside the last door on that floor.

She opened it and motioned for Georgina to enter. "Mrs. Markham," she murmured, her voice devoid of emotion.

Georgina hesitated but then decided she preferred the idea of being in her new chambers to standing in the hall with this foul creature.

She took a step inside and froze. Her mouth fell agape and she had to remind herself to close it.

"It is rather impressive, isn't it?" Miss Gayle said. Georgina thought she detected a trace of condescension in the older woman's words.

Real or imagined, it infused her spine with strength. Georgina turned to the woman with a small frown. "Miss Gayle, have I done something to offend you?"

The housekeeper's eyes went wide for a moment. She shook her head. "Forgive me. I do not know what you are speaking of."

Georgina gritted her teeth. She'd had enough of stern disapproval. The nurses at Middlesex Hospital. The Earl of Whitehaven. The Countess of Whitehaven. She'd not tolerate any more...particularly from a stranger who knew her not at all. "I should hope a woman of your courage and conviction could at least be forthright with me, Miss Gayle."

Miss Gayle blinked back at her in what Georgina thought was surprise. "May I speak frankly?"

Georgina inclined her head. "I wish that you would." She preferred honesty to the false veneer of aloof politeness worn by Adam's mother and older brother.

"The staff is concerned," Miss Gayle finally said.

Well, that makes all of us then.

Georgina waited for the woman to continue.

"There have been..." The maid fell silent.

"There have been...?" Georgina prodded gently.

"Rumors circulating quite freely. One of the maids has a cousin who is employed by the Earl of Whitehaven who mentioned that Mr. Markham had been forced to marry you."

Georgina's heart tightened. She clenched her fingers so tightly it would surely leave marks in the flesh of her palms. Adam's staff was good and loyal. They cared for him and worried that she was an interloper who'd forced his hand.

She glanced away, her gaze colliding with the tall windows at the opposite end of the room. Hadn't she though? Had Adam married her because he truly wanted to? Or had he been driven by a sense of obligation after she'd been relieved of her responsibilities at Middlesex?

The housekeeper continued, twisting the knife of guilt deeper. "It is also being said that you are the source of much contention between

Mr. Markham and his family. Every member of the staff knows just how close he is with the countess and his brothers, and it is—"

"That will be all, Miss Gayle," Adam said in frigid tones.

The housekeeper paled.

Georgina's gaze swiveled to the front of the room. Adam stood framed in the doorway, the muscles in his arms tensed, the fabric of his jacket stretched tight over his skin.

"I—"

"That will be all," he said.

Unrepentant Miss Gayle's glared and, with an insolent curtsy, hurried from the room.

Georgina toyed with the fabric of her skirts, looking everywhere and anywhere but at him as he strode across the room toward her.

He rested his hands on her shoulders. "Look at me," he said, his words a husky murmur.

She glanced up.

"I will never allow anyone to speak to you like that. Do you understand? You are my wife and deserving of respect. I will give Miss Gayle her references and send her—"

Georgina gasped. "No!" She couldn't be responsible for another woman losing her work. Not when she still battled the horrors of being alone with nothing more than false references to her name. She'd wish that on no other woman. She tried again. "Please do not dismiss her. She cares for you."

Adam raised her right hand to his mouth. He brushed his lips across her knuckles. A shiver of awareness coursed through her body.

"You are a good woman," he said solemnly.

Her mind screeched a silent protest at his familiar words. How many times would he hurl that mocking statement at her? It only served as a reminder of her deceit.

She swirled away from him, ripping her hands free. Not for the first time that day, the urge to flee surged like a wave amidst a storm. Adam stood between her and the doorway, and he was looking at her with such gentle concern she wanted to cry and she hated that she wanted to cry because tears were a sign of weakness and…She needed to put some distance between them. Hurrying over to the long window, she pulled back the curtain and peered down into the bustling street below.

Georgina had traveled down a path that could not be undone, and because of it, he would be forever trapped in a marriage that, for him, was nothing more than an obligation. Her throat seized up.

"You should not have married me," she whispered, laying her forehead against the pane.

"I married you because I wanted to, Georgina. I don't give a damn about anyone's opinions or expectations and neither should you." A trace of annoyance underlined his words.

She laughed, shaking her head. "Oh, Adam, you belong to a different world than I do." She glanced over her shoulder at him. "I have to care about others opinions and expectations. You do not. You—"

"Georgina, we now belong to the same world." His jaw flexed as if he were trying to remain in control of his temper.

Oddly, she was not afraid. Adam would not hurt her.

Georgina, however, could hurt him a great deal. All it would take was a whisper of the truth about her lies and he'd toss her into the street. A spasm wracked her body. She had to hug herself to try in vain to stifle the growing shiver. She pictured herself alone in a cold Newgate cell while the guards violated her, while the rats gnawed at her. Bile climbed up her throat.

"Georgina?"

Adam's voice came as if down a long, long hall—distant and faint in her ears.

He pressed his lips to the nape of her neck and the horror receded. She sucked in a deep breath.

Adam pulled her back against his chest and rocked her in a gentle rhythm. "Do you have nightmares?"

She nodded. All the time.

"They haunt me as well. I don't think a night has passed that Fox and Hunter don't pay a visit to my dreams."

145

Oh God. Agony struck her heart like a thousand knives. She knew nightmares. Had lived with them her entire life. And because of her horrible, vile father, Adam's life would never be the same.

Tears blurred her vision. She had to tell him. Now, before they consummated their union and Adam was forever bound to her, a woman he would soon loathe and revile.

She turned in his arms and raised her tear-filled gaze to his. "Adam, I-I n-need…" She took a deep breath and tried again. "I need to tell you about Fox."

Adam pressed a finger to her lips. "Not now. Not on this day. They took so much from both of us. I'll not allow them to ruin this day, too."

Georgina took a step away from him. She threw her palms up. "No! I have to say this."

Adam closed the distance between them. He framed her face between his hands—hands which had caressed and soothed her. "It doesn't matter."

"It does!" she cried. She needed him to listen. Needed him to know every last ugly truth. She should have told him. Long before now, before she'd trapped him into a marriage with his captor's daughter.

He kissed her, effectively silencing her next words. He pulled back, dropping a final kiss on her brow. "It doesn't matter. Not now. Not ever."

Not ever.

Her heart stirred with hope. She was ready to move forward. With Adam as her husband. She'd never meant anything to her father; the day he'd left her alone would forever mark the moment she'd been born again.

Take what Adam offers. Leap on the wings of new beginnings, Georgina. Soar.

Georgina turned around, presenting him with her back. She spoke on a breathless whisper, "Will you undo my buttons?"

Adam sucked in a breath but, with a jerky nod, began to work freeing the long row of buttons. In moments, cool air kissed her exposed back, the modest chemise little barrier to the chill.

Georgina wiggled the fabric past her hips where it pooled in a silken heap, twining about her and Adam's feet. In spite of her undergarments, she felt remarkably bare. How odd, to have been so intimate with him before and yet to feel this modesty now. She made to cross her arms over her breasts, but Adam stayed her with his hand.

"Don't," he begged hoarsely. "I want to see all of you." The rapid rise and fall of his chest indicated that he was as aroused as she was. Georgina shrugged off her chemise and stood before him, shivering with alternating waves of modesty and desire.

A hiss slipped between his clenched teeth. "You are so beautiful."

Really she wasn't. With her large breasts, rounded hips and buttocks, she was really just plump. But when he said it that way, like a starving man offered one final feast, she almost believed it.

Wordlessly, he swept her into his arms and carried her across the room, the tread of his feet quiet on the plush carpet. Then he lowered her to the bed, letting her body slide down his until he had her on her back, open for his mastery. His hard shaft prodded the soft fabric at the center of her thighs.

With a guttural growl, he removed her undergarments, and Georgina was fully naked before him.

A puddle of heat settled between her legs. Georgina bit her lip hard. She wanted him with a wanton longing that frightened her. Yearned to shove him down and press his head between her legs, feel his wicked tongue swirl around her womanhood.

"What are you thinking, Georgina?" he asked, his voice a husky whisper.

Her cheeks flooded with color. Thoughts no good, young lady should have.

"Do you want to feel my mouth here?" His tongue circled the peak of her breast.

She cried out.

"Or here?" He nipped at her neck. She whimpered when he pulled away. He continued to trail feathery kisses along her flesh, until he paused at the threshold of her womanhood. "Or... here?" His breath tickled the curls that concealed the dripping wet desire.

He wedged a knee between her legs, parting her gently. She waited, afraid that any movement on her part would mean an immediate cessation in his loving.

And he did. He looked up at her, a roguish grin on his lips. "Is this what you want, Georgina? Do you want me to kiss you here?" He slipped his tongue between the folds of her womanhood, the caress so faint, so delicate, she feared she'd imagined it. But the puddle grew, and she knew his taunting touch had been real. Her thighs fell open wide, quivering. Aching.

He buried his face between her thighs and plunged his tongue inside. Her hips bucked, and a strangled cry escaped her.

She twisted her fingers in his silken, blond strands, anchoring him to her.

Adam moved his tongue in and out then flicked it over the trembling bud of desire. He claimed it between his lips and sucked hard. She thrashed her head back and forth atop the pillow, incapable of words.

Fortunately, Adam knew exactly what her body craved. He pulled away. The whimpering protest faded on a moan as he shucked off his shirt. The broad, muscled wall of his chest, with the faintest sprinkling of golden curls, was even more impressive than the times she'd seen it during his captivity. His skin now had a healthy olive cast, as if he'd been painted by the sun.

Then he moved on to his breeches. Her mouth went dry. She supposed she should feel a maidenly sense of modesty but hungered for a glimpse of him like a hedonistic wanton. The breeches joined his shirt on the floor.

Georgina couldn't move. The full, swollen length of him was more magnificent than any piece of art. A drip of moisture beaded at the plumed, purplish-blue head. She reached out and caught the bead. She raised her finger to her lips and sucked down the taste of him. It was salty and tasted of raw, masculine vitality.

Adam groaned—the low feral moan of a man ready to possess his mate. He moved over her and settled himself between her legs. "This will hurt for a moment, love," he whispered.

But he closed his lips over the engorged tip of her breast and she forgot anything but the press of his skin against hers. She wanted him. Wanted all of him.

His tip nudged at her threshold. He slipped inside her. Inch by agonizing inch, stretching her womanhood. Georgina circled her legs around his hips, urging him on.

His rock-hard shaft reached the thin barrier. He groaned. "Forgive me." With a guttural moan, he flexed his hips and plunged past that wall.

Georgina's cry blended with his roar of approval.

Perspiration dotted her brow. With his shaft buried deep inside her, she felt like she was soaring through the sun-lit sky.

He cupped her breast and raised the mound to his mouth, worshiping her with his tongue. Georgina gasped, the earlier twinge of discomfort forgotten under his skilled ministrations. She peered at him through heavy lids, watching as he laved first one swollen nipple then the next. There was something heady in watching as he pleasured her.

She raised her hips, and now it was Adam who hissed as if in pain. Then he rocked his hips. Slowly at first then with increasing speed.

Adam flexed his shaft and then thrust in and out of her wet center until anything and everything fell away except her need for release.

Georgina matched his rhythm.

Adam moaned. "That's it, love. Show me how much you want this." The demand was hoarse with desire, and it only made the ache in her center grow and grow until she thought she'd go mad from the wanting.

The movement of his hips took on an almost savage intensity but Georgina moved with him in perfect harmony.

She exploded in a vibrant burst of color. She cried out over and over, her cries melding with Adam's as he stiffened above her, and his shaft throbbed deep within her, emptying the seed of life into her womb.

He collapsed atop her, his chest heaving as if he struggled to catch his breath.

Or mayhap that is me, she wondered with a sated smile.

It was near impossible to tell where she ended and he began.

Her eyes grew heavy, but she fought back the exhaustion descending over her. She didn't want to miss one moment of the rest of her life.

"I love you," she whispered against his chest.

At last, sleep won out. She closed her eyes and let it carry her away.

FIFTEEN

Fox and other Irish sympathizers have purchased premises in Dublin where war materials can be made closer to the site of planned rebellion. They are getting close.

Signed,

A Loyal British Subject

Adam brushed a sweat-dampened tendril off his wife's brow. His lips turned up at the corners.

His wife.

Mayhap he should have been bloody terrified by the hold Georgina seemed to have over him, but he couldn't think of a place he would have rather been than here in his chambers with her wrapped in his arms. When she was at his side, all the anger and pain he'd carried for so long slipped away.

She shifted her hips, burrowing close to him. The rounded flesh of her bottom nestled against his shaft, which roared to life in response.

He groaned, flexing his hips. This uncontrollable desire had more to do with Georgina being the first woman he'd taken in almost two years. First, he'd remained celibate out of respect for Grace, and then he'd battled his baser urges while in captivity.

When The Brethren had allowed him to return to London, and he'd discovered the truth about Grace, learned she'd married some other man, he'd gone off to Madam Touseou's—one of the most popular gentleman's clubs, which had a reputation for the most unique, inventive beauties. Bitter anger had driven him like a man gone mad. All he'd wanted was to lay down some nameless beauty and fuck her until he forgot Grace, Georgina, Bristol, and all the hell he'd endured.

He'd sat down with a bottle of whiskey and eyed a narrow-waisted blonde who had possessed the kind of beauty men went to war over. Except the moment she'd stepped in front of him, all Adam had been able to see was another woman with a slightly fuller figure and brown, untamable curls. Adam's determination to losing himself in the courtesan's arms was killed by images of Georgina Wilcox.

He'd dropped his tumbler and beat a hasty retreat, ignoring the curious stares shot his way.

Now, holding Georgina, Adam was grateful he hadn't turned himself over to empty desire. Not when he could have…this, whatever it was, with his wife.

Adam stroked the corner of her breast, rubbing the tip of her breast between his fingers. In response, the bud puckered and peaked. Even in her sleep, she moaned her need.

She undulated her hips against him.

A hiss slipped from between his clenched teeth. What had he initiated? Georgina had been a virgin. She was surely sore from his earlier possession of her body. But, as much as he told himself to let her sleep, his manhood throbbed with need.

He climbed astride her. Her lids fluttered open and her pouty red lips turned up in a hungry smile. "Again?" she whispered.

He paused, his shaft pressed against the thatch of brown curls that shielded her womanhood. "Do you need to wait?" he asked hoarsely. "If it is too soon, I can wait." His body shook in protest of his gallant offer.

Georgina's response was to wrap her thighs tight around his waist. "I want you, Adam. Make love to me."

He claimed her with a single thrust.

She screamed his name and Adam moved inside her.

At last, he'd come home.

༄

A quiet knocked shattered Adam's slumber.

His eyes shot open. A ray of sunlight burst through the curtains and he draped an arm over his eyes to blot out the glare. With his other arm, he pulled Georgina closer to his side, snuggling her body against him.

Even in sleep, a little moan of approval escaped her.

He closed his eyes again, shoving aside the noise that had intruded on his sleep.

A servant's voice penetrated the oaken door. "I'm sorry to interrupt, sir."

Adam's brow wrinkled.

Christ, what in hell does he want?

The only thing that should have merited Adam being roused the morning after his wedding night was a house fire, and Adam didn't smell smoke.

You simply do not interrupt a man the morning after his wedding night.

Wedding night. His mind conjured up an image of Georgina straddling him and riding him as if he were a prized mare. He stroked her lush thighs. She was going to be well-sated today. Sore, but well-sated. His shaft hardened in anticipation of the rest of the day's pleasures.

Another knock. "Your mother is here."

Adam's shaft wilted beneath the coverlet.

"What is my mother doing here at this ungodly hour?" he muttered under his breath.

Georgina snored. Flipping over onto her stomach, she proceeded to sleep.

God, his wife slept like the dead. Then, considering how little sleep she'd had the night before, was it really any wonder?

He threw his legs over the side of the bed, taking care not to jostle Georgina. As he fished his clothing from around the room, tugging on his wrinkled shirt and breeches, she slept on.

Adam pulled the door open to find the servant with his hand up to knock.

"Do not," he commanded, leaving the red-faced, young man standing there.

Adam's valet stood at the top of the stairway with a jacket outstretched. Adam stuffed his arms into the sapphire fabric.

His butler sidled up beside them, rasping for breath.

Adam started down the stairs.

"Sir, I took the liberty of showing her to your office."

Adam continued his descent. He shot a glare over his shoulder. "You are never to pound on my bloody door again. In the future, I don't care if the king himself is at my damned door. Is that clear?"

"Tsk, tsk, Adam. I'm disappointed. You'd deny entry to both the King of England and me? Where have your manners gone?"

His mother stood in the foyer, arms folded across her chest.

Adam bit back a curse. Dead. He was going to kill his butler. "Hello, Mother. It is so very good to see you." He leaned down and kissed her on the cheek.

She swatted him on the arm. "You are a poor liar."

If she only knew about his involvement with The Brethren. He smiled crookedly.

She wrinkled her nose. "And you are in need of a bath."

Adam bowed low at the waist. "Forgive me," he said dryly. "I was led to believe there was some kind of crisis that merited my immediate attention."

The countess slapped his fingers. "You are incorrigible."

He raised a brow. "You are correct, but I am sure that is not the reason for your visit."

His mother patted her elegant coiffure, casting a glance around the foyer. "I'd rather not discuss this for your servants to hear." She didn't wait for Adam, merely sailed off toward his office.

With a shake of his head, he trailed in her wake. Where his mother was concerned, it mattered not that he was nearly nine and twenty years. He might as well have been a boy of just nine. Then again, considering how she'd suffered him and his scoundrel brothers over the years, he supposed she was entitled to her maternal concerns.

She entered his office and he followed, closing the door behind them. His mother stopped in front of his desk, hands propped on her hips. "How could you simply leave without a word on your wedding day?"

His jaw flexed. "Forgive me for not believing you had anything planned to honor Georgina and I. You and Nick made it abundantly clear how you felt about our nuptials."

She sighed, looking away from him as if guilt wouldn't allow her to hold his eye. "I am sorry I did not organize a breakfast in your honor."

Adam cursed. "It isn't about the breakfast, Mother." How could his family not realize it was their treatment of Georgina he could not forgive? "Surely you cannot think I'd ever allow anyone to disparage my wife, including my own family?"

"No, no, I know that," she said in a very un-countess-like stammer.

Adam was unrelenting. "She is going to face condemnation from most of society. I never expected she would face it from you and Nicholas."

Mother dropped her head, looking properly shamed.

"It is not my intention to make you feel badly, Mother." He walked over to where she stood in front of his desk.

She looked up at him. "I just," she paused. "*We* just want to see you happy, Adam. When you disappeared…" Tears filled her eyes and she shook her head. "You cannot imagine any greater heartbreak than worrying after your child's whereabouts."

"I wrote you," he reminded her. It wasn't altogether a lie. Whenever he'd been off on a mission, he'd be sure to write—until his capture. Then The Brethren had seen to writing his mother.

"But Nicholas believed differently." Her gaze scoured his face as though she were unraveling a puzzle. "He believed there was more to your absence."

Not for the first time, Adam cursed his older brother to hell. He should never have needlessly troubled Mother with his unsubstantiated concerns. Adam forced a smile. "There was nothing more to my absence."

Mother was nothing if not tenacious. "You came home a different person." Her hand fluttered about. "The gaming, the women, the overindulging in spirits."

"I always enjoyed gaming, women, and spirits," he said sardonically.

155

Her lips formed a small moue of annoyance. "You once indicated there was a woman behind your sadness." She squared her shoulders.

Adam propped his hip against the edge of his desk and, folding his arms across his chest, said, "And?"

"Was it her? Georgina," she amended. "Was she the reason for your sadness?"

His body went rigid. Georgina had spoken to him several times about being the adored daughter of two simple servants. Somewhere along the way, her life had turned far off course, and all she'd known was pain. Yet she had emerged from all that darkness as a strong, courageous, kind-hearted woman. Georgina could never be the reason for his sadness.

"There was someone else," he said quietly. "She married another."

His mother made a pitying sound that grated like glass scraped along his flesh. The last thing he wanted or desired was anyone's pity. "What if I told you that Georgina saved me when I desperately needed saving?"

She said nothing for a long while. Instead, she claimed the seat in front of his desk and smoothed the fabric of her immaculate skirts in two long strokes. When she looked up at him, a smile wreathed her face. "Then I would say I will gladly call her daughter. Would you like to speak of her?" She hesitated. "The other woman," she clarified.

Filled with a restive energy, Adam shoved himself up. "I would not," he bit out. Grace was part of his past. He'd come to find peace with her betrayal. He'd moved on. She would always be an aching memory of simpler, less complicated times, but he was content to remember her that way.

His mother looked like she wanted to say something else, so he cut her off. "I imagine there was another reason for your visit today?"

Her green eyes sparkled and she perked up. "There was! We don't have much time."

His head swam with confusion. "Time for what?"

"Why, to prepare Georgina for her entrance into Society!" She hopped from her seat as if a fire had been lit beneath her feet. "She requires a dance instructor, tutor, and the most fashionable modiste. We have several months…" She paused. "Is she a quick study?"

Adam blinked. "A quick study?"

She waved her hand about. "Yes, you know? Do you imagine it will take her more than the three months before the Season begins?" Mother troubled her lower lip between her teeth. "I had hoped we could have her all prepared for the start of the Season, but if you believe she'll need more time then…"

Adam shook his head. "She won't need more time. She is very intelligent."

His mother snorted. "Most men wouldn't have such a pleased little expression when saying their wives are intelligent."

He laughed. "Oh? What of Father?"

She beamed at him. "Your father was different than most men."

He inclined his head. "Then I can only assume I am different than most men."

Mother's smile dipped and sadness came into her eyes. "I miss your father so very much." A little spasm contorted her ageless face. "For twenty-two years I had everything in the world I could have dreamed of. And do you know what?" She didn't wait for him to answer. "As fast as they ticked by, those years may as well have been minutes. Live joyously, every moment of every day that you are blessed with her, because it can all be taken as quickly as you can blink your eyes. Promise me you'll steal any and all happiness you can."

A cold, ominous chill fell over Adam. He told himself it was merely his mother's macabre words, words that really weren't intended to be morbid.

He bowed his head solemnly, shoving aside the cloying unease eating at his insides. "I promise," he murmured. Georgina had known too much heartache—she deserved a lifetime of happiness and he intended to be the person to give it to her.

He showed his mother out. When he returned to his office, he sat behind his desk, staring blankly at the empty room, wondering why he couldn't stifle the unease that lingered like the shadow of a ghost.

Georgina had awakened two hours ago. In that time, she'd taken a warm bath, had a cheery, young maid, Lucy, drag a brush through her tangled knots and help her into a simple, pale yellow dress. She had waited with breathless anticipation for Adam to walk through her chamber door...

He hadn't come.

She had gone down to the dining room and found a large buffet atop the sideboard. Her stomach had rumbled in hunger, but she'd looked around the room...

And he hadn't been there either.

A servant had rushed forward to pull out a chair, but she waved him off with a smile, seeing to it herself. She imagined the young man could detect it wasn't sincere. Georgina forced herself to sit and nibble several links of sausage and a piece of toast. With a napkin, she dabbed at the corners of her lips, and then rose, determined to find her husband—even if he wasn't as determined to find her.

The servant cleared his throat and she looked up.

"If I may? Mr. Markham can usually be found in his office." He dropped his gaze to the floor in deferential respect.

Georgina smiled. "Thank you," she murmured.

His gaze shot up and he returned her smile.

So here she stood, two...no, now three hours, one bath, one meal, and one painful hair-arrangement later, outside his office.

His door was closed as if to say *go away, you are unwanted.*

She stuck her tongue out at the wood. Well, that was fine, she'd been unwanted the better part of her life.

"Did you just stick your tongue out at the door?"

Georgina screeched and spun around. Her hand covered her thundering heart.

Her wide-eyed gaze shot from where Adam stood several feet away, leaning against the wall, to the closed door. "I thought—you...I..." She stopped talking.

He shoved away from the wall and stalked her like a wild beast stalking its prey and, oh God, how she wanted to be caught. Longed to lay herself bare for him. Her wanton desires turned her skin hot with embarrassment.

"Were you looking for me, Georgina?" A teasing sparkle glinted within the depths of his green eyes.

She wet her lips. "I—I may have been," she conceded. She couldn't conjure any real excuse for being outside his office.

"Did you stick your tongue out at my door?"

Her skin grew ten shades warmer. "I—I may have." She could have kicked herself for answering, but doing so would garner even more attention than the whole sticking her tongue out business, so she contented herself with closing her mouth.

Adam tipped her chin up, forcing her to meet his gaze. His breath, a sweet blend of mint and coffee, wafted over her skin. He lowered his mouth and claimed her lips. She swayed on her feet, but Adam was there to steady her. Georgina pulled away. Her lids fluttered open. "I love you." The words spilled from her before she could even try to call them back.

Except she didn't want to call them back.

She loved him. There was no helping it. She had loved him a very, very long time, and would not be sorry for it.

Adam's expression grew shuttered. "I...thank you."

Thank you?

Georgina swore she could hear her own heart rending beneath her breast. She took a deep breath. His love would not come overnight. He'd loved Grace. He could not so easily switch his affections to her, plain and drab Georgina Wilcox.

Pride leeched into her spine, stiffening it. No, not Wilcox. Markham. Grace may have had Adam at some point, but she had given him up. He belonged to her now. He might not love her—yet—but she would do everything in her power to change that.

She smiled up at him as if she'd not just had her words of love offset by a courteously polite response. Searching for something, anything to shift the conversation, she said, "Were you looking for me?"

His relieved-sounding sigh indicated he was just as eager to discuss anything but her awkward profession of love. "My mother came by."

Georgina's stomach twisted into a painful knot. She thought she might rather discuss her words of love than discuss his mother. "I... uh...how lovely."

His lips twitched at her obvious lie. "We discussed your debut."

"My debut?" To her own ears, she sounded like the parrot capable of mimicry she'd once seen at a fair in Bristol.

"My mother wants to help you—help us," he amended.

Georgina wanted to stamp her foot in protest. She didn't want to have a debut. In fact, she'd be quite content to disappear to some far-flung corner of the world to keep reality from intruding on her and Adam's growing feelings for each other. Adam smiled, but Georgina could see the nervous lines of tension at the corners of his mouth and knew her response meant a great deal. She sighed, relenting. She would do anything for him. Even if it meant going out like a lamb to the slaughter.

"I'd be glad for her help," she murmured.

Adam raised her hand to his lips. "I will not leave you alone. We'll do this all together, Georgina. I'm sure the moment my mother left she'd already contacted the most respected dance instructor and tutors."

Tutors?

Dance instructors?

It made sense. Why would Adam ever suspect she'd already been trained in the most popular dances? Why should he think she spoke French, Italian, and a smattering of Latin? Her father had scoffed at her ability to acquire languages, said a lady only had a need for the basic elements of a language. Nonetheless, Georgina was fairly fluent.

Adam only knew her as the battered maid in Bristol. He didn't know that her father was a wealthy merchant or that she'd had her own Bristol version of a Season. She gulped as she faced the growing realization that it would be harder and harder to keep her many lies straight.

Adam nuzzled her neck and her body shivered in heated response. "I want to make love to you," he whispered against her ear.

Georgina's head fell back on a groan and, there for any servant who happened to pass by, Adam swept her into his office. He kicked the door shut with the heel of his boot and proceeded to make love to her.

And Georgina allowed herself to believe that mayhap it would all turn out all right.

SIXTEEN

Fox has earned Emmet's displeasure. He defied Emmet's orders to focus on supplying United Irish veterans with muskets. Instead, Fox believes the cause is best served by determining the identities of The Brethren.
Signed,
A Loyal British Subject

W hen he'd made the claim to his mother that Georgina would not need more than the three winter months to prepare for the Season, Adam had secretly been filled with hesitancy.

Georgina completed the intricate steps of a quadrille with Tony.

He grinned. His wife was a woman of many talents.

Since his tense wedding day, Mother had come around where Georgina was concerned. With her kind spirit and genuine warmth, it would appear Georgina had charmed his mother. Even Nick appeared to be more easy-spirited around Georgina.

But then, Georgina had that effect on people. She said something to Tony, who threw his head back and laughed uproariously. His brother stumbled over his feet and nearly took Georgina down with him. At the last moment, he righted his footing and prevented them from crashing to the floor. They collapsed into a fit of laughter.

Adam smiled. Initially, he'd battled waves of jealousy over Tony's seeming infatuation with his wife. Tony, however, had been Adam and Georgina's greatest ally and, eying him as he moved her down a line of imaginary dancers, Adam could forgive his little brother's seeming fascination. Georgina's quiet hesitancy and fear had lifted,

162

replaced by this gay, sparkling wood fairy. How could Tony not be charmed?

Roses filled her full cheeks, the crimson stain matching the color of her sinfully perfect, plump lips. It would appear Fox and Hunter were no more than a distant memory—for both of them. Oh, the traitorous bastards lingered; Adam suspected they always would. But, for him, the nightmares came hardly at all.

The same could not be said for his wife. There were times Adam awakened in a cold sweat, only to realize it was Georgina gripped by an unshakeable terror. He would take her in his arms, willing her back to him, guiding her with the soothing strength of his voice.

Tony drew to a stop and bowed, murmuring something to Georgina. She spun around. Her gaze alighted on him, her eyes sparkling like a million stars on a cloudless night.

She hurried over to him. "Adam!" She hesitated then dipped into a formal curtsy.

He bowed. "Mrs. Markham."

"Tony was just helping me refine the steps of the quadrille," she explained.

"I think you have well-mastered it, wife." Nor was that a platitude; Georgina moved as gracefully as if she'd done it her entire life. The dance instructor they'd hired had marveled at his student's innate ability.

Georgina had modestly brushed off the man's compliments, but there was no denying she possessed a natural grace and elegance on the dance floor.

Tony sauntered up to them. "Your wife could have given that old instructor lessons," he said with a wink.

She blushed prettily and gave her head a shake. "My head is going to explode from all your compliments."

Tony smiled in response. "Your wife picked up Latin, Italian, and French in almost three months' time. She's as skilled a dancer as any I've seen." He shook his head. "It's hard to believe with all her talent, the one skill she doesn't possess is a singing voice."

163

Adam started. "What…?" Georgina's voice could shame a choir of angels.

Brown, panicky eyes met his, and Adam realized she didn't want Tony to know about her voice. His brow furrowed. In fact, come to think on it, he'd spent so many of his days making passionate love to Georgina and squiring her about London, it had escaped his notice until now that she'd not sung since they'd been reunited.

She had her lower lip between her teeth, worrying the flesh. "I'd imagine there isn't a thing Georgina isn't accomplished at," Adam said instead. Her shoulders seemed to lift on a relieved exhale. The glowing smile was back in place. He held his hand out. "Will you waltz with me?"

Her gasp blended with Tony's guffaw of amusement. "If Mother finds out you've taught Georgina the waltz, her head will spin in circles."

Adam's lips quirked. "When did you start to worry about what Mother thinks?"

Tony inclined his head in acknowledgement. "Touché, Brother."

Adam returned his attention to Georgina. He held his hand out. "Mrs. Markham?"

She gave her head a frantic shake. "Adam, we can't!" she said in a scandalized whisper. "Your brother—"

"Shan't say a word," Tony promised solemnly, crossing an X over his heart.

"See?" Adam murmured.

And, to the strings of an imagined orchestra, he began to twirl her about the dance floor. Her feet struggled to adjust to the unfamiliar movement. They'd not engaged in that particular dance since…since his captivity. Except then they'd had just the small four walls of his prison cell. Now they possessed the wide expanse of freedom provided by the long dance floor.

Georgina's footsteps matched his in a perfect harmony. All the while, her lips moved as she counted a silent one-two-three rhythm. His heart swelled at the endearing gesture.

"What?" she asked. She stumbled a bit.

He caught her to his chest, righting her.

Tony's laugh echoed off the ballroom windows.

They ignored him.

"You are beautiful, Georgina," he said. And he meant it. There'd been a time, long, long ago, that he'd thought her plain and dull. How could that have ever been? She was more vibrant than any person he'd ever met—including Grace. "Are you ready for your introduction to Society?"

She snorted. "I think I'd rather face down a pack of hungry wolves."

He angled her body close to his.

"Not appropriate, big brother. Not appropriate." Tony guffawed from the sidelines of the dance floor.

Adam ignored him. "I'll not let anyone hurt you, Georgina. I promise you that."

She lowered her eyes and it struck him—why should she believe him? All Georgina had ever known was pain. Oddly, the thought did something more than enrage him. It made him want to fill her days with endless joy and wonder. He applied pressure to her waist. "Look at me," he ordered.

Georgina glanced up.

"You do know that, don't you? I will not tolerate anyone being cruel to you—"

She made a sound in her throat. "You cannot control the thoughts and actions of other people." Her eyes fairly bled with hurt.

Her meaning couldn't be clearer. A shiver wracked his frame. By God, he was free, and Fox and Hunter would forever be relegated to a distant memory. He would not let them dictate his actions for a moment longer.

Adam growled. "Can't I?" He'd sworn he'd place himself between her and any and every danger. She was his and he'd not let anything happen to her. Not again. Not when she'd suffered so bloody much.

Her full lips tipped up in a sad little smile. "Oh, Adam, you truly believe that, don't you?"

"With all my heart." His gaze fell to her plump, red lips. An uncomfortable ache settled in his groin as he was seized by a sudden urge to kiss her. He snorted. Sudden urge. It was really rather something of a constant urge.

He glanced over at Tony and found the young blighter eying him with knowing amusement. All his earlier appreciation faded under the weight of wanting him gone.

Georgina stopped counting to say, "Stop glaring at your brother."

Adam seized the opportunity to gather her closer to him.

"He's making a nuisance of himself," he growled. "He—"

"Has been a good brother and loyal friend to me," she interjected, giving him an admonishing look. "Tony has accepted me when most people will not. Even the staff has not—"

Fury bubbled to the surface. "Have they given you a difficult time?" The mere thought of it made him want to storm through the house and summarily dismiss every blasted one of the servants.

Georgina shook her head a little too hastily. "Only at the onset. They've all warmed considerably."

His wife was a miserable liar. He chose to let the matter rest… for now. He would speak with his staff later. When Georgina was not around. That would mean letting her out of his sight, and he did not intend to do that—especially in light of her upcoming entry into Society.

His musings were interrupted by the sudden appearance of his butler. He bore a silver tray with an envelope upon it.

Adam brought them to a slow halt. He released her and sketched a bow.

Georgina fell into a deep curtsy that would have done her dance instructor proud and took a step away from him.

"Can't you see, Watson, my wife and I were in the midst of a very important dance?" Adam said teasingly.

The butler's face may as well have been carved in stone. "I…"

Adam made to take Georgina in his arms when a resolute Watson cleared his throat.

Adam frowned. "What is it?" His earlier amusement faded at his servant's tenacity.

Watson crossed over, coming to a stop in front of Adam and Georgina. "I was told it was of great importance that you receive this note immediately."

With a growl, Adam snatched the note and started. A very familiar, elegant stroke had marked the thick ivory velum. His heartbeat slowed.

"Adam?" Georgina asked hesitantly.

He picked his head up, a wave of guilt filling him.

His wife studied him. "Is everything all right?"

"Everything's fine," he murmured, his mind a million miles from the silent ballroom.

She reached out to him. When she spoke, her words emerged as a halting whisper. "Are you certain? You seem—"

"I said I'm fine," he snapped, jerking away from her touch.

Georgina flinched as though he'd slapped her. Utter silence followed his outburst.

Tony and Watson stared at him with alternating looks of disappointment and dismay. The scorn in their eyes, coupled with his own clawing guilt, rocked him on his heels.

"Forgive me," he said hoarsely. "If you'll excuse me. There is a matter of business I must see to." He sketched a hasty bow and fled.

When he finally reached the sanctuary that was his office, he slammed the door behind him, his heart racing not from the rapid pace he'd set for himself but from the sealed missive in his hand.

He stood there in silence, his rapid breathing and the snap of the fire the only sounds in the empty office.

Then, unable to resist the overwhelming urge, he tore the envelope open.

Grace's scent, a blend of fresh-meadow roses and primrose, wafted from the sheets. His eyes slid closed. He would not, if given the chance, go back and wed Grace. Georgina had come to mean too much to him. Still, Grace represented a far simpler time from before, a time he found himself yearning for in the dead of night when the nightmares came. He pulled out the note.

A log tumbled in the fireplace. The pop of the fire's embers drew him over to the hearth. He stared down into the flames. He should toss the bloody note into the fire and be done with it. There was nothing Grace Blakely, nay Helling, could say that would make her betrayal less painful.

Nor should it matter. He was married to Georgina.

He unfolded the note and read.

Adam, I hope this note finds you well. I wish to congratulate you on your recent nuptials. I must speak with you on a matter of utmost importance.
Ever Yours,
Grace

His lip curled. Apparently, Grace felt no apologies were necessary. Adam held the parchment to the flames.

Leaning his head against the mantel, he watched the fire lick the corners of the note. They curled. Twisted.

Adam gasped and tugged his fingers back, preserving the note. He dropped it to the floor and slammed his booted foot on it, stamping out the fire, then picked it up to study it. He couldn't destroy the note and he didn't care to consider why.

Horribly burned and nearly unrecognizable, all that remained of the parchment were Grace's three meager sentences. Adam sank into the nearest chair, staring blankly down at the note in his hands.

Why should she have contacted him now? What could she possibly have to say to him now that he'd married and finally found happiness?

Adam dropped his head into his hand, crushing the already help-lessly ruined note. His mouth all but begged for the stinging bite of a hot whiskey. He fought back the urge like a man battling a dragon.

All Grace's note represented was trouble.

The last thing he needed in the world was any more bloody trouble.

Georgina stared down at her hands. At her toes. At the marble floor. Anywhere but at Tony's pitying expression.

"I'm sure it was of great importance," he murmured.

"Yes, I'm sure it was," she said, her words halting to her own ears. "He did say as much."

Tony snorted. "You're entirely too forgiving. It was unpardonable for him to speak to you the way he did."

Of course, Tony had no idea that Adam's tone of annoyance was no different from the way she'd been spoken to the better part of her life. Her father's callous words and stinging rebuke had ceased to hurt a long, long time ago...Adam's, however, wielded too much power. The kind that could cripple her with a single unkind utterance.

Georgina managed a weak smile. "Are you trying to create trouble for your brother?"

"Oh, I rather suspect my brother doesn't need my help getting himself into trouble." He held his elbow out. "Come along."

Georgina wrinkled her brow. "I'm not a dog, Tony."

He laughed, the sound deep and husky. The kind of laugh that was going to do funny things to far too many debutantes' hearts that Season. "I didn't snap my fingers or pat my leg, Georgie. Come with me," he tried again, though there was now a note of seriousness in his usually relaxed demeanor. "You must want something before you're shoved off into Society."

This time she did laugh. "First a dog, now a ship?"

Tony waggled his brows, his jolliness returning full-fledged. "I never called you a dog, or for that matter a ship." He held his elbow out again and waited.

Georgina hesitated before placing her arm in his.

"There's a girl," he murmured. "I'm sure Adam will return any moment and," he lowered his lips to her ear, "be madly jealous to discover you've run off with his much handsomer, wittier brother."

"The earl?" she asked teasingly.

He pressed his free hand to his heart. "You wound me! The only accurate thing you've said about Nick is that he is, in fact, an earl."

"And he wouldn't by the way," Georgina added. "Be jealous, that is," she clarified at his puzzled expression. "Adam wouldn't even notice." You had to feel something greater than a sense of obligation for a person to truly care about them. The truth of it knifed through her.

Tony gave her fingers a little squeeze. "You truly have no idea that he is madly in love with you."

Georgina faltered, stumbling against him. "What?" She gave her curls a frantic shake. "No. You are wrong. Adam doesn't love me." Oh, she believed he cared for her, had no doubts that he would always protect her, but he did not love her. A person was surely only capable of one true love—and for Adam that had been, and would always be, Grace.

Jealousy gnawed at her heart.

It took her a moment to realize they had stopped in the foyer. Georgina blinked, glancing around as Tony waited for his carriage to be readied. He looked down at her, cuffing her gently under the chin.

"Georgie, my brother would have to either be mad or blind not to love you. And you'd have to be mad or blind to realize that he's not mad or blind."

She grinned up at him.

"Now come, let us go spend some of your husband's money."

Georgina allowed him to pull her along, allowed her heart to soar on the hope that maybe, just maybe, Adam did love her after all.

SEVENTEEN

Fox and Hunter have a friend within The Brethren of the Lords.
Signed,
A Loyal British subject

T ony wrinkled his brow and turned his bemused expression from the crumbly façade of the storefront to Georgina. "A bookshop?"

Georgina smiled. "Come, Tony. It is not as though I've dragged you off to Sunday sermon. I like to read," she added for good measure.

Tony scratched the top of his head. "Read?"

She waggled her brows at him. "You know. Books?"

"Hmph." He glanced longingly across the street.

Georgina followed his gaze to the men's shop. He eyed it like a young lady picking through an assortment of satin and silk fabrics.

She nudged him with her elbow. "Go."

His face flushed a dull red. "Go where?"

She rolled her eyes. "It's only across the street. I won't leave this shop," she promised.

His lips tilted down in a boyish frown. "My brother will have my head—"

"Your brother won't know. Now go."

He grinned. "I've got to find a woman like you. Sweet, understanding—"

She laughed. "Go!"

Georgina entered the bookshop. She wrinkled her nose at the overwhelming scent of aged books.

"Hullo, miss. Is there anything I might help you find?"

She spun around to face the bookkeeper. Bushy, white, wizened brows stood out on the bald man's face. He smiled at her, which set his fleshy jowls to jiggling.

"Actually, yes. I am looking for a book." He paused, turning back to face her. She tried to recall the name. "It is a collection of art." She realized even as she said it that her words wouldn't be much help.

The old shopkeeper scratched his head. "Uh…"

She saved him from struggling with the hopeless endeavor of finding an untitled and authorless book. "Is there a section for books about art?"

He inclined his head. "Right this way." He didn't wait to see if she followed, merely continued down the long, long row of books. He guided her to the very last corner of the store. "There is your section, miss."

Georgina thanked him then focused her attention on the vast collection of books. She pulled out a copy of Jean-Etienne Liotard's collection. It appeared the small, leather volume hadn't seen the outside of a shelf in the current century. She studied the cover, trailing her fingertips along the title, and made to return it to its forgotten place.

She paused.

There was something so forlorn about placing the book back where it most likely would never see the light of day until…until…who knew? Years, perhaps.

Georgina set the copy of Jean Etienne Liotard's work on the floor. She couldn't abandon the volume in this dusty bookshop.

She continued through the shelves, biting her lip as she rescued an increasing number of art books. Georgina eyed the torn black edition of Guardi's work in her hands and, with a sigh, set it atop the ever-growing stack. It wasn't fair to leave them here, unwanted, unread, and unloved, all because they didn't have a shiny, leather cover and golden lettering.

At last, her fingers settled on a deep red leather binding and she gasped, reaching for it with a fluttery breath. She pulled it into her hands with reverence, remembering that long ago day when Adam was first taken captive and spoke to her of Francois Boucher.

The soft tread of footsteps registered. Georgina glanced up and her smile died on her lips as the stuff of her nightmares materialized like a ghoulish apparition.

The book slid from her fingers.

Jamie leaned against the towering bookcase. "Hullo, Georgina."

A swell of panic climbed into her throat. She shook her head. It couldn't be! Not when she'd finally found happiness and relegated Father and Jamie to the corner of her mind dedicated to old, buried hurts. She closed her eyes, counted to five then opened them.

Jamie shoved himself off the shelving and, with slow, precise steps, walked closer. Closer. Ever closer.

Georgina lurched forward. The neatly built stack of books clattered to the floor. Heart hammering wildly, she spun on her heel and turned to flee.

Jamie blocked her escape.

She opened her mouth to cry out, but he clamped his hand over lips, stifling the sound.

"Shh," he whispered against her ear, his breath hot and tinged with brandy. "Not another sound, is that clear? Your father is across the street speaking with a Mr. Anthony Markham."

Oh God in heaven, her father was here as well, and he had his hands on Tony. If Tony came to harm because of her, Georgina would never forgive herself. In a short time, Tony had become a brother to her.

She nodded jerkily. If she resisted in any way, Adam's brother would be killed. A sick dread filled her stomach, churning with the inevitable sense that her past had intersected with her future. Tears filled her eyes, blurring the shelving. She had come so very close to having everything she'd ever dreamed of. In the end, she'd only deluded herself, and now Adam's brother might pay the ultimate price.

Jamie released her, casting a furtive glance around. When he looked back at her, his crystalline blue eyes burned with anger. "I understand congratulations are in order, Mrs. Markham."

Georgina's mind raced as her life spiraled out of control before her. She'd known Jamie long enough to know he was holding on to a very thin thread of control that prevented him from beating her down in this very public place.

"What do you want?" she whispered, proud at the steadiness of her response.

He cupped her cheek. "My lovely Georgina."

She bit hard on the inside of her cheek to keep from crying out for help. Jamie would most likely kill the old shopkeeper, and then Father would kill Tony in retribution. She waited in silence for him to speak.

Jamie broke the quiet. "We were very disappointed in you, my dear."

She froze. After all these years, they'd discovered that she was the one responsible for sending off Emmet's plans for the Irish revolution. "For what?"

He caught a strand of her hair, rubbing it between his fingers. "Why, for marrying the enemy."

Relief swept over her. They knew she'd freed Adam and Mr. Blakely, but they didn't know the depth of her betrayal.

A muscle ticked at the corner of Jamie's eye. "What, nothing to say?" His brogue, thicker than usual, was a telltale indication of his fury.

Her toes dug into the soles of her slippers in remembrance of the many cruelties she'd suffered at his hands.

Jamie gave the lone lock in his fingers a painful tug. Georgina winced, closing her eyes as pain radiated along her temple. She drew in a staccato series of shallow breaths, knowing he would not hesitate to drag her from the shop and draw her away to his new lair.

He released the curl suddenly. "I am very angry with you, Georgina."

"I'm sorry," she lied. She couldn't care less how Jamie felt about her, but she'd learned long ago that it was a good deal easier to lie and tell him what he wanted to hear.

He glanced around as if to verify they were still alone. "Then it came to me."

A shiver of apprehension raced along her spine. "What came to you?"

"That you can help the Cause."

Georgina stared at him.

Jamie grasped her wrist and squeezed it in a manacle-like grip. "You see, the United Irishmen have had to divide our efforts between amassing our army and trying to find the names of those who would quash our efforts. I want the names of our enemies."

She yanked her arm.

He held fast.

"You'd have me betray my husband and my country?" she demanded. "Why would I do that?"

He tightened his hold and she clamped her lips together to keep from crying out.

"Why, because your husband is far less faithful than you, my dear."

A coldness settled in her heart. She wanted to wrap her arms around herself and rub warmth back into her body, but Jamie's grip prevented movement.

At last, he let her wrist go. Her arm fell to her side.

"I see you understand. Her name is Grace Helling. She is the lovely woman in the sketchpad and," he dropped his voice to a punishing whisper, "if the papers are to be believed, even more stunning than Helen of Troy."

The muscles in her stomach tightened.

"And Lady Edward Helling and your husband have resumed their relationship." He spoke as casually as if discussing the weather yet each word was like a dagger being thrust into her heart. In and out. Twisting. Aching.

"You lie," she whispered.

He grinned. "Oftentimes, yes. This is not one of those times. They appear to communicate through very personal, very detailed notes."

Georgina's breath hitched as she remembered Watson's interruption. The note. Adam's preoccupation. His annoyance with Georgina.

This time she did wrap her arms around her body. The agony of Jamie's cruel revelation was so much greater than any physical pain. Every blow she'd taken paled when faced with this crushing loss. Her knees buckled and she caught the edge of the shelf to keep from falling.

"I expect you to help us," Jamie said.

A bitter laugh bubbled up from her throat. She'd never help them.

"I want an answer, Georgina. Take some time to think on it. You'll see for yourself that your husband is undeserving of your loyalty. When you realize that, I suspect you'll help us."

Then, as quickly as he'd come and shattered her world, Jamie left.

Georgina stood there staring after him, until his retreating form was no more.

She smothered a sob with her hand and sank to the floor, attempting to put together her overturned pile. Except her fingers trembled so badly, her efforts were in vain.

"Do you require any assistance, miss?"

She cried out, her nerves still frayed from Jamie's sudden appearance.

A tall, elegantly clad stranger dropped to a knee beside her. From his perfect posture to the gold signet on his finger, everything about him fairly oozed refined nobility.

The shopkeeper hurried over, but the ominously handsome man waved him off.

It took a moment for Georgina to realize the merchant awaited a sign from her that she was indeed well.

A flood of heat rushed her cheeks. "I-I am fine," she managed. "I-I was merely startled and tipped over my assortment of books." It wasn't altogether a lie. She'd been startled, but more by Jamie's resurrection from the pits of hell.

The old shopkeeper moved on, leaving Georgina alone with the stranger. As she looked at him—at the unfashionably long, black hair, the expert cut of his midnight jacket, even the hard glint in his sapphire eyes—only one word came to mind: dark.

He continued his methodical work, reorganizing her books. A nervous laugh nearly strangled her. Noblemen weren't supposed to see to such menial tasks…in old, unfrequented bookshops, no less.

He looked up from the neat, efficient stack he'd made. "What a large selection you've made, miss."

Georgina didn't comment.

He stood. "Considering our rather odd encounter, perhaps intro-ductions are in order." He bowed low at the waist. "The Duke of Aubrey." The young duke held his hand out to assist her to her feet.

Georgina eyed it momentarily before placing her fingers in his. He helped her up and she reminded herself to curtsy. "Thank you, Your Grace." She tried to place the Duke of Aubrey. Something about his title rang oddly familiar. She scoffed. It was utterly preposterous to think she knew anyone of this man's lofty ranking.

She focused her attention on a book on the shelf. Though highly unlikely that anyone should discover the two of them in Ye Olde Bookshop, it would be a terrible scandal if she were caught clustered behind a bookcase with the illustrious duke.

Except the duke seemed of a different mind altogether and not at all inclined to simply take himself off and leave her to wallow in the misery of Jamie's reappearance. "Have you read all these books, Miss...?"

Georgina froze on the next volume beneath her fingers. "Mrs. Markham," she corrected. When he still appeared to have no inten-tion of leaving, she sighed. "No, I have not read them all."

He held up a single copy. The cracked, black leather showed an abundance of wear. "I highly recommend this copy."

Geoffrey Keating—Foundation of Knowledge on Ireland. Her heart fal-tered then picked up speed. The duke's words contained a subtle hint of knowingness. She fought back an insatiable urge to look around for Jamie. Had the Duke of Aubrey heard her and Jamie's discussion?

Georgina forced herself to accept the copy, marveling that her fin-gers weren't shaking. Their hands brushed and she jerked the book close to her chest. "Thank you for the recommendation." She lowered her head and proceeded to study the title, willing him to leave.

Of course being a duke, the man was clearly accustomed to doing just as he pleased. "You are Adam Markham's new bride."

It wasn't a question.

The bothersome noble tapped his chin. "I wonder that your hus-band has not joined you."

A jolt of sick humiliation coursed through her.

Salvation came from an unexpected source. "He didn't join her because his younger brother insisted on quality time with the lovely young woman."

Georgina spun around, her eyes alighting on Tony. Like a conquering hero, he may as well have climbed off Pegasus with sword and shield in hand. He stood at the end of the row, arms folded in a mock nonchalance, though the tension in his tight smile hinted at the anger just below the surface. Of course, the disconcertingly perceptive Duke of Aubrey was too polite to point out that said "brother" had been suspiciously absent until now.

Tony sauntered down the aisle and stopped next to Georgina, bowing low at the waist. "Your Grace."

The duke bowed in return. "You are Markham's younger brother, I presume?"

Tony gave him a young, cocksure smile. "I am. Anthony Markham." He looked pointedly down at Georgina's scattered pile of books. "Were you able to find the book you sought?"

She blinked at Tony's clear dismissal of the duke. "Uh...yes. I found it. I found a lot of them," she finished lamely.

Tony bent down and filled his arms with the assorted array of art books. "Very well, then we should be on our way."

The Duke of Aubrey claimed her hand in his.

She gasped at the unexpectedness of his touch, shriveling against Tony's side. Logic told her the Duke of Aubrey wouldn't harm her; at least not in a public bookshop. Yet twenty years of living with her father had ingrained certain truths into her—one of them being, men had the ability to inflict pain. Something told her this man was not to be trusted.

At her silent reaction, Tony's body seemed to turn to granite. Even the usually smiling lines at the corner of his eyes had gone hard.

The duke continued to hold Georgina's hand far longer than was appropriate. He raised it to his lips, seemingly unaware of the internal battle she waged to stay calm in his presence.

"Again, Mrs. Markham, I must insist you read my selection."

178

Georgina allowed Tony to lead her to the counter and make her purchases. "What was that about?" he whispered in her ear.

She shook her head. She could feel the duke's intense sapphire-black eyes boring a hole into her back. This wasn't the place.

With the exception of a single leather volume that she insisted on holding onto, she allowed the shopkeeper to bundle her large purchase. Tony steered her from the shop and into their waiting carriage.

"Now, tell me, what was that about?" The carriage lurched forward.

Georgina played with the fabric of the curtain covering the window, clenching and unclenching her hands. She lifted a single shoulder. "I don't know." And she didn't. The Duke of Aubrey was a perfectly lofty stranger who'd seemed in possession of many details about her marriage along with suspicious statements and questions. "I dropped my books and he happened to be present to help me."

Tony snorted. "The Duke of Aubrey doesn't *help* anyone."

Another frisson of unease raked her spine. A silent voice whispered that maybe Tony was right and there was more to the duke's interest. Her exchange with Jamie flitted through her mind and she tried to determine how much the powerful nobleman had overheard.

She took the curl Jamie had yanked only a short while ago, rubbing it between her fingers. "I don't know, Tony. He was there. My books fell and he helped. That's all there is to it." She desperately hoped that was the case anyway.

"Adam won't be pleased when he finds out," Tony murmured.

She dropped the strand of hair and whipped her head around to look at him, letting the red velvet curtain flutter back into place. "Who is he?"

Tony's brow furrowed. "Who is…oh, you mean the Duke of Aubrey." It was his turn to shrug. "Most eligible bachelor in London. Quite the rogue. The ladies adore him. Not that I can understand what they find so appealing," he said sullenly.

Georgina managed a weak smile. "Do he and Adam not get along?"

He scratched the top of his head. "Why would you think that?"

She pointed her eyes to the top of the carriage ceiling. "You said that Adam wouldn't be pleased…"

"Because he'd be jealous."

Georgina felt like she was being twirled in dizzying circles. "Why is he jealous of the Duke of Aubrey?" The carriage lurched to a halt, nearly sending the forgotten book on her lap tumbling to the floor. She caught it before it fell.

Tony leaned over and gave her errant curl a tug. "He'll be jealous that Aubrey was flirting with you."

A warm flutter fanned out in her belly but logic quickly doused the embers of happiness his words elicited. In order to be jealous, Adam would have to feel something more than casual regard for her.

The groom opened the door to hand her down. Holding on to her leather treasure, she took Tony's arm with her free one and climbed the stairs just as the butler threw the door wide.

"You're wrong, you know," she said. "Adam wouldn't mind."

"I won't mind what?"

She gasped and tripped to an awkward stop. Tony righted her and nodded at his brother.

Adam ignored him. He stood silent, at the bottom of the winding staircase, arms folded across his chest. Georgina's heart sped up at the sight of him, all tall, lean, muscular elegance.

Then his question registered.

Tony responded. "The Duke of Aubrey's interest in your wife." A sparkle glittered in his teasing eyes.

Adam's body stiffened and he looked at her through hooded lashes.

Georgina pointed her eyes to the ceiling. "There is no interest."

Tension dripped off her husband's frame; his palpable jealousy, a life force that breathed hope into her that Adam did in fact care for her—even if just a little.

Tony laughed, saying something to Adam, then bent low over her hand. He made his farewell to Georgina and was gone, leaving her alone with Adam.

The six feet between them seemed a chasm as great as the English Channel. It represented an impenetrable breach their marriage could never close. She shifted back and forth on her feet.

"What did Aubrey say to you?" he asked, a ferocious gleam in his eye.

"No." She gave a brusque shake of her head, dislodging a curl. Georgina brushed it back. "Tony has been perfectly gentleman—"

"I referred to the duke."

Oh. Yes. Well that made far more sense. She clamped her lips closed. The duke had said a great deal and, at the same time, nothing at all.

"Georgina?"

"No. He didn't say anything." Which was not an untruth. "Do you know him well?"

Adam looked over her shoulder. "No." He tightened his jaw.

Something about that "no"; the slightest hesitancy in the one word utterance, gave her pause.

Then before she could ask questions on it, her husband turned the conversation. "Are you prepared for your introduction to Society tomorrow evening?"

She recalled her dismal failure amidst the merchants in Bristol. Confronting a room of nobles would be the equivalent of facing a pit of poisonous snakes. "Uh…yes." Though in truth, she'd rather confront a sea of those slithering serpents than the two-legged sort.

Adam's lips turned down at the corners. "You needn't be fearful. You'll—"

Uncomfortable with his confidence in her efforts amidst his world, she thrust her recent purchase into his hands. "I got this for you," she blurted.

Adam studied the title and then met her gaze. "What is…?" He fell silent.

Georgina shifted awkwardly on her feet. His inscrutable expression gave little indication as to his thoughts. She'd expected he would be pleased with her gift. "Did I have the wrong title?" She bit her lower lip. "Do you not like it? I thought it was this one but—What…?" A little squeak escaped her when he swept her into his arms and proceeded to carry her up the stairs. "Adam," she protested. Her gaze darted around for nosy servants.

"I love it." His response was gruff with emotion. With an effortless grace, he carried her down the hall and into his chambers, kicking the door shut with the heel of his boot.

When he set her on the floor, her body slid down his. The flame of desire raged like a fire within. In moments, he'd divested her of her gown and undergarments. She stood shivering beneath his gaze, not from cold but with heated anticipation.

Adam shrugged his jacket off and tossed it to the floor. His shirt followed suit, and then his hands went to his breeches.

Her mouth went dry. She brushed his fingers away with bold insistence. "Let me." Dropping to her knees, she urged his black breeches down around his ankles and then he was naked before her.

Adam stood there, stiff and unbending as a marble statue. His proudly erect manhood earned her notice. How could it not? The magnificent member was at eye level and so incredibly close to her mouth. An urge to taste him overcame her. She leaned forward to kiss his shaft.

He groaned. "What are you doing?"

She hesitated, a wave of uncertainty hitting her. Mayhap her wanton thoughts and actions were better suited to a harlot than the wife of a peer. Still…she said nothing. Instead, she took the tip of him between her lips, drawing the length deeper and deeper until he was buried in her mouth.

He cried out. Any and all doubts died a swift death when he wound his fingers in her hair, urging her to continue.

Georgina's reservations were replaced by hedonistic yearning. She became bolder, flicking her tongue up and down his length. His guttural groan of approval filled her with desire. She'd never imagined that giving her husband pleasure could so consume her with longing.

Adam flexed his hips.

Georgina continued to draw him in and out until he was groaning.

Adam jerked his hips away.

Georgina's eyes fluttered open.

He picked her up and carried her over to the bed. Adam set her down like she was a treasure more precious than gold.

"What are you doing?" she asked when he pulled her atop him.

"Shh," he whispered, guiding her down onto his length.

Her body widened to accept every inch of his enormous shaft. Georgina cried out when he sheathed himself within her center.

Adam rested his hands on her hips and guided her, urging her up. And down. Up. And down. Georgina closed her eyes. Arching her back, she found the rhythm and rode him like a master horsewoman.

"That's it," he cried.

Her hips undulated, taking on a frenzied speed. The inner muscles at the center of her womanhood began to spasm. She ground herself against him, taking him even deeper, and then she was coming on a great, gasping cry and he was joining her, pouring his seed inside her.

He continued to throb, and she accepted all of him, ringing out every last bit he could give. When her body could no longer bear weight, she collapsed atop him. Her long curls fanned out atop his rapidly heaving chest, their breath mingling in a jagged symphony of sated desire.

Adam rested a hand atop her buttocks, caressing the plump flesh, but Georgina couldn't muster any hint of humility.

"I love you," she whispered.

Adam stilled his movements and then resumed his soft massage.

He did not respond.

And Jamie's taunting accusation reared in her mind, intruding on this otherwise perfect moment.

EIGHTEEN

This is the last note I can write. Fox plans to kill Mr. Markham. Please
send help.
Signed,
A Loyal British Subject

Lying on his side, head propped on his hand, Adam studied his sleeping wife. A little snore escaped her slightly parted lips, her breath caressed his chest hair. Her riot of chocolate waves fanned out along the pillow and over his forearm.

He captured a strand of hair. Leaning down, he placed a kiss along her temple. She stirred and burrowed close to him, but did not wake. After their energetic round of lovemaking, he should have been sleeping soundly beside her.

Yet tumultuous thoughts kept rest at bay.

She loved him. The quiet whisper had not been the stuff of his imaginings. Nor was it the first time she'd uttered those words, though Adam had not allowed himself to contemplate the significance or sincerity of her declaration. It was easier to ascribe her feelings to those of gratitude.

Or it had been.

Now he was a man conflicted.

He'd thought he'd loved Grace. Following his captivity, he'd had to weather the truth of her betrayal and it had forced him to confront his feelings for her.

Now he could acknowledge that he'd never truly loved Grace. He'd been enamored of her beauty. Appreciated her wit and intellect.

He had cared for her, and her happiness, and he would always think of her with more than mere fondness. She represented a tie to the different person he'd been.

But he'd not been consumed by this swell of emotion that threatened to drag him under and never let him go.

Adam had attributed their close bond to what they had endured. To the courage and power they'd lent each other to survive.

He'd told himself the paltry emotion of love was fleeting and as easy to grasp as a wisp of London fog. He'd told himself he'd not loved Grace because, as Georgina once said to him, "it simply didn't exist." Which, of course, by extension meant he did not love his lovely young wife.

How wrong he'd been.

She whimpered in her sleep, tossing her head on the pillow. A pathetic little moan escaped her and, even in sleep, the muscles in her body tightened as if she were bracing for a blow.

Rage nearly blinded him. He'd battled Fox and Hunter in his own dreams enough to know what tortured his wife's slumber. He pulled Georgina into his arms, willing her to absorb his warmth and strength, and rubbed a circle over her back.

She stilled as though his body's closeness penetrated the haze of her nightmare.

What had Georgina done before they'd married when the nightmares came? He saw her alone, shaking, crying out…and his eyes slid closed in pain. She'd never be alone again. She made him want to slay dragons for her.

He'd cared very deeply for Grace Blakely.

But he loved his wife.

The silent acknowledgement gave him pause.

I love her. I love my wife.

Adam waited for the whisper of panic that such an admission of weakness should cost him. For years, he had erected a wall around his heart. It had been a deliberate effort on his part. He'd known that to care too deeply could only prove fatal if anyone were to learn of his role with The Brethren which is why, even though Grace had meant a good deal to him, he'd never let her inside.

185

His months in captivity had made him realize that he wanted more than a life devoid of warmth.

"I love you," he whispered against her ear.

He waited for the wave of panic to sweep over him.

His exhausted wife slept on, oblivious to his declaration.

A faint scratch at the door drew his attention. He frowned when the sound increased. "Mr. Markham?"

Silence.

Adam cursed under his breath and set Georgina down, careful to disentangle himself from his delectable wife without disturbing her.

He flung his legs over the side of the bed and walked to the door, dragging on his discarded clothes as he padded across the carpeted floor.

Adam pulled it open. "What is it?" he snapped, holding the door closed lest his butler caught sight of Georgina, resplendent in her nudity.

Watson averted his eyes and handed him a note. "You have visitors, sir."

Adam accepted the envelope but when his gaze landed on the seal, he froze.

"I've directed your visitors to your office, sir. Can I be of any further assistance?"

"That will be all," he murmured.

The gold signet on Adam's finger served as a metallic reminder that he belonged to The Brethren. He always would. Adam tamped down the potent blend of frustration, anger, and disappointment that roiled in his gut. Since his dismissal from The Brethren, he'd enjoyed more peace than he'd ever known and, damn it, he wanted to hold onto it as long as he could.

He took a deep breath. Perhaps he was worrying needlessly. Perhaps "The Sovereign" wouldn't ask anything of him.

As he opened the door to his office, he knew he was being foolishly optimistic.

Cedric Bennett stood at the center of the room with his hands clasped behind him. A stranger with a hard, flint-eyed stare stood beside him.

Adam closed the door and turned around. He bowed. "Gentlemen."

Bennett dropped his arms to his side. "Markham." He held a black leather folio in his right hand.

A frisson of unease ran through him. He forced it aside and strode over to the drink cart stationed alongside his desk. "May I offer you a drink?" He held up a crystal decanter of brandy.

Bennett nodded but the tall, brooding stranger beside him shook his head.

Adam pulled the stopper off the bottle. "Gentlemen, how may I be of assistance?"

"Markham, allow me to introduce a fellow member," Bennett drawled. "This is Lord Edward Helling."

Adam started. Amber droplets splashed the wood surface.

Grace's husband?

So Grace had married a member of The Brethren. The scandal sheets had claimed Grace's was a love match. Her father, Blakely, however, was one of the oldest leaders of the organization.

Now Adam wondered if there were more to their union.

Helling's eyes narrowed, as if he'd detected the direction Adam's thoughts had taken. Adam bristled with annoyance of his own. This was no social call. "Gentlemen…"

Bennett held up a hand. "We're here on a matter of importance."

Damn Bennett and his cryptic tone. Adam handed a glass to Bennett who downed it in one swallow. Adam's own throat burned. He curled his fingers into the sides of the cart to keep from reaching for the bottle and pouring a healthy glass for himself.

"Perhaps you should sit, Markham." Helling's voice jerked Adam's attention away from his thirst for spirits.

Bennett nodded and gestured to the leather sofa.

"I don't need to," Adam said.

Bennett and Helling exchanged a look.

"Say whatever it is that brought you here," Adam snapped.

He'd found peace outside The Brethren. He didn't want any part of their world. Not anymore. He had a wife he loved. A wife who, even now, could be carrying his child. His heartbeat sped at the image of Georgina's belly heavy with child. That was the life he wanted. Not—

Bennett held out the folio.

Adam looked at it. A horrific sense of doom lingered in the air. He told himself he was being foolish. He told himself that.

But he didn't believe it.

"You need to understand," Bennett said. "We were operating under assumptions. Had we known anything with absolute certainty we would have intervened."

Adam hesitated then accepted the packet. The book felt heavy in his hands. He turned it over. A pit settled in his stomach, heavy and nauseating.

"Read it, Markham," Helling said, his tone surprisingly gentle.

Adam glanced at Grace's husband. Pity shone in the other man's eyes.

Adam had enough pity from his family. He didn't need it from this man, too. He opened the folio.

Bennett said, "Had we suspected you were in any danger we would have said something immediately. We were not concerned... until now."

A loud buzz filled Adam ears.

His eyes scoured the first page. He read the notes, until he stumbled over the last sentence on the parchment.

Henry Wilcox, known as Fox. Son of an English merchant and Irish mother. Friend and supporter of the United Irishmen.

He turned the page. Snippet after snippet called his attention.

Wilcox, a wealthy merchant.
Georgina Patience Wilcox. Daughter to the Fox
Jamie Marshall, known as Hunter, orphaned son of an Irish merchant. Raised alongside Georgina Wilcox.

Adam's hands shook. The words blurred together. He turned page after damning page.

No!

The folio slipped from his fingers and tumbled to the floor where it landed with a heavy thump.

Bile climbed to the back of his throat. He choked it down. It couldn't be…If this was right, Georgina was a traitor. She bore the blood of his captor. He stared down at the documents on his library floor.

"You're wrong," he choked out.

They had to be, because if they weren't, the beast of madness would devour Adam. Shred him to pieces. He pressed his fingers into his eyes, trying to blot out the ugly truth.

"I read her file. She seems like a good woman," Helling began. Bennett glared at him. "I wish we were wrong," Helling tossed at his superior. Then turned back to Adam. "But it's true, Markham."

"It's not—" Adam rasped.

Bennett interrupted Adam's defense of Georgina. "It is." His tone was harsh and impatient, as though Adam's show of emotion disgusted him.

Adam raked his hand through his hair. Everything he'd known about her had been a lie. He'd flayed himself alive when he'd left her behind in Bristol. He'd married her against his family's insistence.

Oh God. The biting agony nearly dropped him to his knees. *Lies. All lies.*

Bennett and Helling stood by in silence. He suspected they'd seen a great deal in their work, but had they ever seen a man come undone?

He'd wed a bloody traitor. A sweet, impossibly seductive temptress. Oh, the laugh she must have had at his expense.

He thought back to her rushing into his prison, claiming Hunter had attacked her. What if she'd all along been Hunter's lover? A chill stole over him. The niggling possibility grew and grew, and he tortured himself with the idea of Georgina on her knees for Jamie.

Adam spun away and stormed over to the window. He scanned the streets below. For all the lies between them, she had still been a virgin.

So she had the thin barrier of flesh marking her a virgin, a taunting voice jeered. *That doesn't mean she wasn't well versed in how to use her body to steal secrets from unsuspecting fools...*

Good God, he was going to be sick. He gripped the edge of the windowsill and drew in a slow breath. "What now?" he managed past dry lips.

"Nothing. For now," Bennett said.

Adam shook his head and spun around. "Nothing? You'd have me stay married to this traitorous bitch?"

Helling flinched. His obvious reaction only fueled Adam's humiliation.

Oh, she deserved a place on the London stage, his wife! With her trembling lips and tear-filled eyes, she could make the devil himself feel like a scoundrel and swear to protect her.

Bitterness seeped from him as he stared at Helling married to Grace. Beautiful, loyal Grace. And Adam had been saddled with a conniving woman not fit to touch the heel of her slippers.

Bennett rubbed his chin. "We could have a quick trial and have her hanged."

Adam's gut clenched. The other man spoke as if deciding on which cravat to wear to a soiree, not on the fate of Georgina's life.

Bennett continued over Adam's turbulent thoughts. "Should you like, we can take her with us now." There was a slight hesitation there, as though the man wanted or expected Adam to protest.

Nausea turned in Adam's belly.

They had come here today to claim her. They would cart her off to Newgate and execute her as a traitor. He should have welcomed it. Lined up alongside the gallows and cheered as they hanged her... but God he couldn't. Tortured images flashed through his mind; Georgina's lifeless body dancing at the end of a rope while a crowd of loyal subjects watched on in sick fascination. He wanted to send Georgina to the devil for her treachery—but could not. The matching expressions worn by the Brethren indicated they knew as much. "No."

Bennett arched a brow. "No?"

Adam spun around and took a step forward. Then another. And realized…he couldn't flee. There was no escaping this agony. It lanced through him like the edge of a burning torch held against his skin. It seared him, ate at him until his heart went up in flames…and crumbled into ash.

Except…he touched his chest and his heart beat hard and fast beneath his palm. How could it be? How when he felt dead, inside and out?

"No. No trial." Adam's jaw tightened. "Not yet. I'd like to spare my family the scandal. Surely 'The Sovereign' can make my wife…disappear in a way that isn't so public?"

Bennett and Helling exchanged another look. "We can do that," Bennett said after a pause. "Make her disappear."

The silken promise threatened to cleave Adam in two. Even with all she'd done, when he tried to imagine a world without her in it, he found it a world he didn't want to live in. Adam's breath came in quick, gasping pants. "I don't want her killed."

"What do you want, then?" Bennett said with a touch of impatience.

That she should live somewhere with Fox and Hunter where they would continue to aid the Irish in their quest for independence from England? Let them all keep aiding the Irish on their quest for independence from England.

Helling came around and rested a hand on Adam's shoulder.

He shrugged off the gesture of camaraderie. The last thing in the world he wanted to do was commiserate with Grace's husband.

Helling spoke. "It is imperative that you continue to keep your wife in sight. Attend *ton* events—"

A bitter laugh escaped Adam. "With an Irish radical?"

"I'm not saying you have to present a happy façade to the world," Bennett snapped. "Your marriage really isn't all that different from the rest of Society."

With the exception of my deceitful wife who will hang for her crimes.

He fisted his hands at his side to keep from tossing his head back and railing like a tortured demon.

191

He swiped a hand over his face. "I believe we're done here, gentlemen?"

After a round of polite bows, Bennett and Helling left.

He stood and stared at the closed door, welcoming the solitude. He was alone with the bloody file, his tortured thoughts, and—his gaze snagged on the glimmer of crystal—a decanter of brandy.

He picked up Georgina's file, the bottle of spirits and a lone glass, and sat down to read. His lip curled.

Georgina Wilcox, born 14 April 1782.
It would appear his wife had had a birthday since they'd married. A pang of regret pulled at him. He should know such a detail about this woman who'd come to mean more to him than himself. Then, why would she mention such a minute detail when there were so many other great secrets between them?

He scrubbed a hand over his face. It all made sense. Adam had ignored so many obvious unexplained details: her cultured tone, the ease with which she'd mastered the lessons by the dancing instructor he'd hired for her.

He tossed the pages aside and reached for his tumbler of brandy.

He'd only seen what he'd wanted. It had been far easier to view Georgina as a courageous woman in need of rescuing, because it had given him strength. He'd felt less alone in his hellish prison.

Adam poured himself a healthy glassful and did what he swore he'd never do again...

He drank.

NINETEEN

A bolt of lightning split the black, late afternoon sky. The resounding boom of thunder rattled the foundations of the townhouse.

"Come away from that window, Mrs. Markham," her maid, Suzanne, murmured.

"Georgina," she corrected without missing a beat. An ominous foreboding surrounded her, hinting at doom. "It is a bad omen," she whispered.

Suzanne made a comforting sound. "Come away from that window, ma'am. This is the night you'll make your entrance into Society. Surely you must be excited?"

Georgina let the curtain fall back into place. The young maid couldn't be more wrong.

"I need to prepare your hair, Mrs....Georgina," she amended when Georgina glanced back at her.

Panic crashed into her more forcefully than the next boom of thunder to rattle the windowpane. She'd been well-versed in dancing, proper deportment, and all that was expected of a merchant's daughter. This, her entrance into Society, was something altogether different. Georgina Wilcox did not belong in this world. She was only moving forward with the pretense of belonging because of her husband.

She'd not seen him since they'd made love last evening. When she'd awakened, he'd been gone. He'd not come to breakfast. All day she'd waited for him to make an appearance, but he'd been conspicuously absent. Her pride prevented her from asking one of the servants.

Georgina wet her lips. She needed to see him. She sprinted for the door and yanked it open.

"Mrs. Markham?" Suzanne's voice echoed around her but Georgina ignored her as she all but flew down the corridor.

She raced down the stairs as if the devil himself were chasing her, her breath came fast and heavy.

A large figure stepped into her path.

Georgina shrieked as she skidded to a halt in front of Watson.

"Mrs. Markham." He greeted her as if she were casually strolling through the garden and not racing through the house with her curls undone like a woman bound for Bedlam.

She murmured a greeting and stepped around him. This time, she took care to slow her steps, lest she earn any more suspicious looks from the servants. She paused outside her husband's office and then, before her courage deserted her, pressed the handle.

Georgina peeked inside.

She took a deep breath and entered the quiet room. "Adam?" She closed the door. Silence met her query.

She leaned against the wood panel, a frown playing about her lips.

Silence confirmed her misgivings.

She hated this urgent desire to see him. She'd prided herself on not needing anyone these many years. Only, since she'd met and fallen in love with Adam, she had been forced to confront the truth. She didn't want to be alone any longer. She wanted to share the burdens of life with someone else. Her own strength had helped her survive and yet, it had not been any kind of warm, companion for her over the years.

Another rumble of thunder sounded. She shivered and wished her husband was near to chase away this black doom that surrounded her.

Ugly suspicion nibbled at her mind. Adam's aloofness, Jamie's charges about Grace and Adam resuming their relationship, his mysterious absence on the day she would enter Society. Her gaze alighted on his perfectly neat desk. Not a thing out of place. She glanced over her shoulder toward the door and then back to the mahogany desk at the center of the room.

She walked hesitantly over to the desk. "This is wrong," she muttered to herself. "He's given you no reason to mistrust him."

Guilt twisted about her insides. Unlike she who'd betrayed him from their first meeting.

Still…

She tugged open the first draw and sifted through the papers. Business ledgers.

Georgina moved on to the next and rustled through a series of invitations to events. Her guilt doubled. She shook her head. Snooping on her husband…her fingers brushed an oddly coarse sheet. She pulled out the badly burned page. Most of the words had been destroyed. Her heart froze. Stopped beating within her chest. Withered. And died.

Adam, I must speak with you on a matter of utmost importance.
Ever Yours,
Grace

"Can I help you find anything, wife?"

Georgina screeched. The note in her hands danced through the air and fluttered to the floor, the burned note damning.

To her.

To him.

Adam stood framed in the doorway. He glanced at the sheet and then back to her.

Her lips trembled. Attired in the same clothes as yesterday, he looked a good deal more rumpled. His red-rimmed eyes bespoke a sleepless night.

A wave of heat rushed to her cheeks. Goddess-like Grace flitted through Georgina's mind, and Georgina's heart broke open and bled. "Hello." She bit the inside of her cheek hard to stifle the mortified guilt she felt at being discovered going through her husband's private things.

Adam smiled—a cold mirthless grin that iced her veins. She cleared her throat.

He's merely angry that I'm going through his things. He won't hurt me.

But he closed the door, and when he looked back at her there was such loathing in his tightly clenched jaw that a familiar fear licked at her insides, transporting her back to another home, another man. Her husband took a step forward. She retreated. He continued his advance and she backed away, until her shoulder knocked against the wall. The plaster bit into her flesh, but she ignored the dull, throbbing ache.

Adam drew to an abrupt halt. "You didn't answer me, wife." He studied her through hooded eyes.

Had there been a question there? "Uh, I...I..." She curled her fingers tight into the palms of her hands, making crescent marks upon her flesh.

He tapped the bridge of her nose almost teasing and taunting all at once. "Did you find anything of interest?"

Georgina's heart spasamed. She detested this hard, cruel side of a man who'd once been so gentle. "I f-found a note." She'd not allow him to browbeat her. He had as much to answer for as she did in snooping through his things.

Adam inclined his head. "Did you?" he said, a trace of humor lacing his words. He spun around and fetched said note. "This?" He turned back to face her.

She managed a jerky nod.

"Poor, poor Georgina." Except his faintly slurred words sounded anything but sympathetic. "I hadn't intended to hurt you, dear wife." Again, the hard lines at the corners of his eyes, the tight way in which he held his mouth, belied his words.

Georgina went immobile, hoping he'd leave, wishing him gone. This stranger wasn't the man who'd saved her from an empty existence, who'd battled his family for her honor. Tears blurred her vision and she dropped her gaze to his boots. She'd never expected Adam to hurt her. Father and Jamie, yes. Never Adam. And she suspected it would be easier to feel Adam's fists on her flesh than this subtle game of cat and mouse he played with her.

"Adam, I'm sorry. I didn't mean to—"

He pressed a finger to her lips, silencing her. "What exactly are you sorry for?"

Georgina angled her head, the earlier chill of foreboding surging to life as she began to suspect this was about more than being caught looking through his private letters. She opened her mouth, but the words wouldn't come.

Adam's lips flattened into a single, hard line. He spun on his heel. He turned to his desk, reached under the top and popped open a hidden compartment. He pulled out a leather folio.

"Do you know what this is?" He walked around the other side of the desk.

Her mouth went dry. She looked to the packet in his hands.

"Georgina?" he pressed.

She jerked her gaze back to his and shook her head.

Adam propped his hip on the edge of the desk and flipped it open. He perused the inside contents, a cold smile playing about his lips. "I'm a terrible husband. I forgot to wish you a Happy Birthday, wife. It was only last week."

Georgina's dull mind tried to keep up with her husband's confounding words. "I...uh. That is fine." Tony had known. She'd mentioned it to him when they were walking in Hyde Park. He'd insisted on taking her to Gunter's for ices.

Adam's head snapped up so fast she imagined he'd given his head a nasty jolt. "Tell me, Georgina, I've not heard you sing in so long. Why is that?"

Her gaze shifted to a point beyond his shoulder. She'd not sung since the day that he'd twirled her around his prison. Music and the joy it brought had ceased to fit into her world. "I don't know, Adam," she said quietly. She didn't want to speak about those dark days.

"I feel I don't know enough about you. Tell me more about your loving mother and father. What types of servants were they?"

Warning bells of panic clamored inside her head. "Adam?"

He waved the folio about the air. "Your parents, dear wife. I want to know more about these loving pillars of society. Tell me the sweet tales of how you were the darling daughter of two now-dead angels." The faintly jeering note reached her ears.

Georgina crossed her arms and tried to rub warmth back into them. "Why are you doing this, Adam?" she whispered. Why did he assault her with a barrage of questions about her past? Why—? She sucked in a deep breath.

And she knew. Oh God, she knew. Her chest constricted, making breathing difficult.

Adam smiled the same, ice-cold grin he'd worn since he'd discovered her going through his desk.

Her eyes slid closed. *He knows.*

The world was falling down around her, crumbling into ashes and dust, and she was being sucked into the disastrous heap. Still, she clung to the fragile hope that—

"Tell me, Georgina, what name is given to the daughter of a fox? Or," he took a step closer and leaned down, his breath heavy with the scent of brandy, "the mistress of a hunter."

Stars dotted her vision. His words were more devastating than had he dealt her a swift backhand. Georgina's legs buckled and she stretched her hand out, searching for something, anything, to keep her stable, but found no purchase. She sank into a puddle of nothingness at his feet.

Adam took a hasty step away from her, as if even touching her would forever stain him.

"Adam," she whispered. Except there were no answers. No explanations. Nothing she could say would justify her betrayal. Her love would never mean anything to him, not when her father's blood coursed through her veins. But she needed to make him see reason, needed to try. She held a tremulous hand out to him.

He ignored it, directing his attention to the sheets of paper that had destroyed everything. "Do you know what these papers say, Georgina? Do you?" His tone grew harsher.

She shut her eyes tight against Adam's deadened tone.

"You lied to me Miss Wilcox!" he hissed.

She was no longer that woman. She was his wife. Georgina opened her eyes and again reached for him. She'd wronged him with her lies, but she loved him. She would battle the devil himself for her husband. And had fought two demons to help free him from her father and Jamie's clutches. "Adam, I can explain." The words emerged broken and hollow.

Adam flung the damning folio at her. The papers fluttered and danced about her in a mocking remembrance of the scandalous waltz they'd twirled in his too small room in Bristol...days? Weeks? Years?... ago. Tears seeped from her lashes and fell down her cheeks.

"Lies," he hissed. "Everything about you has been a lie."

She shook her head frantically, scrambling to her feet. "No. That's not true. I love you." That had been the one truth, the truth that mattered more than all others—or it had. To her, anyway.

A sharp, barking laugh burst from his lips. Adam clapped his hands together with slow, precise movements. "Brava, my dear. Brava. An act fit for the London stage. Tell me, what exactly are you looking for? Information to bring to your father and lover?"

Georgina blinked back confusion. "My lover?" she repeated dumbly.

"Yes, what is his name? Mr. Jamie Adleyson Marshall." Adam stormed over to the drink cart and splashed several fingers of whiskey into a tumbler. He raised it in mock salute. "I must commend you on a very convincing show when you came to me teary-eyed following his *attack*. Oh, the laugh you must have had about poor, pathetic Adam Markham who tried to comfort you." His face contorted as if in pain. He downed the alcohol in a single swallow.

Georgina rushed to him and clasped his free hand. "Jamie was never my lover." Her skin crawled at the remembrance of Jamie's vile touch.

Adam wrenched free of her then reached for the bottle. He poured another tumbler full. "To be honest, my dear, if you are indeed who these papers claim, I won't care when you're forced to spread your sweet, beautiful thighs for all the guards in your rotting cell at Newgate."

Georgina recoiled at the vile words spewing from his mouth. The image he'd painted took hold—her on her back in a cold, dank cell while man after man took turns violating her. The horrific images nearly blinded her with terror. She told herself he only lashed out at her because he was hurting. It didn't lessen the agony that threatened to rip her apart.

Adam caught her gaze and held it. He drew in an audible breath. "Is Fox your father?"

Georgina's heart tightened. If that was the only question he had for her then he'd never forgive her. She had many regrets, but she'd already realized she could not help the circumstances of her birth. She squared her shoulders and met his gaze. "He is," she said quietly.

Adam hurled his tumbler across the room. It slammed into the wall behind her, spraying Georgina with amber liquid and shards of glass. She winced, fully expecting him to charge her and choke the life from her as he'd first tried to do in her father's house.

Of course, even in his rage, Adam was a different man than her father and Jamie. He spun away, as if the sight of her made him physically ill, drawing in several deep breaths before speaking again. When he did, his words were flat. "I married you against my family's better judgment. I ignored the very obvious signs of your identity, and for that I am to blame." He turned back to face her. "If you think to hurt my family, by God, I'll see you hang. Is that clear?"

The color drained from her cheeks. *How can I mean so little to you? How, when you are the reason for my every joy, my every smile?*

She managed a jerky nod. "It is clear," she choked out.

He turned as if to leave and panicked words bubbled up from her throat. "What will happen to us?" Would he have her thrown in prison? A wave of nausea hit her at the mere thought of life in Newgate. She considered herself a survivor but she would die if sent to the bowels of Newgate.

Adam spun back around, an ugly grin painting the perfect lines of his face. "Come now. You cannot possibly believe I'll stay married to you." He ran a disgusted stare down her person and appeared to find her as wanting as the rest of the people in her life. "You will continue your role as dutiful, sweet, biddable wife. You owe me that much. I will tell you when the time to end this façade arrives. When it does, do not expect anything of me. No money, no references, nothing. You can hang, starve, or sell your lush body, for all I care."

His words scoured her like a dull blade raked along her exposed and already battered heart. She fisted a hand to her mouth to keep from crying out, unable to sort out which was more agonizing: his cruel words or the emotionless way in which he spoke of her death. She reached a hand out in pleading, but he swatted it away.

"There's nothing left to say. Get ready. We have a ball to attend, dear wife."

With that, he spun on his heel, leaving Georgina more shattered and broken than the lone tumbler lying in jagged shards at her feet.

To keep from descending into madness, she fell back into the role she'd assumed for the past years—that of maid. Georgina sank to the floor and began to collect the tiny bits of glass, gathering them into a neat little pile. She welcomed the sting of pain as the occasional shard punctured her skin, even embraced the flood of nausea that her small drops of blood elicited. They reminded her that she was alive. She'd survived twenty years of being beaten, emotionally battered, and unloved at her father's hands, and she would survive this too.

A sob escaped her. The tears flowed as her body was wracked by convulsive gasps of despair. This was so very different from the hurt she'd known at her father's hands. He was a vile, greedy traitor. Adam was good, and honest, and caring. And he'd made her believe in love. He'd made her believe there was goodness in the world.

Only now did she confront the truth, the ugly reminder that the Lord had decided she was a person undeserving of love and happiness.

She buried her head in her hands, weeping until her ribs ached and her throat burned.

He expected her to don her lovely sea-foam green gown and paste a smile to her face. The urge to run was strong. Her gaze darted around the room in search of valuables. Surely, she could take enough of value and be gone? Flee this world of false happiness and go somewhere...

"If you could go anywhere, where would you go?"

"Why bother, Adam? Dreams aren't real."

"Surely you must have dreams?"

"Dreams are for small children."

"Wouldn't you want to see Paris?"

"We're on the cusp of war with France," she pointed out. *"I hardly think Paris would be my best destination."*

He waved his hand. *"Fine, Rome then, or Greece. Don't you want to see the world?"*

The whisperings of that day were so vivid it was like being transported to the small chambers that had served as Adam's prison.

He'd asked where she would go...but she was in the only place in the world she would ever want to be.

And it was the one place she would never be allowed to stay.

TWENTY

Georgina had tucked herself into the corner of the spacious carriage bearing them to Lady Ashton's ball for her introduction into Society. She had the look of a small fox burrowing within the fabric of her shimmering blue cloak as though she feared he'd reach over and strangle her.

The image she evoked raised the ugly reminder of who she was. Fox's kin—his enemy and captor's daughter.

Adam directed his attention outside to the passing scenery. That way he didn't have to see her ashen cheeks and those wide, wounded, brown eyes. When she looked at him as if he'd torn apart her world, his insides roiled with remorse. Adam reminded himself that Georgina's misery was of her own making. He told himself her tears were the practiced tools of a skilled actress.

None of that mattered; guilt threatened to rip him apart. It only made him that much more enraged…with himself. With her. With all of it. Not even the bottle of whiskey he'd consumed that day had managed to quash the dull hurt.

How dare she look at him as if he'd betrayed her? Not when she'd been the one to deceive him from the moment they'd first met, the one who'd lured him in and trapped him into this sham of a marriage.

Bennett had assured Adam the marriage would be dissolved—either by Georgina's death or upon special orders from the king himself.

The promise should have eased Adam's troubled mind. Instead, whenever he thought of her gone from his life, it felt like his heart had withered and died within his chest. He told himself his reservations stemmed from a fear of the way the dissolution would reflect on his mother and brothers. The words rang hollow in his mind.

The carriage drew to a halt. Adam peered out the window at the long line of guests before them.

He gritted his teeth. Bloody wonderful. Just what he needed: more time alone with his wife.

Wife.

His lip curled and he dropped the curtain back into place.

"Here we are," he said flatly. "Are you prepared to use your skills to charm the lords and ladies this evening?" She opened her mouth to speak, but he cut into her response. "Do you fear being viewed as an interloper?" he asked viciously.

With her grace and elegance, no one could take her for anything but a lady.

That irascible, brown tendril escaped the artful arrangement of curls atop her head. She brushed it back, angling her chin upwards. "I've lived through a good deal more than the haute *ton*. The last thing I fear is their treatment of me."

Ah, how very brave his wife was. He could detect the faint tremble in her words and yet she spoke with resolve and courage.

He gripped the edge of the seat and he blinked back the effects of too much alcohol.

Bloody Georgina for making him turn to the bloody alcohol. He raised a brow. "Am I supposed to feel bad for you, Georgina?"

She tilted her chin back another notch. "I don't want your pity."

Damn her for not giving him the fight he'd been spoiling for since he'd left her alone in his office. It would be far easier to hate her if she were victorious in her deceit. Instead, she appeared broken, and it was playing havoc with his heart and mind.

They didn't speak until their carriage arrived at the front of the line. Adam leaned across the carriage and Georgina flinched. Her gaze darted around the carriage like a battered animal seeking escape. Adam recoiled. He could not forgive her. But he'd never lay his hands on her. How could she believe he'd ever harm her?

Adam held a finger up. "My mother and brothers are working very hard to see you accepted into Society. Do not shame them this night. Is that clear?"

She gave a jerky nod. "H-how…w-what…?"

"Yes?" he demanded when she fell silent.

Georgina studied her folded hands. "W-will you stand beside me?"

"Georgina, it hardly matters if we are seen as a happy couple. Members of the *ton* would be more repulsed if we showed affection. Therefore, our animosity will be perfectly suited."

She flinched. "I have no animosity toward you."

The driver opened the carriage door, saving him from uttering words that would surely crumple her already pained face. He directed his attention toward the front of the townhouse, not even deigning to offer Georgina his hand.

They climbed the steps in complete silence. Adam took great pains to avoid any physical contact with his wife, concentrating his efforts on putting one drunken foot in front of the other. The slow pace he set for himself allowed Georgina to match his stride.

They moved into the receiving line and awaited their turn to greet the host and hostess.

Their names were called. A sea of rabidly curious eyes fixed on him and Georgina. He stole a glance at her from the corner of his eye and found her remarkably composed. It was also the first time he'd seen her in the sea-foam green gown selected by his mother. With the subtle flare of her hips and the lush spill of her bosom, Georgina had the look of a sea nymph.

As if she felt his stare, Georgina looked up at him.

He returned his gaze to the crowd below. The moment they were introduced, Adam and Georgina descended the steps and wound their way through a crush of guests.

Bevies of disapproving scowls were directed at his wife, but the cool contempt did not seem to penetrate Georgina's stoic expression.

His mother and brothers came into focus. Tony raised his hand in greeting and all but elbowed his way through the crowd to meet them.

"Poor fool's been charmed by you. Ten times the fool he is," he muttered beneath his breath.

A graying matron nearby gasped behind her hand, her eyes widened in delighted shock at being privy to such intimate words. The old harridan rushed off, most likely to share good gossip with anyone who would listen.

Georgina's pallor turned a sickly shade of white and she looked at him with accusing eyes.

I will not feel bad. I will not feel bad.

In spite of the silent mantra, his gut churned.

Then Tony was there, beaming a broad smile for Georgina. He bowed. "Hullo, sis! You look even more stunning than usual." He claimed her hand for a kiss. A hissing gasp escaped her. Tony frowned, turning her hand over.

Georgina pulled her fingers back and dipped a curtsy. Red surged to her cheeks. "Thank you," she said softly.

Adam gritted his teeth. On any other day, with any other woman, it should have been him showering compliments on his wife...not his brother. He and Georgina, however, were no more than two souls bound by lies and deception.

Georgina lifted her gaze to his and Adam tore his eyes away. He'd not be duped by the façade of innocence she wore.

Mother and Nick appeared.

Adam greeted his mother with a deep bow and nearly tipped over, flat upon his face.

"Whoa," Nick said, helping right him.

Adam grinned. "Are you here to pay respects to my lovely wife?"

Mother and Nick exchanged a look.

"Come, nothing to say to my beautiful, loyal wife?" he prodded.

Georgina bit her lower lip, tears pooling in her eyes.

"What's the matter with you?" Tony asked, taking a step toward him.

Adam stumbled a bit but closed the distance between him and Tony. So this was how it was to be? He would now fight his brother in public for this lying traitor?

By God, she is not worth it.

He took a step back.

His mother smiled through gritted teeth. "Adam, I must insist that you stop right now." She had the same look in her eyes that she'd had the day he'd collected a basket of frogs and released them during a dinner party at their country estate.

Nick directed a frown at Georgina. "I would like to request the first dance." He shot a look at Adam. "That is, if your husband doesn't mind?"

Adam chuckled. "Not in the least. Take her. Please take her."

Mother's eyes went round as saucers.

Nick glared at him. "Come, join me for refreshments," he said when Tony took a step forward, most likely to lay him flat in Lady Ashton's ballroom.

Said like that, in his very earl-like tone, Adam had little choice but to follow along, leaving his mother and Tony alone with the vicious viper he'd married.

The two brothers wound their way through the throng of guests, Adam taking pains to ignore the greetings and well-wishes directed his way, responding with a glare for anyone without the sense to leave him alone.

Adam reached for a flute of champagne, but Nick plucked it from his fingers swifter than a pickpocket from the Seven Dials. "I think you've had enough," he said between clenched teeth, taking a refined sip of the bubbling brew.

Adam's throat went dry and need gripped him. "Give me the bloody glass."

Nick finished the contents of the crystal flute in one long swallow. A servant materialized as if out of thin air, and Nick placed the empty glass on the tray and waved the young man away.

His brother said nothing for a long while. When he did, his words were so faint they barely reached Adam's ears. "I don't care if you have suddenly realized your foolish error in wedding Miss Wilcox. It is something that cannot be undone. So put a smile on your bloody face, conduct yourself in a respectable manner, and get back to her side."

Without waiting for a response, Nick turned on his heel and disappeared through the crowded ballroom.

Adam stared after him. He would rejoin his wife. But first...

He reached for a glass of champagne.

First, he'd have another drink.

Once upon a time, she'd had grand dreams of her entrance into Bristol's society of merchants. She would be courted by handsome, witty, kind, young gentlemen. They would shower her with flowers and write odes to her otherwise non-existent beauty.

Those dreams had died a swift death when she'd made her debut.

Remarkably, her introduction into London Society would appear to be an even greater disaster. Adam was soused. He was slurring horrible, hurtful things for the ears of any and all who happened to be near and—she glanced around—in this crush, everyone was near.

Then, of course, there were the sneers dripping with noble condescension from the ladies. Georgina couldn't decide which was worse—the ladies' haughty stares or their husbands ogling her embarrassingly plump bosom. She tamped down the urge to fold her arms and shield herself.

Thankfully, Tony had not left her side. Even the Countess of Whitehaven remained staunchly at her elbow.

Georgina would never be able to repay them. She bit the inside of her cheek. Repay them? When her identity was revealed and she was landed in Newgate, all she would bring to these lovely people was greater shame and heartache.

"How about a dance?" Tony asked, not for the first time.

Georgina shook her head. "N-no. Thank you. I..." Her words trailed off as an exceedingly handsome couple appeared on the stairway. They possessed the utter perfection that artists would salivate to replicate on canvas. The tall, muscular gentleman attired all in black had drawn the notice of every single lady in the ballroom.

Not Georgina. Her eyes were fixed on the golden Athena at the dark stranger's elbow. Tall, lithe, and impossibly elegant, she was everything Georgina was not.

Georgina had committed that face to memory many months ago. Grace Blakely.

In this sea of strangers, Grace appeared to be scouring the room, searching, searching, before her eyes alighted on a single person. Georgina told herself not to look, but she could no sooner stop her heart from beating than resist the pull. She followed Grace's violet gaze right to Adam.

He had the look of a man who'd been cleaved in two by a mighty sword.

The pain of their reunion sucked the air from Georgina's lungs. She swayed on her feet.

The countess gasped, reaching out just as Tony did to keep her standing.

"Are you all right?" Tony asked, his voice coming as if down a long hall.

She stared blankly through the crowd at Adam, punishing herself with the emotion in his expressive eyes laid bare for all to see. Regret. Pain. Loss. Anger. He read like a book, and she wanted to rip out the bloody pages and grind them beneath her heel.

"Are you all right, my dear?" This time it was Adam's mother.

Georgina shook her head. "I-I..." She needed to get away from this. From all of this. If she continued to stand there, she would collapse amongst a crowd that would like nothing better than to shred her to pieces. She did what she'd longed to do since their arrival. She walked away. Moving through the crowd. Disregarding the stares. Ignoring Tony calling after her.

There had to be somewhere she could go for some privacy. She darted between perfect strangers and passed down long corridors.

When the din of the crowded ballroom was no more than a distant hum, she glanced over her shoulder, feeling blessedly free. Georgina continued on to the nearest room and shoved the door open.

She shut it behind her. Leaning against the protective barrier, she closed her eyes and sighed.

"Well, well, Mrs. Markham. It would appear we meet again," a cultured voice drawled.

Her eyes popped open. A scream climbed up her throat but went nowhere. She pressed her hand to her pounding heart and stared back at the Duke of Aubrey.

He sat on their host's sofa, drinking the man's brandy, looking for all the world as though it were his own palace. The duke held his glass up in mock salute but made no move to rise.

Georgina clenched and unclenched her hands. A sinister darkness clung to him and the last thing she needed was more of what this hardened man represented. She started to leave.

"Please stay, Mrs. Markham. I find myself in need of good company as well."

She paused. "And you've decided I'm good company?" She couldn't keep the bitter words from spilling off her tongue.

He took a small sip, smiling around the rim of his glass. "I've decided you are better company than most of the people out there."

Her brow furrowed. "Oh, and you've reached such an exalted opinion from all of our meaningful exchanges?" Georgina bit the inside of her cheek, wishing she could call the mocking words back.

The duke laughed.

She didn't know what possessed her to remain here with this stranger, baiting him. Logic told her to turn on her heels and flee to the nearest empty room. Something kept her back. Her toes curled in her slippers at the image of Adam and Grace indelibly burned in her mind. If she returned to the ballroom, she'd have to confront the pain of watching her husband pine for his lost love.

"I like you, Mrs. Markham."

Georgina said nothing. She hadn't quite made up her mind about the duke. She'd heard Tony's low opinion of the roguish peer but had long ago learned to form her own opinions, basing them on more than mere gossip and happenstance.

The duke finished his glass and reached for the decanter. He held it up. "Would you like a glass?"

She shook her head. "No, thank you." She'd seen what spirits had done to her father, Jamie, and now Adam, and had no interest in turning over her self-control, even for liquid fortitude. "I should leave." It would not do for them to be discovered alone together. She nearly choked on a mirthless giggle as she imagined being found with the young duke. Oh, the gossips would just love such a succulent tidbit.

Your husband would only care about how it reflects on his family, a cruel voice jeered inside her heart.

"Yet you stay." He made the observation like a scientist discovering the planetary secrets.

Georgina bit her lip to keep from saying that the only reason she stayed was because she preferred one beast over several hundred.

"Tell me, did you read any of the book I recommended?" he asked.

A stray curl fell over her eye. She brushed it back into place. "I didn't." With her marriage and life falling apart, she'd not put much effort into reading. "Furthermore, it's been but a day, Your Grace." She bit the inside of her cheek at that insolent response that slipped past her lips.

His lips twitched with the faintest hint of mirth. He inclined his head. "You strike me as an intelligent woman. Do you ever give much thought to the revolutionary principles that took shape in Ireland?"

Georgina's heartbeat sped up. Warning bells went off in her head and all her earlier fears of being discovered with Jamie resurfaced. "I-I'm sorry?"

Hard lips twitched upward in a smile. "You do know there was a revolution in France, don't you?"

"Of course I know there was a war," she snapped.

He raised a brow.

Georgina bowed her head.

This man is a duke. He can destroy you faster than a dog finishing off a discarded bone.

"Forgive me," she said quietly. "I—"

The duke waved off her apology. "I don't offend easily." She suspected that was a lie.

He leaned forward in his chair, propping his elbows on his knees. "I am curious what you think about the Society of United Irishmen."

It was hardly the conversation for a young woman and a powerful noble. Women were groomed to discuss polite topics such as the weather and music. But no one had ever asked her where her political beliefs resided. It had always been expected that she ascribe to whatever political ideologies her father held. Father. Jamie. Adam. They all seemed to think that the blood in her veins determined the direction of her heart and mind.

Georgina sidled deeper into the room, drawn by the possibility of speaking her own thoughts. "I believe there were great benefits to the democratic reforms put forth by the society," she began. "I also believe there were merits to the French vision of *liberté, égalité, fraternité*, but powerful men manipulated and distorted the visions and hopes for the people." She looked him square in the eye. "England is great. It is not perfect, but that does not mean I love it any less, Your Grace. It is not blind loyalty that ties me to England. It is a belief that it is a good, fair country." She fell silent, realizing at some point she'd ceased to answer the question and had begun to ramble, carried along by the strong desire for someone to hear her, even if it was just a bored nobleman with too much curiosity.

The duke gave her an enigmatic grin that would have set most ladies' hearts aflutter. "I'm never wrong, Mrs. Markham."

Her lips twitched. She supposed arrogance went along with the esteemed title of Duke. "I beg your pardon?"

He set his glass down on the table beside him and stood. "I said I liked you and you've only confirmed that I was indeed correct about your character."

"And you know all of that from our very concise conversation?" She heard the skepticism in her own voice.

"I imagine your husband will be looking for you."

"He won't..." she started then promptly clamped her lips shut.

"He won't what?" the duke asked gently.

"You are correct. I should be going."

Georgina didn't wait for a proper dismissal, merely curtsied then fled the Marquess of Ashton's opulent library.

She closed the door behind her and jumped when the faint echo of footsteps reached her ears. Squinting down the dark hall, she tried to determine the direction of this newest interloper so she might avoid him…or her.

It was too late. "Hello, my lord," she whispered.

Her brother-in-law, the Earl of Whitehaven, frowned, his familiar emerald gaze going to the door behind her. "I'm looking for my brother."

So much for pleasantries. She brushed her warm palms along her silken skirts. "I haven't seen him since we arrived."

Suspicion darkened his eyes to a dark jade. "What were you doing in our host's library?"

Georgina gave her curls a little toss. "That is none of your business, my lord."

His mouth hung open. Apparently, he didn't expect that meek, biddable Georgina would ever defy his orders. Well, good. The earl could go hang along with everyone else who'd treated her worse than a common street whore. He snapped his jaw closed and took a step toward her.

Georgina held her ground. She'd had enough of men using their strength to bend her to their will.

The earl pointed a finger at her. "I don't know what you did to hurt my brother, but he's begun drinking again. By God, you'll make it right."

Pain and regret clogged her throat. She'd never meant to hurt Adam, yet her lie of omission had turned him from a rational, caring man to a cold, heartless stranger dependent on a bottle.

Her brother-in-law pounced on her guilty silence. "Have you taken a lover?"

"No!" Georgina gasped, pressing a palm to her heated cheek. She could never, ever think of lying with another man. Not after the magic she'd known in Adam's skilled arms.

The earl's lip curled. He leaned down so close she could see the pores of his skin. "I suggest you go find your husband. Now. And, you should know, I don't believe you. Whoever he is, end it. Or I will destroy you." With that dark promise, he spun on his heel and left.

Georgina stared after him. With all those intent on destroying her, she really didn't have much of a chance at survival.

Her shoulders drooped in defeat and she set out to find her husband.

TWENTY-ONE

A dam stared out across the ballroom floor. Dancers twirled and swirled in rapid circles down jaunty lines until his head spun with dizziness.

Or mayhap it was the alcohol. He took another swallow of champagne. His gaze landed on a young lady with a crop of dark curls and his heart lifted.

Until she turned and he realized it wasn't his wife.

And then he realized he was searching for his wife.

He took another drink and found his glass empty.

The raucous laughter and twittering giggles of eager young debutantes made him want to gnash his teeth, clamp his hands over his ears and drown out the repellent din. With his world dashed to crumbling ruins, it seemed unfathomable that anyone should find amusement in anything.

Earlier that day, when he'd confronted Georgina with the file given him by Bennett, a part deep inside Adam had clung to the fragile thread of hope that it had all been a great big lie perpetuated by The Brethren.

Until she'd uttered that two-word confirmation about her father, he'd believed in her. He'd imagined the conversation playing out so very different. He would have presented her the information, asked her for the truth. She would have been shocked and hurt that he could ever think a traitor's blood flowed through her veins. He would fall to his knees, beg her forgiveness, and they would carry on as they'd been before.

How utterly naïve he'd been. A bloody fool was more like it.

An elegant woman moved into his line of vision. Her flaxen hair caught his eye, glinting like spun-gold in the glow of the candles.

Like a deer caught in a snare, Grace Helling froze. Her gaze flitted around the room until she found Adam. Her lips turned up in a tremulous smile. He ripped his eyes away.

While he'd been captive, this woman had married another member of The Brethren. Her laugh, husky and sweet, reached his ears even through the loud hum of conversations. Adam was besieged by the sting of regret and anger. While he'd tied himself to his captor's daughter, Grace had found herself in a perfectly happy, uncomplicated union.

And he wanted that. Not with Grace, but with an undeserving, lying Georgina.

Adam cursed. The graying matron beside him gasped and snatching her skirts away, walked off in a flurry.

He was making a proper ass of himself. The morning papers would quite gleefully report on the scene made by Mr. and Mrs. Markham, but he couldn't drum up the smallest vestige of concern. The sting of Georgina's betrayal ate at his thoughts. At any moment, The Brethren could appear with a determination of her fate. As much as he wanted to punish her, as much as he wanted her to hurt as he was hurting, the thought of her life being snuffed out as easily as the flame of a candle threatened to destroy him.

Adam needed to spend less time wallowing in his own misery and more time keeping a close eye on his wife—Fox's daughter.

A servant appeared, and he handed his glass off to the young man, waving off a filled flute. Walking the perimeter of the ballroom, he searched the crowd, doing a rapid scan for the voluptuous beauty who'd broken his heart. It took him only moments to realize she was suspiciously missing. With a silent curse, Adam headed for his host's alcoves.

When he turned up empty from his search, he moved outside to the empty balcony. The crisp, cool air filled his senses, pushing back the liquored haze he'd put himself in. His eyes struggled to adjust to the thick, starless night.

Then he saw her.

His breath caught. She stood there all tall, lithe elegance, her beauty even greater than he'd remembered. Her lips were turned up in a sorry rendition of a smile.

He only managed one word. "Grace."

If he and Grace were discovered, the scandal would be great—for his entire family. The last thing he could do after all the misery he'd caused was create further heartache. There was also Georgina to consider. It shouldn't have mattered if his wife discovered him with Grace, but—damn him for having a bloody conscience—he cared. He made to leave.

"Don't go!" Grace cried out. "Please."

It was that last pathetic word that halted him mid-stride.

He turned. She held a hand up, outstretched to him as if she'd wrapped a string around him to draw him to her.

And perhaps she had, because—against his better judgment—Adam moved forward, toward the woman who'd once claimed his heart.

He froze in front of her, acutely aware that she was only a few inches shorter than his six foot two.

She cocked her head. "I've missed you, Adam."

Her betrayal should not have mattered any longer, and yet it did. It served as a reminder that the women who had claimed to love him were nothing more than self-serving creatures who only thought of their own happiness. He twisted his lips in an attempted smile. "Not enough to wait for me."

She flinched and a single tear streaked down her cheek. "I thought you were dead. They told me you were dead."

Adam arched a brow. "Oh? Who are they?"

Grace wiped the tear away. "Come, Adam, surely by now you have figured out who I am? *What* I am?" She looked at him meaningfully.

And of course, he knew. Oh, it had taken him some time to piece it all together, but he'd eventually gathered that Grace Blakely was, in fact, a member of The Brethren. It was the perfect ruse. Who would ever expect Grace, the daughter of a Viscount, to be a member of a spy organization?

Adam frowned. "I really don't think there is anything left for us to say. You are married. And I…"

I have Georgina.

"And you are married," Grace finished his thought for him. She reached up and caressed his cheek. "Are you…happy?"

Guilt curled around his stomach as he imagined how Georgina would feel if she discovered him with Grace.

Why do you care?

Georgina was guilty of enough lies and deceit to fill the bloody Thames.

Yet, somehow, for reasons both unfathomable and frustrating, he did care.

He needed to leave.

So why did he stay?

"Did you ever think of me?" Grace asked. The question contained a forlorn note of despair that threatened to run his confounded emotions ragged.

"What do you want from me, Grace? Do you want to hear that I thought of you every day during my captivity?" He scoffed. "That when I found out you'd married, I became a bitter shadow of the person I had been?" Is that what she wanted?

Grace stretched a hand toward him. "No, I…" Her gloved fingers fell to her side. "I loved you. I need you to know that."

He raised a cynical brow. "What good is that supposed to do me, Grace? We're both married." For as long as The Brethren saw fit. His heart convulsed with a painful spasm.

Fool! I'm a bloody fool!

"I just want to know that you're happy." Grace tilted her head back and the rosewater that clung to her skin bathed his senses, carrying him back to a place and time, long before Georgina and her father had upended his world.

He spoke, his words coming out heavy. "Why does it matter?"

Tears clouded her eyes. "It does. I need to know one of us is," she whispered.

Adam closed his eyes.

Grace is also trapped in an empty, loveless marriage.

He'd imagined he would feel elated to know that she was miserable. But he didn't. He wanted her to be happy, because at one time he'd cared very deeply for her. Even now, he still cared. He couldn't just shut the door on all they'd shared.

So he opened his eyes.

And lied to her.

"I'm happy."

She tilted her head. "You're certain. Because I've read that—"

He interjected. "I'm happy, Grace."

She smiled and her violet eyes sparkled with real joy. Leaning up, she placed a faint kiss on his lips. Her breath melded with his.

There was none of the fire that accompanied his and Georgina's lips meeting. Just—

A chorus of shocked gasps and cries penetrated his thoughts. He spun and faced the crowd of spectators.

When he looked back at Grace, he found all the color had leeched from her cheeks and followed her gaze to his fellow Brethren—Edward Helling.

Helling's lips were flattened in a single, hard line. The sea of bleeding hurt in the other man's eyes jabbed at Adam as he wrestled with the unwelcome truth that he was responsible for that look, that pain, that hurt betrayal. Adam glanced away.

His heart fell somewhere in the vicinity of his toes.

Georgina stood just beyond Helling's shoulder. Her full, red lips were rounded in a moue of shock. Had she taken a bullet to the heart, she could not have looked more surprised.

Their hostess, Lady Ashton, stood amongst the crowd. She fanned herself rapidly, eying the scandal unfolding on her balcony. "Oh, my. Oh, my."

Observers continued to appear, including Nick, who quickly took in the scene, and ended it with his ducal authority. "I suggest we all return to our lovely hostess's ballroom. The entertainment within is a good deal more amusing than this dull meeting," Nick said.

Those present shuffled off the balcony with clear reluctance in their slow steps.

With the throng of voyeurs gone, only the two married couples remained.

Grace reached a hand out to her husband. "Edward," she whispered.

As if awakening from a long slumber, Helling gave his head a quick shake and stalked away.

A ragged cry escaped Grace as she ran after him.

Georgina stared down at the tips of her slippers.

"Georgina," Adam said.

She looked up and Adam inclined his head in greeting.

His wife didn't say anything, just continued to stand there with shocked hurt in her soulful, brown eyes. His insides twisted.

Why do I care so much? Why, after all you have put me through, does the sight of your trembling lip make me want to drop to my knees and plead forgiveness for even an imagined offense?

Her voice broke. "Are you deliberately trying to humiliate me?"

He ground his teeth. Is that what she cared about? How this appeared to Society? It doused his sympathy and quashed his regret. "Is this about you? Is it all about you?"

She shook her head. "N-no." A lone tear slid down her cheek.

"No?" He advanced angrily, swiping a hand at the air. "I wasn't betraying you with Grace." Joy lit her eyes, brighter than the moon that peeked from behind the clouds. "Does that make you happy? That you have me wound around your sweet, little finger?"

The happiness in her eyes faded, giving way to the shadow of doubt. "No," she rasped.

"Were you spying on me?" he barked.

Georgina shook her head and curls tumbled out of her artful arrangement of chocolate brown locks. Two long strands of silken hair nestled in the crevice of her full, white bosom.

His breath caught. In spite of it all, he wanted to lay her bare and make love to her until he drove reality from their life, until nothing but sated desire remained.

Suddenly he needed her. Right or wrong. He needed her like a starving man craved food.

Adam started forward. He stopped in front of Georgina. A mere hairsbreadth separated them, but it may as well have been the Nile for all the space between them.

He pulled her into his arms and their lips met in an explosion of angry desire. He yanked her skirts up with one hand then shoved down her chemise. He worked the flap open on his breeches and his shaft sprang free. Georgina moaned and reached down between them to caress his shaft. She took it in her long fingers and stroked him up and down. With a groan, he arched into her skilled hands.

He parted her thighs and—there against Lord Ashton's stone wall, with the tinkling echo of the orchestra playing in the far distance— claimed her, plunging deep inside her welcoming heat.

Her head fell backwards as she bucked against him. Adam thrust, once, twice, their flesh slapping hard in a relentless meeting of skin. "It's not enough," he rasped.

He spun her around and bending her low against the balustrade nestled his manhood at the base of her buttocks. She whimpered, rocking her hips against him, searching.

"I want you." He bit her shoulder.

She cried out.

"I want all of you, Georgina. Even as I want to hate you. I cannot." He slipped inside inch by agonizing inch. "Tell me you want me."

"I do," she whimpered and with a hard thrust he pushed deep. "I've always wanted you."

His eyes slid closed as her words washed over him. She could not ever love him as he loved her. Even with her deception and lies and the truth of her birth…he loved her. And he hated himself for it. She accepted every single inch of him. She squeezed him with clever inner thigh muscles, milking his shaft.

Adam flexed his hips.

Georgina gasped, buckling against him. But he wouldn't let her fall. He gripped the sides of her hips and kept her upright, continuing to grind against her.

She pushed back as if trying to get closer to him, and it felt like blissful revenge that she should ache for him, that she was as tortured as he would be until he drew his last breath on this cruel earth. He would fuck her and leave. But for now he'd take what was his. He pumped his hips again. Hard. Punishing her with merciless strokes. She didn't complain. She moaned loud enough to attract the notice of any person happening to pass by. He didn't care.

"I love you," Georgina moaned, arching against him.

He continued to plow into her, ignoring her breathy declaration.

Her head fell forward as she bowed to his masterful conquering. "I want you. Even if you do not you want me," she breathed.

Adam nipped her lobe hard. He clenched his jaw to call back the words of love on his own lips. He could not bare himself to her. Not again.

She angled her head over her shoulder, looking at him through passion-glazed eyes. "How can someone who hates me make me feel like all I want in the world is right here?"

Ah, Georgina. I hate that you've lied to me. I don't know how we can go on with all the mistruths between us. But I can never hate you.

"No more talking," he demanded, his tone pleading to his own ears.

Adam filled his palms with her pale, plump breasts, rubbing the pebbled nipples between his thumb and forefinger. A spasm coursed through her body, and he felt it all the way to his shaft buried in her hot, honeyed core. It fueled his erection, sent blood rushing to his member.

She flung her head back, and her chocolate curls came undone in a cascade about them. "Yes, Adam!"

Adam grunted, feeling like a primal beast taming his mate. He continued to plow her. Harder. Deeper.

"Tell me you want me," he demanded roughly, gripping her hips hard in his hands. Suddenly, it mattered very much that he knew she wanted him. He needed to know that her body and heart both ached with the same agonizing intensity.

She moaned in response. It wasn't enough. He needed her to say it aloud. Needed her to know that for all her deceit and all her treachery, in this moment he was the one in complete and supreme control. "Tell me, Georgina," he repeated. He pulled out of her.

She raised sooty lashes to look at him. Desire blazed in her fathomless eyes. "Only you. I only want you." Her hips pumped as if seeking him.

He closed his eyes tight as her words washed over him and in that moment he allowed himself to believe the truth of those words. When nothing but lies had ever existed between them, he believed she'd never wanted anyone but him.

He slammed into her on a groan, his shaft convulsed in rippling tides of spent desire. Georgina's body went rigid in his arms as she toppled over the precipice of ecstasy. Their breathy moans blended long after they'd reached sexual release.

Adam pulled away. Dropping her skirts, he stuffed himself back inside his breeches.

Georgina leaned over the balustrade, clinging to it as if it were the only thing keeping her from falling over. She panted roughly, while the round swell of her buttocks was presented to him like a carnal feast. Hunger roared through him and his shaft stirred at the sight.

Adam swiped a hand over his eyes, agony lanced his heart. Georgina had managed to penetrate his every defense. She'd crept inside his heart, mind, and now it would seem he didn't even have control over his body's cravings.

Words of love died on his lips.

He had to sever this connection, or she would use it to destroy him.

"Thank you for that, sweet Georgina."

She sucked in a gasping breath, Adam straightened his jacket… and left with a feeling that he was as cruel and evil as the men who'd imprisoned him.

Georgina heard the steady click of her husband's fast-retreating steps until they were no more than an echo bouncing around inside her head.

She focused on that curt, staccato rhythm for it saved her from thinking about the vile, ugly words he'd hurled at her only moments after demonstrating such beautiful mastery of her body. Stopped her from focusing on the fact that he'd taken her like a common street whore in a place where anyone could have seen them. And that she'd panted and moaned just like the whore he thought her to be.

Georgina became aware of the jagged stone biting into her flesh, cold and unyielding—just like her husband's heart. She shoved herself back from the wall with a gasping sob. Tears fell down her cheeks and chest to stain the ground.

Her hair hung in a riot of untamed curls. She could only imagine the sight she made. If anyone were to see Adam Markham's new wife good and tousled, as if she'd been taken against a stone wall...A cackling laugh escaped her that would surely have seen her committed to Bedlam had anyone heard it.

She buried her face in her hands and wept until her lungs ached. When she'd stumbled upon the tableau of Adam with his former love, her already broken heart had lost another layer. Then he'd confessed that nothing untoward had happened. Even though Georgina had seen them with their lips pressed against each other's, she'd not thought of anything but his denial. What reason had Adam to lie? He'd already demonstrated he had few qualms when it came to hurting her with words. So why not let her believe he had been about to make love to Grace?

He had taken her into his arms and made almost violent love to her body. And she'd let him. Because she loved him and, shamefully, because she'd wanted it as much as he had. Mayhap more.

Now, Georgina had to acknowledge the truth—her husband would never forgive her and most certainly never love her.

She had to leave. The host's library would no longer suit. Drawing in a deep, steadying breath, she swiped her hands across her cheeks, wiping away the evidence of her grief.

Georgina bent down to retrieve her scattered hairpins then set to work righting herself as best as possible.

"Hullo? Georgina?"

At the familiar voice, her body turned to stone. "Tony."

He stood six feet away. He widened his eyes. The horror in blue-green irises so much like Adam's told her exactly how she looked with her flyaway hair and badly rumpled skirts.

When he spoke, his words were surprisingly devoid of emotion. "My brother thought it best if I had your carriage brought round."

Her heart surged. "He did?" For all his anger, Adam had still thought of her.

Tony averted his gaze to a point beyond her shoulder. "Nick did," he said almost apologetically.

"Oh, of course. Thank you," she finished dumbly, as a wave of heat coursed to her cheeks. Of course her husband hadn't thought of her after he'd stalked off. She hated the lash of pain at such a truth.

Tony held out his arm. "I know a way to the entrance that won't take you through the ballroom."

"Thank you," she whispered.

Georgina hurried over and took his arm. She allowed him to steer her on a winding path through the house. They reached the foyer. A servant was waiting to assist her into the almost luminescent aquamarine cloak. Georgina tugged the hood up, relishing even the small protection from any potential witnesses.

She had her foot out the door when Tony called out to her. "I'm sorry," he said gruffly.

Georgina held up a wavering hand in farewell. "Thank you for everything."

He looked like he'd say more, so she fled to the carriage. The middle of Lord and Lady Ashton's foyer in view of gossiping servants was no place to discuss anything.

A footman opened the door to the spacious carriage and assisted her inside.

The door jerked closed with such speed, she gasped. She pushed her hood off.

Her heart puttered to a halt then resumed beating as if she'd run a country mile. She opened her mouth to scream, but the gloved hand of a stranger covered her mouth, drowning out her plea for help.

The horses sprang forward, carting her off to certain doom.

TWENTY-TWO

Georgina whipped her head from side to side, and managed a glance back at her captor before he had her anchored firmly in place. Her eyes widened. She clawed the large hand clamped over her mouth. Her efforts were ineffectual against Stone's sheer strength and power. What a fool she'd been. She should have learned long ago to trust no one. No one but herself.

"Please, don't fight," a third, familiar voice said.

"We won't hurt you," Stone whispered against her ear.

In all her darkest moments, she'd expected her father or Jamie would end her. She'd never expected to face this black devil again who'd surely quash her as though she were nothing more than a gnat on his sleeve. Her teeth chattered. She flailed her arms and legs, and twisted about.

His grip slackened and Georgina bit down hard on his hand. Even through his kid leather gloves, her teeth managed to penetrate flesh. He cursed but still held fast.

She jerked her foot down on his heel, wrestling for freedom. In the thick cloak of the carriage's darkness, her eyes slowly adjusted and the face of her other captor shifted into sharp focus.

The Duke of Aubrey!

Chills wracked her frame as she tried to imagine the bored, lascivious nobleman's intentions. Oh God, what did he want with her? Adam had already made it abundantly clear that he wouldn't care what happened to her. He wouldn't search for her. She was alone. Once again. As she'd always been.

The thought breathed life into her struggles.

"I already said I liked you, Mrs. Markham. I have no intention of harming you," the duke drawled, seemingly bored by her show of protest. He looked to the third man, whose face was concealed in the shadows. "I'd imagine we're far enough away to not attract notice if she screams." He glanced back at Georgina. "They won't, you know. Hear you, that is."

Georgina wrenched her neck, attempting to break free of Archer.

The duke gave a curt nod and Archer dropped his hand.

She sucked in a series of rasping breaths. What sick game were they playing with her?

"I needed to speak with you," the duke said.

The same sense of helplessness she'd known at her father's hands returned. There would be no one rushing to her rescue. If she were to get out of this situation, she would have to help herself. Georgina took a deep breath and collected what wits remained to her. She brushed the black curtain.

The duke frowned. "No need to look outside, Mrs. Markham."

She dropped her hand to her lap.

"A woman of your intelligence must be curious to know what you're doing here."

"I had rather wondered about that," she said. Her husky response seemed to amuse them.

They chuckled and exchanged looks.

Georgina seized the momentary distraction. She reached for the door handle.

The duke yanked her back.

"Don't do anything foolish, Mrs. Markham. You'd be crushed beneath the wheels of the carriage," he said, with a small frown.

Did he speak from concern or had those words contained the hint of a threat? No matter. She'd braved her father and Jamie for the course of her life, she'd not allow one such as this to intimidate her. She tipped her chin up. "What do you want?"

"Tell us about your work for Fox."

Adam's steely promise to see her pay for her sins surfaced. He'd turned her over to these men. She wanted to curl up in a ball and

wallow in the endless depths of her misery, but she was a survivor—
she had no intention of allowing them to…to do whatever it was
they did with the daughters of traitors. "That isn't an answer, Your
Grace."

Stone and Archer chuckled. The duke scowled at them and then
returned his attention to Georgina. "We've spent several years trying
to determine exactly where your loyalties lie."

At his admission, Georgina's stomach turned. For years, she had
been closely watched by these powerful men and had been none the
wiser. "You watched me?" she asked, her voice flat.

"Oh, we did more than watch you, Mrs. Markham," the duke said
matter-of-factly. "We corresponded with you. It took us some time
to realize that the woman penning the notes was in fact 'The Fox's'
daughter. You see, we couldn't quite piece together how someone who
proclaimed their support for the Crown would withhold such a vital
fact."

Staring back at the duke and the aura of power radiating from him,
Georgina knew that if this man sought retribution she would stand no
chance. She was a survivor. She was not, however, indestructible.

Georgina bit her lip.

He leaned forward across the seat, bringing the harsh angles of his
face into sharper focus. "It is now quite clear to all of us. You are loyal,
my dear."

Georgina didn't care to examine what her fate would be if he
believed otherwise. "Who are you?"

He seemed unfazed by the impudence of her question, but
ignored it nevertheless. "Do you know about your husband's role with
the Crown?"

Georgina compressed her lips into a tight line, biting back a stinging retort. The Duke of Aubrey was very nearly royalty and she had
to be mindful of that, but she'd not betray her husband by talking to
him. "If you trust I'm loyal, Your Grace, then surely you must realize
I will not disclose intimate details about my husband to you. Or anyone," she added, glancing pointedly at the other silent figures in the
conveyance.

The duke inclined his head. "Brava, my dear." Adam's mocking use of those very words shot through her brain and her face contorted with pain. She yanked her gaze away.

The duke was far too perceptive not to detect her show of emotion. "Your husband was informed about your father."

Gooseflesh dotted her arms. Understanding dawned, dark and ugly. "You told him," she breathed.

"As I said, you are intelligent," the duke complimented. He did not, however, apologize.

Georgina wanted to reach across the carriage and shake him until he hurt as much as she was hurting. "Why would you do that? Who are you that you would destroy…?"

Our happiness.

The duke arched a single black brow. "Surely you didn't intend to live the rest of your life as a lie? Would you deceive him forever?"

Damn him for being right. Yet…that was just what she'd hoped—that she and Adam could live out their lives with the simple omission of her birthright. She'd even begun to believe that her father and Jamie would dissolve into nothing more than an empty memory… until Jamie had reappeared, dashing those hopes.

Georgina swiped a weary hand across her face. "What do you want?"

The duke didn't miss a beat. "I'd like to enlist your help."

"My help?" How could she possibly help the Duke of Aubrey?

"The Irish radicals are getting close to staging their revolt. I need to prevent that."

Georgina fisted her hands at her side. So this was what the Duke of Aubrey wanted of her. He wanted her to betray her father. Over the years, she'd told herself she hated him. She'd contemplated all the vile atrocities he'd carried out and had readily believed she could see him brought to justice. She just wasn't sure if she could be the person to put the noose around his neck.

"You are quiet, Mrs. Markham," the duke said after a long while.

Georgina traced the seam of her lips with the tip of her tongue. "I didn't realize you'd asked a question."

His lips dipped down, giving him an almost boyish look of annoyance. "Should I be clearer? I'm asking you to reconcile with your father."

She closed her eyes. The sound of her father's fists meeting her flesh echoed in her memory. A faint tremor racked her body. "No," she rasped. After the hell she'd endured at his hands, she could never return. If she did, he would inevitably kill her with no more thought than squashing a nagging insect. "I can't."

Mr. Archer seemed to grasp the direction of her unspoken thoughts for he again broke with propriety and claimed her fingers. His touch was gentle and warm. He interrupted the duke, who was about to speak. "I know you are afraid of him, Miss Wilcox."

"Markham," Stone corrected.

Mr. Archer ignored him. "We need your help. We've learned that Robert Emmet has returned to Ireland and is preparing to assemble his army. The good of the country is at stake."

She pressed her fingers against her temple and rubbed. It would seem all Emmet's efforts were about to come to fruition. What could she possibly do to prevent the Irish insurrection?

"We need you to guide us to Emmet," the duke explained.

"How do you presume I do that?" She'd lost all access to information the moment she'd freed Adam and fled her father and Jamie. "The only reason I had knowledge in the first place was because my f…" A loud hum filled her ears as the enormity of what was being asked of her sunk in.

The duke leaned forward. "We need your help."

She heard the duke's words as if from a distance. "No. I won't."

I can't.

Seeing him again would result in her death. She was sure of it.

"Miss Wilcox, a number of good, loyal Englishmen have died at the hands of these Irish revolutionaries," Archer said.

He exchanged a glance with the duke before continuing. "Our country is on the cusp of war with France. A battle with Ireland would be disastrous."

Georgina directed her eyes to the ink black, velvet curtain. Her mind raced. She couldn't go back there. She'd waited her whole life to escape her father and Jamie's cruel machinations and now with the mission presented to her, they'd undo all hope of freedom.

A chill wracked her frame as she remembered the day Adam had escaped and the beating she'd received.

"Your father is a traitor, Miss Wilcox, and he knows the date and location of the planned event," the duke said quietly, having correctly interpreted the reasons for her hesitancy.

The pit in her stomach grew. All her life she'd known someday she would have to make a decision, that secret notes handed off to the butcher's son were not enough to right Father's wrongs. The time to make that decision had finally come.

"What will you require of me?" she asked, the question flat to her own ears.

The duke exchanged a look with Stone.

Stone spoke. "Hunter recently contacted you, asking for your support."

She tried to conceal a flash of surprise. "How do you—?"

"It is our responsibility to know. The next time you are contacted, meet them. We will provide you with papers containing information. I want you to pass them along to your father. That should solidify your reconciliation."

The muscles in her body strained. Leaning forward, she rested her elbows on her knees and buried her head in her hands. She'd not seen her father since the day she'd freed Blakely. She picked her head up. "This will never work," she said finally.

The duke frowned.

She recalled her father's earliest suspicions and then the moment he'd discovered her role in freeing Adam. "My father will never confide in me. I betrayed him for a second time."

"He will," the duke insisted.

"You don't know," she lashed out. "You don't know that my father never trusted me, that he abandoned me to my own devices. Why should he take me back?"

The duke dusted his hands together. "Because he believes you are an angry, jealous wife. Everyone knows of your discontent from the papers and mention of your husband's former love."

Georgina blanched and dug her fingers into the palms of her hand until she left crescent moons of silent hurt.

The duke seemed immune to her pain. "And you forget. Your father is in desperate need of the information in your possession. The *ton* has already done a remarkable job brandishing about the recent scandal with Markham. Therefore, your father will see what he wants to see. That is your weapon."

He fell silent.

Georgina broke the quiet. "How do you presume I obtain Emmet's plans?"

He inclined his head. "Why, the same way you did in the past, my dear."

She nibbled on her lip. "My husband—"

"Can't know."

A lock of hair fell across her eye. She brushed it back. She couldn't keep this from him. Not when secrets and lies had already destroyed their fragile happiness.

Georgina shook her head. "I can't lie to him, Your Grace."

Archer cleared his throat.

Georgina looked at him.

"Your husband will not let you take on this role," he pointed out gently.

Bitterness coated her mouth with a filmy layer of regret. She saw herself bent over Lord Ashton's balcony while Adam took her with punishing strokes then coldly walked away. "You are wrong. My husband will not care."

"He is angry, but he cares a great deal for you. I'm sure of it. If your husband were to know what we proposed, he'd not allow you take on this mission. No man would," Archer concluded.

They'd not seen the black hatred in Adam's eyes, or heard the vile things he'd said.

"When you are done, when your father has been brought to justice, your husband will forgive you," the duke said.

Georgina managed a small smile. Adam would never forgive her.

But mayhap if I do this, I can prove to him that I am loyal.

Hope stirred within her breast.

"I'd ask that I be able to write my husband a note," she said, her words a faint whisper.

The duke frowned.

Stone interjected. "What kind of note?"

"An explanation. If anything happens to me, I'd want him to know that I was not disloyal in this. I'd want him to know that I was loyal to the Crown."

Archer's mouth flattened. "Nothing will happen to you."

Georgina waited for the duke to speak.

The nobleman's eyes were uncharacteristically somber. "I will see that it reaches him."

Georgina leaned back, sucking in a breath. "How will I be in contact with you? How will I know what information to give? How—"

He held up a finger, silencing her barrage of questions. "Suzanne is to be trusted."

Her brow wrinkled. "My maid?"

"The very same. All correspondences will go through Suzanne. She will serve as your emissary. When you receive your summons from Fox and Hunter, she will accompany you."

It would appear the duke had thought out every detail.

He rapped on the ceiling and the conveyance came to a fluid stop.

She reached for the window curtain. This time no one stopped her and she peered outside. "Where are we?"

Stone answered her question. "The Dials."

She drew in a shuddery breath. No member of the nobility would find himself in the Seven Dials, or if he did…well, then whatever had brought him here would be less than reputable.

"Do you know what I find interesting, Mrs. Markham?"

Georgina inclined her head. "No, but I suspect you'll tell me."

Stone stifled a chuckle with his hand.

"You've not once wondered about your own fate. You've not asked what will happen to you."

Georgina studied her lap. His words weren't altogether true. Since Adam had leveled the threat of Newgate at her, she'd not been able to shake the images of a dank, dark cell from her mind.

"You've done nothing wrong," Archer murmured.

Tears blurred her vision. Adam had suffered unimagined horrors at her father's hands. As had Archer. And others. She clenched her eyes tight.

Two lone drops trickled down her cheeks. "I am guilty by my birthright."

The duke looked at her with an indecipherable expression. "You're not responsible for your father's actions. But you are responsible for yours." He nodded to Stone, who in turn opened the door.

Stone and Archer jumped out.

The duke lingered then took his leave without a final word.

As the carriage pulled away, returning her home, she watched the duke disappear into the faint London fog, unable to quell the sense of doom that lingered in her heart.

TWENTY-THREE

G eorgina sat on the small window seat, staring out at the steady stream of rain beating against the glass pane.

She touched her finger to a single droplet and, through the thin barrier, traced its slow, winding path until it disappeared.

Thunder rumbled in the far distance, making the glass tremble under her hand.

She made the mistake of glancing down at the paper on her lap. Her throat worked reflexively. It had been a fortnight since Adam and Grace had been discovered in flagrante delicato as the scandal sheets had reported, and still the story would not die. The gossips reported on everything from Adam's long nights, to Edward Helling taking separate quarters from his wife, to scorn for Georgina—a mere nurse, a shameless nobody who had dared to enter the upper echelon of Society. The papers quite gleefully reported that Georgina's misery was a product of her self-serving desires.

Oddly, they were correct.

Just not in the way they believed.

Georgina had selfishly scratched and clawed for every sliver of happiness she could, and for her efforts, she'd been punished by the harsh echoing silence of loneliness.

She had no friends.

She dined alone.

She slept alone.

Even the somber staff eyed her with equal parts anger and pity for what she'd wrought on their lord and master. Georgina sighed, the faint breath stirring a single curl that had fallen over her eye. Adam deserved their allegiance. Not the daughter of a traitor and murderer.

Georgina squeezed her eyes shut tight. Her chance of redeeming herself in Adam's jaded eyes was slipping through her fingers. God, how she missed him. She missed his smile, his laughter, his gentle touch, his kind words. This cold, callous man he'd become was not someone she recognized—and in the lies she'd perpetuated through her silence, she'd created this dark, divide between them.

Time was proving that Adam could not move forward because he was stuck in the past, and she feared that was where he would always remain.

"Mrs. Markham?"

Georgina stiffened.

Suzanne stood in the doorway.

"Yes, Suzanne?"

"I've brought you your book."

Book?

Since her world had fallen apart, Georgina hadn't read anything but the London Times and various other scandal sheets. "Thank you, Suzanne. If you could bring it upstairs, I don't much feel like reading right now."

Suzanne frowned. "Mrs. Markham, I must insist. You need to do something."

She opened her mouth to dismiss the maid then the determined glint in Suzanne's brown eyes registered.

The maid thrust a book toward her.

Georgina swung her legs over the side of the seat, her muslin skirts rustling as her slippers touched the floor. She accepted the offering.

The thick leather volume shook in her hands as she studied it. It contained the duke's message.

It is time.

Only moments ago, she'd dreamed of this diversion. Now, she wanted to drop the book, run to her chambers and hide under the thick coverlet upon her bed.

Mouth dry with fear, she looked up at Suzanne.

"Do you need anything else, Mrs. Markham?"

Just my husband. Oh, and if you can manage it, his love and devotion.

"That will be all."

Suzanne pivoted on her heel, but then paused and turned back around. "One more thing, miss." She reached into the flat pocket of her crisp, white apron and extracted a thin envelope. "This arrived for you a short while ago."

Georgina stared at the unmarked envelope. And knew.

She forced herself to take it, knowing without even opening it what it contained.

"When did this come?" she managed to ask.

"A young beggar came round. Said he was given a six-pence if he gave the letter to Mrs. Markham."

Georgina swallowed. "Thank you, Suzanne."

The maid lingered, her deep, brown eyes clouded with what appeared to be a blend of pity and compassion. "You are a good woman, Mrs. Markham."

You are a good woman, Georgina Wilcox.

She fought the urge to clamp her hands over her ears and drown out the words.

I'm not. My misery is testament to my lack of worth.

"Thank you."

Suzanne left, pulling the door closed behind her.

Georgina looked at the ivory envelope and the leather volume. She first opened the book, her fingers flipped through the pages, then stopped. A single piece of parchment had been tucked inside. Mindful that she sat in the window in full view of anyone who happened to be in the gardens on this miserable spring day, she stood and crossed over to the hearth.

A small fire popped and hissed, though the flames failed to warm her.

Georgina set the book on the mantel then opened the single sheet she'd retrieved from inside the copy of the cleric poet Pádraigín Haicéad's work.

A note will arrive. Fox and Hunter will request a meeting at Ye Olde Bookshop.

You are to go. They will be looking for 3 names. You are to give them the following: Marcus. Roberts. Mooring. You know no further details than those names found in a secret compartment in your husband's chambers. Burn this when you've committed it to memory.

Georgina crumpled the orders into a tight ball and threw it into the blaze. The orange and red flames nipped at the edges of the paper before swallowing the sheet.

She gave herself another moment in front of the fire to gather her courage. But she could not ignore the second missive, though she knew what it contained. Georgina broke open the non-descript seal with badly shaking fingers, withdrew the note, and then she began to read.

My dearest Georgina,

I hope you've thought hard on what I said. Your husband does not deserve your loyalty, and I believe you know that. We are looking for three names. These men are members of The Brethren of the Lords, the secret organization your husband belongs to. If you obtain the names, you are to meet us in three days at the spot we last met.

Ever Yours,

Jamie

She tossed the parchment onto the embers and the charred remnants of the duke's note.

"Hello, wife."

Georgina cried out and spun around.

Adam leaned against the wooden frame, his arms folded under the broad-expanse of his muscular chest.

Fear rivaled joy. The damning scrap of paper being licked apart by the flames crackled.

"A-Adam." She tossed her chin back, though, determined to not be cowed by the steely set to his jaw.

He shoved away from the door and kicked it closed behind him.

Georgina remained rooted to the floor and prayed the note from Jamie would be destroyed by the time he reached her.

Adam stopped before her. His towering form cast a shadow over her. He snagged a strand of her hair and rubbed the curl back and forth between his thumb and forefinger. "You appear guilty of something, wife."

How did he manage to make the word "wife" sound like a curse?

She snatched the strand back, wincing at the tug on her scalp. "According to you, I've been guilty since first we met."

He inclined his head. A smile played on his lips. "Ahh, how very true." He peered over her shoulder into the fire. His eyes narrowed ever so slightly, but when he looked at her, his gaze was curiously blank.

She gripped the edge of her skirts. "What do you want, Adam?"

He clasped her cheek with his right hand and caressed her.

In an attempt to stop him, Georgina touched her fingers to his wrist. "I said what do you want, Adam?"

He bent down, and the potent bite of whiskey was so strong on his breath, she nearly tasted it. "Is that an invitation, dear wife?"

The haze of passion lifted. Georgina slapped his hand away. "You are drunk," she said, the words bearing more than a faint trace of accusation.

He sketched a mocking bow. "As I have been since I discovered my lovely wife is a—"

"Have you come here merely to hurl insults at me?" She had wronged him, but she would not grovel, nor would she spend the rest of her life wallowing in shamed remorse. "I've not seen you in a fortnight. Something must have prompted you to seek me out."

Adam stood in silence. A log crumpled in the hearth, sending off a smattering of sparks and embers. His wife was nothing if not astute.

He had sought her out, and not to exchange barbs. Against his logic and better judgment, he missed her. He missed the sound of her voice, the satiny smoothness of her skin. He even missed the defiant tilt to her chin when she challenged him. Loneliness, greater than anything he'd known during his captivity, gripped him until he felt like an empty shell of a man.

In the dead of night, when he returned from his clubs, he would wander up to Georgina's chambers and sit at the edge of her bed, watching as she slept. Every night, her head thrashed violently against the pillow and a piteous whimpering escaped her lips. And every night, he would stroke the sweat-dampened strands of hair off her brow until she stilled.

When dawn broke over the horizon, he'd slip from her rooms, his wife none the wiser, and head to his office to waste his hours trying to convince himself he was wrong about her. Georgina could not be a scheming temptress sent to trick secrets out of him. He had to be wrong. When he managed to convince himself of it, he'd reach for the damning file and punish himself with the truth of her birth.

Then he'd reach for the bloody bottle of whiskey.

Part of him wondered—if, on that day they'd first met, she'd confessed her real identity, would he have felt this same, gnawing resentment?

His gaze wandered from her luminous eyes and came to rest on her fragile neck.

I wrapped my hands around her flesh. I very nearly choked the life from her.

At the memory, tightness settled deep in his chest and spread through his body.

The answer was simple—he'd never have trusted her. Nor, following his assault, had he given Georgina any reason to believe he'd not do her harm if she shared the truth with him.

She brushed away the lone curl that had a tendency to escape the serviceable knot at the nape of her neck and continued to stand there in silence.

He'd never met a person capable of such utter stillness. The women he knew were besieged by what seemed like an insatiable need to talk over any stretches of quiet. Not his wife. What had been done to her that she should have learned to stand as quiet as a forest creature hiding from encroaching hunters?

The niggling of doubt came again. Mayhap her role with Fox and Hunter was less clear than he'd assumed?

He shoved the hope aside. It was only desperation that made him see castles in the sky.

Adam jerked his chin toward the fireplace. "I thought I saw you throw something into the fire."

The color seeped from Georgina's cheek. She shook her head quickly. Too quickly. "No. You are mistaken."

He clenched his teeth. She was a dreadful liar. How had she managed to aid Fox and Hunter all these years without being discovered? "Am I, Georgina?"

His eyes alighted on a lone book atop the mantle. Adam frowned and reached behind her.

Georgina folded her hands in front of her, casting her gaze to the floor demurely. He flipped through the pages. "A rather odd choice," he murmured, setting it back down.

Her head shot up, her dainty chin jutting out in a mutinous line. "You don't even know what I like to read, so why should it seem odd?"

Adam started. Georgina's words bore an accusatory tone and, God help him, she was correct. He didn't know a thing about her tastes or preferences in literature. He knew so very little about her...and most of what he did know had turned out to be lies. "I imagine if I'd bothered asking, you'd have merely lied."

She jerked as if he'd backhanded her.

His hand quivered with the need to touch her, to drag her close, bury his face in her crown of curls and plead forgiveness.

He did none of those things.

"Why are you here, Adam?" she asked, her tone surprisingly resolute.

"It is time we put in an appearance at a ball."

Georgina shook her head. "No. I'll not go. I'll not perpetuate this lie."

"Tsk, tsk. What's one more, dear wife? Surely you can feign contented wife? You did a remarkable job at battered maid."

The palm of her hand connected with his cheek in a loud crack. His head whipped to the right. Adam flexed his jaw and brushed his fingers over the stinging flesh.

Georgina stared at him, her eyes full moons in her pale, white cheeks. She held her hand out as if warding him off and took a step back, stumbling over her skirts. In her haste to get away, she nearly retreated into the burning hearth.

"Georgina!" he bellowed, grasping her by the forearm and pulling her to safety.

Georgina cried out, wrestling her arm free. "I'm s-sorry," she stammered, slipping underneath his arm.

He froze.

Christ. She thinks I'm going to hit her.

Nausea turned his stomach. "Come here, Georgina." He reached for her.

She swatted at his fingers and danced artfully away.

"I'm not going to hurt you," Adam said, a gruff edge to his words.

She spun on her heel and fled as if the gates of hell had opened and unleashed a stream of fire.

Adam stared after her, sickened. How could she believe he would ever lay his hands on her? Since he'd discovered her betrayal, he'd wavered between wanting to throw his head back and roar in anguish and shaking her until she swore all of this had been a horrible misunderstanding. But he would never, could never, strike her. He might've been a beast, but he was not so depraved as to descend into the cowardly behavior of beating his wife.

Still, her apprehension had not been feigned. She'd been terror incarnate.

And once more a maelstrom of doubts snuck back to the surface.

Watson appeared at the door. "Sir, you have visitors."

Adam cursed. The last thing he wanted at this moment was company. "Tell whoever it is I'm out."

"Shame, little brother. You'd lie to your brother and mother?"

Nick stood beside his mother, who frowned when she got a good look at him.

Watson took that as his cue to leave.

"Coward," Adam muttered beneath his breath. He threw his arms wide. "Come in, come in! How very good it is to see you," he said, his tone coated in sarcasm.

His mother hurried to his side and leaned up to kiss him. She paused, wrinkling her nose. "You smell like you've been bathing in spirits," she said, her lips turned down in motherly disapproval.

Adam bowed. "Guilty as charged."

Nick settled himself into the leather sofa and folded his leg over his knee. "I'm glad this is amusing to you, little brother."

Adam quirked a brow.

"Nicholas," his mother murmured. She gave a slight shake of her head.

Ever the earl, Nick ignored her. "You married Georgina against our better wishes. We all but pleaded with you to set the woman aside, but you were adamant. You were insistent. It is now clear to us—"

"And all the *ton*," mother said beneath her breath.

Nick ignored her and continued, "...that you merely married Georgina because you were nursing a broken heart for Viscount Camden's daughter."

Adam ground his teeth, fighting the urge to cross over, drag Nick up by the lapels of his coat and throw him from the room. Nick knew nothing about what plagued Adam but believed he possessed some kind of insight that gave him leave to speak candidly about Adam's marriage.

"That's right. I'm bitter because I loved and lost Blakely's daughter," he mocked.

The truth has more to do with the fact that I loved and lost my own wife.

Mother stifled a gasp behind her hand. "Adam, you are destroying your reputation."

He spun on his heel. "Is that what has you worried, Mother? My reputation?" He snarled the last word at her.

Nick surged to his feet. "Do not speak to her in that tone."

Tears filled his mother's eyes and a wave of guilt hit him. "We are worried about you, Adam," she whispered. "I wish you'd never met that woman. Either of them. But you did, and you are married to Georgina. You must put aside your differences. If you don't, it will destroy you." A hauntingly prophetic note hung on those last words.

Adam shoved down the unnerving sensation roiling in his gut. He bowed his head. "I'll try."

For as long as I'm wed to Georgina.

His heart turned over at the thought of her absent from his life.

"No more whiskey," Nick instructed.

Adam nodded. The moment Georgina had fled his office like a scared rabbit he'd decided he'd taken his last drink. He'd wallowed in spirits long enough to know they were not erasing any of the bleeding hurt. "No more spirits," he pledged.

Mother clapped her hands, a smile on her face. "Excellent! I shall call for tea so we might celebrate!"

She rang for a servant, who materialized almost instantly.

When the servant hurried off, Nick looked Adam square in the eyes. "I was determined to not like Georgina from the moment you all but dragged her from Middlesex Hospital. I'd decided early on that she was unworthy of you, brother."

A defense sprang to Adam's lips.

Nick held a hand up. "I believe I was wrong. To have faced down the gossips as she did that night took real courage. I think you can give this marriage a go. Even if you still love another woman."

I don't still love another woman. The only woman I love is my wife.

All he said, however, was, "Thank you."

Nick nodded. Tension seemed to leave his broad shoulders and he managed a half-grin for Adam. "Tony bade me give you a message."

"Oh?"

"He said you're a bloody fool, and he can't come around because if he did, he would lay you low."

Adam grinned. "Oh, he did, did he?"

Nick smiled back. "He's quite taken with your wife."

Adam was saved from answering by the reappearance of the servant with a tray bearing a steaming porcelain pot and three fragile cups.

As Adam sat down to take tea with his family, he was forced to silently acknowledge to himself, that Tony wasn't the only one taken with Georgina.

TWENTY-FOUR

Georgina wished her orders from the duke had come another day.

She wished Jamie's note had never arrived.

If they hadn't, she would have remained ensconced in her chambers and wouldn't have been on the main level of the house. If she hadn't been on the main level of the house, she wouldn't have heard the voices coming from her husband's library.

The earl exclaimed, "You merely married Georgina because you were nursing a broken heart for Viscount Camden's daughter."

Adam's reply ripped through her. "That's right. I'm bitter because I loved and lost Blakely's daughter."

Georgina stood, back pressed against the wall outside the library. She fisted a hand against her mouth, biting the top of her hand to keep from crying out as she listened to the very candid exchange between brothers and mother.

"Excellent!" the countess said. "I shall call for tea."

The words jolted life into Georgina's petrified legs, jerking her from the trance that had held her immobile. Nothing, however, could drive back the easy camaraderie between Adam and his family as he'd so casually spoken of his love for Grace. It shouldn't have come as any great surprise that he still loved her. Georgina had watched him toil over a sketchpad, filling page after page with the woman's haunting beauty.

What cleaved Georgina's heart in two was the loathing Adam reserved for her. She could never win his heart. It had seemed like an impossibility before when she'd been Georgina the maid. Now…nothing she could do or say would ever ease the repugnance her husband had shown since he'd learned the truth of her paternity. Choking on a sob, Georgina ran down the hall and all but collided with a servant.

"Mrs. Markham. I'm so very sorry," he stammered.

She continued her flight to the foyer.

Watson appeared. "I need the carriage readied," she ordered, giving him her destination.

He inclined his head and hurried to do her bidding.

Suzanne appeared, standing at her elbow. "Steady, Mrs. Markham," she whispered in quiet, soothing tones.

Folding her arms under her breasts, Georgina hugged herself. When she'd gone downstairs to Adam's office, she'd intended to apologize for striking him. And she'd wanted to see him one more time before she went off on her mission. She wanted possibly the last memory she would have of Adam to be warmer, something she could carry with her in lieu of courage. Her hopes had been dashed yet again—all she was left with were the hurtful, ugly words between brothers who'd seemed united in their disapproval of Georgina.

She wished Watson would return with the news that something was wrong with the conveyance. A broken axle, a missing wheel, a horse in need of a new hoof.

Whoever was in charge of granting Georgina wishes was remarkably poor at what they did, for he reappeared and held the door open.

Georgina gulped down a wave of fear and passed through the door and down to the carriage with Suzanne trailing behind her.

The moment they pulled away, Suzanne began to speak. "Do you remember your orders?"

Georgina nodded. "I committed them to memory."

"Good," Suzanne said. "You mustn't be obvious in your defection. They will be suspicious. You must tread a fine line between wavering loyalty and anger for your husband. Anything else and they will know you are false."

The woman continued spewing a sea of orders and instructions until Georgina's head was swimming.

The carriage rocked to a halt.

"We've arrived." Suzanne rapped the ceiling. The carriage door opened and the tiger handed Georgina, and then Suzanne, down.

"I'm going to the bookshop. Why don't you t-take some time to yourself."

"Oh, I mustn't," Suzanne insisted, playing her part to perfection.

Georgina waved her hand. "Truly, I'll be fine."

Suzanne sank into a deep curtsy, her eyes wide with very believable, yet feigned, appreciation. "Very well. Thank you ever so much, Mrs. Markham!" She hurried off to go wherever her orders had indicated she should be.

Georgina peered down the street. First left. Then right. Drawing in a fortifying breath, she faced the door and entered Ye Olde Bookshop.

The wizened merchant appeared almost instantly. His eyes lit with recognition. Most assuredly due to the great amount she'd last spent in his establishment.

"Good day. How are you?"

Georgina pasted a smile to her face. "Very well," Georgina lied.

"I've recently acquired new books on art."

"Just splendid," she forced out. Her life was in shambles and soon, most likely forfeit. The last thing she cared about was books.

He proceeded to carry on a conversation for one, his voice a droning buzz, so that all she wanted was to clamp her hand over her ears and demand he leave her to her misery. She followed him down the long aisle, coming to stop at a very familiar row of books.

This is where I last saw Jamie. Where I first met the duke.

She expected to feel the stirrings of fear and trepidation. Instead, she felt a peculiar nothingness. "Thank you," she murmured and watched as the merchant hurried off.

Georgina stared at the vast stretch of volumes, the titles a blur of leather. How she longed for this mission to be over.

And then what? Nothing will have changed with Adam. You shall still be the traitorous daughter of the infamous Fox.

To give herself something to do, she touched book after book, counting them as she went.

One hundred and six. One hundred and seven. One hundred and...

"Hullo, Georgina."

Eight.

Her finger froze on one hundred and nine, toying with the gold lettering. "Jamie." She didn't bother to look at him.

I lied, her mind screeched. *I am afraid.*

Jamie sidled up beside her. He clasped book one hundred and nine and plucked it from the shelf. She peeked at him out the corner of her eye. He leafed through the pages, skimming the words. "You came," he said.

Suzanne's reminder knocked around in her brain. "I wasn't going to," she lied. "I...I shouldn't be here." She turned on her heel as if to leave, and a large part of her prayed that he'd let her go and never bother her with his and Father's contemptible efforts again.

Jamie placed himself in front of her, blocking her path. "Don't go." He took her hands in his.

Georgina's insides tightened with revulsion. Remembering the day he'd forced his attentions on her, she had to fight the urge to throw off his touch. "I c-can't d-do this, Jamie. He is my husband."

He raised her gloved fingers to his lips then pulled back the thin mint green fabric and placed a lingering kiss on the inside of her wrist.

Bile climbed up her throat and she had to swallow several times to keep from being sick at his feet.

I can't do this. I can't do this. I can't do this.

He spoke, seeming wholly unaware of her repulsion. "But you are here, Georgie. You are here, because you know he loves another woman and is undeserving of you."

She managed a jerky nod, praying he'd release her.

He tugged her glove all the way free and continued to hold on to her. He stroked a path over her palm with the pad of his thumb. "And you want to hurt him, don't you?" Jamie didn't allow her to respond, just lowered his head and kissed her.

Georgina gasped at the absolute shock of his assault, but he took her mouth falling open as assent. He raped her mouth, sullying her tongue with his assault. He cupped her buttocks in a hard, unrelenting grip and squeezed the soft flesh.

This time it couldn't be helped—she gagged.

She jerked back, colliding with the shelving. A lone book tumbled to the floor, landing with an almost soundless thump.

Jamie's pale blue eyes were glassy with desire.

"We can't. Not...not here," she managed, praying he believed that to be the true reason for her denial. She fought the urge to wipe her mouth, to scrub away the taste of him. "I don't have much time."

That seemed to sober him. He nodded. "We're looking for names of those men and women assisting the Crown."

"Women?" she squeaked.

Jamie patted her head as if she were a small girl. "Yes, my love. Men and women form part of this organization. We've already identified three members of the society. We need the others."

"Will you hurt them?" she couldn't keep from asking.

His lips twisted in a chilling rendition of a smile. "Do not worry about them."

Georgina bit down hard on her lip and, fearing he could read the lies in her eyes, forced her gaze to the floor. "I found a list." Not wishing to appear too obvious in her deception, she sought to cast doubt. "But it had nothing on it aside from several names. There was nothing else on it."

Stop repeating yourself, Georgina.

A glimmer blazed to life in his eyes. "What were the names?"

She shook her head. "Surely this isn't the information you seek."

He took her hard by the shoulders, his fingers biting into the smooth flesh of her arms until tears stung her eyes. "Give me the bloody names and I'll determine if it is information useful to us."

"Marcus, Roberts, and..." Her mind spun.

Think. Think, Georgina. What is the name? What is it?

"And?" Jamie insisted.

"Uh…Mooring."

Yes, it is Mooring.

Jamie grinned and, for a moment, looked like the same young boy who'd come to live with her and her family. When she'd learned he would be living with them, Georgina had twirled in circles with the excitement of having a brother. Until he slapped her. She'd been just seven and still remembered her fat, bloodied lip. She had stared back at him with fear before running off to hide. She'd been hiding ever since.

Jamie's next words brought her back from the distant memory. "You have done well, my dear."

"I can't do any more, Jamie. This is the last time I can help you."

He trailed the tip of one finger along her lower lip. "Do you know, Georgie? I don't believe you."

Terror zigzagged through her like a bolt of lightning. She opened her mouth to plead her innocence, but he tapped her lips to keep her silent. "I believe you want to help the Cause. I believe you want to punish your husband."

She closed her eyes and prayed he would believe her lies. "I loved him so much. I gave up everything for him."

"And he's repaid you by fucking his former lover."

Georgina gasped with pain at the image his words evoked.

"Will you continue to help us?"

She tamped down the agonizing regret threatening to shred her to pieces. "He is still my husband." Jamie was cruel, evil, and conniving but he was not a simpleton. He would be suspicious if she were to capitulate too easily.

"And you still have your father to appease."

Odd, how for the first time in her life he was uttering those words as if they meant something.

Georgina hesitated and then gave a curt nod. "I will."

He patted her cheek as if she were one of the queen's terriers. "Good girl."

Georgina couldn't let him leave, not without finding out something, anything that might be of use to the duke. "Does it ever feel hopeless to you?"

Jamie raised a brow.

"The plan for Irish independence?" she said hurriedly.

"We're not alone. There are those with great wealth and power who support the Cause, Georgina."

Her heart kicked up an exited rhythm and she had to bite the inside of her cheek to keep from asking for names.

Her silence was rewarded.

"If you need to find me or are in need of support, Lord Ackerly can be trusted."

Georgina blinked, certain her ears had deceived her. Excitement made her giddy. How easily he'd handed over a name! It gave her a heady sense of power.

He grabbed her, wrapping a vise-like grip around her wrist. "If you deceive us again, Georgina, there will be no forgiveness. Do you understand what I am saying to you?"

Moisture dampened her palms. She'd known the moment the duke had enlisted her help that what was really at stake was more than her happiness; it was her life. Her throat constricted and she struggled to force any words out.

"Mrs. Markham?" Suzanne called from within the bookshop.

Georgina quelled a surge of relief and forced her eyes wide in feigned fear. "It's my maid!" she gasped, her eyes darting around the aisle.

Jamie stiffened. He seemed to want to say more but must have feared the risk of discovery, for he slipped down the aisle and out of sight.

Georgina sagged against the shelving, pressing a hand against her galloping heart.

"Mrs. Markham?" Suzanne called again.

Georgina detected a thread of panic in the maid's tone. She tried calling to Suzanne but couldn't get the words out. Now that Jamie was gone, she was overwhelmed by a maelstrom of relief, fear, and anticipation. Her skin tingled until she wanted to scrape her fingernails along her flesh and drive the frayed nerves from her body.

She knew the moment Suzanne found her. The maid gasped. "We must get you out of here."

Georgina closed her eyes, not wanting to see the questions in the other woman's gaze. She must have noted the stark violet marks left on her forearms by Jamie's fingers. She touched the corner of her bruised lip, wincing. Or mayhap her swollen lips. The memory of Jamie's kiss entered her mind and a hysterical giggle gurgled deep within her chest. She shivered.

Suzanne whispered something to her, but it was lost to the loud droning in Georgina's ears.

The maid took her by the arm and steered her out of the shop and to a waiting carriage. The hum of mundane street sounds played out like the errant screech of a violin chord—deafening. Georgina stepped forward.

"Mrs. Markham!" Suzanne cried, pulling her back just as a phaeton came whirring by.

The fog lifted and Georgina crashed to the ground. She landed on the pavement with a pained *oomph*. The passing horses kicked a spray of dust and dirt into her eyes, momentarily blinding her.

Several gentlemen hurried forward to offer their assistance, but Georgina climbed to her feet before they could reach her. Throwing propriety to the proverbial wind, she raced to the opened carriage door and allowed the tiger to assist her inside. Then, saints be preserved, the door closed, and she found herself alone with Suzanne.

"Are you all right?" Suzanne asked.

Georgina glanced out the window at the passing scenery. "I have a name for you," she said. "Lord Ackerly."

She didn't answer the maid's question, because Georgina had a sinking feeling she'd never be all right again.

For the first time in a fortnight, Adam hadn't gone out to take dinner at his club or attend some other *ton* function. Seated behind his desk, he stared down at the note he'd received from his superior. It seemed Fitzmorris needed to meet with him on a matter of some urgency.

At a different point in his life, at a time before Georgina, those words would have galvanized him into motion. Now the whole blasted organization could go hang. Where had they been when he'd been taken captive? With their far-reaching influence, they'd been unable to spring him from Fox and Hunter's clutches.

The only person he cared to see was his bloody wife.

So, of course, this would be the one night she'd gone out.

He pulled the watch fob from his jacket pocket and, for what was surely the hundredth time that day, consulted the piece. Thirty minutes past six.

Where in hell is she?

Folding up Fitzmorris's note, he placed it inside the hidden compartment on his desk and rose.

Someone had to know where Georgina had gone.

"Watson!" he bellowed, striding out of the room. "Watson!"

He nearly collided with the old, graying man. "Yes, Mr. Markham?"

"Where in the hell is my wife?"

Watson angled his head as if Adam had just asked him to fetch the king's crown and not the woman he was married to. A nugget of guilt jabbed at him. His disregard had been abundantly clear, not only to his family and the *ton*, but his staff as well.

"Watson?" Adam prodded with a trace of annoyance.

"She went out," the butler blurted.

Adam briefly closed his eyes. "Yes, I had rather guessed that. Where has she gone?"

"A bookshop."

"A bookshop?" Adam repeated.

Watson nodded. "Yes, a bookshop."

Well, now that they'd cleared that away..."When did she go to the bookshop?"

The corners of Watson's mouth tipped down ever so slightly. "I'm not sure sir."

"You're not sure?"

Watson nodded. "I wasn't aware I was to keep track of Mrs. Markham's whereabouts."

Adam growled at his butler's subtle disapproval.

For all anyone knew, his wife may as well have gone out hours ago. An inexplicable fear ate at him. He told himself to take a deep breath. When that made no difference in staving off his dread, he made himself take another. There had to be something more to Georgina's absence. His heart slowed, panicked hurt blinding him.

Good God, what if she's left me?

Adam pointed a finger at Watson. "I want my horse readied and the address of the establishment."

Watson bowed his head. "Very well, sir." He hurried to do Adam's bidding.

Not even ten minutes later, Adam stood in the foyer, preparing to head out in pursuit of his wife when Watson opened the door.

Georgina swept through, her maid in tow.

She jerked to a stop at the sight of him. Her cloak was drawn tight about her, the billowing hood concealing her face.

His knees all but knocked together in relief. "Where did you go?" The harsh demand conveyed none of that to his wife, however.

Her body went rigid. "I went to a bookshop." Her words were nearly lost in the muslin fabric of her cloak.

Watson made a move to retrieve it, but she waved him off and proceeded up the stairs.

Adam's mouth fell open. Now that Georgina had returned, all his fears had abated, and he was left feeling more than a little foolish.

"Are you dismissing me?" he barked, taking the steps two at a time to keep up with her swift pace. He didn't like his sweet wife discharging him as if he were nothing more than a wayward servant.

Georgina didn't pause in her long, slow climb. "Please, Adam. You mustn't pretend there is anything we have to talk about."

Her words brought him up short and, by the time he'd collected his confounded emotions, Georgina had gone. The tall maid he'd employed for Georgina paused to shoot him a long, black look before hurrying after her mistress.

It was only as he stared bemusedly after them that he realized— Georgina hadn't returned from her shopping with any purchases.

Doubts ran rampant.

Something was decidedly suspicious about his wife's behavior, but Adam was too bloody confused too examine the reason for his apprehension. He couldn't, however, turn a blind eye to her activities.

If she were betraying him again, God help her, because there would be no mercy on his part.

TWENTY-FIVE

Seated behind his desk, Adam stared down at the second letter Fitzmorris had sent round. There was a greater note of urgency in this missive. The other man requested an audience on the morrow. Adam sighed, tossing the sheet onto his desktop. He'd pay Fitzmorris a bloody visit and be done with him.

The day Adam had been dismissed from The Brethren, his role within the organization had been amputated. Like a petulant child, he delighted in ignoring their bloody summons. Except now, he needed the diversion, something to keep his mind from the state of bloody confusion Georgina had plunged him into.

Fighting the urge to bury his head in his hands, Adam gripped the side of his desk. He and Georgina had managed to co-exist in a relatively peaceful existence, which was a tremendous feat considering he'd wanted her thrown into Newgate not too long ago.

Now he didn't know what he wanted for her.

Or them.

If Georgina had pleaded with him, professed her innocence, he suspected it would have fueled his hatred. She did none of those things. Rather, she moved through their household like a ghost. Her head lowered in an abject misery no one could possibly feign. It made him feel bloody guilty. He told himself he had nothing to feel guilty over—it was Georgina who had deceived him—but it made no difference. His stomach roiled with agony until he wanted to reach for her, beg her forgiveness. Until he had to shake his head and think on the ludicrousness of such flawed thinking.

It is Georgina who should be pleading on her lovely knees for absolution.

He told himself that but, since he was being honest with himself, he could acknowledge that he didn't wholly believe it.

The day she'd returned from the bookshop, her arms empty of purchases, warning bells had sounded in Adam's ears. All signs had pointed to Georgina being involved in some clandestine act. He'd watched her quite closely over the next week, only to find that she didn't go anywhere or interact with anyone. It only attuned Adam to the fact that her existence was a lonely one...and his guilt swelled.

Adam sighed. He would get nothing accomplished this day.

He needed to see her. Adam made his way upstairs and nearly collided with her maid.

The tall woman's cheeks were heightened with a splash of red. Her chest heaved as if she'd been running through the house and, when she spoke, her gasping words echoed his thought. "Have you seen Mrs. Markham?"

The warning bells blared louder. He shoved down the concern radiating from a point deep inside him. "I'm sorry?"

The maid frowned. "As you should be," she muttered.

Adam blinked. Surely, he'd imagined the affront. "I beg your pardon? What's your name?"

She tossed her chin back in a show of defiance. "Suzanne. If you'll excuse me, sir. I have to find Mrs. Markham."

Had he just been dismissed by a servant? He shook his head. The world was going all topsy-turvy on him. "Just a moment," he commanded in the tone that had frozen traitors in their tracks.

Suzanne spun around, planting her hands upon her hips. Fire danced in her eyes. "Yes, sir?"

Adam's thoughts spun.

Am I really going to address her impudence? Christ, I've gone stodgy.

"Where the hell is my wife?" he barked.

She gave her head a toss. "If I knew that, sir, would I be asking you?"

He strode down the hall toward Georgina's rooms, asking over his shoulder, "Have you searched her chambers?"

The maid pressed her lips into a firm line. "Yes, sir," she said, but not before Adam saw the way she pointed her eyes to the ceiling.

Adam paused outside Georgina's chambers and threw the door open.

Suzanne hovered in the doorway.

Adam strode through the immaculate room, knowing implicitly what his wife's maid had already verified—Georgina was not here.

He frowned, turning in a slow circle. His gaze landed on her armoire.

Adam threw open the oak doors and began tossing aside dress after dress, examining the contents until they littered the floor in a colossal heap of satins and taffeta. He stomped over the garments, his boots crinkling the expensive fabrics.

"What are you looking for?" Suzanne asked, suspicion lacing her words.

Adam ignored her question. He stopped beside Georgina's faultlessly made bed and tugged the coverlet off, tossing it to the ground.

The maid gasped.

A familiar red leather book peeked from beneath Georgina's pillow. Adam frowned and picked it up, turning it over in his hands. Absently he looked through the book when one particular page snagged awkwardly on a lone scrap of paper.

His heart quickened.

"Sir?" Suzanne pressed.

Adam removed the sheet and unfolded it to read the damning words. His stomach felt as if he were being pitched around the deck of a small vessel on a stormy sea.

Four o'clock.
Ye Olde Bookshop.
Leave your maid.
Ever Yours, H

H.

An image surfaced of Georgina wrapped in Hunter's arms, the other man lifting her skirts and fucking her while she cried out with longing for the man who'd stolen Adam's freedom and destroyed his life.

A filmy layer of pain and fury descended over his eyes, blurring his vision. His fists tightened convulsively around the paper, crinkling it into an unrecognizable ball. With a roar that tore from somewhere deep within his heart, Adam tossed it across the room and slammed his fist into the coverlet.

Goddamn her.

"Sir!" Suzanne cried when he spun around and all about flew from the chambers.

He raced down the stairs, bellowing for his carriage.

Four o'clock.
Ye Olde Bookshop.
Leave your maid.
Ever Yours,
H

Georgina stared across the bustling street at the bookshop.

It had been ten days since she'd had her first and last meeting with Jamie. She'd not heard hide nor hair from him or the duke.

Until this morning. She'd had to work quite hard to slip out without Suzanne noticing. The maid clung to her side like an aged vine wrapped about an old oak. Now, part of her wondered at the wisdom of setting off alone. The duke had made it quite clear that Suzanne was to accompany her everywhere.

He'd not however indicated what she should do if Jamie requested a meeting and ordered her to leave Suzanne behind.

She'd had the better part of the day to analyze the prudence of her intended actions. In the end, she had rationalized that if she were to provide the assistance the Crown needed then she would have to take these added risks. Thus far, she'd only obtained a solitary piece of information for the duke—the name, Ackerly. She'd pledged to help the Crown and her efforts had proven ineffectual.

No longer.

Squaring her shoulders, she set off across the street and entered the bookshop. Georgina managed a quiet greeting for the merchant, who tried in vain to engage her in conversation. Her nerves were too frayed to muster pleasantries and she wandered in silence down the long rows.

She stopped in front of a shelf and stared at the book directly in her line of vision. Othello.

Her lips turned in a sorry rendition of a smile. Shakespeare's work seemed very apropos. *Take note, take note, O world, To be direct and honest is not safe.*

With a sigh, Georgina set it aside.

In the nearly three weeks since Adam had discovered her betrayal, he'd tempered the stinging vitriol he directed her way. He'd also not indulged in spirits since the day in the library when she'd slapped him. Their names had also appeared less and less in the scandal sheets, though that had more to do with their retreat from Society's peering eyes.

Her husband had not warmed to her, however. He made no move to touch her or engage in any real conversation outside of rapid questioning as to where she'd been and what she'd done each day. Georgina knew Adam's questions stemmed more from suspicion than any real interest in how she spent her days.

She had tried to weave her way back into his good graces. Lord knew she had tried. In spite of the toe-curling awkwardness of seeking out a man who couldn't care less whether she lived or died, Georgina would join him in the library, the parlor, or his office whenever she could.

On one occasion, she'd slipped into the parlor and found him with a sketchpad in his hands—his head bent low over the page, tousled blond locks falling over his eye.

Reminded of the things that had united them during the days of his captivity, Georgina had slid behind the pianoforte and begun to sing. Adam had jerked his head up, his erratic movement sending the sketchpad falling to the floor.

He'd glowered at her with such dark annoyance that she'd fumbled with the keys, creating a discordant, grating noise. She'd closed her mouth, risen clumsily to her feet, and stormed from the parlor.

Georgina had long ago realized that she would not be able to win back her husband's affections. Even if he forgave her, she would always be Fox's daughter and that could not be undone.

Her heart tightened at the truth of her silent acknowledgement. Georgina shoved her sorrowful musings into a deep corner in her mind. She could not think about this. Not now. She needed to be prepared for her meeting with Jamie.

The minutes ticked by and her nerves stretched so thin she had to bite her lip to keep from throwing her head back and screaming. Nearly two hours later, Georgina began to suspect Jamie had no intention of coming. Nonetheless, she continued to wait. And wait. And wait.

Until there was no choice but to accept that Jamie wasn't honoring the meeting. With a sigh, Georgina snatched the copy of Othello and carried it to the front counter.

The owner of the shop smiled at her, displaying an uneven row of yellowing teeth. "Very different than your usual selections," he observed.

If the thought there was something suspicious in the hours she'd spent in his store, he did not give any indication of it. She turned her money over to him and accepted her purchase. "I was feeling the need for a change."

He scratched the top of his bald pate. "Isn't the most happy of Shakespeare's work."

He had her there. But then the book fit her mood perfectly.

Georgina bid him good day and hurried off with her purchase under her arm. She stepped outside, squinting into the fading sunlight for a sign of her driver. Catching sight of him, she began walking forward.

"Good day, Georgina," Jamie said, and moved directly into her path.

Her recently purchased book tumbled into a puddle of black and brown sludge. She gasped.

Jamie held his elbow out. "Come with me, Georgina."

Georgina shook her head, fighting a burgeoning sense of panic. She couldn't accompany him, not alone, and not in this very public fashion. The gossips would sharpen their teeth on such delicious fodder.

She took a step away from him.

"Don't even think of it, my dear." Jamie smiled through tightly clenched teeth.

For anyone passing by, they'd only see a compellingly handsome gentleman with an affable grin. Only Georgina had the experience to know that this smile preceded his most vicious attacks.

Memory of the duke's admonition that she take Suzanne with her everywhere surfaced. Georgina swallowed back her growing apprehension. "I-I…"

He extended his elbow. A courteous offer from a gentleman assisting a lady across the street.

Georgina's stomach curled into a tight ball of tension that made her mouth go dry. She was besieged by the ominous thought that if she joined Jamie, she would never return. The flecks of gold shooting fire in his pale blue eyes, the vein throbbing at his temple…all pointed to a palpable, dangerous fury.

"N-no. I have to—"

"If you care even a bit for your husband, I suggest you accompany me, Georgina."

She placed her hand on his arm and allowed him to guide her across the street.

All the while, she sought out her driver. When she found him, any hope of salvation died a swift and painful death. The young man stood with his back to the street, engrossed in a conversation with a pretty maid.

Jamie rested his hand against the small of her back, applying subtle pressure. He led her to a black carriage. "Get in."

Georgina bit the inside of her cheek and allowed him to assist her inside.

The door closed and the conveyance rattled off, carrying Georgina away from the bookshop. No one knew where she had gone. She'd left no note to indicate that she'd received a summons from Jamie. When she didn't return that evening—and, casting a glance at Jamie from beneath hooded lids—it was a certainty that she wouldn't return, no one would note her absence. Not her husband, nor her staff.

Suzanne!

She sent a silent prayer to a very busy God that her maid had discovered her absence. Why, even now the young woman might be alerting the duke—

"I'm disappointed in you, Georgina," Jamie said, interrupting her spiraling thoughts. He leaned over and gripped her chin, forcing her closer so that his hot breath wafted over her skin.

She bit her lip to keep from crying out.

"Very disappointed," he murmured. He relinquished her so suddenly she pitched backward, slamming her head into the wall of the carriage.

She curled her fingers into the fabric of her skirts as she sought to hide the terror growing in her breast. She didn't speak, knowing Jamie was toying with her like the cat who'd trapped the mouse. No, she wouldn't give in to that fear. It would only heighten the sick pleasure he took in torturing her.

"Do you know why I'm disappointed?"

She wet her lips. "No."

Georgina had a sinking feeling she knew exactly what had pushed Jamie to the brink of madness. She prayed she was wrong but knew in her heart that he'd discovered her deception. There was no other accounting for the about-face from their last encounter. It was why he hadn't contacted her over the past ten days. Why he'd instructed her to leave Suzanne behind.

She unfurled her fingers. With infinite slowness, she inched her hand along the edge of the seat.

Jamie grabbed her before she'd even grasped the handle. He squeezed her wrist.

A hiss of pain escaped her as tears flooded her eyes.

"Lying bitch," he snarled.

"Jamie," she implored.

He backhanded her across the face. A loud thrumming resonated in her ears.

She gave her head a clearing shake. "Please."

Don't hurt me. Let me go. Tell my husband I love him.

Jamie dusted his hands, as if by touching her he had forever sullied his person. He reached for the curtain and directed his attention outside, seeming to study the passing scenery. He spoke in a chillingly, cheerful voice. "Do you know that I insisted you were loyal? I went against your father's better judgment. I attested to your honor."

"I am honorable." She cradled her throbbing cheek within her hand. It was true. She just happened to be loyal to those other than Jamie and the Irish Republicanism.

Jamie's nostrils flared. The curtain fluttered back into place. "Do you take me for an idiot?" he exploded.

"I—" Her protestations were rewarded with another cruel slap. This time to the opposite cheek.

"Enough. Not another word until we reach our destination."

She wanted to ask where they were going, but Jamie's muscled biceps rippled through the fabric of his coat, and his countenance shone with barely suppressed rage. She'd find out nothing else from him. All she would do was invite another assault.

The silence, only broken by the swift-moving wheels and the occasional whinny of the horses, was more torturous than even Jamie's taunting barbs. The quiet fed her fear and led her thoughts down the path of regret.

She should have left Father and Jamie long, long ago. During his captivity, Adam had continually prodded her, encouraging her to go, asking why she remained. She'd thought the information she passed to the Crown absolved her of wrongdoing. Helped save honorable lives. In the end, nothing she'd done had ever really mattered.

She'd thought herself brave. The truth was sick and ugly. Georgina had been a coward all her life. She'd allowed her father and Jamie to browbeat her, had stood silent while Father rained vitriolic disapproval upon her head until she'd become a shell of the young girl she'd once been. Over time, her shoulders had drooped a bit more, and her expectations in life had become much less.

It hadn't been until Adam that the spark of life and laughter had been rekindled. Through his gentle encouragement and caring, she'd been born again into a woman she didn't recognize. He had taught her to smile and to dream.

She closed her eyes.

I will never tell him. I will never be able to hold him and thank him for showing me the strength I carry within. I will not tell him that he set me free. I will never see him again.

They will kill me.

The four words froze her beating heart, stilled the blood coursing through her body. She went numb as she faced the certainty of her own demise.

What will I have accomplished? What will be my mark on this world? A husband who detests me. A father who will most assuredly be the one to put a gun to my temple—and only then if I am fortunate.

Her stomach heaved, bile climbing up her throat.

She concentrated on drawing in long, even breaths until the wave of nausea passed.

And then she waited.

TWENTY-SIX

Adam had thought there could be no greater pain than having learned the truth about Georgina's paternity.

Except as Jamie Adleyson Marshall smiled down at his wife, intimately stroking her lower back, Adam realized he couldn't have been more wrong. He watched from within the confines of his carriage, thankful for the protection it provided, for allowing him to take in every single, mind-numbing, aching moment as his wife betrayed him with his captor.

Hunter whispered in Georgina's ear and her response made the other man smile. Even with the distance separating him, the man's pearl white grin caught Adam's attention from across the street, and he wanted nothing more than to climb out of his carriage, punch Hunter in the face, and shove every single, blasted tooth down his bloody throat until he choked on them.

Georgina paused. Her body went ramrod straight, and Adam leaned close to the window, peering through the curtain. For an infinitesimal moment, in his heart of hearts, he believed she was going to turn around and leave Hunter. But the moment passed and Hunter was handing Georgina up into the carriage.

Adam rapped on the ceiling. The orders had been clear to his driver when they'd parked the conveyance across from Ye Olde Bookshop. The moment Hunter's carriage left, he was to follow.

All the while his conveyance carried him toward his lying wife and her lover, Adam flayed himself with the humiliated hurt he'd opened himself to at Georgina's hands. Since they had first met, she'd done nothing but deceive and trick him. When he'd confronted her in his library those four weeks ago, she'd looked at him through teary-eyes, lips aquiver in a very believable, heart-rending tableau of a woman wronged. Adam had hardened his heart...but the doubts had seeped in and had continued to eat at him.

Now he could no longer turn from the truth of it—Georgina's loyalty did not lie with him and England. Instead, she'd pledged her heart, mind, and soul to venomous monsters who would gladly have killed him if it hadn't been for Stone's timely intervention.

Adam stared out at the passing scenery, expecting to see the ordinary streets give way to the darker, seedier parts of London. Instead, the carriage rumbled along through the bustling London wharves, eventually drawing to a halt beside a large warehouse. Hunter stepped down and reached inside.

Adam gnashed his teeth, battling the sting of jealousy as Hunter placed his hands around Georgina's waist and helped her down. Adam shouldn't have cared. The two of them deserved each other. He should have considered himself well and truly blessed to have uncovered the truth of her deceit, and left it at that.

But, as he watched Hunter guide her down the side of the large building, Adam had to acknowledge that he cared—a great deal more than he liked. He sat within the confines of his carriage, his body numbed. Visions slashed through his mind like the swift edge of a blade. Georgina in Hunter's arms. Hunter laying her down and working her skirts up around her supple hips. Her smiling up at him.

Adam had promised Georgina that there would be no redemption if she were to again betray him. He waited for the murderous rage to consume him. It didn't come.

Pain lanced him to the core. Georgina might have betrayed him but, damn it, he wanted her—all of her—and he would have rather lopped off his left arm than see her walk out of his life without a backward glance.

He dropped his head into his hands as the truth intruded with an agonizing viciousness.

I did this. I drove her back to Hunter's arms.

Adam had threatened to have her hauled off to Newgate. He'd not bothered to hide his loathing from her. And he'd taken her like a trollop on a balcony where anyone could have witnessed.

He yanked his head up. Regardless, it was time he had closure. The moment Georgina had walked across that street and into Hunter's carriage, everything between them had died. It would do Adam little good bemoaning all he could have done differently.

But before he put Georgina from his life, he needed to see her—and Hunter.

As Georgina descended from the carriage, she cast a desperate glance around at her surroundings. Carriages littered the streets. Men moved freely along the pavement. If she called out, surely someone would rescue her?

She didn't want just anyone, however. She wanted her husband.

With the hopeful dreams belonging to a foolish young girl, she imagined Adam striding down the street, blocking Jamie's path, and plucking her from his clutches.

Jamie led her down the side of the building and a rat scurried across the path before them, a high-pitched squeak escaping the hideous creature.

Georgina took a hasty step backward. She wanted Adam, but right now she would accept aid from the devil himself if he offered.

Jamie took Georgina by the arm, the pads of his fingers biting into the soft flesh as he steered her through what appeared to be an empty warehouse.

She blinked, trying to bring the dark surroundings into focus.

"Come along." Jamie gave her a nudge, propelling her forward.

The click of his boot-steps and the shuffle of her delicate slippers broke the eerie echoing silence. The swift pace he set for them kicked up dust, and Georgina wrinkled her nose, fighting back a sneeze in vain.

"Achoo!"

Jamie glared down at her, tightening his grip on her upper arm. "Quiet."

He shoved her through a door.

Georgina stumbled, tripping over her slippers, but caught herself.

Jamie pointed to the lone sofa in the room. "Sit."

Pride urged her to resist his laconic orders.

The will to survive drove her into the stiff leather seat.

Jamie tapped his finger along his jaw, studying her as if she were a species of insect he'd never seen before. With a growl, he turned away from Georgina and walked over to the heavily curtained window. He didn't pull back the thick, red velvet, merely stood there in silence, his gaze fixed on the fabric.

Georgina used his distraction to study her surroundings. Perched on the edge of a brown leather sofa, she peered around the spacious office within the factory. There was little doubt this was one of her father's holdings, though she'd never been inside his warehouses. She'd known he had buildings in Bristol and London but hadn't put much thought into how he spent his days—she'd just been so very grateful for his absence.

She looked on with no small amount of curiosity. Or awe for the vast wealth demonstrated in the Aubusson carpets or the wall-length shelves of leather books. Instead, her stomach churned at the prospect of facing her father, and she had to quell the urge to look over her shoulder to see if he lurked in the shadows of the room.

Time marched to the tune of the tick-tock, tick-tock of the tarnished silver clock atop the vast, mahogany desk. Jamie did not utter a single word. He stood in the exact same pose, as still as one of Da Vinci's marble works of art. His biceps tensed so tightly, the muscles strained the expensive sapphire fabric of his coat.

Jamie had never been one to keep his rage in check. Over the years, he'd exercised his anger and frustrations quite freely. This unpredictable figure—rage seething beneath the surface of his immaculate façade—was, oddly, more threatening.

Georgina inched to the edge of her seat, casting surreptitious looks between Jamie's back and the door, measuring the distance. A good six feet separated them and, with the added obstacle of the desk, she suspected she had another foot or so advantage.

The leather creaked beneath her and she winced.

Jamie spun to face her, his gaze narrowed into near impenetrable slits.

When Georgina had been a small girl, she'd watched the kitchen cat corner a mouse. The fat, white and black spotted creature had pranced and danced about, occasionally hitting the tiny mouse with its paw. Georgina had stared on with a sick fascination as the cat had hunkered down, his intense gaze honed in on the motionless mouse. Then the creature had made one desperate attempt to flee. The cat had taken him between his teeth, shaking him with a frenzy, until the poor thing had gone still.

Georgina now felt a remarkable oneness with that tiny, forgotten mouse. She forced herself to take a breath. She would not lie in wait for Jamie to devour her. "I imagine I've done something to displease you. But then that would be nothing new, would it?" She forced her chin up.

Jamie folded his hands in front of him. "It isn't just me you've displeased."

Father.

"Your father is quite disappointed in you, my dear."

Bitterness made her rash. "But then, have I ever really pleased my father?"

Jamie turned around to face her, though the desk remained a protective barrier between them. "Do you realize you've not yet asked what caused our anger?"

Georgina had a strong suspicion she didn't need to hear the revelation. "Is it my dismal entrance into London Society?"

A sharp bark of laughter escaped him. His eyes, however, were dead of all emotion. He strolled out from behind the desk.

Georgina stole another glance over her shoulder.

"Don't even think about it," he commanded.

Her head shot around. "Think about what?"

She burrowed within the folds of her seat when Jamie flew across the room, closing the distance between them. He leaned forward, bracing his arms on either side of her seat. "Do you take me for a bloody fool?" he snapped.

Spit landed on her cheek and Georgina itched to wipe the filth away. "You're not a fool, Jamie. A traitor and a cruel beast, but not a fool."

Jamie's face froze, but then, as though her words amused him, he smiled. "If you didn't believe I was a fool, why would you run so quickly back to the Crown with the name I gave you?"

She started.

"Yes, my dear." The words were hardly an endearment. "We gave you a false contact. Poor Ackerly was physically removed from his townhouse and thoroughly questioned."

Georgina's eyes went wide as the dawning horror settled in. "He isn't a Republican." Of course, they'd given her a false name to test her loyalty.

How could I have been so naïve?

Jamie confirmed her worst fears. "That's right." He chuckled. "Though after the questioning he received, I'd imagine he isn't too fond of the Crown."

Georgina closed her eyes.

This is bad. This is very bad, indeed.

She had thought, at worst, mayhap Jamie had learned of her connection with the Duke of Aubrey, but she'd hoped he'd only been speaking on suspicion of guilt. The truth was a deal more troubling— they had trapped her in her duplicity.

"Hmm? Nothing to say?" Like the kitchen cat, his paw was out.

No. There is nothing to say.

He lowered his brow to hers, his breath brushed her nose.

She remained motionless and a pit settled in her stomach.

If he has lascivious intentions, there is no one to prevent Jamie from forcing himself on me. I would be helpless to stop him.

The hot, feral gleam in his eyes indicated that he had followed the exact direction of Georgina's thoughts. He rubbed his thumb along her lower lip, his gaze dropping to study the plump flesh.

A whore's mouth, her father used to say. Georgina had never known what her father had meant—until just now.

Jamie lowered his lips, and Georgina cringed, biting the inside of her cheek when suddenly he stopped.

"Do you know I would have given you everything and anything you ever desired, Georgina? Do you know I would have dressed you in the finest silks and satins, adorning you like a queen?" He cupped her jaw with one hand. "You're no longer a stuttering child, afraid of her shadow." His words sounded like a lover's endearment.

Georgina broke contact with his heated gaze, lowering her eyes. "You know those things never mattered to me, Jamie," she said with a trace of sadness and regret. "I just wanted to live a normal life."

Please God, spare me his advances.

There was no God. Jamie took her lips in a hard, punishing kiss, his assault, a gross violation. Shivers of revulsion wracked her frame, and she pulled back, trying to dislodge him. Jamie wrapped a hand around her head, anchoring her in place, and Georgina could not fight him.

He wrenched his lips away from hers with enough force that she collapsed against the firm back of the sofa.

"Where is my father?" she asked, wishing for the first time that Father was near. She'd rather deal with his anger than Jamie's vile touch.

Jamie blinked back the cloud of desire. "Have you missed us?"

"How could I not?" She threw the words mockingly at him. Jamie was more a child to Father than Georgina had ever been— or ever wanted to be. They were both sick and twisted in their machinations. "You've always been so very devoted and loving to me."

"Finally, I hear the truth from your lips."

Georgina gasped and shoved Jamie backward. Her gaze flew to the door. "Adam!"

He stood there, a towering golden god, more powerful than the avenging archangel Gabriel, a pistol trained on Jamie's black-blooded heart.

Then Adam's words registered.

And hope died in her breast.

273

Georgina clambered to her feet, taking a step toward him. "Adam!"

His gun didn't waver from the man who'd held him captive, who'd beaten and bloodied him. He moved his gaze from Hunter to his wife, and for one endless moment, swore her eyes radiated love, joy in seeing him, and something odd—relief.

Adam tightened his grip on the pistol to keep from tossing her over his shoulder and storming off like a conquering lord from long ago. The male part of him, blinded by hot jealousy, said be damned with how Georgina felt about Jamie. It mattered not at all when faced with his hungering love for her.

Except Adam had spent the better part of the past month reconciling himself to the truth about his wife's loyalties. He forced himself to look away from Georgina. No, it was better to look at the snake Hunter who held his wife's heart.

"We meet again, Hunter," Adam drawled.

Hunter made a move to open the front of his jacket.

Adam waved his gun. "I don't think that's a good idea...but then, perhaps it is. I'd like nothing better than to shoot you through your heart."

The other man paled. "P-please." His badly shaking hands fell uselessly to his sides.

Energized by the terror etched on Hunter's face, Adam lowered the pistol, pointing the barrel at the front flap of Hunter's breeches. "Do you know, every day you held me captive I would spend my time imagining all the ways I would eventually kill you? Some days I decided I would do it quickly, so I could rid the earth of your evil." Adam dropped his voice to a near whisper, relishing the way Hunter's body quaked. "Most days, though, I decided I would take my time and make your death a slow, painful one."

Like a cornered rat, Hunter's gaze flitted between Adam's pistol and the door.

Adam grinned. "Are we expecting company, Hunter? Is it perhaps my dear father-in-law who you expect to step through the doors and rescue you?" His gaze landed on his wife. Her soulful, brown eyes made wide circles in her face and her skin had the same deathly pallor as Hunter's.

You made me fall in love with you and you broke my heart, Georgina.

His grip tightened on the pistol. He'd not utter those words aloud and give Hunter any bit of victory in these final moments.

Georgina moved toward him, but Hunter captured her wrist, pulling her to his side. "Surely Georgina means enough to you that you'd let me live?" Hunter wheedled.

Georgina made a move to free herself from his grip. "Adam, I love you," she rasped. "Do not listen to him!" She looked at him with pleading eyes.

God, how he wanted to believe her. Wanted to trust her words.

Then Hunter pulled her sweet buttocks against the vee of his thighs, and leaned down close so his lips fairly brushed her ear. "You would abandon me to save yourself, Georgina?" His voice broke. "After all we've shared, you would betray me, too?" He looked at Adam, pain reflected in his eyes. "Do you know Georgina can sing? She has sung to me every day since we met. She has a voice like an angel."

Adam winced as he remembered waltzing her around his small prison. He'd once thought the very same thing about sweet, harmless Georgina.

Georgina swatted at Hunter's hand. "You lie," she cried, her face contorted with rage, quashing all memories of the innocent young maid who'd come to Adam's rooms and cared for him.

Hunter continued. "She would cook for me. She knew my favorite dish was lamb and every night would—"

Adam held his hand up. He couldn't take anymore. Not if he were to retain any semblance of his sanity. Georgina's willingness to transfer her affections from Hunter drove her betrayal home like a nail through his heart.

For the first time in a very long time, Adam didn't want to kill Hunter. Instead, he felt a remarkable kinship with this man who loved Georgina too. He, like Hunter, knew what it was to love a woman so self-serving she'd say and do anything to achieve her goals...and her father's goals.

Adam lowered his pistol. "Get out," he commanded hoarsely.

Hunter's eyes went wide.

He waved his gun. "Before I change my mind. You two are deserving of the Crown's punishment, however it will not be at my hands."

Right or wrong, I love you too much, Georgina, to turn you and your lover over.

He'd sooner wrap the noose about his own neck than watch anyone do that to her, even if that was what his deceitful wife had coming.

Hunter reacted first. He took Georgina by the arm and pulled her toward the doorway, beating a hasty retreat around Adam.

Georgina dug her heels in. She gave her curls a frantic shake. "Adam, y-you—"

He jerked his chin toward the door. "Go!" he barked.

Go! Before I change my mind, kill Hunter, and take you with me.

Hunter leaned down and whispered something close to her ear.

As if she'd stared the mythical Medusa in the eyes, Georgina went motionless. A small, quivering smile turned her lips. "Goodbye," she said hoarsely then walked out beside Hunter, Adam's bruised and bloodied heart going right out the door with them.

TWENTY-SEVEN

Adam stepped out of the warehouse and squinted into the last vestiges of the setting sun. He pulled his watch fob out and consulted the time. Funny, it felt like he'd spent eternity in the bowels of hell, when it had been but a thirty-minute exchange.

He scanned the busy surroundings, searching for his coach. It sat motionless across the street, waiting for him, but Adam turned on his heel and walked away. He needed to walk. With a heavy tread, he made the long trek down the street, his pace slow. He concentrated on placing one foot in front of the other, because if he didn't, he would go mad at the loss of Georgina.

Adam had thought he'd loved Grace, but that had been nothing compared to this all-consuming fire that licked at him and scorched him from the inside out. His love for Georgina was so great he'd betrayed his country, The Brethren, and his own family. Even knowing she would go off and continue her work against the Crown hadn't been enough to turn her over to his superiors, because when he imagined a world without her smiling in it, he knew he would go mad.

Mayhap he already had. He paused, glancing back at the empty warehouse. Where would she go? Would she ever think of him? Or had she truly only used him to serve her own purposes? The questions swirled through his brain until it felt like he was running in dizzying circles. A carriage pulled up alongside him, spraying him with bits of gravel and refuse from the street.

The door opened. "Get in."

Adam stared up at the Duke of Aubrey.

Aubrey glared down at him. "I said, get in."

Adam's numbed hurt gave way to fast-growing rage. He welcomed any diversion that would keep him from thinking of Georgina, even if for just a moment.

Aubrey held up a hand, displaying the familiar signet belonging to The Brethren.

Adam climbed into the coach.

Into the very crowded coach. Across from him, Aubrey sat beside Bennett and another man. This one a stranger.

The carriage lurched forward.

Aubrey wasted no time with social niceties. "You may know me as 'The Sovereign'."

Adam started. So this was the infamous leader of the organization: the powerful Duke of Aubrey, whose name appeared in scandal sheets linking him with notoriously disreputable widows. It was a stroke of genius. Who would ever suspect that one of the most notable rogues in London served in one of the most exalted positions with the Crown?

"What do you want?" Adam growled. He'd already deduced the reason for Aubrey's unexpected appearance—"The Sovereign" wanted Fox and Hunter...and Georgina. His superior had surely come for Georgina.

Aubrey drummed his fingertips along the edge of his knee, giving him an air of relaxed calm. The stiff tension in his broad shoulders and the hard set to his square jaw belied the duke's attempt at feigned nonchalance. "I spoke to Fitzmorris earlier this morn," Aubrey said. "He claims he requested several audiences. Did you meet with him?"

Adam shook his head. He'd been otherwise engaged uncovering the truth of his wife's deception.

Aubrey cursed. "Where is she?" he barked.

"I don't suppose you're speaking about my mother, the Countess of Whitehaven?" he asked with forced levity.

"Don't play games," Bennett snapped. "Where is she?"

Adam bit back a stinging retort. His entire world had been blown to pieces, and why? Because he'd devoted everything he was to The

Brethren. They wanted Georgina. Well they were going to have to wait until the good Lord came again, because he wasn't turning her over. The Duke of Aubrey, Bennett, and the nameless bastard could all go hang.

"Markham?" Aubrey urged.

Adam prayed Georgina had had enough time to make her escape, because The Brethren had discovered her deception.

"You have nothing to fear from Georgina Wilcox. She's not here. She's gone," Adam said woodenly.

Bennett and the stranger exchanged looks, and the first frisson of doubt unfurled in Adam's gut, along with the awful feeling that he'd committed some irreparable harm.

"What do you mean, gone?" the unfamiliar figure pressed.

"Who are you?" Adam asked the nameless stranger.

The man waved his hand as though to say it didn't matter who the hell he was. "I said, where is she?"

Adam had exhausted his store of patience for that day. "Go to hell," he spat.

The man reached across the carriage and gripped him by the lapels of his coat, jerking his frame against the squabs of the coach. He gave him a hard shake. "By Christ, you'll answer me!"

Aubrey settled a hand on his shoulder but he shrugged it off.

Adam remained stoically silent. He'd not give Georgina over to this ruthless bastard.

He released Adam with a black curse and reached for the handle of the still-moving carriage. Panic made Adam's heart speed. This stranger was so determined to get his hands upon Georgina he'd risk life and limb by jumping from a moving conveyance.

"She's not here," Adam barked, effectively ending the stranger's intentions of climbing out and hunting Georgina like a cornered beast.

Aubrey spoke. "Where is she?"

Adam met the duke's icy stare. "I freed her."

The tension seemed to drain out of the duke's stiff shoulders.

"Finally something's gone right," Bennett mumbled in his gravelly tone. "Where is she then?"

Adam stared back at the expectant expressions of the three men. Why would The Brethren want Georgina freed? Unless to lead them deeper into the web of traitors...

"Markham?" Aubrey prompted.

"She's with Hunter," he said, between clenched teeth.

A deathly silence filled the carriage. Only the clip clop of the horses' hooves split the quiet.

The stranger roared and launched himself across the cramped coach. "By God, I'll kill you."

Bennett wrestled him off Adam and shoved him back into his seat.

"Enough!" the duke commanded.

Adam looked through narrowed eyes at his superior. "She is my wife. Surely you cannot think I'd turn her over to you?"

Aubrey ran his fingers through immaculate, black hair. "You didn't know. I expressly forbade Fitzmorris from meeting with you, but he defied my wishes. But you never met him."

Adam had already said as much. A loud humming filled his ears as he tried to make logic of the other man's outrage. "Why did Fitzmorris want to see me?" When the duke remained silent, Adam demanded again. "Why did he want to see me?"

Aubrey looked from Adam to the others. "She didn't tell him."

With a growl, the tall stranger swiped a hand over his eyes. "Of course she didn't tell him."

"Tell me what?" Adam demanded. When Aubrey remained stoically silent, he directed the question to Bennett. "Tell me what?"

"That she is working for us," the stranger spat.

The dull humming in his ears grew and he gave his head a shake, to no avail. Nausea roiled in his stomach, bile climbing up his throat. "No." He'd heard them wrong. Georgina wouldn't be helping The Brethren. She was a traitor—

"We enlisted her help," Aubrey finally answered, his tone quiet.

Even if they spoke the truth and Georgina was now in fact helping The Brethren, that hadn't always been the case. Some of the tautness left his frame. Adam hardened his jaw. "That doesn't pardon her of the wrongs she's committed. She has probably only done so to save her own neck." He'd not be so foolish where Georgina was concerned. Not again.

The stranger spoke. "You are wrong. Miss Wilcox has been helping us for many years now."

The last shred of Adam's patience fell away. "Who the hell are you?"

"He's speaking the truth," Aubrey said. "For more than four years, Miss Wilcox has aided The Brethren. Her efforts have proven invaluable."

The growing unease stirred in his gut once again and he tried in vain to tamp it down. He dug his fingers into his temples and gave his head a frantic shake. "Lies." The denial tore from his throat, hoarse and guttural. "You lie." They had to be lies, because if they weren't, that would mean Georgina had been loyal to him and the Crown. That would mean when she'd insisted on her innocence she'd been telling the truth. And that would mean he had turned her over to Hunter's clutches. His stomach pitched. *Oh God, I'm going to be sick.* "Back. We have to go back," he rasped. "I left her with him."

Aubrey cursed and banged on the roof of the coach, calling out new orders.

Disdain seeped from the stranger's eyes. "You bloody fool." Guilt knifed away at Adam's insides. He pressed the heel of his palms against his eyes and tried to blot out the horror of what he'd done. This was so very different from the betrayal he'd felt when he'd learned of Georgina's birth. This was a hell of his own making, born of his insecurities and unwillingness to see his wife for the beautiful gift she was. And because of it, he'd placed her life in the hands of that monster.

Aubrey dropped a hand on his shoulder. "We will get her back."

"And, God willing, she'll be alive," the stranger spat.

Adam's heart shriveled in his chest.

She has to be alive. She has to.

She had to live because he needed to spend the rest of his life atoning for all the ways in which he'd wronged her. Sucking in a ragged breath, he closed his eyes and saw her as he'd left her—pleading with him in words and through the depth of emotion in her eyes to protect her.

And what did I do? He'd walked out on her, abandoning her to the clutches of Hunter and Fox. His mind screeched a protest. Unable to bear the images he'd conjured, he banged his head against the back of the carriage in a slow, punishing rhythm. Fox would not kill her. He couldn't kill her. What manner of man could? That was, if Georgina was even Fox's daughter.

His eyes popped open. "Is she the daughter of Fox?"

The stranger spat on the carriage floor—a crass reminder of what he thought of Adam. "Is that all you care about?"

"No. I..." At one time, that might have been the case. He swallowed hard, holding his palms up. "No, it isn't."

Aubrey took mercy. "An anonymous informant has been notifying The Brethren of Emmet's plots and plans for a number of years. This person identified Fox and Hunter as key figures for us to watch and follow."

Georgina.

Georgina was the informant.

"For years we've suspected Mrs. Markham's loyalties were not her father's. We'd purposefully arranged several missions over the years to ascertain her dependability."

Adam's stomach tightened. Bennett and Fitzmorris had dismissed his claims that he'd been drugged and betrayed because they'd known it to be fact. Because they'd orchestrated his capture.

As if sensing the direction of Adam's thoughts, Bennett gave a curt nod. "We sent you in to determine her faithfulness to the Crown. There was another man before you." He jerked his chin over at the stranger. "Nathaniel Archer was the first."

Adam looked at Archer, whose eyes brimmed with loathing. A disgusted laugh bubbled up from Adam's throat. The other man couldn't hate him any more than Adam hated himself.

He pulled back the curtain, just as the warehouse came into focus.

He didn't give a damn about The Brethren or that they'd sacrificed his safety and well-being as part of a mission. There'd be time enough for those recriminations later...For now, all he cared about was getting his wife back.

The carriage hadn't even drawn to a stop when Adam opened the door and leaped to the ground. He faltered but was on his feet in moments and running toward the factory. The three men followed in his wake.

The crack of a gunshot split the mundane street sounds and his body jerked to a stop so suddenly that someone crashed into his back, nearly sending him pitching forward.

The echo of the shot danced around his mind. Stars dotted his vision.

Georgina!

Georgina knew particular things with complete certainty. The sun rose every morning. The sun set each evening. Men were driven by avarice and greed.

Adam had walked out on Georgina, abandoning her to Jamie's evil and, as Jamie tugged her through the empty warehouse, she faced another absolute certainty—her life was forfeit.

Jamie stopped, shoving her down atop a wooden crate. "Sit."

Then like an evil spirit materializing through the fog, Father appeared. He didn't so much as utter a greeting, and Georgina knew enough to remain silent and draw as little attention to herself as possible while Jamie and Father conversed.

The occasional name reached her ears. They mentioned France several times and Georgina knew they were plotting their escape. She wasn't so foolish as to believe they'd so freely talk in front of her. That is, unless they didn't plan on her being alive much longer.

Georgina used the time they spent in distracted conversation searching for anything with which to arm herself, focusing on survival, because if she didn't, the hurt of Adam's abandonment would destroy her faster than a bullet to the heart. Except the thought had crept in and there was no shaking it free.

How easily he'd believed the worst in her. Just like everyone else in her life, he'd only seen her failures and shortcomings—in this case, her greatest crime was the blood in her veins. As much as she loved Adam, as much as she would fight the devil himself for him, she meant nothing to her husband.

"You've disappointed me, daughter," Father called out.

Georgina's lip curled, and she remained seated, hands folded atop her lap. "That is nothing new, Father."

He tipped his head in acknowledgement. "Your grandmother died at the hands of those English monsters. They took turns raping her and, even with that, you would betray me with the British. You would marry one of those bastards."

Pain lanced her heart. "What those men did to your mother was unpardonable, but not all Englishmen are like them. My husband is not like them."

He roared and made a grab for her, but Jamie stayed his efforts. "You slut." Her father's lip peeled back in a snarl, giving him a look of a beast frothing at the mouth. "All these years stealing information and sending it to the British."

Georgina sucked in a breath and she flicked her gaze about the room in search of escape.

Jamie continued to restrain him. Father fought against his hold but at his age, he was no match for Jamie's strength. "Do you know what the best part is, daughter?"

She met his gaze. "No, but I suspect you'll tell me."

He licked his lips like a dog savoring a tasty morsel. "You aren't even married to the bastard."

The ground went out from under her. She shoved herself to her feet. "Liar."

"You stupid chit." A black, ugly laugh bubbled past his lips. "You married him before you were twenty without my consent." He gave a mocking bow. "And I'd sooner send the both of you to the devil than consent to my whore daughter marrying an Englishmen who is trying to destroy the Irish republic."

Georgina folded her arms across her stomach, every muscle in her body tight with the ugly truth of his words. She'd never been married to Adam. She closed her eyes. How very glad he would be when he found out.

Jamie cried out. "No!"

Georgina's eyes flew open and her heart froze. Her father leveled his pistol at her breast.

"How does it feel knowing you spread your legs for the enemy, all without the benefit of marriage?"

She'd always known he would eventually kill her but had hoped she would be brave when the time came. A shudder wracked her frame. Then another. And another.

In spite of all the misery she'd known, she would always choose life. She wanted to live, to see Adam one more time, to smell the salty Bristol sea air. She didn't want to die alone on this warehouse floor. She held out a hand. "Please, Father."

He slapped her across the cheek.

Georgina landed hard on her knees. Blood trickled from the corner of her split lip. She scrambled away, attempting to put distance between them.

Father laughed and kicked her in the small of her back.

Georgina's body screamed with agony. She bit down hard on the inside of her cheek refusing to beg this man for mercy.

Adam. God. Anyone.

Father pressed the pistol against her temple.

She closed her eyes, scenes playing out in her mind like the one Drury Lane production she'd seen in her life: Adam twirling her about his cell. Around the ballroom. Adam laying her tenderly on the bed, his eyes and body for her alone.

The crack of a gunshot filled her ears.

She touched her fingers to her head. There was no pain. Or blood.

Her eyes flew open.

The gun slipped from Father's fingers as he crumpled to the floor. Georgina's gaze fixed on the small round hole in his head.

"I had to," Jamie said, his voice hoarse. His gun remained pointed where her father had last stood.

"Georgina," Adam cried.

Georgina fought back the cobwebs that cluttered her brain. Her eyes strayed back to Father's dead body. Shouldn't she feel more than this peculiar numbness?

"Georgina."

There it was again. Adam's voice. Jerking her eyes away from Father's body, she searched for Adam. Except...why would Adam be here? Adam didn't love her. He didn't even like her.

Her husband charged forward. The emerald green of his irises glinted with emotion.

Tears flooded her eyes, blinding her. "Why are you here?" she called out.

"I don't want you," Adam said. "Do you hear?"

Her heart plummeted. His words cut through her like the tip of a rapier but then he stuck a finger in Jamie's direction. "I want her," Adam finished.

Her ears were playing cruel tricks on her. In her plunge into madness, she had dreamed the possessive undertone to Adam's pronouncement. Tears seeped down her cheeks and she let them fall, the salty drops filling her mouth, choking her with the bitter taste of regret.

I want to go back to the first day. I want to walk into his chamber and tell him who I truly am. I want to begin without this wall of lies between us.

Jamie's already-fired pistol lay uselessly at his feet. "She's mine," he hissed.

Adam waved the gun in his hand at Jamie's chest. "By God, I'm not walking out of here without her by my side. Leave, Hunter, while you can."

A cold smile twisted Jamie's handsome face into a mask of terror. "You're going to have to kill me. Because I'm taking her. She belongs to me." Jamie grappled for Georgina and she shrank away from him.

Adam cocked his pistol...

Click.

Jamie's eyes widened. A demonic laugh ripped from his chest. Adam tried again. The useless weapon clicked.

Georgina's heart raced. She inched away from Jamie, seemingly forgotten as he reached into his boot. Even in the dim warehouse, the silver handle of his pistol glinted.

He lifted one shoulder in a small shrug. "I told you she's mine, Markham," he said, glee laced his words. He pointed his gun at Adam's chest and the world came to a screeching, silent halt.

Adam's gaze alternated between her and the barrel of Jamie's pistol. His throat bobbed up and down but was it fear? Regret?

"Forgive me, Georgina," he said hoarsely. "It was my duty to protect you."

Georgina shook her head, unable to speak past the emotion that clogged her throat. "No." He couldn't die. Not like this. Not at Jamie's hands, attempting to rescue her. She didn't want him to blame himself. Not if these were to be his final moments. "I love you, Adam."

Adam closed his eyes. "Georgina—"

"Silence," Jamie snapped, and waved the pistol from her to Adam as if he hadn't yet made up his mind who he wanted dead first. "Don't worry, Markham. I'll take good care of your lovely wife. Wait a moment. How could I forget? She's not your wife."

Fury sparked in Adam's emerald gaze. "What are you talking about?"

She inched closer, dimly registering Jamie's words. So close. She was almost there.

Jamie spoke, making her freeze. "Ahh, but then you don't know. Of course you don't." Jamie inclined his head, gesturing broadly at Georgina with his free hand. "Why, you aren't married."

Adam blanched. His skin went an ashen gray.

She'd not allow Jamie the twisted joy in repeating the whole sordid story. "I had not yet reached my majority when we wed. We required my father's consent."

Adam held her stare. "It doesn't matter. We'll marry again."

A sob bubbled up from her throat. Why would he marry her? Why, when he hated her so?

Jamie roared, leveling his gun on Adam.

Then the world righted and began spinning only this time it was moving out of control, in fast-moving circles. Georgina shoved to her feet. "No," she cried, tripping over her skirts in her haste to get to Adam. She leaped in front of him.

The sharp retort of the pistol echoed off the warehouse rafters, followed by another, and another.

Georgina's body jerked in stunned surprise. Oh God. She'd always imagined her father and Jamie receiving the justice they deserved, but to witness it, to see her father fall beneath the weight of the bullet, and now...this. Jamie dying before her eyes. A sharp twinge in her chest made breathing difficult.

Jamie clasped a hand to the blood blossoming on the front of his jacket as it turned the sapphire fabric black. "I love you," he choked out. Blood spewed forth with his hideous pronouncement. He slumped to the ground, coughing and gurgling.

Georgina swayed, lightheaded from the sight of Jamie dying. A stabbing pain radiated out to her chest.

Adam took her against his side and pressed her face in his chest.

Georgina pulled back as Jamie pitched forward.

Dead.

TWENTY-EIGHT

After he'd been taken captive, Adam had believed he wouldn't know peace until Fox and Hunter were dead by his hand. Staring down at Hunter as the blood seeped from his pale, lifeless body, Adam realized the stark truth—killing them wouldn't bring him peace.

Only Georgina could do that.

The duke shouted something.

"What the hell took you so long?" Adam snapped.

"Markham," Aubrey murmured.

Bennett strode through the room. "He's dead," he confirmed, jerking his head over to where Georgina's father lay.

Adam's heart spasmed. He loathed Fox for the hell he'd put him through but now, the horror of his captivity seemed secondary to the love he had for Georgina. Fox was still her father and this was still a loss for her.

He looked at her.

She'd fixed her wide-eyed stare on Hunter's dead body and clasped a hand to her chest.

Adam frowned at the ashen hue of her skin and took a step toward her. "Georgina…"

She pulled her fingers back. She stared unblinking, at a thick, red stain on her fingers.

A loud humming filled his ears. "Georgina?" he repeated, his voice came as if down a long hall.

She held her bloody fingers toward him. Her beautiful, bow-shaped lips formed a small moue of surprise. "I…" Her eyes rolled back in her head and she collapsed.

Adam caught her to him. His heart slowed to a halt then picked up a pounding, hard rhythm as he lowered her to the floor. With shaking fingers, he explored the blood-soaked fabric, searching for a pulse.

No. No. No. No. No.

He struggled to breathe.

Ah, God, no. Please, I can't…

He found her heartbeat; threadbare and slow but still beating. Adam yanked his cravat off and pressed it against the steady outpouring of blood, trying in vain to stem the flow.

There was so much of it.

"Help," he cried out. "She needs a doctor."

He swiped his blood-stained fingers over his face. He'd not survive this.

He pulled Georgina against him and rocked her back and forth. Tears blinded him. He blinked and forced the drops to fall, clearing his vision so he could see what his insecurities and foolishness had wrought. "Why?" he rasped against her temple. "Why would you place yourself in front of a bullet for me? Why, Georgina? Why?" *Why, when I hurt and betrayed you? Why would you give your life for me?* He dimly registered the commands barked out by Bennett, Archer, and Aubrey but couldn't fight his way through the thick fog of confusion.

Archer clasped Adam's shoulder. "We have to get her help." He reached for Georgina.

Adam snarled at him. "Get the hell away from her." Wisely, Archer fell back. Adam wouldn't let anyone else touch her. Nobody.

Aubrey looked to Bennett and Archer. "See to this," he said quietly and motioned to Georgina's family. "As discreetly as possible."

Adam rose, taking great pains not to jar Georgina. They moved through the warehouse, out the doors, and into Aubrey's carriage. Georgina remained still. Her eyes were sunken against the porcelain white of her skin.

As the carriage rattled on, Adam raised Georgina's fingers to the light. Blood marred the tips of her fingers and the underside of her nails. Nausea roiled in his gut.

He remembered back to his captivity when Georgina had cared for him; how the sight of blood had made her weak-kneed. His eyes slid closed. Until the day he died, he would forever remember the sight of her life-blood seeping onto the coach floor.

He growled. "Surely the driver can move faster."

Aubrey gave the command and the carriage sprung into motion. Adam cradled Georgina to his body and prayed. He prayed to a God he didn't even think he believed in anymore. But for Georgina, he'd trade his soul to the devil if it might save her.

It seemed ten lifetimes passed before the conveyance reached its destination. He dimly registered the door opening. Aubrey leapt from the carriage and reached up for Georgina's prone form. Adam handed her over, but when his feet were on the ground, he swiftly reclaimed her and followed the duke up the steps to the white townhouse.

The front doors were thrown open before they'd reached the top step. "We need a doctor," Aubrey instructed the stoic butler as they sailed through the entranceway. The aged servant gave no indication that there was anything untoward about bloodstained men carrying an unconscious woman into the duke's home. "And then we need warm water and strips of cloth."

The butler nodded and hurried off.

Adam followed Aubrey up the stairs and into an empty chamber. For the first time since he'd exited the carriage, Adam allowed himself to look down at Georgina. His heart fell.

She's dead. Adam hung onto her limp frame.

"Hand her to me," Aubrey said.

Adam's chest seized and his legs crumpled beneath him. The other man rescued Georgina before Adam carried her to the floor with him. The duke laid her down on the floral coverlet.

"She's dead," Adam said, his voice hollow.

Aubrey shoved back the sticky, wet fabric of Georgina's modest gown. He pressed his fingers to her chest. "She is alive," he said quietly.

"But for how long?" Adam rasped.

Everything unfolded in a blurry haze. The doctor came and attended to Georgina. He shook his head and Adam tossed him physically from the room.

Another doctor came with the same grim pronouncement—Georgina had shed too much blood.

This time Aubrey ushered the man out before Adam got to the old doctor.

The third doctor came; a tall, young, non-descript fellow. He examined Georgina.

Adam sat at the edge of a chair beside her bed. "Can you save her?" he asked hoarsely.

The doctor studied the front of her shoulder. Then the back. "I'll not lie to you. Her condition is dire," he said bluntly. His mouth set in a firm line. "I'll do everything I can to save her."

For three days, the doctor did just that. When fever set in and Georgina's body shook from chills he laid cold compresses on her wrists, her ankles, her brow. Through it all, Georgina writhed and screamed.

Then the nightmares came and Adam tortured himself with his wife's plaintive whimpers. Her head tossed and turned as she battled the demons in her sleep. At those times, the only thing he could do was crawl into bed beside her and wrap his body around her until she eventually stilled.

He lay beside her, head propped up on his elbow, and simply studied her. Memories poured over him like a gentle rain.

"Are you Eve?"

She angled her head. "My name is Georgina."

Adam touched his lips to Georgina's sweat-dampened temple. The eerie pall of silence punctured by her harsh breathing served as a bleak reminder that if she didn't awaken soon she most likely never would. He drew in a shuddery breath, willing her to hear him, needing her to come back to him.

"There are so many things I want to say to you, things I want to do and see with you. I want to dance with you in the moonlight until your cheeks are flush with color." He caught a long, curled tendril and rubbed it between his fingers. "I want to sit with you in the still of the night until the sun comes up." His throat worked. "And I want to have a family with you. I want to have feisty daughters with your heart and spirit and my...No. I don't want them to have any part of me, Georgina. I want them to be just like their mother."

Adam spoke until his throat was hoarse and still the words kept coming. "My beautiful, perfect Georgina. You've known so little happiness. If you come back to me, I will spend the rest of my days filling your life with joy." He lowered his brow to hers, rubbing it back and forth. He would spend the remainder of his life endeavoring to deserve her. There were so many wrongs that could never be forgiven.

He directed his gaze to the ceiling. "Please let her live. If you let her live, I will be anything and everything you want me to be. Just let her live."

There was no lightning from above. Adam curled into a ball at his wife's side and sobbed. Great, big, gasping breaths tore from his chest.

"I don't want to live without you."

He wept until his lungs burned, and only when he couldn't cry anymore, did he sleep.

Georgina struggled to open her eyes and when she did, promptly closed them against the sun streaming through the window.

When she'd been given her first horse some years ago, she'd taken a tumble off the beautiful creature. Her arms and torso had bore nasty greenish-blue bruises for the hard fall she'd taken. Her body felt much as it had that long ago day.

What happened?

She forced her eyes open once more and made a move to push herself up on her elbows. Her shoulder screamed in protest, and a wave of agony robbed her of breath. Georgina fell back against the pillow.

Father.

Jamie.

...Adam had walked out on her.

In the span of moments, she'd lost every single person in her life. She closed her eyes, revisiting the scenes from the warehouse. *Jamie saved me. He killed Father.* Her heart tightened painfully. She struggled to recall the events that had transpired after she'd placed herself between the bullet Jamie had intended for him. Only then did she become aware of the tall, muscular figure pressed against her side.

She froze. Her heart flipped over.

Her husband.

A bitter smile played about her lips as she remembered her father's damning revelation. Adam wasn't really her husband.

In sleep, the hard lines around his mouth had relaxed. A stray golden lock hung over his eye and she ached to brush it back. She wanted to remember him like this forever, for in this moment they might have been any couple in love, sleeping peacefully in their bed, wrapped in each other's arms. She wanted this moment before she forced herself to accept the truth. Adam had never loved her.

Life had reminded Georgina what she'd deluded herself into forgetting...dreams did not exist.

Adam's eyes flickered open and closed. Then popped open.

"Georgina!" he gasped. He lurched upright.

The sudden movement sent a lightning-quick pain up her arm.

He scrambled to his knees. "Forgive me. Are you—?"

She shook her head. "I'm all right." Except she wasn't. She didn't understand why he occupied the spot beside her. She scanned the foreign surroundings and struggled to place her location. "Where am I?"

"The Duke of Aubrey has a townhouse on the outskirts of London." Adam ran a solemn gaze over her face.

She struggled for some hint of affection but his face was set in a stoic mask. *Silly ninny.* Adam didn't care for her. He'd made it abundantly clear on Lord Ashton's terrace how little she meant to him, and in the warehouse...she'd never be able to forget how easily he'd walked out on her.

"You shouldn't be here." She squeezed the words out through dry lips. "We aren't even married." No, he'd made it perfectly clear that he didn't want to be wed to her.

Adam's face contorted. "I don't care about that. I told you the day…" He faltered. "The day you were shot I would wed you again."

She looked away as an internal battle waged inside her. The foolish part of her wanted to accept that which he offered and go on pretending she was the cherished wife of a man who'd nearly been killed by her father. Except…

She'd been foolish for too long. She would not allow him to wed her out of a misbegotten sense of guilt. "No." Her one word response blared in the silence of the room. Nor could she wed a man who'd believed so ill of her. Even if she had given him earlier grounds to do so. There was too much they could not recover from.

A pained sound rumbled from Adam's chest. "You don't…" He seemed to be searching for words. "No," he repeated back. "You said no," he said more to himself. Adam sucked in an audible breath. "For days I considered what I might say to you. I would tell you how unworthy I am of you and your love." He raked a hand through his hair. "I would beg your forgiveness. There is nothing to say. Nothing but, please forgive me."

Adam *would* do anything for her—but out of guilt. He wore it etched in the tired lines of his rugged cheekbones and the sad twist of his lips.

She could not trap him—not when fate had freed him. Not when fate had freed them both.

No. There were only three words that he could give her. Three words Adam would *never* utter. Not to her. Not when there was beautiful Grace, who had the added advantage of not being the daughter of a traitor.

So she said nothing but, "I need to rest, Adam."

Adam cleared his throat and stood. "Of course, of course." He reached a hand to her and she turned on her side. "We will talk later," he pledged quietly.

There was nothing left to say.

ᐧᐧᐧᐧᐧ

One week later, Georgina requested a meeting with the Duke of Aubrey.

She stared across the wide surface of the immaculate, mahogany desk at the powerful nobleman who'd controlled her fate these many years now. He sat, his gaze trained on a sheet in front of him as though either uncaring or disinterested in her presence. She gritted her teeth, tired of commanding gentleman.

Georgina cleared her throat.

The duke picked his head up. He stood and studied her from hooded lashes. "You should still be resting," he chided.

Georgina gave him a tight smile. "I never took you for a nurse-maid, Your Grace."

He inclined his head. "Or a spy."

She remembered the carriage ride the evening she'd fled Lord and Lady Ashton's. Her smile dipped. "Or a spy." Yes, gentlemen did not become spies. It was seedy and dark and not the endeavors pursued by powerful noblemen.

"Please sit." He motioned to the smooth, brown leather sofa by the hearth.

Georgina slid into a seat. She set down a sealed note she'd carried here. "Thank you for the clothing and for allowing me to convalesce here."

He claimed the chair opposite her. He waved off her thanks. "Mrs. Markham, as you know, I'm indebted to you far beyond several gowns and shelter."

Which brought Georgina to the reason for her visit. "I cannot stay here any longer."

"I assure you my staff is the soul of discretion. Your presence here has gone, and will remain, undetected if that is your—"

Georgina shook her head. "No. It is more than my reputation. I…"

Am tired of living a lie. Her entire life had been a lie. The truth of her parentage, her role in helping The Brethren, her marriage to Adam. All of it. She was tired of the mistruths and deception. She wanted to start anew. Nay, she needed to begin anew. And it had to begin by freeing Adam. Her heart seized.

The duke spoke. "I gather you want to return to your husband."

She laughed. The sound bitter and empty. Her husband. Dear, loyal Adam, who continued to pay her visits, sketching at her bedside, bringing flowers. She cleared her throat. "No."

The duke blinked. "No?"

She smoothed her palms over her skirts. "You know he is not my husband."

The duke sighed and settled his long, muscled arm on the back of his seat. He tapped his fingers along the top of the chair. "I can see that your marriage is made legal."

Her lips twisted wryly. Of course he could. A step shy of royalty, with a large dose of power at the Home Office, the duke could accomplish nearly everything. Seeing to the legality of her sham marriage should prove little obstacle.

"I don't want to remain married to Adam," she said bluntly.

The duke's fingers stilled.

Even if Adam somehow desired a true marriage with her, how could she marry the man who'd left her so callously, believing the lies of another? *Because you were never truthful with him,* a voice taunted. Yes, she hadn't been entirely honest, or at all honest with him, but after the hell she'd endured at her father and Jamie's hands, she deserved more than an empty marriage with a man who thought so ill of her.

Georgina continued. "I only ask you help me leave. Beyond that, I will never ask anything else of you, Your Grace." She reached for the note at her side and handed it to him. "Could you give this to my h... to Adam." He wasn't her husband. Only in her heart would he remain that way.

The duke studied the note in her fingers a moment and then took it. "I am so very sorry for how all this turned out," he said quietly.

Georgina rather suspected the Duke of Aubrey apologized to no one. "Will you help me?"

Two hours later, she left.

297

TWENTY-NINE

Adam stepped into the Duke of Aubrey's library and glanced around for Georgina. Disappointment twisted his gut when he found only the duke standing in the corner of the room by a floor-length window. They exchanged bows, before the duke moved over to a wingback chair and sat.

Adam remained standing.

"Sit," Aubrey murmured.

"I don't feel like sitting." His gaze flickered over toward the door. *Where the hell is she?*

Two days ago, Georgina had asked Adam to leave the Duke of Aubrey's townhouse. She had insisted that, as they were not married, it was highly improper to remain as guests in the duke's home together. Willing to do anything to earn her forgiveness, Adam had granted her wish and taken himself home, though it didn't prevent him from visiting. He did. Every day. She was always ensconced in the music room or library.

Aubrey interrupted his musings. "We should speak about your captivity."

Adam's gaze whipped forward.

The duke motioned to the chair opposite him and Adam slid into the seat. His hands curled into tight fists and he had to force his fingers to relax. The horror of those days in Fox and Hunter's clutches, the fear that he'd not live to see beyond the small chamber walls, had faded but still crept back into his mind's eye at the oddest times. He suspected they would always haunt him.

But the dreams had shifted. In his deep, troubled sleep, he no longer saw the chambers in Bristol but rather the inside of a dark warehouse, with Georgina lying limp and bloodied on the hard floor. He shoved the thought aside.

"What is there to say about...about...?" Adam couldn't force the word out. "For my service with The Brethren, I was handsomely repaid by losing months of my life to Fox and Hunter." He leaned forward in his chair, fairly seething. "Tell me, Your Grace, at what point did you decide my life was expendable? Was it all along?"

Aubrey's lips turned down at the corners. "You knew when you pledged your service to The Brethren that your life belonged to the Crown."

"Yes, but I did not agree to becoming bait." The words ripped from Adam's chest as he allowed the bitterness he'd kept buried to spew to the surface. "I lost everything. My family. My life." *My sanity.* "And it was all a game to you."

The duke made an impatient sound. "Surely you trust this wasn't a game?"

"My life was inconsequential to The Brethren. My service meant nothing when—"

"I considered what we could have learned from Miss Wilcox and made a decision that was in the Crown's best interests." There was no apology in the duke's words.

Adam looked away. The rub of it was that he did see value in the duke's plan.

"Markham, I do not argue that you endured hell to benefit the organization, but didn't anything good come of it?"

Georgina.

He would never have met Georgina. Some other poor, hapless member of The Brethren would have been at the mercy of Fox and Hunter, and Georgina would have been there to care for him. Adam would have married Grace.

A viselike pressure tightened about his heart at the rewrite of history which erased Georgina from his life.

The duke reached inside his jacket. He pulled out a folded note and handed it over. "When Miss Wilcox agreed to help us lure her father out, she asked I give you this if anything were to happen to her."

Adam stared at it a moment and then took it. His fingers tightened reflexively about the letter.

"I understand you cared very deeply for my sister-in-law," Aubrey said.

He glanced up. Odd, he hadn't given much thought to Grace's familial connection with the duke. After his reunion with Grace at Lord Ashton's ball, Adam had finally been able to lay to rest all the tumultuous yearnings he'd thought he had for Grace.

Now she existed as nothing more than a distant memory of a past that belonged to some other man he no longer knew.

Thoughts of Georgina drove back all memory of Grace.

He needed to see his wife.

"Markham?" Aubrey prompted.

Adam shook his head. "I cared very much for Grace, but I love my wife, and I would like to see her." He made to rise.

Aubrey held up a hand. "She's not here."

"I can see that," Adam said with a touch of impatience.

"No," Aubrey said, his tone firm. "I mean she is not here. She left."

He froze. "What do you mean she left?"

Aubrey withdrew a second note. "One more thing. Miss Wilcox asked that I give you this as well."

Adam stared at it. Dread pooled in his gut. *Why would Georgina give me a letter?* His mouth went dry as a niggling fear crept in. "Her name is Mrs. Markham."

"You know by now that you were not married. Not in the eyes of the Church of England," Aubrey said with surprising gentleness.

Adam slammed his fist down. "We were married in the eyes of God, and that is all that matters."

The Church of England could go hang! He tore open the envelope in a frenzied panic and scanned the succinct note.

Adam,
You have always done what is right. For England. For your family. For
me. I cannot allow you to sacrifice any more of your happiness. Not out
of any misplaced guilt or obligation. If I let you, you would spend the
rest of your life married to me for all the wrong reasons.
This is for the best. For the both of us.
I will always love you.
Ever Yours,
Georgina

He fisted the note and it crumpled in his fingers. Oh God.

I have lost her. And with her goes my heart and soul.

His legs knocked against the edge of the chair and he sank into the leather folds. How could she believe this was for the best? How, when she was his every reason for living?

He hadn't even told her how much he loved her, how she'd breathed happiness and life into his existence. How had he not realized until just now that he would endure a lifetime of captivity in a small, barren chamber so long as he had Georgina at his side. He buried his face in his hands.

Aubrey settled a hand on his shoulder. "She is a good woman."

What a bloody fool I've been.

He'd never deserved her.

Adam picked his head up. "Where is she?"

He looked up when Aubrey remained stonily silent. Shoving the duke's hand from his person, he snarled his next words, "You won't tell me?"

The duke's jaw set at a stony angle. "The Brethren is indebted to Miss Wilcox. It would be wrong of us to not honor her wishes."

Adam leapt to his feet and snarled. "Her wishes? You speak about being indebted to Georgina. Where is The Brethren's loyalty to me? After all I've suffered for this organization, you'd take my wife from me."

"We didn't take your wife from you," Aubrey said. A muscle in the corner of his eye twitched indicating the powerful nobleman's magnanimous attempt at patience was waning. "Your wife left of her own volition."

The words hit Adam like a blow to the chest. He spun on his heel and stalked from the room. Even as he left the duke's townhouse, Adam could admit he was responsible for his own misery. Not Hunter, Fox, Aubrey, or any other member of The Brethren could shoulder responsibility for Georgina leaving.

With his coldness and harsh disregard, Adam had driven her away and by God, he wanted her back.

And he would get her back.

THIRTY

3 days later

Adam stared up at the façade of Bristol Hospital. His cloak swirled about his feet as he climbed the steps. He knocked.

A short moment later, the door opened. A young man with an empty shirtsleeve pinned up greeted him with a frown on his hard lips.

Adam handed the man his card. "I'd like to speak with the lead nurse."

The servant stared down at the card, his expression impassive. With a curt nod, the servant motioned him inside, and then went in search of the woman.

Adam clasped his arms behind his back and paced the pink marble foyer. His gaze searched the sterile space and guilt burned like acid in his throat. It had taken him but one meeting with Aubrey to deduce Georgina's whereabouts. The duke hadn't come out and directly given him her location but had alluded to it in such a way that made Adam believe that perhaps the Duke of Aubrey wasn't the total, heartless bastard he'd taken him for.

"Sir?"

He froze mid-step.

The young man bowed. "If you'll follow me?"

Adam walked beside the servant. They moved through the silent, cheerless halls. With each step he took, his anxiety doubled.

What if she isn't here?

Or worse, what if she is here and turns me away?

They paused at a dark paneled door. The servant motioned him inside.

A plump, matronly woman of non-descript years stood in the middle of the room, hands clasped in front of her rounded belly. She dismissed the servant with a slight nod. All the while her attention remained focused on Adam. "I am Nurse Catherine. You requested an audience with me, Mr. Markham?"

Adam rocked on the balls of his feet. He glanced around the room and searched for the right words. He expected after the three days it had taken him to travel to Bristol Hospital, he should have found some words, any words that would be adequate for Georgina. Then, what could one say or do after all the heartache he'd caused his wife?

"Mr. Markham?" she prodded.

He coughed into his hand, humbled to admit to this stranger that he'd come to find his wife...who'd left him. "Forgive me. Do you employ a woman by the name of Georgina Mar—Wilcox?"

The faintest tick appeared on the woman's right eyelid and he suspected if his role with The Brethren hadn't required his strictest attention to detail, he might have not detected the telltale gesture.

But he did.

And he knew with a certainty he'd wager his very life on that Georgina was here.

"It is my understanding she might be here," he pressed.

Nurse Catherine arched a single brow. "You have misplaced your wife, Mr. Markham?"

His back stiffened at the condescension in the older woman's tone, but he did not respond to it. She couldn't possibly loathe him any more than he loathed himself.

"And you believe she is here," she went on.

"I do." He knew she was here.

The nurse's hand fluttered about the base of her severe chignon. "Forgive me, sir, this is a most unusual meeting. I don't know a woman by that name."

"Oh?" he drawled.

The corner of her eye twitched again.

Yes. Georgina was here. He'd rather maintain a semblance of gentlemanliness and not storm Nurse Catherine's halls in search of his wife.

Her lips compressed into a tight line. "What do you want, sir?" Impatience danced in her eyes.

Adam held his palms up. "I love my wife. I need to see her. I need to know if she is here, and that she is safe."

Nurse Catherine's hands tightened, rustling the fabric of her stark, white dress. "May I speak plainly, sir?"

He inclined his head.

"If your wife is here, and I'm not saying she is, it would indicate that she ran away from you. What would make me trust that your intentions are driven out of love and a sense of concern for her well-being and not out of a desire to bring her back home where you can continue to hurt her?"

He strongly suspected his answer was paramount to being granted an audience with Georgina. He knew the only thing Nurse Catherine would respond to was truth. "I wronged her. I believed the worst things about her and because of that, drove her away. My life is incomplete without her."

She took a step toward him and ran her gaze over his face. "It took your wife leaving for you to realize your life is incomplete without her?"

Adam accepted the lash of her disapproval. It was no less than he deserved. He couldn't expect this woman to forgive him when he couldn't forgive himself. He spoke quietly. "If after she hears what I have to say, if she chooses to remain, I promise to leave and never return."

Being able to lie without remorse was one of the many skills he'd acquired in his work for the Crown. Now that he'd found her, not even the mighty Lord could keep him from her.

"I don't suppose you are aware of the condition Miss Wilcox was in when she last came to me?"

His heart thudded painfully. He tried to force words out past numbed lips but they lodged in his throat. He shook his head once.

"She was badly beaten," she said with a bluntness that made him flinch. "In all my years caring for people I have never seen a woman more battered and bloodied than the day Miss Wilcox arrived on my doorstep in the middle of the night."

The world tilted on its axis. Adam's knees buckled beneath him, and he sought something, anything to grip on to to keep from falling to his knees. His hands found purchase on the back of a scarred, wooden chair.

"It was done at her father's hands." Nurse Catherine continued to flay him with the truth. "She was brought here by an honorable gentleman some months past."

A loud humming filled his ears as he pieced together the woman's words. The timing...the nobleman...

It had to have been after she'd freed him. Yes, it would seem he had found his freedom that day, but Georgina had paid the ultimate price. He pressed the backs of his hands against his eyes to blot out the horror of imagining Georgina at the mercy of Fox and Hunter.

"Her ribs were fractured," the nurse continued, her telling cold and methodical. "Her eyes so swollen she was unable to open them for more than a week."

Adam struggled to swallow past a wave of emotion. Not for the first time, he wished Georgina's father had lived so Adam could beat him with his bare fists. Pummel the bastard for the way he had abused his daughter. "Thank you for caring for her. I can never repay your kindness." Such hollow words.

"It wasn't kindness that drove me to help Georgina," she snapped.

The muscles in his body went taut. That there had been another person there to help Georgina, when it should have been Adam protecting her, pricked at his heart.

"So I'll ask you again. What do you want with Miss Wilcox?"

"I love her."

I need her. I am nothing without her.

Nurse Catherine continued to study him, seeming to weigh the veracity of his promise. "I will call her." His heart leaped. She held up a finger. "I understand you are a powerful man and that you are of noble birth, but I will not let her leave this place unless she wishes it."

Adam watched the woman as she rang for a servant. She asked for Georgina.

He waited.

THIRTY-ONE

G eorgina poured water into a glass and handed it to the young
woman, Madeline. When she'd arrived back at Bristol Hospital
asking Nurse Catherine for work, the woman hadn't hesitated. She'd
even found a home and position for Georgina.

"Here, sit up." Georgina gently guided the woman forward and
held the drink to her lips.

The woman took several sips before settling back into the bed.
"You are an angel, Miss Wilcox."

Georgina winced. "I'm no angel."

I'm just a woman, flawed and imperfect.

"Are you Eve?"

Adam's taunting whisper curled around her brain, the memory of
their first meeting as clear as a clean Bristol sky.

"Miss, are you all right?"

She gave her head a clearing shake. "Forgive me," she said. "I'm
fine."

"Miss Wilcox?"

Georgina jumped at the unexpected intrusion and she scrambled
to her feet. "Yes?"

The young maid, Jane, smiled. "Nurse Catherine has requested
your presence in her office."

Her heart raced. Georgina lived in constant fear that one day
Catherine would find Georgina guilty for the crimes of her father and toss
her from Bristol Hospital. Then Georgina would be well and truly lost.

Jane cleared her throat and Georgina started. "She just said it was an urgent matter, miss."

Oh God, an urgent matter. While Georgina made the long trek to Nurse Catherine's office, she told herself it could be anything or nothing at all but the worst possible scenarios played out in her head.

The young maid scurried off.

Georgina leaned against the wall and closed her eyes, willing away memories of Adam though they refused to stay buried. He was everywhere. There was no escaping him.

She knocked on the door.

"Enter," the woman called.

Georgina opened the door, but hesitated at the threshold. "You wished to see me?"

She gestured her forward. "My dear, there is someone who requested an audience with you."

She furrowed her brow. The only people who would ever have a need for her were Father and Jamie—and they were both dead.

"Hello, Georgina." That deep baritone that haunted both her dreams and nightmares filled the room.

She spun around and her hand flew to her breast.

Adam!

In her darkest moments she imagined he'd forgotten about her. She'd tortured herself with the truth—he'd surely not thought of her. Only he was here now. Her mind went blank and she searched for words. "Adam." *Why are you here?*

An indecipherable look passed over her face.

Odd, she should know him so very well and yet he may as well be carved from stone for the stiffness to him. She wet her lips. "Why you here?" Then a niggling of fear pebbled in her belly. Gooseflesh dotted her skin at the sickening possibility that he'd come for no other reason than to retrieve her, to bring her to justice, to…She took a step back, toward the door.

He stretched a hand out. "Don't go," he said hoarsely. "Please."

Please. This man who'd endured countless days of torture at her father and Jamie's hands had never pleaded once. Now he would beg her. To what end?

Georgina nodded once.

"May I speak to my wife alone?" he said quietly.

Georgina's lips twisted. "I'm not your wife." He'd not wanted her. She hated the inherent weakness in her that the pain of his betrayal should still ravage her heart.

He closed the distance between them. He stopped a hairsbreadth apart from her. "You are my wife and I'd like to speak to you alone."

Catherine interjected. "If Georgina will not speak to you, I will have to insist you leave, sir. I merely allowed this extraordinary meeting because I believed you were her husband. However—"

"I'll speak to him," Georgina said. She looked back to Adam. "I'll speak to you, but when you are finished you must leave."

He hesitated and then gave a curt nod.

Nurse Catherine walked toward the front of the room but paused at the doorway. "If you require anything, Georgina…" She closed the door behind her with a soft click. The meaning was clear. If he were to harm her, Georgina need just call out and help would be there.

Adam would never lay a hand on her. He'd inflicted a different kind of pain—the kind which would never go away.

"What do you want, Adam?" She didn't allow herself to look up his towering, lithe form. His moss-green eyes could weaken a woman's resolve and Georgina was not willing or able to turn herself back over to him. He'd hurt her too greatly, and she feared if she welcomed him back into her life, she would always be on a steep cliff that she could teeter over at any moment. She wasn't strong enough to survive another fall—not at his hands.

Adam brushed her jawline with his fingertips, directing her chin up. Warm shivers radiated out from the point of his touch.

She closed her eyes, hating her body's awareness of him, hating herself for her weakness.

"Look at me," he ordered.

She bit the inside of her cheek. "Why are you here?" she tossed back.

Ah, she'd always been bold and proud. He admired her now more than ever. Framing her face between his hands, he lowered his brow to hers. "I have thought of you and nothing else since you walked out of my life. I lied awake and imagined what I would say to you when I found you again and now you are here," The muscles of his throat worked. "*We* are here. And I am remarkably without words." He drew in a shuddery breath. "Nothing I can say would be adequate to convey how sorry I am—"

Georgina shoved his hands off her person. Was that was this was about? His sense of remorse? She spun away from him. "If you've come to apologize, there is no need. We were both wrong. I was wrong to lie to you and…"

You were wrong to believe the absolute worst of me. You were wrong to abandon me with Jamie.

Folding her arms beneath her stomach, she hugged herself tight.

Adam rested his hands on her shoulders and turned her to face him.

She shrugged him off and proceeded to speak. "I do not know for what purpose you've come. I've already told you the reasons for my lies."

"I know—"

Georgina glared him into silence. "You asked why I lied to you about my father and yet your treatment of me from the moment you discovered the truth, confirmed the need for my deception." She shook her head sadly. "It is as I said, you would have only seen Fox's daughter and…what was it you called me? Hunter's whore?"

Adam jerked as though he'd been run through with a blade. His throat worked. Hunter's mistress. He'd called her Hunter's mistress. Mistress. Whore. She was right. It was all the same. He'd debased her with his words and tone. His neck heated with shame.

Georgina continued, either unaware or uncaring of his own tortured thoughts. "In the beginning, I painted a world of make-believe for myself as much as for you. It was easier to share a world with you where I was the loved and cherished daughter of two honorable people, rather than the useless daughter of a man who loathed me."

Ah God, he needed her to stop talking. He would forever bear the nightmares of his short time in captivity and yet his brave, courageous Georgina had lived her whole life in such a state. He held his palms up. "I didn't know."

"Of course you didn't," she scoffed. "Would you rather I showed you my scars?" She held her right hand up and displayed the white scar between her thumb and forefinger. "Should I have told you how my father stabbed me with a fork?"

His heart cracked. He wanted to clamp his hands over his ears and drown her words out. "No!" Nausea burned in his belly at the hell she'd endured.

"Would you have rather I told you that when I ran off chasing rainbows, my father had a servant fetch me then proceeded to beat me for my foolishness?"

He sucked in a shuddering breath. "Oh God, Georgina." His words were an entreaty. He tried to gather her into his arms but she shrugged free of him.

"There is nothing more for either of us to say or do, except move on."

He growled. His cloak snapped angrily at the alacrity of his movement. "I cannot live without you."

She smiled back at him sadly. "At one time, I would have given anything and everything to hear you utter those words. Now it is too late. There is too much for us to overcome." He reached for her, but she held up a staying hand. "You never wanted to marry me. Your one and only love is Grace. You married me out of a sense of obligation, and that obligation is the only reason you're here."

His patience snapped. "Do not presume to know what brings me here, love." He'd not thought of Grace since the last he'd seen her on the balustrade and had his needed good-bye. "I'm here to tell you what

I should have told you a long time ago. I love you, Georgina Patience Wilcox, and I'm asking you to marry me. Again." He dropped to a single knee and withdrew the signet ring from the front of his jacket pocket.

Georgina gasped and her hand flew to her mouth. Hope soared in his chest and he allowed himself to believe for an infinitesimal moment she intended to capitulate and accept his unworthy hand.

Then her glance slid away. "I lied to you about something else, Adam."

He froze.

"I once told you that I didn't dream, but that was a lie. I did dream. I used to dream there would be a man who would fall in love with me." Her lips turned up in a heartbreaking smile. "In my dreams, I would be a mother to these incredibly plump, angelic babies with rounded cheeks and sweet giggles."

He was lost in the dream of those children. He wanted those babies. He wanted them with her. Only her.

"Let me give you—"

Grace touched her fingers to his lips. "I spent the past days warring between anger for your total lack of faith in me and my love for you." She sucked in an audible breath. "You broke my heart, Adam." Those words were flat. Matter-of-fact. "You ruined that dream beyond repair. I can't marry you."

A vise like pressured tightened about his lungs making it difficult to draw in a breath. Adam came to his feet. "No," That one word utterance was wrenched from deep inside his soul. Determination coursed through him. He had not found her only to lose her. Not again. Fate had already separated them too many times. "You can." *You have to, because I am nothing without you. I am an empty shell of a man when you're not near.*

She shook her head, dislodging a single strand of chocolate brown hair. "As much as I love you, I cannot wed you."

He didn't move.

Georgina brushed the loose curl behind her ear. "There are too many lies. You'd never truly be able to forgive me for being your captor's daughter and I would always be waiting for you to realize you couldn't truly be happy with me." She turned her palms up. "It is easier this way."

This was easier? Than what? Having his heart pulled from his living, breathing body? A muscle ticked at the corner of his mouth. "You're wrong. It doesn't matter to me who your father is. I thought it mattered, but it doesn't." And it didn't. He'd only just fully realized that now.

Tears filled her eyes. A fat, lone tear trailed down her cheek. It was followed by another, and another. She swatted at them as though embarrassed of the show of emotion. "Please go," she begged.

Adam's jaw flexed. She thought he would leave and never look back. But then, he'd never given her much reason to believe in his constancy. He gave a curt nod and walked stiffly to the doorway.

Georgina watched him go and wanted to plead with him to forget every foolish word she'd just uttered.

He looked at her once more before he left. "This is not over, Georgina Markham."

Her legs gave out beneath her and she wilted to the floor like a dying flower. A spark of gold caught her eye and she reached for the signet Adam had left behind.

She knew Adam leaving was for the best, but she could not keep herself from wanting him. She would always love him.

Georgina buried her face in her hands and wept.

THIRTY-TWO

G eorgina went through her morning ablutions. The sun glared into the small chambers she kept here at the hospital. The rays bright and unforgiving. She stole a glance at her reflection in the bevel mirror. She barely recognized the wan creature with dark circles under her eyes in an uncharacteristically pale face. Following Adam's swift exit the previous afternoon, she'd been unable to sleep or think. He occupied her every thought.

In the dead of night, she'd lain awake staring up at the small crack across the ceiling. Fool, fool, fool. She'd sent him away. How many hours of how many days had she dreamed of Adam loving her, loving her even with knowing about her connection to Fox and Hunter? Her pride, her fear of being hurt again by Adam, had driven her motives.

She pinched her cheeks hard, trying to send some blood flowing through her white skin. Her efforts proved futile.

Georgina opened the door and stopped.

A simple sketch hung on the wall. She walked up to it, studying— she squinted—what appeared to be a meal of roast chicken and potatoes.

Georgina walked down the hall until she came upon another drawing. This one of Bristol Hospital's front façade.

She continued and found sketch after sketch: a woman's hands, a songbird...a woman. Her breath caught. Georgina drew to a halt, her gaze riveted to her own image. It was a rendering of Adam's cell, with her kneeling beside his chair, rubbing his wrists. She yanked it from the wall. Her heart raced as she studied the picture.

Nurse Catherine appeared. She looked at the page clutched in Georgina's fingers. "It is very odd, you know. There are these sketches throughout the hospital. Perhaps you should follow them and see where they lead."

Georgina angled her head.

The kindly, older woman gestured down the long hall and Georgina continued walking. The sketches were everywhere. There was the moment Adam had twirled her around his prison cell, forever memorialized in charcoal. That scene gave way to his ballroom when he'd danced her around, with Tony laughing on the sidelines.

The images led her all the way to the foyer.

She stumbled to a halt. A vibrant rainbow had been painted on the white wall above the hospital's entrance. Periwinkles, daisies, and pale peach and pink roses lay scattered on the floor, beneath the painting. Standing amidst the blooms, peppermint in hand, stood Adam.

Her throat worked. "What are you—?"

"I thought long and hard about what you said. I thought about when I fell in love with you and realized it was a collection of moments. From the moment I first met you, you began to work your way into my heart. Your place there grew and grew, and now..." He held his hands up. "Now you fill all of me. Heart, mind, and soul. I am nothing without you. A time long ago, Georgina, you went chasing rainbows. All these years, I was the one waiting at the other end. I know I'm not much of a treasure, but I love you. I know I've wronged you, but—"

"Be quiet," Georgina rasped. She buried her fist against her mouth, attempting to stifle a sob.

Adam's hand fell quivering to his side, the children's treats tumbled to the floor.

"I love you," she choked out. She ran the remaining distance between them and launched herself into his arms. Adam wrapped his arms around her.

He pressed his lips hard against her temple. "Marry me. I will spend the rest of my life making amends, Georgina."

Tears fell unchecked down her cheeks. She drew back slightly and, leaning up on tiptoe, passed her gaze over his face. "I don't want you to spend the rest of your life making amends. I want you to spend it simply loving me."

A glimmer lit his moss-green eyes. Adam smiled; that gentle expression filled with hope, peace, and the happiness she'd searched for. "Forever, Georgina. I promise you, forever."

EPILOGUE

Georgina caressed her swollen belly and reached for another peppermint.

Adam glanced up from his sketchpad. A golden curl fell across his eye, lending him a boyish look, so very different from the dark, tortured man she'd first met. He grinned at her. "Are you well?"

Georgina arched her back and continued to stroke the place beneath her heart, where her and Adam's child rested. She smiled back at her husband. "Indeed."

Adam returned his attention to the drawing in front of him.

Georgina leaned her head against the chair. Most of her life had been spent dreaming of a different life—a husband, a family. Of simple happiness.

She closed her eyes. A smile played about her lips as she realized that *this* moment was what dreams were made of.

The End

BIOGRAPHY

Christi Caldwell is a USA Today Bestselling author of histori-
cal romance novels set in the Regency era. Christi blames Judith
McNaught's "Whitney, My Love," for luring her into the world of his-
torical romance. While sitting in her graduate school apartment at the
University of Connecticut, Christi decided to set aside her notes and
try her hand at writing romance. She believes the most perfect heroes
and heroines have imperfections and rather enjoys tormenting them
before crafting a well-deserved happily ever after!

When Christi isn't writing the stories of flawed heroes and heroines,
she can be found in her Southern Connecticut home chasing around
her feisty six-year-old son, and caring for twin princesses-in-training!

Visit www.christicaldwellauthor.com to learn more about what
Christi is working on, or join her on Facebook at Christi Caldwell
Author (for frequent updates, excerpts, and posts about her fun as a
fulltime mom and writer) and Twitter @ChristiCaldwell (which she is
still quite dreadful with).

OTHER BOOKS BY

CHRISTI CALDWELL

"Winning a Lady's Heart"
A Danby Novella

Author's Note: This is a novella that was originally available in A Summons From The Castle (The Regency Christmas Summons Collection). It is being published as an individual novella.

For Lady Alexandra, being the source of a cold, calculated wager is bad enough...but when it is waged by Nathaniel Michael Winters, 5th Earl of Pembroke, the man she's in love with, it results in a broken heart, the scandal of the season, and a summons from her grandfather – the Duke of Danby.

To escape Society's gossip, she hurries to her meeting with the duke, determined to put memories of the earl far behind. Except the duke has other plans for Alexandra...plans which include the 5th Earl of Pembroke!

"A Season of Hope"
A Danby Novella

Five years ago when her love, Marcus Wheatley, failed to return from fighting Napoleon's forces, Lady Olivia Foster buried her heart.

Unable to betray Marcus's memory, Olivia has gone out of her way to run off prospective suitors. At three and twenty she considers herself firmly on the shelf. Her father, however, disagrees and accepts an offer for Olivia's hand in marriage. Yet it's Christmas, when anything can happen...

Olivia receives a well-timed summons from her grandfather, the Duke of Danby, and eagerly embraces the reprieve from her betrothal.

Only, when Olivia arrives at Danby Castle she realizes the Christmas season represents hope, second chances, and even miracles.

"Forever Betrothed, Never the Bride"
Book 1 in the Scandalous Seasons Series

Hopeless romantic Lady Emmaline Fitzhugh is tired of sitting with the wallflowers, waiting for her betrothed to come to his senses and marry her. When Emmaline reads one too many reports of his scandalous liaisons in the gossip rags, she takes matters into her own hands.

War-torn veteran Lord Drake devotes himself to forgetting his days on the Peninsula through an endless round of meaningless associations. He no longer wants to feel anything, but Lady Emmaline is making it hard to maintain a state of numbness. With her zest for life, she awakens his passion and desire for love.

The one woman Drake has spent the better part of his life avoiding is now the only woman he needs, but he is no longer a man worthy of his Emmaline. It is up to her to show him the healing power of love.

"Never Courted, Suddenly Wed"
Book 2 in the Scandalous Seasons Series

Christopher Ansley, Earl of Waxham, has constructed a perfect image for the *ton*–the ladies love him and his company is desired by all. Only two people know the truth about Waxham's secret. Unfortunately, one of them is Miss Sophie Winters.

Sophie Winters has known Christopher since she was in leading strings. As children, they delighted in tormenting each other. Now at two and twenty, she still has a tendency to find herself in scrapes, and her marital prospects are slim.

When his father threatens to expose his shame to the *ton*, unless he weds Sophie for her dowry, Christopher concocts a plan to remain a bachelor. What he didn't plan on was falling in love with the lively, impetuous Sophie. As secrets are exposed, will Christopher's love be enough when she discovers his role in his father's scheme?

"Always Proper, Suddenly Scandalous"
Book 3 in the Scandalous Seasons Series

Geoffrey Winters, Viscount Redbrooke was not always the hard, unrelenting lord driven by propriety. After a tragic mistake, he resolved to honor his responsibility to the Redbrooke line and live a life, free of scandal. Knowing his duty is to wed a proper, respectable English miss, he selects Lady Beatrice Dennington, daughter of the Duke of Somerset, the perfect woman for him. Until he meets Miss Abigail Stone…

To distance herself from a personal scandal, Abigail Stone flees America to visit her uncle, the Duke of Somerset. Determined to never trust a man again, she is helplessly intrigued by the hard, too-proper Geoffrey. With his strict appreciation for decorum and order, he is nothing like the man' she's always dreamed of.

Abigail is everything Geoffrey does not need. She upends his carefully ordered world at every encounter. As they begin to care for one another, Abigail carefully guards the secret that resulted in her journey to England.

Only, if Geoffrey learns the truth about Abigail, he must decide which he holds most dear: his place in Society or Abigail's place in his heart.

"Always a Rogue, Forever Her Love"
Book 4 in the Scandalous Seasons Series

Miss Juliet Marshville is spitting mad. With one guardian missing, and the other singularly uninterested in her fate, she is at the mercy of her wastrel brother who loses her beloved childhood home to a man known as Sin. Determined to reclaim control of Rosecliff Cottage and her own fate, Juliet arranges a meeting with the notorious rogue and demands the return of her property.

Jonathan Tidemore, 5th Earl of Sinclair, known to the *ton* as Sin, is exceptionally lucky in life and at the gaming tables. He has just one problem. Well…four, really. His incorrigible sisters have driven off yet another governess. This time, however, his mother demands he find an appropriate replacement.

When Miss Juliet Marshville boldly demands the return of her precious cottage, he takes advantage of his sudden good fortune and puts an offer to her; turn his sisters into proper English ladies, and he'll return Rosecliff Cottage to Juliet's possession.

Jonathan comes to appreciate Juliet's spirit, courage, and clever wit, and decides to claim the fiery beauty as his mistress. Juliet, however, will be mistress for no man. Nor could she ever love a man who callously stole her home in a game of cards. As Jonathan begins to see Juliet as more than a spirited beauty to warm his bed, he realizes she could be a lady he could love the rest of his life, if only he can convince the proud Juliet that he's worthy of her hand and heart.

"A Marquess For Christmas"
Book 5 in the Scandalous Seasons Series

Lady Patrina Tidemore gave up on the ridiculous notion of true love after having her heart shattered and her trust destroyed by a black-hearted cad. Used as a pawn in a game of revenge against her brother, Patrina returns to London from a failed elopement with a tattered reputation and little hope for a respectable match. The only peace she finds is in her solitude on the cold winter days at Hyde Park. And even that is yanked from her by two little hellions who just happen to have a devastatingly handsome, but coldly aloof father, the Marquess of Beaufort. Something about the lord stirs the dreams she'd once carried for an honorable gentleman's love.

Weston Aldridge, the 4th Marquess of Beaufort was deceived and betrayed by his late wife. In her faithlessness, he's come to view women as self-serving, indulgent creatures. Except, after a series of chance encounters with Patrina, he comes to appreciate how uniquely different she is than all women he's ever known.

At the Christmastide season, a time of hope and new beginnings, Patrina and Weston, unexpectedly learn true love in one another. However, as Patrina's scandalous past threatens their future and the happiness of his children, they are both left to determine if love is enough.

"Once a Wallflower, At Last His Love"
Book 6 in the Scandalous Seasons Series

Responsible, practical Miss Hermione Rogers, has been crafting stories as the notorious Mr. Michael Michaelmas and selling them for a meager wage to support her siblings. The only real way to ensure her family's ruinous debts are paid, however, is to marry.

Tall, thin, and plain, she has no expectation of success. In London for her first Season she seizes the chance to write the tale of a brooding duke. In her research, she finds Sebastian Fitzhugh, the 5th Duke of Mallen, who unfortunately is perfectly affable, charming, and so nicely...configured...he takes her breath away. He lacks all the character traits she needs for her story, but alas, any duke will have to do.

Sebastian Fitzhugh, the 5th Duke of Mallen has been deceived so many times during the high-stakes game of courtship, he's lost faith in Society women. Yet, after a chance encounter with Hermione, he finds himself intrigued. Not a woman he'd normally consider beautiful, the young lady's practical bent, her forthright nature and her tendency to turn up in the oddest places has his interests...roused. He'd like to trust her, he'd like to do a whole lot more with her too, but should he?

"In Need of a Duke"
A Prequel Novella to "The Heart of a Duke" Series by Christi Caldwell

In Need of a Duke: (Author's Note: This is a prequel novella to "The Heart of a Duke" series by Christi Caldwell. It was originally available in "The Heart of a Duke" Collection and is now being published as an individual novella.

It features a new prologue and epilogue.

Years earlier, a gypsy woman passed to Lady Aldora Adamson and her friends a heart pendant that promised them each the heart of a duke.

Now, a young lady, with her family facing ruin and scandal, Lady Aldora doesn't have time for mythical stories about cheap baubles. She needs to save her sisters and brother by marrying a titled gentleman with wealth and power to his name. She sets her bespectacled sights upon the Marquess of St. James.

Turned out by his father after a tragic scandal, Lord Michael Knightly has grown into a powerful, but self-made man. With the whispers and stares that still follow him, he would rather be anywhere but London…

Until he meets Lady Aldora, a young woman who mistakes him for his brother, the Marquess of St. James. The connection between Aldora and Michael is immediate and as they come to know one another, Aldora's feelings for Michael war with her sisterly responsibilities. With her family's dire situation, a man of Michael's scandalous past will never do.

Ultimately, Aldora must choose between her responsibilities as a sister and her love for Michael.

"For Love of the Duke"
First Full-Length Book in the "Heart of a Duke"
Series by Christi Caldwell

After the tragic death of his wife, Jasper, the 8th Duke of Bainbridge buried himself away in the dark cold walls of his home, Castle Blackwood. When he's coaxed out of his self-imposed exile to attend the amusements of the Frost Fair, his life is irrevocably changed by his fateful meeting with Lady Katherine Adamson.

With her tight brown ringlets and silly white-ruffled gowns, Lady Katherine Adamson has found her dance card empty for two Seasons. After her father's passing, Katherine learned the unreliability of men, and is determined to depend on no one, except herself. Until she meets Jasper…

In a desperate bid to avoid a match arranged by her family, Katherine makes the Duke of Bainbridge a shocking proposition—one that he accepts.

Only, as Katherine begins to love Jasper, she finds the arrangement agreed upon is not enough. And Jasper is left to decide if protecting his heart is more important than fighting for Katherine's love.

"More Than a Duke"
Book 2 in the "Heart of a Duke" Series by Christi Caldwell

Polite Society doesn't take Lady Anne Adamson seriously. However, Anne isn't just another pretty young miss. When she discovers her father betrayed her mother's love and her family descended into poverty, Anne comes up with a plan to marry a respectable, powerful, and honorable gentleman—a man nothing like her philandering father.

Armed with the heart of a duke pendant, fabled to land the wearer a duke's heart, she decides to enlist the aid of the notorious Harry, 6th Earl of Stanhope. A scoundrel with a scandalous past, he is the last gentleman she'd ever wed...however, his reputation marks him the perfect man to school her in the art of seduction so she might ensnare the illustrious Duke of Crawford.

Harry, the Earl of Stanhope is a jaded, cynical rogue who lives for his own pleasures. Having been thrown over by the only woman he ever loved so she could wed a duke, he's not at all surprised when Lady Anne approaches him with her scheme to capture another duke's affection. He's come to appreciate that all women are in fact greedy, title-grasping, self-indulgent creatures. And with Anne's history of grating on his every last nerve, she is the last woman he'd ever agree to school in the art of seduction. Only his friendship with the lady's sister compels him to help.

What begins as a pretend courtship, born of lessons on seduction, becomes something more leaving Anne to decide if she can give her heart to a reckless rogue, and Harry must decide if he's willing to again trust in a lady's love.

"The Love of a Rogue"
Book 3 in the "Heart of a Duke" Series by Christi Caldwell

Lady Imogen Moore hasn't had an easy time of it since she made her Come Out. With her betrothed, a powerful duke breaking it off to wed her sister, she's become the *tons* favorite piece of gossip. Never again wanting to experience the pain of a broken heart, she's resolved to make a match with a polite, respectable gentleman. The last thing she wants is another reckless rogue.

Lord Alex Edgerton has a problem. His brother, tired of Alex's carousing has charged him with chaperoning their remaining, unwed sister about *ton* events. Shopping? No, thank you. Attending the theatre? He'd rather be at Forbidden Pleasures with a scantily clad beauty upon his lap. The task of *chaperone* becomes even more of a bother when his sister drags along her dearest friend, Lady Imogen to social functions. The last thing he wants in his life is a young, innocent English miss.

Except, as Alex and Imogen are thrown together, passions flare and Alex comes to find he not only wants Imogen in his bed, but also in his heart. Yet now he must convince Imogen to risk all, on the heart of a rogue.

"Loved By a Duke"
Book 4 in the "Heart of a Duke" Series by Christi Caldwell

For ten years, Lady Daisy Meadows has been in love with Auric, the Duke of Crawford. Ever since his gallant rescue years earlier, Daisy knew she was destined to be his Duchess. Unfortunately, Auric sees her as his best friend's sister and nothing more. But perhaps, if she can manage to find the fabled heart of a duke pendant, she will win over the heart of her duke.

Auric, the Duke of Crawford enjoys Daisy's company. The last thing he is interested in however, is pursuing a romance with a woman he's known since she was in leading strings. This season, Daisy is turning up in the oddest places and he cannot help but notice that she is no longer a girl. But Auric wouldn't do something as foolhardy as to fall in love with Daisy. He couldn't. Not with the guilt he carries over his past sins...Not when he has no right to her heart...But perhaps, just perhaps, she can forgive the past and trust that he'd forever cherish her heart—but will she let him?

"Seduced By a Lady's Heart"
Book 1 in the "Lords of Honor" Series

You met Lieutenant Lucien Jones in "Forever Betrothed, Never the Bride" when he was a broken soldier returned from fighting Boney's forces. This is his story of triumph and happily-ever-after!

Lieutenant Lucien Jones, son of a viscount, returned from war, to find his wife and child dead. Blaming his father for the commission that sent him off to fight Boney's forces, he was content to languish at London Hospital...until offered employment on the Marquess of Drake's staff. Through his position, Lucien found purpose in life and is content to keep his past buried.

Lady Eloise Yardley has loved Lucien since they were children. Having long ago given up on the dream of him, she married another. Years later, she is a young, lonely widow who does not fit in with the ton. When Lucien's family enlists her aid to reunite father and son, she leaps at the opportunity to not only aid her former friend, but to also escape London.

Lucien doesn't know what scheme Eloise has concocted, but knowing her as he does, when she pays a visit to his employer, he knows she's up to something. The last thing he wants is the temptation that this new, older, mature Eloise presents; a tantalizing reminder of happier times and peace.

Yet Eloise is determined to win Lucien's love once and for all...if only Lucien can set aside the pain of his past and risk all on a lady's heart.

Made in United States
Orlando, FL
12 February 2022

14763675R00183